A note on the author

Douglas Skelton was born in Glasgow. He has been a bank clerk, tax officer, taxi driver (for two days), wine waiter (for two hours), journalist and investigator. He has written several true crime and Scottish criminal history books but now concentrates on fiction. *Thunder Bay* (longlisted for the McIlvanney Prize), *The Blood Is Still*, *A Rattle of Bones* (also longlisted for the McIlvanney Prize), *Where Demons Hide* and *Children of the Mist* are the first five novels in the bestselling Rebecca Connolly thriller series.

Also by Douglas Skelton

The Davie McCall series
Blood City
Crow Bait
Devil's Knock
Open Wounds

The Dominic Queste series
The Dead Don't Boogie
Tag – You're Dead

The Janus Run
An Honourable Thief

Death Insurance (novella with Morgan Cry)
Springtime for a Dead Man (e-short story)

The Rebecca Connolly series
Thunder Bay
The Blood Is Still
A Rattle of Bones
Where Demons Hide
Children of the Mist

CHILDREN OF THE MIST

A REBECCA CONNOLLY THRILLER

Douglas Skelton

First published in Great Britain in 2023 by
Polygon, an imprint of Birlinn Ltd

Birlinn Ltd
West Newington House
10 Newington Road
Edinburgh
EH9 1QS

www.polygonbooks.co.uk

1

ISBN 978 1 84697 625 4
eBook ISBN 978 1 78885 586 0

British Library Cataloguing-in-Publication Data
A catalogue record for this book is available
on request from the British Library.

Typeset by Biblichor Ltd, Scotland

In memory of Stephen Wilkie, the big guy

1

The mist made ghosts of the trees.

It draped itself over and around the woodland like a lover, enveloping the trunks, branches and pine bristles in a dewy embrace and brushing Fergus MacGregor's face like a phantom kiss. He sat on the recumbent log – *his* log it had once been in his mind, now it was *theirs*, his and Shona's – and listened for the first sound of her approach, but heard nothing yet. No matter, he had arrived purposely early for he loved these moments alone in this part of the old Scotland where the modern world, marked by the road along the loch side, did not intrude. It was by no means a busy road, although it had its moments in the summer months, but it was a roaring motorway compared to the silent calm of the forest, where the only regular sound was the breeze wafting through the branches. Not this day, though, for to all intents and purposes the world itself had fallen silent.

He glanced at his watch. She was still not late, and even though he relished his time alone in the Black Wood, the thrill of anticipation he always felt when he was about to see her, to hold her, just to be with her, fluttered in his stomach. He loved these trees, he loved these paths, this mist, and the wildlife he had seen and wished to see, but, when it came down to it, he loved her more.

Which is why he was here, for he couldn't leave without saying goodbye to the place that had been his sanctuary for so many years, the place that had given him comfort, that had helped him find himself when life seemed intent on keeping that true self hidden. He knew he had to leave, much as it pained him. He knew it would pain others – his mother, his brother. He was unsure about his father because he had not shown much caring lately, and Fergus suspected there was a slim chance of him showing any after he was gone. The simple truth was that they, he and Shona, had to leave. They couldn't stay here, not the way things were between their parents. Sooner or later the stresses of whatever bad blood lay between them would rip them apart. It had already begun. She had been warned off, as had he, but they had defied the orders, knowing that love can act as a vaccine against the viral effects of hatred. But they also knew it can be weakened. They had agreed that, if they were to have a future, they had to leave this valley, even though it was their home.

He thought he saw something move, just on the periphery of his vision, a dark disturbance in the grey, but when he focused he saw only the mist and the shades of the trees. A deer, perhaps, navigating the dense undergrowth. He held his breath, listened for the faint sound of its movement, but heard nothing.

He smiled. Perhaps he had glimpsed one of the phantoms of the woodland's wild past, when the MacGregors roamed this land. He had often imagined them moving silently through this old forest, perhaps even among these very trees, hunting for game to bring down, cattle to steal, men to rob or food to feed their families, their very name banned by an angry king, manipulated by powerful men with designs of their own. And here, in the wild fastness of the Highlands, they joined those others who had been put to the horn – made outlaws, for one reason or another – and became wraiths who could appear from the mist and vanish back into it when their deeds were done. Children of the Mist, Sir Walter Scott called them, and they have been known thus since. As a boy, he had been held enraptured as his grandmother and father told him the history of their family name. That was when his father was different, of course. Fergus had been so fascinated by the stories that he had set out to learn as much as he could about his clan kin of Rannoch.

And now, as he sat on the log, he felt them there with him, watching him – their flesh, their clothing, their weapons all part of the mist and, by extension, part of him. Would they understand what he was doing, he wondered? Would they, too, condemn him for his love, as his father seemed to? Would they disapprove of him turning his back on family and home? Or would those MacGregors of the past understand everyone has a right to happiness, and that Shona was his conduit to that? He scanned the greyness around him, hoping to catch a flash of plaid or a clink of metal against harness, but if the Children of the Mist were present in the thin place between the past and the present, the physical and the ethereal, they kept their own counsel on the matter.

His watch told him it was time, and he thrust the past from his mind to focus on the pathway leading to the road, for that was the direction from which Shona would come, and that was the future. The flattened trail, still hard from the frost, petered out in the gloom. He felt anticipation rise further as he watched avidly for the first sight of her.

At last, a shadow formed in the mist. But the smile that had widened on his lips died when he saw that the person approaching was not Shona. A glare eclipsed the joy that had thrilled his blood as he moved to intercept the newcomer.

His voice was harsh as he said, 'What are you doing here?'

2

Five years later

The man's eyes bore a mixture of shame and sadness. They were a blue that might have been striking at one time but were now diluted by too many years and perhaps too many disappointments. He sat in an armchair that looked slightly worn but was still comfortable. It seemed out of place in this nicely furnished modern cottage. He had caught her looking at the ragged corners and said that it was his favourite chair, a hint of apology in his voice.

'The cat,' he went on to explain, his accent still bearing traces of his native Lancashire even though he had lived in Scotland for thirty years. 'Tibby, she was called. My wife named her. She'd had a cat with the same name when she was a girl. Tibby.' He paused, lines around his eyes crinkling as he recalled both human and feline with fondness. 'We never could get her to use a scratching post. Cats have a mind of their own, don't they?'

Rebecca Connolly looked around the room, expecting to see the man's pet curled up somewhere.

'She died,' he said, catching her glance. 'Just after Christmas.'

'That's a shame.' The words felt lame. What do you say? When she was a child, she'd had dogs; she had loved their black Labrador Retriever Ben so much that when he'd died while Rebecca was in her late teens, she'd been inconsolable. She'd never had a pet since.

'She was Melanie's cat, was Tibby. She never had much time for me.' His eyes were drawn to a framed photograph sitting in a modular bookcase against the wall to their right. Paperback books and ornaments filled the other boxes, but this photograph sat on its own, placed where it was easy for him to see from his chair. It showed him as a younger man, with a fair-haired woman, her face broad, her eyes blue. She was in the foreground, her head resting on his shoulder as he held her from behind. They were smiling: wide, happy, beaming smiles.

'Mr Simmonds . . .' she began.

'Harry,' he said.

'Harry.' She gave him a smile. 'You know why I'm here?'

He hesitated. 'Would you like tea or coffee first? I have some nice cake, too.'

'I'm fine, thanks, Harry.'

He seemed disappointed and she instantly regretted her refusal, wondering if he had bought the cake especially for her visit. She hoped not. She hoped it was something he had bought for himself. She didn't want to be yet another disappointment.

'You know your daughter has been in touch with me, don't you?'

His face crinkled slightly. 'Yes, but she shouldn't have bothered you.'

'She's worried.'

'I'm fine.' He gave her a slight smile. 'Honestly. Ann shouldn't have contacted you.'

'Tell me about this woman, anyway.'

He jerked a shoulder. 'She's just a friend.'

'A friend you've never met in person.'

He sighed, looked back at the framed portrait of his wife and shifted slightly in the chair. 'Ann is blowing this all out of proportion.'

'She doesn't think so. And from what she's told me, I don't think so either, Harry. Just tell me about it. Let me hear it from you.'

'So you can do a story?' An ever-so-slightly defensive tone had crept into his voice. 'Put my name in the papers?'

This wasn't for the press. She was doing some legwork for a London-based TV production company making a series for Channel 4 on romance scams, one of the benefits of the two true-crime books written by her boss, Elspeth McTaggart, about cases in which Rebecca herself had played a prominent role. The production company was preparing a documentary feature for one of the streaming channels on the first case, in which a man's body was found on Culloden Moor in period Highland dress. But it was slow going, so in the meantime it threw the Highland News Agency some work. If a programme strand they were working on had a connection to the Scottish Highlands, they hired Rebecca to do the digging, which normally involved finding and having preliminary chats with potential interview subjects. For this series, the producer wanted cases from the length of the country, and had placed stories in local newspapers appealing for people to come forward. Harry's daughter, living in Elgin, had responded after spotting the item in the *Highland Chronicle*, and the company had then reached out to the agency. Using a local researcher was cheaper than sending one up from London. Ann would have been with her today to help convince her father to take part, but she had broken her leg in what Rebecca had begun to call a freak skateboarding incident. She had been showing off her skills – what she called her Marty McFly special – but had tumbled off, landed badly and fractured her tibia.

Rebecca said, 'If this person is what I think she is, then I believe she needs to be exposed.'

'And what do you think she is?' Harry's tone was stronger now. He'd no doubt had a similar conversation with his daughter and was prepared to stand his ground.

He can be a stubborn old sod, Ann had warned her. *That's the problem.* She was also worried that her father was beginning to show early signs of dementia and feared the worst regarding the individual who had contacted him via social media.

Rebecca paused, took a breath. She could fudge this, but now was not the time. 'I think she's a scammer, Harry. I think she's conning you out of your money.'

Her opinion didn't surprise him, and the slight shake of his head seemed pre-prepared. 'She's just a young woman in trouble.'

'Are you sure?'

He opened his mouth to say something, then thought better of it. Instead, he found the photograph on the bookcase again and stared at it for a few moments while gathering his thoughts.

'Mel was a good person,' he said eventually. 'She believed in helping people. Friends, family, strangers. If there was an appeal on the telly, she gave, didn't matter what it was. Water in Africa, food for the starving, wildlife, children in need. Those awful adverts where they show donkeys in distress. If there was a phone number and she caught it, she picked up the phone and gave. She wasn't religious, neither of us are. She didn't do it because she thought it would bring her salvation, she did it because she had a good heart.'

He stopped, his eyes still lingering on the photograph, as if somehow he could will it to come to life.

'I wasn't so charitable,' he went on. 'I wasn't heartless, but I would say to her that there was such a thing as being too caring, too generous. She didn't listen, though.'

Ann had explained that her father had not been the warmest, the most loving figure in her life, but Rebecca saw genuine pain in his eyes as he looked at his wife's photograph.

'How long has Mel been gone, Harry?'

He paused as if calculating, but Rebecca had the feeling he knew how long it had been down to the minute. 'Four years. She was here one day, gone the next.'

That was the way of it, Rebecca knew. A person can take one breath and slip away before the air has left the body. A minute, a second, a millisecond, a single breath – a final breath – and life is gone.

'I'm so sorry,' she said, once again aware of how hollow such sympathy can be. She didn't know this woman, she didn't know this man, yet the words sprang from her lips. It wasn't that she didn't feel for him, it was just that the words themselves seemed so utterly lifeless. He shrugged them away, not to dismiss them but more to say that death is part of life. Pets die. People die. Of that, Rebecca was already well aware, far more than she should have been at her age. His shrug also signified that life goes on. She was aware of that, too.

'And so this woman you met online, you think helping her is in some way keeping Mel's memory alive?'

'No, nothing like that,' he said. 'To be honest, I've never thought about it in that way. I think she would approve, though.'

'Even if this woman—'

'Her name's Ashley.'

It almost certainly wasn't, but Rebecca didn't go there. 'So even if Ashley is a scammer, you think Mel would approve?'

'You don't know she's a scammer.'

'Harry,' Rebecca said gently, 'she very likely is.'

'Yes, but you don't *know*, do you? You don't know her, do you?'

'How much money have you given this person, Harry?'

He looked away again. His daughter wasn't sure of the exact total he had sent this woman, if it even was a woman. The production company had sent Ann some briefing notes about these people, and often there was no way of knowing their true gender or nationality. They latched onto their marks through dating sites, or trawled social media platforms, hiding their true selves behind profile images lifted from the internet, either of innocent people or, regularly, porn stars. They claimed to be in the USA or even in the UK, but they were generally somewhere in Africa, Russia or the Middle and Far East. They struck up conversations via direct messages, lured the victim in, then hit them with a sob story and asked for money. Nobody knew how much of that money filtered through to organised crime or even terrorist groups. Many of them were just young people on the streets, forced into that life by poverty and hunger.

'She's had an unhappy life,' said Harry.

Of course she has, Rebecca thought. 'In what way?'

'Her parents died in a car crash in Africa when she was very young, along with her younger brother. She was brought up with an aunt in Virginia. She has known sadness.'

'And her boyfriend's just cheated on her, right?'

He looked surprised. 'How did you know that? I didn't tell Ann that.'

'Harry, believe me, this is common. It's the yarn these people spin.'

According to the research material, the tragic backstory was a common thread, as was the cheating boyfriend.

He sighed. 'Miss Connolly . . .'

'Rebecca, please.'

'Rebecca, I know you mean well, but please believe me when I say everything is fine. Ashley is what she says she is, I know it.'

'That's the thing, Harry, you really don't. You know what she wants you to know, and that is very likely all fake. The thing is, she may not even be a woman.'

'She is.'

'How can you be so sure?'

'Because I've spoken to her.'

It was Rebecca's turn to be surprised. His daughter hadn't mentioned this.

'She phoned you?'

'Through the social media site. I'm on there to see pictures of my grandchildren and I share pictures I take on my phone of around here.' Besides his daughter, Harry had a son who lived

9

in Abu Dhabi with his wife and two children. 'You can do voice calls on it, you see. So she called me.'

'But not a video call?'

'No, she tried a couple of times but her signal is poor.'

She wouldn't want him to see her, naturally. Chances were, she looked nothing like the profile picture she was using.

'Can I see her?' Rebecca asked.

Harry thought about that for a moment before he picked up his phone from where it had been resting on the arm of the chair. He flicked through the screen before he handed it over to her. The profile image was of a very beautiful black woman, maybe in her early thirties, gazing at the camera in a confident manner, her glossy dark hair loosely curled around her shoulders, her smile easy and natural. Rebecca read Ashley9951's profile.

Am Ashley, 35, and am looking for good friends. Nude requests will be blocked. Not here to play games.

Rebecca scrolled through the images the person had posted. Rebecca had seen a number of these profiles and this one was typical, while at the same time different. There weren't that many pictures, but they were all selfies and what background there was visible was nondescript. A wall, a doorway, a street that could be anywhere. The clothes she wore were modest, which was unusual for these things. Generally they were of the woman in a variety of poses, showing off their shape and some times a lot of flesh. Ashley had plumped for what looked like genuine selfies in T-shirts and jeans that revealed little. Rebecca was impressed. She looked like she could very well be real.

She memorised the screen name so she could send a link to London later, then handed the phone back to Harry, who glanced at it for a moment before placing it face down on the arm of his chair again.

'So how long did you chat before she asked you for money?' Rebecca asked.

'She didn't ask for money,' said Harry. 'That's why all this is such a waste of time.'

'But you did send her money?'

'Yes, but she didn't ask. I had to practically demand that she take it. We had been talking for weeks, months maybe.'

'What about?'

'Life. Her life. My life. She told me about her aunt, who is unwell, and her boyfriend who cheated on her with the woman she thought of as her best friend. How she missed Ghana, even though she loved America. She had very few friends; too many people made fun of her accent, which she couldn't shake off, she said. She talked about her job and her boss, who was hitting on her all the time. Then she was sacked because she refused him . . .'

Jesus, she really piled it on, Rebecca thought. *Family dead, auntie ill, boyfriend no good and a predator boss. There was a country and western song in there somewhere.*

'So I offered her some help, that was all,' Harry continued. 'Just to bide her over until she got a new job.'

'But she didn't ask you for cash at all?'

'No, it was my idea. She didn't want it. That's why I know she's not a scammer.'

3

'You think he'll appear on camera?'

Rebecca had pulled off the road to make the call. The signal was weak and occasionally Leo's voice sounded as if he had taken a dive into the grey waters to her left. She had driven a few miles from Harry's cottage, which was set back from the road beside Loch Rannoch, because she didn't think it right that she linger in his driveway. She also didn't want to make the call when she got back to the rented accommodation because Stephen was there and this was supposed to be a holiday to coincide with her birthday. She didn't want to be seen doing too much work. He knew she was following up on this story – it was why they had chosen this part of the country for their break – but they had made a pact that neither of them would bring their respective professions into their personal lives, if they could help it. Stephen, a lawyer, seemed to be finding that far easier than she did, to be honest.

She stared at the loch stretching towards the opposite bank, misted by a sheen of light rain, as she spoke to Leo Cross, who was somewhere in London. He preferred video calls, perhaps because he had spent his professional life in front of and behind cameras, but Rebecca told him it was too much for the limited bandwidth in this part of the Central Highlands. She had no idea if that was true, and was aware she was using an excuse scammers like Ashley made, but she simply did not enjoy making face-to-face calls, even though Leo was quite possibly the most attractive man she had ever set eyes on. She felt a twinge of guilt because she knew that even while she was sitting in this lay-by, with Highland drizzle spattering her windscreen, talking to Mr Handsome in London, her own significant other – who was no Quasimodo, it had to be said – was in a cottage a few miles down the road, probably preparing her lunch. At least she hoped he was because she was starving.

'At this point I would say no.' She flicked her wipers on to clear the windscreen. 'He doesn't think he's being scammed.'

'Can't his daughter convince him?' Leo had the kind of mellow voice you hear on TV, persuading you that something you don't want is actually desperately needed in your life – a cleaner home, fresher breath, a sparkling toilet. In fact, Leo Cross had been a TV presenter before he had set up on his own and had – Rebecca had learned while doing some research of her own – voiced advertisements for such varied products as dog food, hair gel and erectile dysfunction. She didn't know him well enough to ask him which of the three he desperately needed himself.

'Unlikely, I'd say,' she replied.

'They don't get on?'

Rebecca thought about her conversations with Harry's daughter. She had detected a slight edge when Ann spoke about her father but had put it down to the woman's concern that Harry was being ripped off.

'Oh, they get on, as far as I know,' Rebecca said. 'They just don't see this Ashley9951 in the same way.'

'And she wasn't there today?'

'No. She's laid up at home. Her husband works offshore.'

'Okay, so what's your take on it? Is it worth pursuing?'

Rebecca paused to consider this, watching in her rear-view as a car pulled in behind her. 'I think so. This person has been clever in the way she's handled this – compared to others, anyway. I'd say for her it's a long game.'

'If it is a *she*,' said Leo. 'But, yeah, most of them get right to the point pretty quickly. Target the sad and the lonely, a little bit of flattery, exchange of photographs, maybe some flirting, a bit of sexting. I'm looking at this Ashley's profile now.'

A middle-aged woman had climbed out of the car, carrying a large wreath, and was crossing the road towards a path leading into some dense woodland.

'So far, so typical,' he said. 'Not many pics posted, first one . . . four months ago. Tell me again, when did she get in touch with Harry for the first time?'

'Four months ago.'

'Yeah, as I said, so far so typical. She sets up the account, does a trawl, finds his profile. Older man, no obvious pics shared of a wife. Maybe he's followed other fake accounts back in the past, though not necessarily interacted with them. She follows him, he follows back.'

'Some people just follow back automatically,' Rebecca said. She was not a fan of social media. Those accounts she had were for use professionally rather than for sharing her own thoughts and images. Even so, sometimes she was not as careful as she should be, for these sites were the bridges under which trolls lived. 'Then she sends a direct message – Hi, how you doing, I'm Ashley, who are you? Blah-blah-blah.'

'Did she try to move him onto any other social media platform?'

Rebecca's research had told her that scammers try to move the mark onto certain other sites where it is harder to trace back and very little is done to shut them down.

'Just a suggestion near the start of the conversation,' she said, 'but he didn't go for it.'

'Why not?'

'I don't think he's on any other platform. Not sure he even knows others exist.'

Another car had pulled in behind and a further two women had alighted from it. They both opened umbrellas against the light rain and Rebecca watched them follow the first into the woods.

'And his wife is dead?' Leo asked.

'Yes.'

'Any clues about their relationship?'

'He seems to still mourn her, but his daughter said he was not the best of husbands, really.'

'Abusive?'

'No, nothing like that. Cold, I suppose. Distant.'

'But you had the impression he missed his wife?'

'Yes, very much.'

Leo made a rumbling sound in his throat, something she had learned he did when he was thinking. 'Some people are like that. They find it difficult to show how they feel about someone.'

Rebecca didn't answer because that was something she understood.

'I feel this is perfect for our show, Rebecca,' said Leo. 'This Ashley is quite something. I think we really need this one.'

There was a silence on the other end of the line during which Rebecca presumed he was studying the profile again. Her wipers swept away the rain to reveal a man and a woman on foot, wrapped in waterproof gear, rounding a bend in the road ahead of her then turning onto the woodland path. Okay, she thought, what's going on here?

Leo broke the silence on the line. 'Did you do a reverse image search?'

'No, not had the chance.' She peered into the pathway opposite. But the forest had wrapped itself around the people who had entered it.

'I'll do it. Leave it with me.'

He was pledging to take the profile image Ashley had posted, and possibly some others, and put them through a digital search engine to see where else they had been used.

Leo asked, 'And you say she has made calls?'

'Yes.'

'And they connected okay?'

'Harry didn't mention any problems.'

'So he's spoken to her?'

'Yes.'

'But not seen her?'

'No.'

'So he doesn't know if she matches the pics on her profile?'

'No. But he did speak to a female.'

'See, that's where she's different. Scammers often don't like to make voice-only calls. If you claim you're from the US but have an African or East European accent – or barely speak English, in fact, judging by some of their messages – it gives the game away. As for video calls, quite often it's forget about it, baby. Mysterious technical problems come up. Or they're a means to draw the mark into some sexual blackmail, get him or her to perform an act of personal gratification on camera.'

'Personal gratification?' she asked, her voice dancing with laughter. 'Wow.'

A slight laugh, almost embarrassed. 'I'm being polite.'

'I prefer the term onanism, myself.'

'It's my turn to say wow! Where did a millennial like you pick that up?'

'We have dictionaries in Scotland, you know. It's not all *och aye, the noo.*'

He chuckled, and Rebecca watched a man climb from a car which had pulled in ahead of her. Although he was wearing a coat, she could see the dog collar at his neck. The minister paused to check he had left enough room for her to pull out, smiled through the windscreen at her, then pulled his coat tighter around him and stepped across the road. She felt her reporter's nose twitch. What was going on in those woods?

16

'Ashley admits she's from Ghana but is living in the US,' said Rebecca.

'Clever. That covers any language issues. Did you see any of the direct messages?'

'No, not yet. I said I would go back, though. Have another chat.'

'And he was okay with that?'

Her wipers began to scrape at the glass, so she clicked them off. 'Seemed to be.'

'I take it he's kinda lonely.'

She laughed. 'What are you saying, Leo? That a man would have to be lonely to want to speak to me again?'

He realised what he'd said and grew flustered. 'No . . . well . . . no! I meant . . .'

'You know, cos I'm quite a catch. My boyfriend thinks so, anyway.'

Her boyfriend. It sounded so ridiculous when she said it, and yet that was what Stephen was, although he had never actually said she was a catch. She was sure he thought it, though. At least, he'd better.

Leo realised she was winding him up. 'Yeah, I'm sure he does. Sorry, you know what I meant. It was basically a non sequitur – I meant him talking to this Ashley. She really didn't ask for money at any point?'

'No, he made the offer. She refused three times.'

'Very biblical,' he said. 'Yeah, that's unusual. They tend to put the bite on fairly quickly. And, in fact, ask straight out – I need a gift card to help pay my rent, or keep my internet going, or pay my college fees or medical bills.' Rebecca knew all this, but she didn't think he was mansplaining. His absent tone told her he was merely giving voice to his own thoughts. 'She's clever, this one. Do we know how much he has given her?'

'He won't say.'

That throat rumble again. 'What are his finances like?'

'He's no Bill Gates but he seems comfortable. Nice house. He was a civil servant all his life so he probably has a decent pension.'

'So he could have parted with some hefty change . . .'

'Maybe.'

'What do you think?'

'He wouldn't admit it completely, but my gut says yes, he's sent her a fair amount. The way he talked about his wife giving to charity made me think he thought he was honouring her memory. His daughter thinks so, too.'

She heard an exhalation of breath. 'Rebecca, I really need this bloke on the show.'

'I'm working on it.'

'He hasn't blown you off yet, though?'

'No. He seems like a decent guy. He's defensive about all this, but that's to be expected. I said I would go back to see him tomorrow, let him think about it.'

'Okay, good. Keep that door open.'

The call ended. She sat for a moment, watching the soft rain smear across the windscreen again, but she didn't click the wipers back on. Instead, she gazed across the road towards the pathway.

4

The path below her feet was springy but firm enough not to cause concern over any moisture breaching the integrity of her shoes, which was just as well because when calling on Harry she had elected not to wear the stout walking boots she'd had on all weekend. Walking boots and leggings did not say professional; black flats and jeans did, at least as far as she was concerned. She followed the trail through the trees, remaining watchful for the people she had seen entering the forest, thankful that the branches above offered some sort of shelter from the rain that seemed to not quite fall but hang in the air before draping itself over whatever was below. She wore a grey hoodie underneath her black thigh-length coat and she pulled the hood up to protect her hair. She wasn't particularly vain – well, perhaps she was as vain as the next person, as long as the next person wasn't a reality TV star – but she didn't enjoy getting wet.

The trees here seemed different to those she'd seen on forest walks near their rented cottage. When she reached out to touch the bark it had an unusual texture. At least, she thought so. This was something her father had taught her. Don't just look, touch. Some places existed in the modern world, yet carried trace elements of the past. She recalled him on family holidays touching old stones, rocks and trees, as if this tactile response could transport him back in time, or uncover some deep secret. She smiled at the memory. There had been a time when thinking about these times with her father contributed to her melancholy – not depression; she believed she had never been depressed – but no longer. He had been taken too soon, but she had come to terms not only with his death from cancer but also the other deaths she had experienced since then.

Occasionally, in the dark of night when all was silent, she would listen for the cry of a child who had never breathed for itself, never seen daylight, never felt a mother's touch. Sometimes she heard it, somewhere in the shadows of her mind, but she knew it was just a longing for a different past. Or maybe a different present. She knew she should not feel guilt: the miscarriage was nobody's fault. That didn't prevent her from wondering if there had been anything she could have done to prevent it. Over the years she had analysed, sifted, scrutinised. But she had done nothing. It was an accident of chromosomes, that's all. A conversation regarding children had not yet come up with Stephen, thank God. Hell, they still hadn't used the L-word.

There was a stillness in this forest that spoke to her. A feeling that here was a part of an ancient world untouched by the modern. It was a thin place, she was sure – where the planes of the physical and the spiritual are in harmony and are occasionally glimpsed. She wondered if those spectres of the past caught sight of her in the present and believed they had seen a ghost.

Voices very much of the present drifted between the boughs of the trees and she finally caught a glimpse of the figures, all standing in the centre of a small clearing. She eased to a halt when she felt she had a decent view of them, making no attempt to move any closer. She hoped none of them would look back and see her peering at them, but she was in a dense enough portion of this forest that she was confident they wouldn't spot her. This wasn't voyeurism – these people weren't dogging, for goodness' sake – this was professional interest. At least, that's what she told herself. Her boss Elspeth would have called it being a right nosey bugger . . .

That's what we do, she would add. *That's a reporter's job. I have to be nosey on behalf of those people who either can't be or don't want to be.*

The six people were clustered around a log, lying on its side, against which was propped a wreath. One woman had a comforting hand on the shoulder of the woman Rebecca had seen carrying the flowers, who now stood as if to attention, her face stiff as though she was holding emotion at bay. The minister was reading from his Bible. Rebecca heard his voice – deep, sonorous – but not the words.

It was a memorial service of some kind, clearly. Someone connected to the woman who had carried the wreath. A husband? A child? Something had happened here, perhaps. But what? Rebecca's nose really itched. She knew she would have to find out, but there was no way she was going to intrude on this moment. She could be a nosey bugger, but not insensitive; she already felt uncomfortable witnessing this personal moment. This was a big, wide valley but a relatively small community. Somebody would know.

She began to edge back along the path, careful not to move too quickly and attract attention or make any noise, which was easy given the carpet of pine needles underfoot. As she retreated, she spotted a man standing far off among the trees. He wore a long thick coat tied tightly around his waist by a heavy black leather belt and a woollen hat pulled down over his ears. From this distance, she couldn't guess whether he was young or old, but she saw a smudge of white bristles on his chin and jawline. She could tell he was tall and powerfully built, and he was watching the memorial with interest. She glanced at the clearing again, where the group were hugging each other, the minister shaking hands. There was no sign of the man when she looked back. One second he was there, the next he was gone. As if he was one of those misty spectres she'd imagined lurking between the trunks and the boughs.

So, who the hell was he?

5

By the time Rebecca had driven through the village of Kinloch Rannoch at the eastern end of the loch, the soft rain had faded to a mere suggestion of moisture and some texture began to ripple the solid grey that had filled the sky. Rebecca had never visited this part of Perthshire, so when the job from Leo had come up, it was Stephen who suggested turning it into a week's holiday. As a child he had visited the area regularly with his parents, renting a converted post office which formed part of an estate a few miles outside the village. He had tried to book that property, but every one of their rentals, all converted from other uses, was fully booked. He had found this two-bedroom cottage set on a small hill just beyond the village, among mature pine trees but with an unrestricted view across the valley towards the mountain of Schiehallion, at that moment hidden in low cloud and hanging mist. The road leading to the house was fairly steep, and suspension-threateningly rough in places, but negotiable by her non-off-road vehicle as long as she remembered to keep the car in low gear and resisted the urge to hammer the accelerator.

When she pulled onto the flat space at the side of the cottage, she saw the quad bike belonging to Catherine McIntosh, her sheepdog Buster sitting obediently in the attached trailer. Rebecca gave the dog a pat on the head, which he accepted with what she had learned in the past two days was his usual equanimity, and walked into the cottage. She saw Catherine's mud-crusted wellingtons just inside the front door and heard her cut-glass tones coming from the kitchen to the right, where Rebecca found her at the small circular table, a coffee cup in front of her and the tell-tale crumbs of fruit cake on her plate.

Stephen was closing the oven door when she came in and he dropped the padded mitt he had been wearing on the surface as he straightened. 'Hi! Lunch won't be long. Microwave soup and I've just popped some crusty bread in the oven.'

Rebecca sat down and nodded a greeting to Catherine, who nodded back as she sipped her coffee. 'Sounds great. If there's any coffee left in that pot, I'll have some.'

Stephen picked up the glass coffee pot from the filter machine, hooked a mug from a wooden tree on the work surface, placed it in front of her and began pouring. 'Can you manage the milk and sugar yourself, madam, or do you need me to do it?'

She smiled. 'No, I can manage, thanks.'

Stephen took the pot back. 'Good, because I was wondering what your last servant died of.'

'Blunt force trauma,' Rebecca said, pouring milk from a small white jug into her coffee. 'For backchat.'

Stephen laughed. 'All go okay with your guy?'

'Yes, but I'll need to go back.'

'That's why you get the big bucks.'

This was one of the things she liked about him, this acceptance that her work could often bleed into her private life, just as she accepted that being a busy solicitor meant he often had work to do when he might otherwise be seeing her. Neither of them complained, bitched, moaned, whinged or sulked when plans had to be changed. She was resolved to not allow this story to intrude too much on their holiday, though, because she intended to enjoy her birthday for the first time in years. She didn't normally mark the day but for some reason she wanted to celebrate it now. She didn't know if having someone else in her life had something to do with that.

Catherine didn't ask where she had been or what they were talking about. She knew Rebecca had work to do but didn't ask what it was. She seemed to be the least inquisitive person Rebecca had ever met, and that made Rebecca very curious. Not that it took much to make her curious.

The woman was perhaps in her fifties, but years of working outdoors had weathered her face. She would have been beautiful when younger; in fact, she remained striking, and her voice betrayed her southern English roots. The only things Rebecca knew about her were that she owned the land on which the cottage sat, she had inherited the sheep farm from her late husband, and she was the daughter of minor landed gentry in Surrey – all gleaned during a conversation in the village shop between Stephen and a shop assistant when she had asked where he was staying. Sometimes Rebecca thought he would make a good reporter, but then asking questions is also a major part of a solicitor's job.

Catherine was wearing what Rebecca assumed was her customary uniform of thick blue waterproof jacket, a grey fleece underneath and a brightly coloured scarf that would have Rupert the Bear stamping his foot in envy. Her trousers were of heavy tweed and the socks Rebecca could see were so well insulated they could ward off an ice age. The afternoon before, as the grey light of the damp day was giving way to the gloom of approaching night, Rebecca and Stephen had sat in small foldaway garden chairs on the cottage's small porch, wrapped in thick coats and sipping mugs of hot chocolate, watching Catherine and Buster gather some sheep and then drive them into another field at the far end. Witnessing human, dog and machine work in harmony had been an almost hypnotic experience for Rebecca.

Nodding at the crumbs on the plate, Rebecca said, 'How did you enjoy Stephen's fruit cake?'

Catherine mopped up the remains with a finger, licked them away and said with a wink, 'It was adequate.'

'Adequate?' Stephen had begun wiping down the sink with a paper towel. 'I'll have you know *Bake Off* wanted me to appear, but I knocked them back because I didn't want to demean my art.'

Rebecca leaned closer to Catherine and said in a stage whisper, 'Don't listen to him. He didn't even know what *Bake Off* was until recently. He doesn't watch much TV.'

Catherine smiled. 'Quite right, too. Horrible little dictatorial device. I much prefer the radio. But the cake was rather good. It must be handy having a man who can cook, darling.'

Rebecca had learned that Catherine called everyone darling, perhaps because she couldn't remember their name. She seemed to be a hard worker, but an air of vagueness hung around her like old perfume.

'Oh, he can't cook,' Rebecca said. 'Fruit cake is the extent of his culinary expertise.'

'Hey,' Stephen objected, 'I resent that. I also make mince pies.'

'True,' Rebecca conceded, 'but not as successfully as fruit cake.'

'You certainly knocked them back at Christmas.'

'I didn't want to offend you . . .' Rebecca leaned towards Catherine. 'So needy. It's embarrassing.'

'Men are all the same, darling – they need strong women to bolster them. Ron was exactly like that. I swear if he hadn't married me this whole farm would have gone to ruin.' Catherine smiled again and pushed her chair away from the table. 'And I'd gathered your man was no chef when he revealed it was microwave soup. I'll drop some real soup off later and protect your body from all those additives. Anyway, I must be about my business. I only came by to deliver some more logs for the fire. You'll have noticed how cold it is at this time of the year. There should be enough to see you through the week, but please shout if you need more. Stephen here was good enough

26

to help me stack them in the shed at the back, then practically begged me to come in and sample this fruit cake, which I now freely admit was excellent.'

'Ah, it's gone from adequate to rather good to excellent,' Stephen said. 'The truth will always out.'

Catherine walked to the kitchen door. 'It's the aftertaste, darling. It really is quite potent.' As she passed Rebecca, she said in a stage whisper, 'I see what you mean about being needy. Quite unbecoming in a handsome man like him.'

Stephen beamed, but Rebecca gave him a withering glance. 'Don't preen, that's also unbecoming.'

Stephen was handsome – not Leo Cross-telly-handsome, but in a more battered way. He had played rugby as a young man and still retained the physique and a nose that was slightly askew.

Catherine was in the hallway pulling on her wellingtons and Rebecca ignored Stephen's still grinning face to ask about the events of the day. 'I saw a very curious thing on the way back from my appointment, Catherine.'

'The valley is full of curious things, darling, and not just some of the visitors.' Catherine stooped to hold a boot steady and wriggled her foot inside. 'You'll have to be more specific.'

'I was on the south side of the loch and I saw a group of people taking a wreath into the woods, where they held some sort of memorial ceremony. Would you know what that was about?'

Catherine straightened and stamped the other foot further into the wellie. 'Was it the Black Wood? Down by Carie?'

Rebecca shook her head. 'I don't know what it was called. I was driving back towards Kinloch Rannoch and had pulled off the road. I followed the people down a path. There was a minister there.'

'That would be Tom Lester. And the woman with the wreath would be Frances MacGregor. Did they lay it in a small clearing, beside an old log?'

27

Rebecca nodded. 'So, what's it all about? Was it a memorial ceremony?'

Catherine paused for a brief moment. 'Yes, for her son Fergus. He disappeared five years ago. She lays a wreath there on the anniversary of when she last saw him. The boy loved this entire valley, yet he left home one morning and was never seen again.'

'No word at all?'

'Not a thing.'

'And no trace of him?'

A head shake. 'The entire wood was combed, search parties went up into the hills and along the lochside, appeals went out for anyone who might have seen him, but nothing. It was as if the Black Wood had simply eaten him up.'

'And was this kind of thing out of character for him?'

Catherine glanced at Stephen, standing behind Rebecca. He tilted his head in an apologetic way. 'Welcome to my world, Catherine. I have to endure this all the time.'

Rebecca felt embarrassed. 'Sorry, Catherine, it's an occupational hazard. I'm a reporter and when something piques my interest I can't help myself.'

A guarded look crossed the woman's face, one that Rebecca was well used to, and the airy demeanour was gone. People often closed down when they learned she was a journalist. 'What newspaper do you work for, darling?'

'It's a news agency – the Highland News Agency?' Rebecca didn't know why she couched that as a question, as though she was asking Catherine if she'd heard of it. 'But honestly, this isn't a story, this is just my natural nosiness.'

Catherine considered this briefly. 'Well, it's no secret really, darling, it was reported at the time. Even had some TV people here. Such pests, they were. I didn't really know Fergus that well.' She thought about that. 'No, didn't really know him at all. I knew him by sight, of course – we know most locals, at least by sight – and from what I understand he was a nice lad, very studious, fascinated by the history of Rannoch; and there's a lot of that.'

'How old was he when he disappeared?'

Catherine's cheeks puffed. 'I couldn't say for sure, early twenties maybe.'

'So, what do you think happened?'

Catherine laughed. 'I have no idea, darling! I told you I didn't know him or the family, apart from a nod and a hello.'

Rebecca had expected that, so wasn't disappointed. 'And he loved this Black Wood? Why is it called that?'

'I was once told that it's because that part of the woodland around Rannoch is all pine, ancient pine. They say other trees such as birch, aspen or oak can be more colourful, but personally I find these old trees more appealing. It's one of the few remaining parcels of the old Caledonian Forest that once covered much of Scotland. It's Scots pine.'

'Isn't that the national tree of Scotland?' Stephen asked.

Catherine seemed surprised he knew that. 'Yes, well done, darling.'

Stephen flushed a little. 'I read as well as bake.'

'None of the trees in the Black Wood were hand-planted. They're all native and protected now, but there are attempts to expand it. Some of the trees at its heart are three hundred years old – granny pines, they call them. I think that's why young Fergus loved the place so much. Those trees have seen a great deal. Perhaps he felt he could tap into all that history somehow. So I'm told anyway. Seems strange, I know, but that seemed to be the way of it.'

It didn't seem strange to Rebecca. 'I saw a man there,' she said. 'He kept himself a little back from the ceremony. He seemed a little . . . off.'

'In what way *off*?'

29

'Well, like a homeless person, you know what I mean?'

Recognition glinted in Catherine's eyes. 'That would be Cormac. He's not homeless, he just looks it. He lives in a small cottage up on the hillside just beyond the edges of the wood. Keeps very much to himself.'

'Does he have a farm? A croft?'

'He makes a living, such as it is, carving wood, creating ornaments and knick-knacks for tourists. The village shop sells them, as do some outlets in Pitlochry. He's not Rannoch-born – his accent is Irish, although no one knows exactly which part because he's never talked much about himself. He doesn't talk much at all, in fact. I don't think I've exchanged more than ten words with him in all the years I've been here. Fetched up here about thirty years ago, bought his cottage, made no friends, told no one about himself – and believe me, there have been many who've tried. We are a varied community, a mixture of Rannoch-born and incomers, and we get on very well by and large. But Cormac is a loner, doesn't mix, doesn't even go into Kinloch Rannoch unless he can help it, and even then only for supplies.'

'So what is he, some sort of recluse?'

'Yes, I suppose he is. And we respect his lifestyle choice.' She stamped her feet properly into her boots. 'But I have to be off now – lots of work to do. Thank you for the cake, Stephen, it really was lovely.'

'My pleasure, Catherine . . .'

Catherine opened the door. 'Are you thinking about doing some sort of story, darling?'

Rebecca had been turning the scant information over in her mind and was surprised by the question. 'No, not really.' Then she reconsidered. 'Well, I don't know.' She then reconsidered again. 'Probably not . . . I'd need something new.'

Catherine nodded. 'I think it best to leave well enough alone. Raking over dead ashes might generate heat that can still burn.

Whatever happened to poor Fergus is a mystery and likely to remain that way. People really don't want someone poking around their little bags of secrets, do they?'

'And are there secrets here, Catherine?'

She stepped into the daylight and paused for a moment to look up at the sky, where pools of blue flooded through the broken clouds, and then across to Schiehallion, more of it visible now, although mist still clung to its summit. 'There are secrets everywhere, darling, even in paradise.'

She gave them a dazzling smile and turned to her quad bike. Rebecca closed the door and turned back to Stephen, who was regarding her with a smile that was almost mocking.

'What?' she asked.

'No, I'm not really doing a story. Well, I don't know if I'm doing a story. Probably not, but I'd need something new.' His smile grew into a grin. 'I know you, Becks. You're not going to let this lie without sticking your nose in.'

'I have no intention of sticking my nose into anything,' she protested. 'Apart from that bread you have in the oven.'

Stephen laughed and turned back into the kitchen. She couldn't blame him for doubting her, for she knew she had sounded as convincing as a government minister on breakfast TV.

6

It was cold in this house.

Frances MacGregor dropped her car keys in the bowl on the polished dark-wood surface of the table by the door, took off her damp coat and hung it on the curved hook of the rack, then pulled off the solid shoes she had worn for the service and slipped her feet into the slippers waiting beneath the table. This was routine. No, this was her ritual. The tiny habitual actions that she performed every day, every week, every month.

It was cold and silent in this house.

She moved down the hallway and into the kitchen. She filled the kettle and clicked it on. She took two mugs from the overhead cabinet, placed a tea bag into each, rested a spoon in one, then stood back, leaned against the work surface on the opposite side of the room and waited for the water to boil. Another routine, another ritual performed every day, every week, every month.

The memorial in the Black Wood was a ritual, but an annual one. She refused to think of it as the day Fergus vanished, for there was a permanence about that word. Vanished suggested that he would never reappear. She couldn't think of him as dead, for that was even more permanent. No, she liked to imagine him alive somewhere, living life, finding a happiness that he had never found here.

And yet, she still organised the wreath and asked Reverend Lester to do a reading, and invited friends to attend, although over the five years their numbers had dwindled. No matter, she would continue with the routine – the ritual – until she was no longer able, even if she was the only one there. The wreath would be laid. Fergus would be remembered, no matter what.

She carried the mugs of tea into the sitting room, where Dan was in his usual position in his armchair, reading the news on his tablet, his earphones clamped to the side of his head, the jack plugged into the CD player on a shelf beside him. She didn't need to hear the music to know what he was listening to. Her husband used classical music as a means of keeping the world at bay, especially today. He looked up and nodded his thanks as she set one of the mugs on a small table beside him. She acknowledged him with a brief smile and moved beyond to the section of their open-plan living room that housed the dining table. It could seat six but only she and Dan used it now. Their younger son, Rory, was away now and Fergus was . . . well, wherever Fergus was. They didn't speak much to Rory now. He had more or less turned his back on them, and they him. He had let them down in so many ways and they could not accept him cohabiting with that slut. She knew Dan struggled with his conscience – after all, Rory was his son and had always been his favourite – but she felt no such weakness of resolve. Rory had broken not only man's laws, but God's, and she could not accept that. Fergus had been her jewel; Rory, a disappointment.

It was cold and silent in this house and it felt empty. When the boys had been here, there was often noise: music from their rooms and either she or Dan telling them to turn it down; the TV blaring; phone calls to and from friends; doors slamming, footsteps, laughter, arguments, disagreements, sulks. Bridges were burned, rebuilt, burned again and built again, for that was what families do.

But some bridges could never be rebuilt because the waters – the emotions – which had torn them down were too strong.

She sat at the table, sipped her tea and stared through the large picture window towards the rear garden. Spring wasn't far off, although you wouldn't know it with the temperature. It would come, though, and the garden would resurrect itself. Life, hidden in the sleep of winter, would awaken and reach out to the warmth of the sun.

But not here, not inside this house. She glanced at the back of her husband's head, still bowed over the pages gleaming from his tablet, still cut off from her and this day within a world of crisp, clear digital notes written by a long-dead composer.

The central heating boiler firing broke the silence as it kept the air temperature comfortable, yet it was cold in this house.

Cormac had seen the young woman looking at him as he watched the service in the clearing. He hadn't joined it. He never did, for he knew he wasn't part of their world, not really. He recognised that people in the glen were in the main kind and tolerant, but he did not feel as if he belonged in their community. He did not feel as if he belonged anywhere, and yet he had remained here for thirty years simply because he had nowhere else to go.

Home.

He thought about the word as he trudged through the bracken, automatically following a path that only he knew, his hands thrust deep into his coat pockets, woollen cap clamped on his head. There was a time he couldn't have worn such a hat, as his hair was unruly and thick, but it was sparser now. He was still far from bald, but he could at least now protect his head from the elements.

Home.

He should have regarded his cottage as his home. He owned it. He lived in it. So why did he see it only as somewhere he stayed, as a shelter? He certainly didn't think of County Tyrone as home, not any more. He had been away for thirty years. Home was somewhere you could return to, and he knew he could never go back there. Or, rather, *should* never go back. He wasn't a displaced person, but he felt out of place wherever he was, apart from in the Black Wood.

These old trees had seen a lot over the years. People, events, blood. He knew every part of the forest, even better than the rangers and conservation officers who tended the place. He had walked these paths by day and by night. He had seen things they wouldn't, natural and unnatural. He had watched the crossbills nest in early spring and extract the seeds from the pine cones with their curious intersecting beaks. He had held himself very still to study deer as they fed, fearful even to breathe lest he startle them. He had listened to the percussive music of the great spotted woodpecker and searched the boughs for sight of its white and black plumage with a flash of red. He had hunkered down and studied the movement of ants as they busied themselves to and from their home in mounds of pine needles.

And he had seen other things that were not part of this world. Shadows that flitted in the mist and in the darkness, figures that were no longer men but images of the past, played out in flickering light like an old film on a wrinkled screen.

And so he had been alone here and yet not alone, for the land around him was filled with wonders.

And, as he emerged from the edge of the forest and headed across an open plain of brown heather, the roof of the cottage and its outbuildings visible on the far side, he knew that someone was waiting for him there.

7

Stephen was having a break, but that didn't mean he didn't keep in touch with his office in Inverness. His secretary/assistant/office manager/bodyguard Elaine was still at her desk every day and was more than capable of keeping the day-to-day business of the practice ticking over. He had arranged for another solicitor to cover court appearances, handle any emergencies or rush to the side of clients if they found themselves the focus of the Inverness police, but he had still promised to call in every day and as this was Monday, he made his first call just after they had eaten the soup (cream of chicken for her, carrot and coriander for him). He had grimaced when Rebecca insisted on dunking the crusty bread into her bowl but, as she pointed out, you can take the girl out of Glasgow et cetera et cetera.

He moved into their bedroom to make his call, leaving her to sit by the open fire in the living room, her laptop on her knee. Thankfully, Catherine had Wi-Fi installed – reluctantly, she had told Stephen, because she believed if people visited this area they should enjoy it with as little intrusion as possible from the twenty-first century.

Rebecca opened a search engine and typed in 'Fergus MacGregor'. A few links popped up, but she clicked on the BBC site first. It was a fairly brief entry, more or less outlining what Catherine had already told her. Other sites, a mixture of red tops and broadsheets, supplied a little more on the case.

Fergus MacGregor was twenty-two when he disappeared. He had recently graduated in history from the University of the West Highlands and was looking for work while also researching a book on the clans which had clustered around Rannoch. His parents, Frances and Daniel, were both Rannoch-born, and they and their two sons lived in a converted steading on the northern side of the loch.

Fergus had told his parents he was going into Pitlochry for the day to meet a friend, but he never arrived. His car was found parked in a space near the Black Wood the following morning, but there was no trace of him, despite an extensive search led by rangers with the Forestry Commission, police, local volunteers, firefighters and even mountain rescue.

From what Rebecca could tell from the reports, Fergus had been well-liked. The family had mostly maintained a stoic silence, broken only by the youngest son, Rory. Rebecca found a photograph of the woman she recognised as Frances standing beside a young man on what looked like the road beside the loch. Obviously a snatched shot. Her face was stiff as she stared into the middle distance, the young man – the caption told her it was Rory – hunched into a black leather jacket with a grey hood covering his head. Another report, in a red top, carried quotes from an emotional appeal Rory had apparently made on the BBC's *Reporting Scotland*.

'Wherever you are, Fergus, get in touch,' the transcript read. 'Mum's worried about you. I'm worried about you. We need to know you're okay. We need to know you're safe and well.'

The report ended with a quote from the police officer in charge of the case, who was at the time based in Perth. Detective Chief Inspector Val Roach had commented, 'This is a puzzling case.' Well, Rebecca thought, it's a small world – though, as some comedian had once said, she wouldn't like to paint it.

Roach had continued: 'Mr MacGregor was a well-liked, well-respected young man and this disappearance is out of character. We would urge anyone who may have any inkling about his current whereabouts to please get in touch. All information will be treated in the utmost confidence, but the young man's family are very worried.'

The report ended with a number for any potential witnesses to call.

Rebecca reached for her phone, found the name in her contacts and hit the call button. It rang for a few seconds, then was answered.

'I thought you were on holiday,' said Val Roach from her office, now in Inverness.

'I am,' Rebecca replied.

'I was looking forward to a whole week without you pestering me. Or is it simply that you miss me?'

DCI Valerie Roach had a playful side, but there was often a hard edge, as Rebecca had discovered during one of their earliest encounters when the police officer had threatened to arrest her if she did not divulge a source. Relations between them had settled now to something that may have been respect, perhaps friendship, but certainly mutual recognition of utility. In short, they each used the other when the need arose.

'Of course I miss you,' said Rebecca, 'and it pains me that we are apart.'

'Uh-huh.' Roach made the two syllables sound like *go screw yourself*. 'So what do you want, Becks?'

'Why should I want something?'

'You always want something.'

'I might just be phoning to say hello, how you doing, hope you're well.'

'Yeah, but you usually only do that when you want something.'

'Well, I'm hurt. People think reporters are heartless, but we feel pain. If you prick us, do we not bleed?'

A stifled laugh drifted down the line. 'Okay, okay, I'll apologise before you go into a soliloquy. So, why have you called?'

'I want something, of course.'

The laugh was open now. 'Fine, shoot.'

'Does the name Fergus MacGregor ring any bells?'

'Vaguely.'

'Young man, twenty-two, went missing five years ago today in Rannoch?'

'Oh, yeah – I remember. It was just before I transferred up here from Perth. Not a great time in my life, thanks to the Bawbag.'

Roach had moved from Perth to Inverness when her marriage had broken down, her scientist husband leaving her to live with his research assistant. His *much younger* research assistant. They were married now, with one child and another on the way. Roach had taken to calling him Bawbag, a Glasgow term for the scrotum more commonly used to disparage another person.

'So, what can you tell me about it?'

There was a pause, and Rebecca heard Roach sipping something. She was fond of her coffee and took a thermos of her own brew into work with her, so in Rebecca's mind's eye the DCI was sitting at her desk in the divisional headquarters, her black hair cut short and threaded with grey, wearing her usual black suit and crisp white blouse, drinking from the flask's silver cup as she searched her memory. There was no doubt in Rebecca's mind that she would call up details of the case, for Roach had a mind sharp enough to cut steel.

'Not much to tell, or that I can remember without cue cards. Young bloke, as you say, vanished while apparently on the way to Pitlochry for the day. His car was found beside Loch Rannoch, near to a path he often took into some woods.'

'The Black Wood.'

'That's right. He was obsessed with the place and, having been in there, I can understand why.'

'It's beautiful.'

'Yes, it is. Anyway, the feeling was he had hurt himself, but we found no trace of him apart from his car.'

'No blood? No sign of violence?'

Roach paused and when she spoke her tone of voice had changed, had become more businesslike. 'Is this an official inquiry? What's your interest?'

It was Rebecca's turn to consider. What was she doing here? She was in the area on one story, a paying gig, and she was supposed to be on a break the rest of the time. Should she really take up precious time following a story that nobody was paying for?

'Curiosity, that's all. I saw a memorial service this morning, apparently the family do it every year, and it piqued my interest. So, I did a bit of internet digging and saw your name in a news story.'

'Just curious, eh?' Roach's voice was heavy with sarcasm.

'Yes.'

'I'll bet. Your curiosity generally leads to some kind of story.'

That wasn't true. Over the past few years she had followed a number of trails that led nowhere, but she wasn't about to undermine her reputation by admitting that.

'Okay,' Roach said, 'but whatever I tell you is completely off the record – clear?'

Rebecca felt excitement build. Whenever Roach spoke off the record she would reveal something that only the police and those directly involved knew.

'Clear,' she said.

'I mean it, Becks, you can't repeat what I'm about to tell you.'

'I'm not on a story, Val, I told you.'

'Yeah, and I'm not the best-looking cop in HQ.'

Rebecca had seen a few very attractive police officers in the divisional headquarters, men and women, but given Roach was co-operating she wasn't about to burst her bubble.

'I promise I won't use any of it,' she said, knowing Roach had to hear the words. It was a ritual between them.

'Okay, fine.' Roach was satisfied. A mutual trust had grown between them from that early, shaky start – she knew that if Rebecca told her she wouldn't use it, she wouldn't. At any rate, Rebecca still wasn't sure what the information was and how she could use it. Roach paused again, presumably for another mouthful of coffee.

'Anyway, he wasn't going to Pitlochry, or if he was, he wasn't meeting that friend, who told us he hadn't spoken to Fergus for two weeks and had made no arrangement to meet.'

'So who had he told he was going to Pitlochry? His parents?'

'Yes. They said they didn't know why he would lie, as it was out of character for him.'

'So why did he?'

'If we knew that we might have found him. That's if it's true he actually said it in the first place.'

'You suspect they might have been lying?'

Roach adopted an appalling French accent. 'I suspect everyone and everything.'

'Yeah, okay, Poirot . . .'

Rebecca recalled Catherine's words about secrets. She suspected there were some involved here. There always were.

'So what do you think happened?'

'Not a clue,' admitted Roach. 'It's a mystery.' She paused. 'Right up your street.'

8

Cormac felt responsible for the animals temporarily in his keeping. Tempted though he was to speak to them, to make a connection, he knew it was not a good idea. They were injured creatures needing some care and attention before they were sent back out into the wild; they were not pets. Keeping his distance meant that they could not imprint themselves upon him, or vice versa. He found them himself, or locals brought them to him, for word that he had what amounted to a small animal hospital had got around over the years. He accepted each wild charge wordlessly, and those who found them and brought them to him understood this, often depositing the poor creature at the gate to his garden and then leaving swiftly. Even the local vet gave her services for free when necessary, for often the injured animal was too far gone to be saved.

He didn't have many animals this morning – a jackdaw with a broken wing, a pipistrelle with a similar injury, a hedgehog that had been injured by a family dog and, rarest of all, a pine marten that had become entangled in some carelessly discarded wire. He had them housed in a series of cages in what was once a garage beside the cottage; his old open-back truck was left on the rough driveway, although he only used the vehicle when he needed to because he preferred to walk. Wheels could not take him through the Black Wood or up into the hills.

He had begun caring for the animals of the wood when he found a young deer caught on a barbed wire fence. He assumed the poor creature had tangled its back legs when attempting to leap over it. Cormac had heard its screaming early in the morning and was at first puzzled as to what it was. He had dressed hurriedly and stepped through his front door into a thick mist, and it had taken him some time to trace the source of the heartbreaking cries. The small roe buck seemed to understand he was there to help, for he allowed Cormac to hold him while easing the jagged wire from his flesh. The deer's haunches were deeply scored and streaming blood, so Cormac carried it back to the cottage and made it comfortable in the empty garage while he cleaned and dressed the wounds. Once inside, the stricken beast became alarmed, so tending to the damage was not easy. He collected some foliage and twigs and made a makeshift bed, placed some water in a bowl and left the creature alone for the rest of the day and overnight to heal a little before he set it free. He did not have the first clue as to what he was doing, but the thought of seeking professional help hadn't occurred to him at the time. He avoided speaking to people when he could; the vet and the storeowners were the exceptions. For a long time, the only meaningful, if non-verbal, contact he'd had was with the lost and broken creatures in that old garage. That was until he met Fergus.

He had watched the boy many times from the cover of the trees as he wandered in the Black Wood alone. He did not approach him, for he knew the dangers such conversations held, but he did observe him over the years, and it was not until Fergus was in his late teens that they began to acknowledge each other and, gradually, exchange a few words. It was clear to Cormac that the young man was equally as fascinated by the Black Wood and this common ground made him more comfortable in striking up an acquaintance, although he never invited Fergus back to his home.

That wasn't the case now, though, for Fergus was in the cottage, sitting in his chair by the fire, probably staring into the flames, lost in a world of his own making. Sulking, more to the point.

They had become embroiled in their usual argument earlier, soon after Cormac had returned from the wood. He knew he should not have said what he did, but he felt forced to and Fergus had reacted with his usual irritation.

'No!'

How he put so much force into that one word amazed Cormac, but it did not stop him from emphasising his original comment.

'Your mother has a right to know, Fergus,' he had said, for as usual he was moved by the woman's obvious sense of loss at the memorial. She did not weep, she did not wail, but her grief was evident in every movement and in the stiff way she held her head, as if she was holding back the emotion.

Fergus's response was vehement. 'We've been through all this before! How many times have I to say it? No! They can't know. They can't see me like this.'

And so it went on, back and forth, just as it had done the year before and the year before that and the two before that: Cormac trying to get the young man to agree to let his family know where he was living, Fergus refusing to even consider it, for reasons best known to himself. The argument grew heated, as it always did, and finally Cormac left him to stew. The rest of the year they got along perfectly, neither saying very much but when they did it was friendly, pleasant even, and Cormac had begun to appreciate having company. But on this day, the anniversary of the attack, it always deteriorated into a sullen silence that lasted for hours before Cormac apologised. It was always Cormac who did this because he knew in his heart that he should not have broached the subject at all. Fergus had made his views very plain. The thing was, Cormac really did believe the boy should be at home with his family. His wounds hadn't been that bad, just some bruising really, and tending to a human was not that much different to tending to an animal, but Fergus no longer wished to be seen. Cormac recognised that the boy had aged in the five years and, if he was honest, he didn't look good. He had also developed a bad limp.

As he poured water through the bars of the pine marten's cage – the wee thing would be ready to leave soon, he realised – Cormac recalled that day five years earlier, when he had carried the unconscious Fergus from the clearing to the cottage where he had tended his wounds. He had been groggy for days afterwards and Cormac came to believe he should have alerted someone, but Fergus pleaded with him to say nothing to anyone. He had hidden him from the search parties and even lied to police officers when they came to his door.

No, he hadn't seen Fergus.

No, he hadn't seen anyone else in the Black Wood.

No, Fergus had never told him that he intended to go anywhere.

All lies. All lies. All lies.

He knew in his heart that he had made a mistake. He should have taken the boy to the village or his parents, not hidden him away as he had done. But Fergus had begged him for protection, for sanctuary, and he had reluctantly agreed, although he knew there was a strong element of self-preservation in that decision. People would think he had done this, they were bound to. After all, he hadn't reported it right away, had he? No, he had carried the boy away, and even though it was an attempt to help him, they wouldn't see it that way. Someone else they might believe, but not him. Not Cormac Devlin.

Not with his past.

9

Rebecca wandered around the clearing, again marvelling at the silence that enveloped the wood so completely. Stephen stood at the edge, leaning against the trunk of a tree and flicking through a little booklet on the Black Wood he had found in the cottage, every now and again reading out something of interest to her. She listened to him, but as was her habit, her mind was filled with questions about what might have occurred here five years before.

She had just finished her call to Val Roach when he appeared from the bedroom, her sheepskin jacket in his hands. 'Let's go, then,' he said.

'We going for a walk?' she asked.

He threw her the jacket. 'Yes, to the Black Wood. I know you want to go back, so we might as well do it now.' He glanced through the living-room windows. 'It's shaping up to be not a bad afternoon, and we would go for a walk anyway, so it might as well be there.'

She felt a wave of warmth wash over her – this was one of the reasons why she was so comfortable with him – and she almost blurted something out, but that would never do. There was no way she was going to say it first. In her eyes, that was a bit needy. It was okay if he said it to her, but not the other way around. It was a distinction she didn't understand herself, but it was there and he would have to live with it. She did give him a long kiss before shouldering on her jacket.

She stooped to read the card attached to the wreath Mrs MacGregor had laid.

For Fergus. Always in our hearts. Come home to us.

Did she believe her son to still be alive? If so, why a memorial service? Rebecca raked at the moss and fallen pine needles with her foot, as if she might find something they had missed years before.

Stephen turned a page in the booklet. 'It's protected now, but it's nothing short of a miracle that the place is still here. Mankind has done everything it can over the centuries to destroy it. They've hacked and chopped and burned.' He looked up and glanced around, then craned his neck to gaze at the tree tops waving in the breeze above them. 'I didn't know Perthshire was known as Big Tree Country, did you?'

'Of course. Everyone knows that.' She smiled.

His look was sceptical as he returned to reading. 'It's home to deer, red squirrels and pine martens.' He studied the branches around him again. 'I've never seen a pine marten.' He breathed in. 'It's quite a place. I can see why this fellow Fergus loved it so much.' He fell silent and when she looked up she saw him studying her and smiling.

'What?'

'You've found your *wa* again,' he said.

She gave him a disparaging grimace, but she knew what he meant. He had said this the previous October. It had been unseasonably warm, she remembered, and she and Stephen were sitting beside a ruined bridge overlooking a river near to Loch Ness, watching rabbits – some brown, but a few white or black – scamper about. The water tumbled over rocks and there was the occasional leap of a salmon in the foaming waters. Stephen was at the time reading James Clavell's *Shōgun* and had watched her for a few minutes before he declared that he thought she had found her *wa*, a spiritual harmony. She had no clue if it was real or something the author had made up, but she could not help

47

but agree. Despite the reason they were now standing in the Black Wood, she felt there was something peaceful about the place, something that acted as a balm to the soul.

'So what are you gonna do now, Butch?' Stephen asked, moving to her side and giving the wreath a glance.

She took a deep breath of the pine-scented air. 'I don't know. We're on a break.'

'Uh-huh,' he said, nodding as if she had solved one of the great mysteries of the universe.

'And I've already got a story to follow while we're here.'

'Uh-huh,' he said again, still nodding as another cosmic conundrum was cracked.

'And time is money and I've no idea if there's a market for something that has no new angle.'

'Very true, very true,' he said, his voice grave, his face straight. 'So we'll just leave it all here, then? Keep walking for a while, go back to the cottage, fool around a little before we make dinner – and by *we* I mean *me* – then I'll give you a thrashing at chess and we round off the evening watching the latest James Bond flick on DVD?'

All of that sounded good, especially the fooling around part, although his prediction of a solid victory at chess was ill-founded – her father had taught her well and she said so. Stephen burst out laughing. 'Seriously, Becks, who are you kidding? Yeah, we'll do all of that, but your mind will be on this story.'

'No,' she argued. 'I can't follow this up. There's no revenue in it.'

'How do you know?'

'There's nothing new. Newspapers, magazines, whatever, all want something fresh. Rehashing old cases is just a cuttings job and they have junior staff to do all of that – they won't pay me to do it.'

'But what if you find something new?'

'Stephen, we're supposed to be on holiday.'

His smile was broad and seemed genuine. 'Give me a break, Becks. I know you. I see it in your eyes, hear it in your voice. That nose of yours is twitching. You know there's something in this and you won't be satisfied until you either find it or are finally convinced that it's a dead issue.'

She knew what he said was true. She had felt the tingle when she first saw the people gathering earlier that day for the memorial. It had intensified when she had listened to Catherine relate some of the facts. She knew she was hooked when she placed the call to Val and had readily agreed to come back here when Stephen suggested it. Once again, as she stared at his handsome, slightly battered rugby player's face she felt something she did not know how to deal with. This man understood her as nobody else had since her father. Not even her mother understood her quite as well as Stephen. She felt that warmth spread through her again, and again felt the urge to say the L-word but forced it back. Instead, she reached out and touched his cheek.

'How did you get to be so smart? University?'

'I was born smart,' he said. 'University just taught me how to drink and throw a funny-shaped ball.'

'Okay, so, as you're so smart, where do you think we should start?'

'We?'

'What are you going to do? Sit in the cottage and watch James Bond by yourself?'

He smiled.

10

Harry had seemed slightly confused as he opened the door to Rebecca, trying to place her face, though it had only been a few hours since she had been with him.

'I'm not here about Ashley,' Rebecca said with a smile, when Harry mentioned he was surprised to see her again so soon. Lines puckered on his forehead and his eyes darted towards Stephen, standing a couple of paces behind Rebecca. 'This is Stephen,' said Rebecca. 'He's my . . .' She hesitated slightly, as ever unsure how to describe him. Using 'boyfriend' made her feel like a teenager, 'partner', in her mind, was premature and a bit lame, 'lover' was out of the question. In the end, it was Stephen who stepped into the breach.

'I'm her minder,' he said, with a grin. 'Nice to meet you – is it okay to call you Harry?'

She had seen him do this before. As a lawyer he could be tough, even taciturn and businesslike – something she had witnessed herself when they first met regarding a client of his and a miscarriage of justice. Yet she had learned that when the situation demanded it he could be blokey and open.

'Of course, but I still wonder why you're back, Ms . . .' Harry appeared to be searching for her name.

'It's Rebecca,' she reminded him. She could be blokey too.

He nodded in acknowledgement. 'I mean, if you don't want to talk about Ashley, I don't see what . . .'

'I wondered . . .' Rebecca began, then amended, '*we* wondered if you could perhaps help us with something else. Tap into your local knowledge.'

Harry's frown deepened. 'About what?'

'Fergus MacGregor.'

Harry's face cleared, as understanding dawned. 'Ah,' was all he said, then, 'You'd better come in.'

He stepped back to allow them to pass. 'You know the way,' he said, as he closed the door and Rebecca turned right into his comfortable living room, with the view of the loch through some trees at the bottom of his steep garden. While Rebecca sat down on the two-seater settee, Stephen stood at the picture window.

'Quite a view,' he said.

'Yes,' said Harry, 'we would have preferred to see the mountain, but we're on the wrong side of the loch.'

Stephen turned, smiled and took a seat beside Rebecca. 'They call the opposite side the smooth side, right? And this side, the southern bank, is the rough side.'

'Some do, son, some do. Not me, though. You been reading up on the area?'

'A little bit. I found that in a book about the history of the area.'

'Aye, son, but can you do the Gaelic?'

Stephen held up his hands. 'Wouldn't even attempt it. I'm a Scot but not a Gaelic speaker.'

'*Slios Minh* over there, *Slios Garbh* here. At least, that's what a local guidebook told me when I moved here.'

Rebecca felt some astonishment. She wasn't a Gaelic speaker either, but Harry's pronunciation sounded spot on, despite his underlying Lancashire accent. Harry smiled at her. 'You don't live here for so long without picking a few things up. Some tea?'

Rebecca would have declined but Stephen got in first. 'That would be lovely.'

'I've still got some cake, too, if you're up for it.'

Rebecca thought she heard a slight accusatory tone in his words, given she had declined the offer that morning but admitted to herself she could have imagined it.

'Even lovelier,' said Stephen. 'Can I give you a hand?'

'No, you're fine, thank you,' Harry assured them as he walked to his armchair and plucked his mobile phone from where it rested on the arm, then headed to the door. 'I won't be long.'

Rebecca gave Stephen a look. 'What?' he said.

'You're a different person when you're away from Inverness, do you know that?'

'Different how?'

'Well, you're . . .' She sought the correct word. 'Charming.'

He laughed. 'Are you saying I'm not charming at other times?'

'Yeah, you were a real Mr Smooth when we first met.'

'That was business.'

'And you didn't trust me.'

'Not an inch.'

They'd had this conversation before and had reached an understanding: he didn't talk about his work and she no longer expected him to. Rebecca was satisfied that, despite what he had said, he did now trust her; it was simply that his own ethics dictated that he did not talk about his clients, except in a very broad sense. He could discuss the limitations and deficiencies of the Scottish legal system for hours, he could dismiss or praise the abilities of other lawyers, judges, sheriffs and police officers, but he would not tell her about any of his cases.

'Anyway,' he said, sitting back, 'I charmed you, didn't I?'

She sniffed. 'You wore me down, more like.'

'Not the way I remember it.'

Rebecca took her notebook from her bag and set it on her lap. 'I can't help your self-delusions.'

A laugh rippled through his body and he dropped his voice. 'Did you see the way he took his phone with him?'

'I did.'

'Bet he thought you would go poking around in it if he left it.'

'I think you'd win that bet.'

Stephen twisted slightly to stare straight at her. 'Would you?'

She held his gaze. 'Would I what? Go poking around in his phone?'

'Yeah.'

'No!'

Stephen let the thought sit between them for a moment, then turned away again. 'Okay, good.'

'Did you think I would?'

'No.'

'Then why did you ask?'

'I was joking.'

Rebecca's body tensed and she felt irritation gnaw at her. He hadn't been joking. He had actually wondered if she would have nosed around in the man's personal phone.

'I don't think you were, Stephen.'

He sighed, as if he knew he had spoken out of turn. 'I was, actually. Sorry, I know it was a bit lame. I've never been with you when you're on a story like this and I don't know what you do.'

'Intruding on someone's privacy is not part of it,' she snapped.

'Really?' His smile was quizzical and slightly nervous at the same time. 'It could be argued that intruding on somebody's privacy is exactly what you do.'

'What's that supposed to mean?'

Their conversation was being carried out in little more than a whisper, but her growing anger was clear, if not in her voice then in the way she had reared back, edged forward to perch on the settee to glare directly at him. The thin lips and gritted teeth also helped complete the picture. Stephen recognised it and held up a placating hand.

'Look, I'm sorry, this is new to me and I spoke out of turn.' He jerked his head to the door. 'Harry will be back in a minute, so let's just drop it, okay?'

She heard Harry's footsteps heading down the hallway from the kitchen and she sat back again, but resolved to pick this up again later. Harry reappeared through the doorway with a tray carrying three mugs, a teapot, milk, sugar and a plate of pre-sliced chocolate cake. Stephen rose to help him lay it carefully on the coffee table in front of them.

'Take a seat, Harry, I'll be mother,' he said. 'What do you take?'

Harry didn't argue and lowered himself into his armchair. 'Milk and two sugars. Are you allowed to say that these days? I'll be mother?'

'Well, I'll not tell anyone if you don't,' Stephen said, dropping some milk into a mug, giving the teapot a shake, then pouring the liquid into it. Rebecca, still seething, watched as he hooked two spoonfuls of sugar in and gave it a stir, then handed it to Harry. 'Cake?'

Harry nodded and Stephen slid a knife under a slice and placed it on a small tea plate, then handed it to him. There was silence for a few minutes as Stephen poured Rebecca's tea – he knew how she took it – and handed it to her, as well as a slice of cake so large she could feel her hips widening by just being in close proximity. She didn't meet his eyes as she set the plate on the arm of the settee.

She forced her annoyance down and concentrated on the matter at hand. 'Do you remember the disappearance, Harry?' He seemed confused again. 'Fergus MacGregor,' she explained. 'He vanished a few years ago?'

Light dawned. 'Oh, yes – terribly sad, all that,' Harry replied. 'The search went on for quite some time, I recall, even this far along the loch.'

Harry's home was closer to the western tip, the real head of

Loch Rannoch. The 'kinloch' part of Kinloch Rannoch meant 'head of the loch', but it had been misnamed when the village was planned centuries before.

Stephen had settled beside her again and sipped his tea. He hadn't taken any cake, she noticed.

'Did you know him or his family?'

Harry had taken a bite of cake and he swallowed before he answered. 'Not know, exactly. They live on the other side of the loch, but obviously when all this happened we came to know them by sight.'

'What was the feeling of the community?'

'The feeling? In what way?'

'Well, what was said about it? Was Fergus's disappearance a shock?'

'I would say yes, but such a thing is always a shock, isn't it?' He took a mouthful of tea. 'Look, Ms Connolly . . .'

'Rebecca,' she urged with a smile she did not feel. She thought she and Stephen were beyond that mistrust. 'Or Becks, if you'd rather.'

'Rebecca, why are you interested in this? Has something happened?'

She told him about it being the anniversary of the young man's disappearance, and witnessing the memorial service.

He frowned again. 'And you think there's some sort of story in this after all this time?'

'I don't know,' she said, truthfully. 'The fact is, I'm a curious person. I couldn't do this job if I wasn't – in fact, there are too few journalists out there who aren't curious enough, if you ask me. They accept what they're told without question and don't apply a hefty dose of scepticism, then don't ask the questions that should be asked. At the moment my nose is bothering me, as my mother used to say, and that's all.'

Harry smiled. 'My wife used to say that, too. I'd never heard that expression till I met her.'

'So, really we're having a conversation is all. I'm not going to quote you.'

He eyed the notebook on her lap. 'But you're taking notes.'

She closed the notebook. 'Force of habit, Harry – sorry.' She put it back in her bag, along with her pen. 'Can we start again?'

'What do you want from me? I didn't know the family at all before this, just to see in the village, and I only knew them because of their pictures in the paper and on the TV.'

'I'm just looking for a local perspective. After all, people talk, Harry, it's natural. Did you hear anything about Fergus, maybe why he would want to leave?'

He sat back in the armchair, sipped from his mug again as he considered. 'I really have no idea, Rebecca. If Mel was here, she might be able to tell you more – she was with the SWRI and I'm sure there would be talk there.'

'What about the family? Did you hear anything about them?'

'I know the mother is very religious. Mel told me she had seen her at church but had never spoken to her. They had two sons, Fergus and his younger brother.'

'And there were no whispers as to why Fergus would want to disappear?'

'No. Everyone was surprised by that. Of course, there are fears that he's lying dead somewhere, but the search parties couldn't find him. That doesn't mean he's not in some forgotten part of a forest somewhere. There was a case down the valley years ago when the body of a young man was found in the middle of a Forestry Commission plantation. He'd been shot and he'd lain there for a couple of years, I think, before someone stumbled on his remains. That was drug-related, something to do with Glasgow gangsters, I think. It's still very sad – a young life lost. Any life, I suppose.'

His eyes wandered to the photograph of his wife and she could see his attention drifting slightly.

'But nobody would have been searching for that young man, would they?' She brought him back to the matter in hand. 'There were searches organised for Fergus.'

'Oh yes. As I said, they were extensive – police, mountain rescue, dogs, even a helicopter for a time. They searched all along this side of the loch, up to the mountain, combed the woodlands, the fields, the high moorland. They checked Tower Island, in case he was there, but nothing.'

'Tower Island?' Stephen asked, startling Rebecca a little because she had half-forgotten he was there.

'You must have seen it out on the loch. It's a crannog, an artificial island, with a tower built on it, although that's from the nineteenth century, I think. It has a Gaelic name, which I won't attempt. *Slios Minh* and *Slios Garbh* are about as far as my vocabulary stretches, and I can't tell you if they're accurate, but in English the island is called the Isle of the Gulls. Anyway, I hear it was one of the places that young Fergus loved and he often rowed a boat out there.'

Rebecca stored that away. 'And there's nothing you can tell me about the family that might be of interest?'

'All I know is that they built up the farm that her husband inherited and they now own a fair bit of land around here, plus some cottages that they rent out to holidaymakers.' He paused, considering his next words carefully. 'You might want to track down his younger brother.'

'Rory, right?' Rebecca recalled seeing his name in the cuts online.

'Yes, that's right. The two boys were different from one another. Fergus, from what I could gather, was studious, quiet, but Rory was wilder. Drink. Drugs, even. But I couldn't swear to that. All that happened after Fergus vanished, so perhaps the lad was badly affected by it. Who knows? As I say, I don't know them, but you hear things, you know?'

She knew. That was why she asked people like Harry about stories. Sometimes all you get is rumour, but rumour is a start. 'And does Rory still live with his parents?'

'No, he moved away a year or two ago. I think he might be in Pitlochry. Or was it Perth?' His forehead crinkled. 'I really can't remember, but he's not in Rannoch now, I know that. He was the only one who spoke to the press, I remember. I know his family were quite annoyed by that. They resolutely refused to comment on it, no matter who asked. They kept their silence then, and they still don't say anything.'

Rebecca knew that if she was going to pursue this, then she would have to speak to the family. She felt the familiar dread of having to approach people who would not welcome her with open arms but knew she would do it when the time came. If the time came. She was still unsure as to what she was doing here.

11

Harry thought he had sensed a coldness develop between the reporter and her boyfriend. Either something had occurred while he was making the tea, or the man had little interest in what they were talking about. Nothing was said between them as they left, which seemed very strange to him, but he swiftly dismissed it from his mind. Young people can be touchy, he knew. His daughter had been the same. In fact, she still was, to an extent. He had not been pleased that she had contacted that TV company about Ashley because it was not her business and he knew what he was doing.

He tried to watch TV – some daytime drama on the BBC that followed a mindless quiz – but he could not concentrate. His mind was not on the disappearance of Fergus MacGregor or even any residual guilt over discussing it with the young woman – what was her name again? It momentarily escaped him, but then it hit him. Rebecca, of course. Everything he had said she would easily find out from anyone in the glen.

His mind was on his phone. Ashley normally messaged in the morning and then at night, but he hadn't heard from her since the day before. The morning messages had puzzled him at first because of the time difference – five hours between Scotland and the east coast of the USA – but she had explained that she didn't sleep much at night – insomnia had hit her when her parents died – and as she was no longer working she caught up on sleep during the day. He understood that because his sleep was fitful, and had been ever since his Mel had passed. After forty-two years together, he just couldn't get used to not having her lying beside him.

Actors on the screen mouthed words he did not hear, propelling a plot he had not even begun to follow. Their dialogue, the storyline, the movement on the screen were merely wallpaper and white noise. That had started after Mel died, too. Lack of focus, he supposed, the inability to connect.

Ashley had changed that. He didn't think he could have explained it to that reporter, so he didn't even try. He understood her scepticism; he had been suspicious himself at first. Why would such a young woman want to spend time talking to an old man on the other side of the world? He had been frosty with her in those early stages, but she had persevered and gradually the warmth of her messages had thawed him out.

She was funny. She was caring. She was very bright. Yes, her English was broken sometimes and that concerned him. He had looked it up and found that English was spoken in Ghana, but she said she had grown up speaking the Akan dialect with her family, so English was very much her second language. That was another reason why she found it hard going in the States, she told him. There were people who made fun of her accent, told her to go back where she belonged. Her boss, the one who had wanted to sleep with her, had told her that he should never have given her the job, he should have given it to an American.

His eyes moved from the TV screen to the phone resting on the arm of his chair. When he hadn't heard from her that morning – after Rebecca's first visit – he had sent a message, but she hadn't replied. Nothing from her that morning, nothing from her the evening before. She had missed one or the other before, but never both. It just wasn't like her.

He thought about his daughter and Rebecca. Had they contacted Ashley, maybe? Put her off? He knew they meant well, but they should not be interfering. He was not some doddering old fool; he knew what he was doing. Ashley was just a poor girl who needed help, who needed someone to talk to. A father figure, he supposed. That was all. She was on her own – okay, there was her auntie, but she never really said much about her except for times when she was called away from chatting to do something for her around the house. She said the woman resented her presence, resented having an unwanted relative in her house, especially now that Ashley was out of work. She was in a strange country, away from everything she had ever known. She was seeking – what was it they called it? – the comfort of strangers. Mel had read a book called that once, *The Comfort of Strangers*. She had loved it, but Harry's tastes ran more to historical fiction. Give him a book with a sailing ship on the cover and he was happy.

He picked up the phone, clicked on the social media app, checked to see if there was a message alert, hoping that he had somehow failed to hear it, but there was still nothing.

Where was she?

12

Rebecca chafed as they drove back along the lochside towards Kinloch Rannoch, her face turned away from Stephen to stare across the water to the far bank. She had thought about insisting on taking the wheel but had decided against it. She was angry, not petty, and she didn't enjoy driving that much anyway, so she sat, stared and seethed.

Somewhere across there Fergus MacGregor had lived. Five years ago on this very day he had left his family home, climbed into his car and driven round the loch, parked at the Black Wood, then perhaps walked to that clearing. And then – what? People vanished every day, Rebecca knew that, and not always through acts of violence. If he was planning on moving on, for whatever reason, then why leave his car where he did? It was possible he met someone there and left with them. If so, who? And why no word? From what little she knew about him, he seemed a level-headed young man. So was he likely to find himself in the kind of situation that he needed to hide himself away for years?

And was there a story here?

Certainly it had kindled her curiosity, but that wouldn't be enough – there was smoke in this story but as yet no fire. She had to find something newsworthy in order to interest the media. Had she known about the five-year anniversary, that might have been enough, but that moment had passed. As much as she would like to follow her nose unpaid, she had matured over the past few years. When she'd worked at the *Highland Chronicle*, she had scoffed when her then editor had held her back from following through on stories that might lead nowhere. She now knew that such fishing expeditions affected the bottom line. She still didn't like it, but she knew it was a simple fact. The Highland News Agency was a business and it had to make money to survive.

But there was something here, she could feel it. It was indefinable – a flutter, a niggle, a whisper – and she knew she had to spend a little more time on it before the itch could be scratched. After all, the research for Leo Marks apart, she was technically on holiday. Even so, she had to bounce this off somebody other than Stephen, who she was still not talking to.

She saw him glance at her as she took out her phone. He would be wondering who she was calling but he'd find out soon enough.

'Bored already?' Her boss seldom said hello these days, answering with variations of curt sentences, scathing comments and, on one occasion, singing the chorus of 'Hello' by Lionel Richie. The year before, Rebecca had discovered that Elspeth McTaggart knew a bit more than expected about hallucinogenic drugs, and sometimes wondered if she was still experimenting with such substances.

'No, I'm having a wonderful time,' Rebecca said. It was only a tiny lie, for until half an hour before she really had been. She heard a slight cough from Stephen and she gave him a cold look, but he was staring straight at the road, his face stony.

'Is there an issue with the work for Leo?'

'No. All okay. The guy is friendly enough, but I may have to work on him a little to get him to agree to appear on camera. There's something different about this particular scammer and Leo is very excited about it.'

'Yes, well, Leo is a showbiz type and gets excited by the light coming on in the fridge,' Elspeth dismissed. She was very unhappy with the progress being made on obtaining a commission for the documentary on her book about the Culloden case, and never missed an opportunity to disparage the industry and those who made their living from it. 'So just calling to give me a sit rep?'

Despite her state of seethe, Rebecca almost laughed. 'Sit rep?'

'Yes, situation report.'

'I know what a sit rep is, I do watch the telly, I just didn't expect you to say it.'

'What can I say? I'm all for the jargon. So what's the happs? Why are you calling your boss when you're supposed to be having a break and enjoying lots of guilty pleasures with Stephen?'

Rebecca let that pass. 'I may have stumbled onto something else here, but I'm not sure if I should dig further into it.'

'Down there in Rannoch?'

'Yes.'

'And you don't know whether to follow it up?'

'Yes.'

'When you're supposed to be on holiday and enjoying lots of guilty pleasures with Stephen?'

Rebecca sighed inwardly. 'Yes.'

Elspeth tutted. 'Becks, I applaud your dedication to the profession, but seriously you need to lighten up. I thought when you got together with Stephen that you might start to enjoy life a bit more.'

'I do.'

'Yes, and perhaps say that too!'

Rebecca was surprised by Elspeth even suggesting that there might be the prospect of marriage. Her boss had never been a proponent of matrimony, having been through what turned out to be a sham with a man, and was now in a civil partnership with a woman named Julie who was more than a match for her – although it had not yet led to wedding bells. However, Rebecca decided not to pursue that subject, not with Stephen sitting beside her and not while she still burned over what he had said in Harry's sitting room. 'Do you want to hear about the story or not?'

Elspeth's voice was weary as she said, 'Fine, go ahead.'

Rebecca told her what she knew so far and Elspeth only interrupted when something was unclear. It didn't take long because, frankly, Rebecca didn't know that much. When she was finished, Elspeth fell silent, the only sound on the line the click of her lighter. Julie could not have been in the vicinity because she had been waging a long war over Elspeth's need to smoke. The cigarettes now only came out when she was not around.

'You'd need something new,' Elspeth said.

'I know.'

'That means a ton of digging.'

'I know that, too.'

'And you're supposed to be on holiday and enjoying lots of guilty pleasures with Stephen.'

'I'm aware of that, Elspeth.' Rebecca's tone sharpened. 'But it's my time, isn't it? And if I want to look into this on my time I'm allowed to, aren't I?'

'Okay, okay, don't work yourself up into a lather. That's Stephen's job . . .' Sometimes talking to Elspeth was like being in a bad 1970s porno movie. 'Speaking of Stephen, have you run this past him? How does he feel about you spending your quality time with him on what may turn out to be a dead end?'

'He's okay with it.' That was true, she reasoned. After all, it had been his idea to come out this afternoon and see what they could uncover. Anyway, right at this moment, and in the mood she was in, how he felt didn't matter. She didn't say that out loud, though.

'So what do you want – my blessing?'

Rebecca hesitated for a beat, wondering if that was indeed what she wanted, but she covered it by saying, 'I need your help. I need to find the missing man's brother, Rory MacGregor. It seems he went off the rails a bit after all this, but he was the only one who spoke to the press – the parents remained silent throughout. He may be willing to speak to me, if I can find him. I don't want to ask Val Roach . . .'

'She wouldn't tell you anyway.'

That was true, Rebecca thought. 'But you may be able to at least find someone who can give me a steer. As I say, he got into trouble, maybe he got into more and it might have been reported. Could you open the Encyclopedia McTaggartia and see if you can track down an address? He's moved away from Rannoch and is now in Perth, maybe.'

'Maybe?'

'Yes, maybe.'

'Perth's a big place.'

'What's life without a challenge?'

Elspeth grunted. 'That's right, throw my own wisdom back at me, I just love that.' She paused, presumably to draw on her cigarette. 'Okay, I'll do it, but listen to me, Becks, you need to get some down time. You've not had a holiday for, how long is it?'

Too long, Rebecca admitted to herself. She had spent some time in Spain, where a friend owned a bar. She had come back tanned and refreshed but that had been over a year ago. She needed this break but that little voice in her ear kept telling her she should not ignore Fergus MacGregor. She didn't say any of that, of course. 'It's been a wee while and I promise I'll get some down time, too. I won't overdo it. I just need to see if there's anything in this.'

'Fair enough, Becks, but do you want some serious advice?'

'Do I have a choice?'

'Not really. Don't screw this up.'

'Elspeth, I don't even know if there's a story here yet, so . . .'

'I don't mean that. I mean Stephen, and you know it. Don't screw it up with him by being little miss worker bee all the time. You're into him in a big way, I can tell.'

'Elspeth . . .'

'No, I'm talking and you're listening and not interrupting. Being dedicated to the job is fine, and I appreciate all the hard work you do. Frankly, I don't pay you enough.'

'You can say that again.'

'What part of not interrupting needs an interpreter? But just in case your command of language has deserted you, I'll repeat – do not screw this up with Stephen. Work life is one thing, but you need a personal life and until he came along you didn't have one. We all need someone, Becks, other than friends. You need him and he needs you and there's a part of you that knows it, no matter how much you deny it. You've been a happier person since he came along and you have been good for each other. Hang onto him. Hang onto each other. Promise me you will do that. I know you, Becks, you will look for some way to bugger up what could well be the best thing to ever happen to you. Apart from meeting me, of course.'

Rebecca waited a beat before she said, quietly, 'I won't do anything like that, I promise.'

When Elspeth rang off, Rebecca could tell she didn't believe a word of it. She couldn't blame her for that because she found it hard to accept herself.

The rooftops of the village were in sight when Rebecca spotted the sign to a small white church set up on a rise to the right.

'Stop here,' she said, immediately regretting how tersely the words had come out, so added, 'Please.' It didn't help much, she realised. Stephen did as he was asked and they sat in silence, staring at the attractive church building, its pointed bell tower etched against a hill draped in brown heather and a blue sky only slightly hazed by the now thin cloud.

Finally Stephen exhaled and said, 'Look, I didn't mean that back there.'

'Yes, you did,' Rebecca said.

'No, I didn't.'

'It sounded as if you did.'

'I was making a joke.'

'Then I wouldn't consider a second career on the stand-up circuit if I were you.'

'You can't honestly believe that I would think you would nose around in the man's phone.'

She twisted in the seat to face him. 'I don't know what I believe, truth be told. Let's be frank here. You've made no secret of the fact that you don't trust reporters.'

'With good reason.'

She had to concede that. 'Granted, but I'm not just any reporter. Okay, I accept that you don't tell me anything about your work . . .'

'We've been through that.'

'Yes, we have and, as I say, I accept it. But when you suggest that I would be so underhand as to do something like that . . .'

'A joke.'

'Even as a joke, it hurts. God knows that reporters get a bad press these days. We're either liars or government mouthpieces or incompetent or all three. The profession is under attack from politicians, would-be politicians, armchair politicians, people with axes to grind and, not the least, by the people who own and run the media. Real news has been marginalised, cheapened and diluted by a reliance on press releases and a mainlining of celebrity pap. I've never hacked, stolen, misrepresented or lied to get a story. The only electronic device I've used to get information is a computer or phone. When you make a crack like that – whether or not you meant it – it upsets me. How would you feel if I pointed out that because you knowingly represent guilty people and help get them off that makes you complicit in their crimes?'

'That's an oversimplification of—'

'Is it? Is it really? Hurts though, doesn't it? It hurts when you're trying to do your job and trying to do it well and someone comes along and casually casts aspersions on how you do it. Especially when it's someone you—' She brought herself up short.

He waited for her to finish, but when she said nothing further, he asked, 'Someone you what?'

Shit, she thought. She had almost said it. She couldn't say it. She shouldn't say it.

'Someone you like,' she said, her words as limp as a soggy digestive. 'Like' was such a teenage word, demeaned by social media. What was worse was that she knew from the look in his eyes that he had sensed she was going to say something very different, something from which you don't walk away unscathed – something she was not ready to face.

'Fine,' he said. 'I apologise. I shouldn't have said what I said, even as a joke. Lame, though it was.'

'Fine,' she said, her mind already turning over this new wrinkle in their relationship. Not what he had said about her raiding the information on Harry's phone, but what she had almost blurted out in the heat of the moment for the second time that day. Why then? Why not when they were in bed? Why not afterwards, in those soft, tender moments when they held each other, sometimes in silence, sometimes talking about inconsequential things? Why did she almost say it when she was angry at him?

Rebecca, what is wrong with you?

Stephen was studying the sign that declared the name of the church, the times of services and the minister's name, Thomas Lester. 'Are you going to see the minister?' he asked.

She dragged herself from her thoughts and nodded.

'Shall I come with you or wait here?'

'No, you go back to the cottage. I'll walk back.'

It wasn't far – a stretch of the legs, as her dad used to say – and the exercise would do her good. The time apart would be good, too. She fretted that Stephen might argue the point, insist on waiting for her, but thankfully he nodded. 'Okay,' he said, 'you're the boss.'

Something told her he was relieved by the prospect of being apart, too. They had just had their first real argument and Rebecca felt guilty about making a big deal over what was probably a stupid comment badly delivered. She had taken it way too seriously and Elspeth's words bounced around in her mind. Was she beginning to screw this up?

She climbed from the car, shouldered her bag and was about to walk away when the passenger window slid down.

'Becks?' Stephen said. She leaned in to face him. He held her eyes for what seemed like a very long time but was probably only a second or two. 'I like you, too,' he said, then the window closed and he pulled away towards the village.

Stephen knew he had made a mistake as soon as he had opened his mouth. He had been kidding, but Becks could be touchy about any perceived attacks on her integrity. As she said, journalists get enough grief from the mainstream media haters without getting it from friends. He had known that and yet he had still said it.

As he drove back to the cottage, he wondered if he had really believed it – that had he not been there, she would have peeked at the man's phone. Did he think she was capable of that?

No, he decided. While it was true he had little trust with regards to the media as a whole, he knew Rebecca guarded her integrity jealously, simply because she actually had some. He had learned she was driven, that once her mind was set on a story she would not stop until she had either tracked it down or found there was nothing in it. While a part of him felt she might take such dedication too far, the fact was, he loved the woman. He hadn't expected to, but there it was. It was his intention to tell her, perhaps on her birthday.

The problem was, he didn't know how she would respond. He'd thought for a second there she was going to tell him how she felt, but he could have been wrong. He could have said it as he left her outside the church, but it wasn't the right moment; he didn't know why. It was not something that came easily to either of them. He had told only one other woman he had loved her, and he had also believed she felt the same in return, so when he realised she didn't, it hurt. It hurt a great deal.

The problem was, Rebecca reminded him very much of her, not in looks but in other ways. And his fear was that history might repeat itself.

13

The Reverend Tom Lester had a broad, open face, but it clouded when Rebecca identified herself as a reporter. She was used to that. People often became guarded when they heard what she did for a living, even when she was not on a story. It was a sign of how distrusted those in her profession could be.

She often recalled a wedding she had attended with Simon, another solicitor with whom she'd had a relationship a few years before. It was a rather fancy affair – she needed a positive credit reference just to take a seat in the church – and they ended up driving two people from the service to the large country hotel for the reception. She vaguely recognised them as they walked ahead to the car and, in a hushed tone, Simon told her that they were the stars of some TV soap or other; and he then warned her not to even think of reporting on their presence at the wedding. Frankly it hadn't even crossed her mind, but she responded with a curt *why the bloody hell would I?* The couple were married and, even if they hadn't been, Rebecca had no interest in peddling or reading celebrity gossip. In the back seat, the passengers mentioned another actor who was gay, but for some reason best known to himself kept his sexuality secret. It was the female celeb who let this slip and she was quickly hushed by her husband, with a brief nod in Rebecca's direction. She wanted to tell them she didn't give a single damn about the guy's sexuality, but she merely pretended not to hear. It was an example of what people thought: that all reporters were on the lookout for a story and could not be trusted. And while she knew many reporters who would run with anything they heard, not all would. Certainly, she wasn't like that. And yet here she was, while she was supposed to be on a break, talking to a local minister about a family tragedy.

The church was empty when she'd walked in and she took a moment to admire the bare stone walls and the exposed roof beams. Sunlight prismed through the large stained-glass window over the apse. She was not religious, but she recognised the feeling of calm these old churches offered, far less so than modern buildings. How many people had come here to worship? How many weddings? How many funerals? How many had perhaps sought sanctuary here from storm, flood or oppression? And when there was no mortal here to witness, did they return and rest in these old, polished wooden pews?

It was while she was standing in the aisle, soaking in the peace, that Tom Lester emerged from a doorway behind the pulpit carrying a bucket and a mop and dressed in civvies – an old pair of jeans, a baggy cardigan over a polo shirt. He showed no surprise at seeing her; he was probably used to casual visitors in the old building and he nodded to her in a friendly manner.

'Afternoon,' he said as he walked down the aisle towards her.

'Hi,' she replied.

He stopped before her and set his bucket and mop down. 'Just visiting, or can I help you with something? Despite this' – he waved a hand at his clothes and the bucket on the stone floor – 'I'm the minister here. Tom Lester.'

He looked younger than he had that morning, she realised, but perhaps it was the clothes and the smile, which he had not borne at the memorial. His hair was thick but shaved tight at the sides and showed no signs of greying. She put his age at early forties – perhaps older if he had a decent skin care regime and hydrated properly.

'Rebecca Connolly.' She held out her hand and he shook it. 'I was looking for you.'

His head tilted inquisitively. 'Really? How can I help you, Ms Connolly?'

'Rebecca, please. I wanted to talk to you about Fergus MacGregor.'

He took a very small step back and the smile faltered. 'I see. And your interest is what?'

'I'm a reporter, with the Highland News Agency.' She handed over a business card that she had already taken from her bag. He studied it carefully, the smile completely gone now. When he looked up, she saw that familiar shadow of suspicion in his eyes.

'I saw the memorial this morning,' she said before he could tell her he couldn't help.

'I see,' he said, then looked down at the card again as if it could answer his next question. 'And what is it you want to know, Ms Connolly?' He was still being purposely formal to keep a distance between them. 'I'm not sure I can help you.'

'I'm only looking for background.'

'To what end?' He flicked the wrist of the hand holding the card as if he was using it to fan himself. 'You're with a news agency? Do you plan selling the story somewhere?'

'I don't know,' she said, truth always being the best approach. 'At the moment, I'm just interested.'

'Why?'

'Why not? A young man vanished without trace five years ago and his family have had no answers. The world has moved on, the search parties have moved on, the media has moved on, but the fact remains.'

'The mystery, you mean.'

'If you want to put it that way.'

'And you think you can clear it up?'

'I have no idea. As I said, at the moment I'm merely interested.'

'Curious.'

'Yes.'

He flicked the corner of her card with his thumb, then sat down in the nearest pew. 'So what do you want to ask me?'

She sat in the pew opposite him, considered taking out her notebook but deciding against it. She was not looking for quotes here, just information. She nodded at the bucket and mop in a bid to break the ice a little. 'Cleaner's day off?'

He followed her gaze briefly. 'She's on holiday,' he said.

'So am I,' Rebecca answered.

'And yet you're following up a story?'

She would not mention that she already had Harry's story on the boil, too. 'As you say, I'm curious.'

A suggestion of a smile. 'Just as well you're not a cat.'

'If I was, my nine lives would sadly be depleted by now. What can you tell me about Fergus, Reverend Lester?'

'Very little. I wasn't here five years ago. I arrived the year after he vanished.'

'But you know the family? Frances, his mother?'

'Yes, she's a member of my congregation.'

'Her husband wasn't at the memorial this morning . . .'

'No, he chooses not to attend.'

'Why?'

'You would have to ask him.'

'Do you think he or Mrs MacGregor would speak to me?'

'Honestly, I doubt it. As far as I'm aware they've never spoken to the media.'

'Why not?'

'They're very private people.'

'Even though it might help them find their son?'

'There was enough publicity at the time and it didn't help. Speaking to them is merely voyeurism. And their other son did speak, I gather.'

'Rory.'

'Yes.'

'Do you know where he is now?'

He stared at her for a moment, considering whether to answer. 'Perth, I believe.'

Good, Harry was right, 'Where do the MacGregors live? I know it's the north side of the loch – the smooth side, right? – but that's all.'

'I don't think I should tell you that.'

She hadn't expected him to, but if you don't ask you don't get. And with that in mind, she said, 'Would you be willing to ask them if they would speak to me?'

He thought this over. 'Again, what good can speaking to you do?'

It was her turn to consider – then she sat forward into the aisle, clasping her hands in front of her. 'Look, I can't say that speaking to me or someone like me can help in any way at all. But five years have passed and people have forgotten about Fergus, if they ever noticed his story in the first place. I can't promise that any media outlet will run a new appeal for information – I don't even know if I'll approach them yet – but my instincts tell me there is something here that needs to be aired again. If Mrs MacGregor didn't speak at the time, but she does now, it might be enough to hook the media.'

'As I said, isn't that simply voyeurism?'

'To an extent yes, I won't lie to you. But at the moment, poor Fergus is a name on old newsprint or tucked away in a corner of the internet. Someone, somewhere, might have further information, but without publicity they'll not be found.'

'And is that likely?'

'Appeals on cold cases are run all the time. Often they generate new leads.' She could see he was still reluctant, so she made a gamble. 'The memorial this morning wasn't that well attended. A handful of people.'

He nodded.

'I'm betting that even in the four years you have been here you've seen the numbers drop off.' She could tell by the look in his eyes she had hit the mark. 'It's natural. People lose interest, wonder what the point is; they stop attending. And that's locals – think of the wider world. If Fergus is out there, people will have forgotten the publicity five years ago. That's why I believe it's important that such cases be kept alive.'

'And if he doesn't want to be found?'

'Don't you think he owes it to his family at least, to let them know he's still alive? A word, a message, a phone call – even through a media outlet – to give them some peace of mind.'

He rose and reached out to grasp the mop handle again. She didn't think he was dismissing her; he was merely moving while he thought. He breathed deeply, unconsciously twisting the handle in a circle.

'I'll speak to Mrs MacGregor, ask her if she'll talk to you. But if the answer is no, I need you to promise me that you will accept that and not pester them at all. And if you do run some kind of story, that you will treat it with the utmost respect. We are dealing with people's feelings here. Grief. Loss. They are powerful forces and not to be taken lightly.'

Rebecca knew how powerful those forces could be. 'I promise,' she said. She stood up and held out her hand again. 'Thank you, Reverend.'

He shook it and nodded. 'I am trusting you, Ms Connolly.'

'Thank you for that,' she said again, then had another thought. 'There was another person there this morning, kept himself back from the main group. I understand his name is Cormac?'

The minister became guarded once more. 'Leave Cormac be, Ms Connolly.'

'I just wondered if he was paying his respects and, if so, why did he keep himself more or less hidden?'

'Cormac is a poor soul and you must leave him out of this. Do not approach him, do not disturb him. If you do, you will not get any help from me in any way.'

'But I understand he practically lives in the Black Wood. It's possible he saw something and—'

'Ms Connolly, listen to me.' Tom Lester's voice took on a hard edge. 'Cormac is a member of this community and we care for him. He's not had an easy life and you must go nowhere near him, do you understand?'

She nodded.

14

When Cormac finally re-entered Hill Cottage, he heard Fergus call him from the kitchen. The young man was in his usual chair by the fireplace. He never left the cottage in daylight; since the accident, he was not keen to be seen outside. It was not an attack; it was an accident. Fergus had insisted on this and Cormac had reluctantly agreed, to keep the peace. Fergus had taken to sleeping in the chair rather than the bed that had been made up for him in the corner of the kitchen, but Cormac often heard the front door opening and closing in the dead of night and Fergus's distinctive dragging step as he took some exercise.

Cormac dropped some carrots he had taken from the food store out back and laid them on the broad kitchen table, then faced the young man, waiting for him to speak. He knew what was coming, but he also knew not to rush it. Words could be difficult for Fergus. Before the accident, he had been talkative to the point of garrulous, telling Cormac of the history of the area and stories of the MacGregors, Menzies and Robertsons who had lived in Rannoch hundreds of years before. Now his moods were changeable, and he seemed to go to a darker place where his speech would slur until it became practically unintelligible. Cormac suspected he was seeing what had happened less as an accident and more as an attack.

Cormac knew it was, of course. For he had been there.

So he waited until Fergus was ready to speak. It took a minute or two. He looked at Cormac, then at the floor, then back again. Finally, he took a deep breath and said, 'I'm sorry for my behaviour earlier.'

'It's okay,' Cormac said.

'No, it's not okay,' Fergus replied. 'It's just that this day is difficult for me, you know that, right? The . . . accident . . .' His voice trailed away and he looked at the glowing coals in the grate.

Cormac felt something clutch at this throat when a tear glistened on the young man's cheek. 'Fergus, don't fly off the handle, but I still think that you should speak to your mother at least.'

Fergus shook his head and the tear trickled faster downward to drip from his chin. 'No, I can't.' He looked back and his eyes swam. 'We've left it too long, you see.' He thought about what he had said and amended it. 'I've waited too long. I can never go back. Not now. Not after all this time.'

Cormac understood how he felt. He could never go home either. 'Then we'll say no more about it. I'll make us some stew and then you can tell me about the battle with the clan of the yellow hair.'

Fergus's face contorted into a lopsided grin. 'You've heard that story so many times, Cormac. You must know it by heart.'

Cormac opened the pantry door and took out some soya chicken pieces. He was a vegetarian and since he had been in his care Fergus had become one, too. Cormac could not tend to his animals knowing that he feasted on the flesh of their relatives. He busied himself, filling pots with water, but turned back to Fergus when he heard him speak again.

'Was she there, Cormac?'

Cormac feigned misunderstanding, for he was uncomfortable again. 'Who?'

'You know who. Was she there this morning? At the memorial?'

Cormac hesitated to tell him, for he didn't know how he would react to the disappointment. He considered lying, but he had never done that with Fergus and he could not begin now. He knew of whom he spoke, of course. The lassie. Shona. The one Cormac had often seen him with before the accident.

'No,' he said. 'She wasn't there.'

Fergus nodded once and resumed his study of the glowing fire as silent tears burst from the corner of his eye to cascade down his cheeks.

Shona Everton glared at her father as she had glared at him so many times before. It sometimes felt that their entire relationship had been one long glare. Her mother had been his third wife and she had been happy with him, although the marriage had lasted only twelve years before she was taken from them. Alexander Burnes had grieved for a long time. And while Shona might not have any true daughter–father feelings for him, she recognised that he had loved her mother, even if he had somehow resented the fact that Shona looked so much like her and yet was not her.

Her half-brother Raymond was listening to their conversation with that so very serious expression of his, the one that told her he sympathised with her position but there was no way he would ever fully back her against his father. She would rather Ray wasn't present, but she supposed even half-hearted support was better than none at all. When she had told her brother what she had just told their father, there had been the usual explosion of rage – over the years, Ray's temper had not eroded – but she had made him promise not to say a word until she came back home and delivered the news herself. She was confident he would never betray her confidence. He feared, respected, loved his father, but he had a strong sense of loyalty to her. It had often proved useful in what seemed like the ongoing war against Alexander Burnes.

'It's happening, Alex, whether you like it or not,' she said, the words strong. She had never called him father, not even as a child. 'Get used to it.'

He regarded her across his desk with an expression that contained both disdain and concern. It was one he had managed to perfect over the years. She believed the latter part was feigned, while the former was his true feeling.

'I didn't want you to marry him in the first place, as you know,' he said, his cultured tone carrying a lazy quality that suggested he should be reclining on a parliamentary bench in a double-breasted suit. 'But you have only been wed for two years, my dear. To throw in the matrimonial towel suggests a lack of determination and application, and that, my dear, I will not have. The Burnes family never allows failure.'

She clicked her tongue. 'This from a man who had two failed marriages before you married my mother. And who can say how long that might have lasted.'

She was both delighted and disturbed to see real pain in his eyes at the mention of her mother. 'I will thank you to keep your dear mother out of this. She would have been most distraught over the failure of your marriage after so short a time.'

'She would not have wanted me to stay with a man who had treated me so badly either.' Her husband, Richard 'Call Me Rick' Everton was a shit of the first order. She knew one or two of her friends had dismissed his first affair as youthful exuberance. They recognised the second one was pushing his luck somewhat too far, but the third was a lethal blow to any hope of wedded bliss.

'Shona is right, Dad,' said Ray, his own accent cultured but, unlike his father's, at least bearing some trace of heather and haggis. 'Rick isn't husband material. We kind of knew that when they got married and . . .'

Alex's slow gaze resting on his son was enough to smother his support as soon as it took breath. Satisfied that Ray would not speak further, that same gaze swivelled back to Shona. She was of sterner stuff and the days of him imposing his will upon her were over. The last time had been five years earlier and it was something she would regret for the rest of her days.

'This divorce is happening, Alex,' she said. 'I'm not looking for your approval. I'm only informing you out of courtesy.'

He pursed his lips, sat back in his big chair, his elbows resting on the arms and his fingers threaded just below his chin, his index fingers making a steeple. She wondered how many times she had seen him do that, as if he was praying for guidance in dealing with his troublesome daughter. Behind him she saw the green of the lawn, carefully tended by old Donald, who lived in a small cottage on the grounds, then beyond it a small lochan and then the beginnings of the brown heather of the great Rannoch Moor. If she had stood on a chair on the roof and craned her neck, she might just catch sight of the railway line leading to Rannoch Station and the north. Not that she had ever tried that, of course.

When he spoke next, his words were soft but she sensed the strain behind them. 'Shona, what is it about this day that you feel forced to bring me news that you know will irritate me?'

She knew what he meant, of course. It had been this day two years ago that she had told him that she had married Call Me Rick in Bermuda. And it had been this day three years before that he had prevented her from starting a new life with the person she thought was the love of her life. She still thought of him that way.

'Coincidence,' she said, but she knew that wasn't true. She had been married two weeks before she told him. She could easily have sent him a text or called on the day of the wedding, but she didn't. She could have come to Scotland when they came back from the Caribbean, but she didn't. She had waited until this particular day to tell him. To punish him for his part in what he had done five years before. Similarly, she had thrown

Call Me Rick out the week before but had waited this long before she came north.

An eyebrow twitch told her he found her explanation hard to believe, but he let it pass. 'And you have proof of Richard's infidelity?'

'All three of them,' she said. Despite everything, he had raised her well enough that she knew never to act without reason or weaponry. And she had enough on Call Me Rick to take him for everything he had, not that she would. She was not that malicious. She would take just enough to make him smart a little, but she was certain he would find some willing slut to rub some salve into his wounds.

Alex breathed deeply, his lips thinning. Was that anger she saw? And who was it directed at – her or Call Me Rick? Alex Burnes was big on loyalty. She knew that he had never cheated on any of his wives; it was one of the traits she found admirable in him. He had many other faults, and they had led to the collapse of the first two marriages, but he believed in fidelity in marriage, in business and even in his staff here at the house. Many of them, like old Donald, had been with the family for years.

'Very well,' he said eventually. 'It's true I held no great affection for Richard, and I believe I told you so when you began to see him and when you finally informed me of your marriage. However, I resolved to support you after my, em, errors of the past.' His errors of the past. That he had regretted his actions she had no doubt, but this was the first time he had ever acknowledged it. 'So I must support you in this also. After all, you are my daughter.'

The words *more's the pity* sprang into her mind, but she left them unsaid. She wasn't that cruel.

'But if you are doing these things to hurt me for some reason, Shona, then rest assured you are not. You're only hurting yourself by insisting on submitting to your rash impulses.'

She let his words lie between them for a moment. She knew she had been impetuous in the past. Call Me Rick was merely one example of a number of actions of which she was not particularly proud, including going a bit wild after Fergus's disappearance. 'I'll try to remember that,' she said, her words heavy with sarcasm.

He blinked away whatever hurt he felt and swivelled his chair so that he caught his profile, which was always his best feature. Her mother had told her once that it was his profile that had first drawn her to him. It was strong, purposeful, like how you might imagine a Roman general's profile to be: a rock-face full of nooks and crannies. The flesh under the chin was beginning to sag a little now, but not that much, and there were jowls forming to knot the once straight jawline, but he was still a handsome man, even she had to admit. Ray had inherited his looks, too, although there was a slight weakness in his features and sometimes a cruel twist to his mouth.

Alex cleared his throat a little. 'How long will you be staying?'

'As long as I'm welcome,' she said.

He turned his face away from her. 'You're always welcome, Shona, you know that. This is your home.'

She heard something in his voice that she hadn't heard before, or had at least dismissed. Was that tenderness? Was he mellowing in his old age? Was it this day having an effect?

Was his guilt bearing down upon him?

15

What's going on?

Rebecca's thoughts rushed like the waterfall tumbling down the sheer rock beside the road. When she left the Reverend Lester, she walked into the village proper, passing another church, the village general store, then a narrow bridge crossing the River Tummel, which flowed from the loch to link with the man-made Dunalastair Water further east, and continued in an occasional white-water frenzy through the valley. At the town square she had paused to study what she thought was a war memorial in front of the Victorian facade of the Dunalastair Hotel, but learned it was a monument to a Highland minister, then continued on until she reached the smaller bridge facing the waterfall.

She kept herself to the verge in case a vehicle heading for the village careered round the corner of the country road while her mind raced.

So, Rebecca, what the hell is going on?

You're supposed to be on holiday, for goodness' sake, and here you are not only following up the story for which you're being paid but starting to dig around another that may never bring in any income. She should stop this now, before it goes any further. It wasn't as if she didn't have enough to do when she got back to Inverness. There were court cases to cover, human interest pieces to write for the weekly magazines, a couple of feature commissions from the nationals to follow up. Did she really have the time to pursue another story?

She had been more or less warned off twice, once by Catherine, then again by the minister. Rebecca was capable of arguing the public interest position when it was merited (even when it wasn't), but she was unsure if she had a leg to stand on here. If the family had wanted the press involved, they would have asked. And by all accounts, they were private people who didn't welcome such intrusion in their lives.

But . . .

There was that familiar flutter in her stomach to deal with. There really was something here, she knew it. As she had said to the minister, if Fergus was out there somewhere, then he owed it to his family to let them know he was alive and well. And if he wasn't, perhaps there was someone out there who knew what had happened to him, and it was possible that fresh appeals could bring them forward. It had happened before.

You're kidding yourself, Becks. There's something more at play here and it's not your reporter's nose.

The little voice in her mind was Elspeth's. While she tried to ignore it, she knew she couldn't. Was she running a little bit scared? Was she afraid of her own feelings?

It was Stephen, of course. Don't sabotage this, Elspeth had said, and even though Rebecca had dismissed the idea she knew within herself that it was possible. She thought about their history. They had met over a story – surprise, surprise – and his suspicion of her profession had been very apparent. However, as time progressed the air between them defrosted. Eventually, he asked her out. What the hell, she had thought, she had nothing to lose, and her friends Chaz and Alan had been nagging her to find a personal life. She'd had dates, of course – she hadn't taken the veil – but none of them had led to anything. She did have reservations. He was older by a few years – he was in this early thirties and she was in her late twenties. Her previous relationship with Simon had made her a little gun-shy. He hadn't been abusive, hadn't been inattentive; in fact, he had been completely the opposite: he had been too clingy. She needed her own space and Simon didn't understand that. Then, of course, she had found herself pregnant and that had brought a different perspective to life, for a time anyway. He, of course, wanted to get married – he was that kind of guy – but she had held back, unsure that marriage was for her. She had told nobody else about the pregnancy, not even her mother. Most people still didn't know. And then came the miscarriage.

If she was being honest with herself, she had been on a downward spiral after that. She functioned. She carried on working. She laughed, she joked. But inside she had been hollowed out by loss and regret over the child that never saw light.

Then there was her father, who had taught her so much, taken by a horrible, pernicious disease that knew no conscience. And her job, which she loved. Her enthusiasm was sapped by accountants with balance sheets for a soul and second-rate yes men who had lost whatever integrity they'd ever had.

That dark hollow became a black hole, sucking all the life from her, and she didn't even realise it.

But she had come through it somehow. And then she had met Stephen.

So what's going on then, Becks?

Chaz's voice this time. They had met for the first time on the island of Stoirm, which she had visited against orders to follow up a story. The bosses at the *Highland Chronicle*, her employer at the time, much preferred their reporters to be in the office, hitting the phones, than travelling across the sea on what could be a wild goose chase. It hadn't been a wild goose chase, but the story she found was not what she had expected. Chaz was the local stringer for the paper, providing photographs and news snippets – not that there was much of that on Stoirm, that particular story and its aftermath aside. He was a professional photographer now, living on the mainland with his husband, Alan. They had been married on the island and Rebecca had travelled back for the ceremony. She had dreaded the return, for her father had been born there and had left when he had uncovered a family secret hidden for decades: that his grandmother had been someone who disposed of unwanted newborns by drowning them in a bucket. Rebecca had found out and had been horrified. It may have happened many years before, but she was still disgusted that the same blood ran in her veins. Such was her shame, she had never told anyone about it – not Elspeth, or Chaz, or Alan.

So what's going on, Becks? Are you really so afraid of intimacy that you will use any excuse to pull away from Stephen? You almost said it earlier, didn't you? The 'L' word? It almost sprang unnoticed from your lips, didn't it? What's that all about?

It wasn't a fear of intimacy. She had been intimate with Stephen for some time. In fact, they had been intimate like bunnies. And she had been intimate with Simon, too. The pregnancy had been no miracle.

That's physical intimacy, Becks – Alan's voice now, always a smart arse. *You shy away from emotional intimacy.*

She considered this. Was it true? Was she afraid of being close to someone? Was that why she kept her secrets so close? Was she afraid that if she opened up then she might just actually share something of herself, not just physically but emotionally? Was she scared of being happy?

Get yourself sorted, Becks. Another friend's voice, an old one from Glasgow.

Her phone rang and she fished it from her coat pocket, glanced at the screen and recognised Leo's number.

'Hi,' she said.

'Hi, I've reverse-image checked Ashley's photo,' he said.

Damn it, she had meant to do that herself when she got back to the cottage but had forgotten.

'And?'

'No matches, as far as I can see.'

That surprised her. 'How unusual is that?'

'Very unusual, but not unheard of. It may well be her own pics she has used, although that does seem unlikely. The thing is, it makes this story even more interesting to me. Can you go back and see your guy?'

She didn't tell him she had left him less than an hour earlier, but it did raise another thought.

'Sure, no bother.'

'Work on him, get him to agree to appear on camera.'

'I'll do what I can. But listen, can I run something else past you?'

'Sure, what's up?'

Rebecca had not planned to raise this with Leo and was thinking off the top of her head. 'Is there a chance of pitching an idea about missing people to the channels?'

A dismissive grunt. 'There have been things like that before.'

'Yeah, but let's be honest, TV isn't a hotbed of originality, is it? I mean, how many shows are there with celebrities going baking, sailing, skateboarding or eating worms?'

She knew he couldn't argue. He himself had once criticised the plethora of such programmes, especially on a respectable channel. 'True, but telly people are all looking for a reason to say no. They'll look at what's been done in that line and want a fresh approach. Why do you ask, anyway?'

How much should she tell him? Keep it vague, she decided. 'It's something I've stumbled on here.'

'A missing person?'

'Yes, five years ago.'

'A child?'

'No, man in his early twenties, I think.' She had no idea how old Fergus was, so she guessed.

That grunt again. 'An adult. It would be better if it was a child.'

She understood what he meant, but she still felt shock ripple through her. Sometimes the media can be heartless, forgetting that they are dealing with real lives. It's what looks good on the page or the screen; what plays. Optics are everything.

Leo asked, 'Any evidence of murder?'

'Not really.'

'Pity. Murder sells.'

If it bleeds, it leads, was an old saying in newspapers. Obviously it was the same with TV.

'Might be a podcast in it,' Leo continued, but she sensed he was merely throwing her a lifeline. 'We're looking into a few of those. There's revenue to be had, so maybe we should talk about it some more.'

'Yeah, sure,' she replied. 'Let me dig around and I'll get back to you.'

After she hung up she began to walk along the road back to the cottage. She knew Leo was not being purposely callous, he was merely telling her the way it was. After all, she had given him no real details and to him the people involved were very much in the abstract. She wondered if she was the same and realised with some measure of shame that to an extent she was. She saw the story she wanted to tell and she went for it. It didn't mean that as time went on she didn't feel for those involved, but she knew she had to detach herself in order to perform. Did she detach herself too far?

And had that filtered through to her private life? Maybe that was what was going on.

16

Nights were once a morass of troubled dreams for Cormac, but those dark times were long in the past and hundreds of miles away now. At first he had found his pills kept the anxiety at bay, but he stopped taking them. With Fergus and his animals to take care of, he had decided the medication was no longer necessary.

He still didn't sleep well, but he was used to that. Even when he was taking the pills, memories would find him. He realised now that you can't hide from your own past.

During the day, when memories stole up on him, he could walk them away in the Black Wood, or tend to his wild charges or toil in his workshop. He found wood on the forest floor or washed up on the loch shore – gnarled branches that had been stripped of their bark and bleached by water and sun – and turned them into something strange and wonderful. He did not know from where this ability to transform worthless timber into art came and he did not question it, accepting it as a gift from God. That's what the Reverend said of it, as if he had been touched by the Almighty. Cormac liked that idea, as if He had forgiven him for his past.

On any given night he could grab a few hours' sleep, he supposed, but it was never deep, his senses always remaining just below the surface and the least noise bringing him instantly alert. He might hear the bark of a fox or the cry of an owl and his eyes would spring open. He enjoyed hearing the sounds of the night creatures beyond the cottage's walls. He had a kinship with them.

But this night he remained awake, for he knew he would have to leave the cottage. He had bade goodnight to Fergus. The cottage was small but it had two storeys: below were the sitting room and the kitchen, above, two small bedrooms, heavily coomb-ceiled, and a small bathroom. Fergus had declined the use of the other bedroom, preferring to spend his time in the warmth of the kitchen, where the fire glowed hot and red. Cormac had headed upstairs, as if for bed, but he sat in an old easy chair in the corner, still fully clothed and his boots on, waiting.

It was just after midnight when he heard what he expected to hear.

Step, drag.

Step, drag.

Fergus was moving downstairs, the trail of his right foot distinctive on the kitchen's worn linoleum. Cormac didn't know what had left him with that distinctive gait but presumed it was the result of the accident. The lad seldom budged from his chair but every year, on this night, he would roam around the ground floor, restless, the near dead foot scraping through the house, and then head out, and Cormac would follow him, even though he knew where he was going. Sure enough, as he craned forward in his chair with his ear cocked to catch the tell-tale movement below, he heard Fergus go from kitchen to hall, and then the front door opening, then Fergus stepping over the threshold and onto the gravel path outside.

Step, drag.

Step, drag.

Cormac rose and looked from the window. He scanned the narrow path leading from the front door to the garden gate, and then the track that led through the plantation to the road. Fergus, his outline blurred by a film of mist but wearing

Cormac's thick winged coat, a scarf around his jaw and a hood pulled over his head, was stepping onto the grass to make less noise, but the foot left a trail in the damp turf.

Cormac watched him move down the slight incline to the gate and then vanish from sight into the shadows of the conifers. He let Fergus get a little further before he himself stole down the stairs, grabbed an old hooded waterproof jacket from the row of hooks in the hallway and eased out of the house. It was silent here on the hill; the slightest noise could alert the boy that he had a shadow other than his own.

Anyway, he knew where Fergus was going.

Shona stood in the doorway watching Ray in his home gym. Her brother liked to keep himself fit and she had to admit he made a good job at it, for some reason tending to do his home workout later at night when the house was asleep. During the day, he would be out on the estate, mostly working but also ever watchful for something he could shoot at with the gun he kept strapped to the rear of his quad bike. The gym was in the basement, so any noise he made was unlikely to disturb anybody. It was a large room kitted out with the best equipment money could buy, for Shona had to admit that Alex never shirked on flashing the cash for his children. Ray had top of the range gear here – a water-resistance rowing machine, three treadmills for some reason, a bench press, racks with weights and bar bells, other gear with functions of which Shona had no clue. The far wall was covered with floor-to-ceiling mirrors, all the better for him to admire himself while he flexed, extended, sweated and strained. He had always been like that, ever since she could remember: exercising, playing sport, even helping staff chop wood for the fires, delighting in his body. She had often caught him as a teenager with his sleeves rolled up, admiring the bulge of his bicep as he stood in front of a mirror.

She had been unable to sleep, so had wandered around the house. She had never been particularly happy here, but she liked to pad through the hallways in the still of the night. As a teenager she would imagine she was in a Gothic romance, moonlight streaming through the large Victorian windows as she flitted around in the silence like a ghost in a flimsy nightgown, even though she was actually wearing a T-shirt and tracksuit bottoms. She had been a child then, and she had learned quickly that romance didn't last, although the Gothic part could be very real.

That was until she met Fergus and her life changed. It was as if the sun had finally broken through the cloud when they first encountered one another at a Hogmanay dance in the village hall. He had asked her to dance, she had accepted, and she danced with nobody else for the rest of the night. In her mind it became like a scene from *West Side Story*, but she knew the reality was a bit more mundane. It wasn't a bolt from the blue; the attraction grew over the course of the night, and the following days and weeks. She found him easy to talk with, easy to smile with, easy to be with, and when she went home at the end of that first night it was with the memory of his kiss at midnight. Ray had been there, too, and he had glared at Fergus as they left. Ray glared at any boy who happened to look twice in her direction and this one had actually locked lips with her in a public place. Fergus didn't seem to mind, for he winked at Shona as Ray practically dragged her to the waiting car.

Lurking in the doorway, she thought hidden in the shadows at the base of the narrow stairway linking the gym to the upper floor, she watched Ray stand before the mirror, a hefty-looking dumb-bell in each hand, doing what he had told her once was a bicep curl. He was wearing only a loose pair of joggers and an old *Star Wars* T-shirt, and his muscles bulged like Jabba the Hutt's chins. He had obviously stepped his regime up while she had been away with Call Me Rick. Both arms hung loose by his sides, then he brought the weights up to chest height, then slowly lowered them in a movement she had heard him call *controlling the negative*, which she presumed was the pull of gravity. He looked down at his swollen biceps, then back at the mirror for an overall body check. He really did love himself, and she was certain there would be women who would be attracted to such an overly honed physique, although she never heard Ray talk about them. Shona didn't find the look attractive at all. She had to admit he looked good in his work clothes and casual wear, but when he put on a suit it was a bit like sausage meat packed into a skin. Formal wear simply did not sit right on his frame, unlike Call Me Rick, on whom a suit hung well. He also looked good out of it, as his succession of conquests would no doubt agree.

'Enjoying the view?'

She looked up and saw Ray staring straight at the reflection of the doorway in the mirror while still flexing and extending both arms. She could just about see her own outline, a darker shape in the shadow. Of course he'd seen her, that was why he was preening in such a way. He always did try to impress her with his body. Nevertheless, she felt her face flush with embarrassment, as if she had been caught being a peeping Tom. She stepped into the gym and affected a nonchalant manner.

'I've just arrived,' she said, looking around at the equipment as if she had the slightest interest.

His smile told her that he knew she had been there for a few minutes. 'Fancy giving a workout a try?'

She pretended to give it some thought. 'Nah, there are better ways to get hot and sweaty.'

It was his turn to flush, as she knew he would. Ray always became embarrassed when she spoke about sex. 'Yeah, well,' he said, hiding his reaction by bending over and placing the two dumb-bells on the floor, 'you'll not be doing a lot of that at the moment.'

'You think so?' she said, a teasing smile on her lips. 'How do you know I've not got someone lined up? Or a friend with benefits?'

He stretched his back, arching his spine a little, then rotated his shoulder muscles. 'Not you. You're a one-guy gal, always have been. Took you three years to take up with Rick after—'

He stopped short, unable to say the name, and covered the near gaffe by peeling off the sodden T-shirt, picking up a towel hanging over the hand rail of the treadmill beside him and wiping the sweat from his body. There was a silence between them for a few moments.

'He does love you, you know?'

At first she thought he was talking about Fergus, and her head snapped back towards him in shock and not a little rage.

'Dad,' he explained, perhaps realising he had inadvertently wandered onto thin ice. 'He really does love you.'

She refused to accept that. 'I was always more part of Mum than I was of him. I'm like an inheritance, something handed down to him that he takes care of but has no real connection to. You're his pride and joy.'

Ray shook his head. 'You're wrong. You're a Burnes and he only wants what is best for you. He always has.'

'Yes, that was very evident five years ago, wasn't it?'

He knew what she was talking about but obviously refused to discuss it, so concentrated on wiping himself down, even though he looked dry to her. She suspected he was still showing off for her.

'And Call Me Rick wasn't right for me either, according to you,' she said. 'Nor any other boy I happened to be attracted to.'

A sly smile crept across his lips as he realised he was on firmer ground. 'I was right about Rick, though.'

She recognised he had been, but she wouldn't say it out loud.

'Dad will get this Rick thing sorted out. Don't worry.'

'I don't want it sorted out,' she said. 'I just want a divorce.'

'That's what I mean. He'll see to it all, you know that.' He dropped the towel and reached for the dry T-shirt hanging over the rail of the treadmill beside him. The fabric ballooned over his chest as he pulled it on. 'Rick's a fucking arsehole, a major dickhead.'

This time she had to agree. He was indeed both of these things.

'I really should head down to London and rip his head off.'

'Why? He didn't cheat on you.' Three times, she reminded herself. Christ, how sappy had she been taking him back twice?

'No, but he cheated on you and that's unacceptable.' He had picked up the damp towel again and was twisting it as if it was Call Me Rick's neck. 'You cross one Burnes, you cross them all, right?'

She gave him a smile. 'It's a kind thought, Ray, but not necessary. I'll divorce him, I'll tell all his friends that he has a tiny little willy that he doesn't know how to use properly, and that will hurt him far more than any head-tearing. He'll have to pick up some floozy somewhere to prove me wrong and, hopefully, catch something.'

Again, Ray reddened. He really didn't enjoy her talking about sex.

'Well, maybe so,' he said, 'but I'd still enjoy five minutes with him – just him and me and maybe a soundproofed room.'

She knew it was just the elevated testosterone talking – gym rage – but he was capable of making rash moves when the Burnes name or their possessions were threatened. She knew of two occasions when he had threatened people with a shotgun: the first, when someone had accused his father of cheating him in a business deal; the second, when a walker had wandered onto their property and made the mistake of arguing the Scottish right-to-roam legislation. On each occasion Ray had made sure that there were no witnesses to the threats, but Alex still smoothed things over with cash. She had little doubt there had been other occasions when money had talked people out of action.

'Calm down, Big Arnie, there's no need for torture and maiming just yet,' she said. 'But hold that thought – if he turns difficult over the divorce, then I may get back to you. If only you'd be as willing to back me up with Alex.'

'I back you up when you're right,' he said. 'And he's not always wrong. Sometimes you can be a right stroppy cow.'

She skipped away and laughed. 'Only sometimes? I must be slipping.'

'Lighten up with him, Shona. He's a good man.'

Of that she was not so sure. 'I can't forgive him, Ray. I can forgive all the other stuff – the coldness, the sometimes open disdain, the cruelty . . .'

'That was all in your mind, Shona. You missed your mother and you blamed him. What you didn't realise was that he missed her just as much as you, perhaps even more. He had finally found the woman he loved and she was taken away from him. And he finds it difficult to reveal his emotions. It's the Burnes way.'

'The Burnes way,' she said, her mouth twisting as if it tasted something bitter.

'Yeah, you hate it, but you're a Burnes, Shona. The way you don't forgive shows that.'

The idea offended her, but she knew there was truth in it, though she refused to accept it. 'As I say, I can forgive that – not forget, but at least forgive. But I can't forgive what he did five years ago.'

He grew uncomfortable again.

'I can never forgive that,' she went on. 'I loved him, Ray. I loved Fergus.'

He flinched again at the name, and his eyes dropped.

'You just don't get it, do you?' She waited for an answer, but he seemed to have found something of huge interest on the floor. 'Of course you can't. Maybe you will someday, when you find someone you care about more than you care about the Burnes name and all that goes with it. And when Alex does everything in his power to come between you, then maybe you'll get it. Until that happens, if it happens, don't talk to me about your father caring for me because he proved that he didn't.'

Ray rallied in defence of Alex Burnes. 'He does, Shona, you're just too pig-headed to see it.'

She fell silent, knowing that there might – just might – be some truth in that, but she *was* too pig-headed to admit it. 'He has a commitment to honour. He promised my mother that he would care for me and I'll make sure that he does just that. And that he never forgets what he did.'

17

Rebecca lay on her back, eyes open, staring at the shadow on the ceiling. Both she and Stephen were city folk and the pitch black that comes with rural life – there were no street lights for miles, it seemed – unnerved them, so they left on a small table lamp in the cottage's hallway. The light shining through made patterns above her. Stephen was on his side, his breathing deep and even as he slept. Thank God he wasn't a snorer, she thought. That would have been it, as far as she was concerned.

When she'd returned from the village, they'd cleared the air. He apologised – again. She apologised for being so touchy. He added another for good measure. She kissed him and one thing led to another and they ended up in bed, spending the rest of the afternoon touching and fondling. She did enjoy that sort of thing; it was something she had forgotten during her self-imposed celibacy. Or was it that she simply enjoyed touching and fondling him in particular?

Once again, she pulled herself back from that brink. She had already stared into the abyss during her period of self-examination by the waterfall, where she hadn't exactly found her *wa* but she had reached some kind of decision. She had to be more open to the possibilities of life. Work to live and not live to work, as they say. They being Elspeth, Chaz and Alan. Even Val Roach had hinted at it.

She hadn't heard anything from the minister and she wasn't holding out much hope that Frances MacGregor would wish to talk. Elspeth hadn't got back to her either, but she hadn't expected a result on Rory MacGregor so soon anyway.

The question on her mind as she looked at the plaster ceiling into which someone had carved little swirls, a decorative touch that for some reason impressed her, was whether to continue with the story. Her new found determination to redress her life/work balance suggested that she should not, or at least wait until she was back on duty, as it were. However, that would mean having to travel back and forth from Inverness to the glen, or simply working the phones, neither of which filled her with enthusiasm. She was in place, on the scene, and she should follow it up now. *If* she was going to follow it up. It kept coming back to that. Wasn't Harry's story enough to be doing while on holiday? Stephen didn't seem to mind. Until their little disagreement, she'd felt he was actually enjoying being on a story with her. But that really wasn't the point, was it?

She had been asking herself a lot of questions that afternoon but had come up with precious few answers and that frustrated her. She liked to have certainty and she wasn't finding it. Being open to life's possibilities was not easy.

Shona was still restless. She wandered the corridors of what her great-grandfather had grandly called Burnes House. Alexander Burnes the First had a yen to put his name on whatever he could, like a dog marking his territory. His house, his company, his charitable trust, his endowment at his old alma mater, the University of Glasgow. His son, Alexander the Second, had expanded the empire and continued seeding the name across the commercial world. His son, the third of the name, and the man Shona insisted on calling, to his annoyance, Alex, had expanded even further. To his credit, he had made his own way in the world of finance and had built his own brand to such a height that he could leave the interests he had inherited to others, although he still retained some measure of control. He had a duty to the Burnes heritage, he had once said. That was what she'd meant when she'd told Ray earlier that she was a mere inheritance to which he felt he had a duty but no real attachment . . .

Looking around her, she realised that the rambling old house was the exception. It had been passed down through the various Alexanders the Great and, like all the Burnes before him, Alex loved this place. It sat on the edge of the moor like a sentinel. As a child, she had thought it huge, but as an adult she saw that it was not as vast as she had at first thought. Yes, there were eight bedrooms, four public rooms, a large kitchen and various outbuildings, as well as an expansive estate with properties dotted around it – now mostly rented out to holidaymakers, adding to the Burnes coffers. Fishing and shooting rights also generated some income. Shona had grown up around the sound of gunfire so was used to it, though she never herself had wielded a shotgun at anything that breathed. It was Alex and Ray who were the enthusiastic shooters. She preferred non-lethal clay-pigeon shooting and had become a more than proficient shot. But there was something about this house she also loved, perhaps revealing that Burnes blood did course through her veins. She had spent her earlier years in London, where Alex was based, and was five years of age when she travelled to Perthshire for the first time. She had a memory from that first day, holding onto her mother's hand as they stepped from the car and looking up at the facade of the house with its twin turrets and large windows that reflected the clouds scudding across the blue sky, hiding what was within. It was the one thing that she and Alex shared, their affection for this house, and she knew that she would always return here when she could, this visit being a perfect example. As soon as she had decided to toss Call Me Rick aside like the garbage he was, she knew there was only one place to seek distance, to seek sanctuary, even though it meant having to be with Alex again.

She climbed the wide staircase that diverged right and left midway and admired the moon shining through the huge double window. It cast silver light on the stairway, split by the beams of the window into a large cross, as if it was targeting her. She turned right to reach the upper landing, walking with the ease that comes from a long acquaintance. She meandered along the dark corridor towards her own room. She paused at the window beside her bedroom door and looked down on part of the lawn, where loomed a stand of Douglas fir trees. Spectral mist hung low over the lawn as frost formed on the grass and the branches of the trees. The sky was clear and the moonlight was bright. It was a full moon – the Death Moon. March marked the end of winter.

A movement in the shadows at the base of the trees caught her attention, and she initially thought it to be a fox or a deer. She strained to see clearly, but the mist and the shadows combined to smear her vision. Her breath caught slightly when she made out someone wearing a bulky coat, with a hood obscuring their face.

Then the figure's head rose and – she was certain of this – fixed on the upper floor. Her bedroom window. She stepped back into the shadows of the hallway and watched, for some reason holding her breath as if the watcher would hear it. It wouldn't be old Duncan, the gardener, at this time of night. Tony, the gamekeeper, perhaps, out to catch the foxes before lambing was in full swing. But he would be away from the house, looking for their den, not standing in a copse of trees staring at the house. It was the coat that finally triggered her memory. She had only seen Cormac a few times and she was certain that it was his. What the hell was he doing here, looking at the house? The figure was immobile for what seemed like an age then, finally, it turned. Whoever was there walked back through the trees to be swallowed by the night and the mist.

18

Harry had become increasingly concerned about Ashley. There had been nothing from her and he sensed she was in trouble. She hadn't said anything in her most recent messages but he had sensed there was something going on behind her words. He knew she'd had trouble with her old boss, knew she had encountered racism where she lived – what was wrong with the world? When did everything become so polarised? Perhaps it had always been like that but people were now more open. So much hate, so much fear, so much mistrust. Racism, sexism, misogyny, misandry, all very much to the fore. He didn't remember it being like that until comparatively recently. Social media was partly to blame, of course, providing a wider platform from which bile could spew. Before, folk could only scream at their walls, or perhaps from a platform at Speakers' Corner. The media and the politicians had a lot to answer for, too. They had become increasingly entrenched in whatever position they chose to take in order to increase profits or garner votes and often were not letting something as inconsequential as the facts get in the way. If truth was the first casualty in war, then God help the country when the next one comes because that body had already fallen.

The screen of his phone lit up and he snatched at it eagerly, swiping it to life and thumbing in his four-digit pin to unlock the screen. Yes – the tell-tale icon of a message on the social media platform.

She called him dear. She had called him 'baby' for a time until he pointed out that it wasn't appropriate, given their age difference. She had said age was just a number, but he said he felt uncomfortable with it, so she had stopped with profuse apologies.

Hi, where have you been?

He thumbed carefully because he didn't like to make mistakes. She often made spelling or grammatical errors in her messages, and though he never corrected her he did feel a duty to perhaps educate her, if only by example. He immediately regretted being so blunt with his message, as it sounded like an accusation and she had proved touchy in the past. This time, she seemed to accept it.

So sorry dear. I been not able to txt. No credit

He frowned. No credit? He had sent her a gift card for £50 two weeks ago. It should have lasted longer than this.

My auntie's son, he use my phone and use up credit

Ah, Harry thought, that explains it. Her cousin was trouble, he had learned during their conversations, and had made sexual overtures to her. Harry had suggested that she should move out and find her own place, but then she lost her job, so that was that.

I got top up today and txt u right away dear. How are u today? *People have been asking about you.*

Again, he hadn't meant to be so blunt about it, but the message was sent before he had properly thought it through. He waited for a response but none came. He stared intently at the screen. She was still online, just not responding. He gave her a few moments – he had already been abrupt enough – but eventually he couldn't help but fire off a new message.

Are you there?

He watched the top of the screen. Finally, he saw the confirmation that she was typing.

Yes I am here. Whose been asking? What they say?

He hesitated, not sure what to tell her, finally deciding that it was best to be upfront. They had both agreed early on that they would always be truthful with one another. She had said that honesty was what she prized the most in friendship. She had been hurt too often in the past to accept it any longer. This poor woman had been through a lot in her young life and he would do his best to honour their mutual commitment to sincerity.

They think you are not real

Why think that?

Reporters. They are looking into online scams

Another pause in the exchange and he feared she had taken offence, thinking he was accusing her.

Do u think I am scammer?

No

What u tell them?

That I don't believe it

That good dear cos u know I not scammer. I yur friend

I know

107

I don't ask u for nothing just friendship. When you send me
money & buy me things I not ask for that
I know that and I told them

Another pause, during which Harry regretted even telling
her about the reporter's questions. More than that, he should
never have spoken to Rebecca Connolly in the first place: he
should have refused to see her. Damn his daughter for interfering. He was a grown man and he could speak to whom
he pleased, message whom he pleased, give money to whom he
pleased without her butting in. He felt his old anger towards her
rising, remembering her as a teenager when she spoke out of
turn. Mel had often chided him about his anger and he had
fought to suppress it, but he believed strongly that children
should not question their parents.

Will u do something for me dear?
Of course
I do not want you to talk to them again. Can u do that?
They want to turn u against me I don't no why.
I have already told them they are wrong
That is good dear cos I am no scammer. Just a
girl who needs a friend like u. A kind caring man
who I can depend on and will care for me
I do care for you
So u will not speak to them again. Promise me?
I promise

He had already decided not to take part in the TV show. He
liked the reporter, but this was his private life and he was not
going to have it aired all over the country and beyond. No, he
would politely decline to speak any further on the matter when
she contacted him.

That is good dear. I been having more troubles lately here and I
don't need that worry

What kind of trouble?

U dont worry about it. I will deal but things bad here.
My auntie, my cousin and there are people here who
dont like me cos I am not American. I told you that

Yes

So I need to deal with all this and dont
want to feel u are talking about me

I won't. But you need to tell me what is happening

She was offline before he hit the arrow to send his last
message. He heard nothing further from her that night.

19

Elspeth phoned just as they were having breakfast, the valley on the other side of the window basking in soft spring sunlight, sharpening the edges of trees ready to bud and highlighting the browns of the heath. The sharp tip of Schiehallion pierced the blue sky, a touch of candy floss mist still clinging to its slopes. The mountain reminded her so much of Ben Shee on the island of Stoirm and she was intrigued to find that both peaks carried similar legends. Schiehallion, in Gaelic, Sidh Chailleann, had been translated in a number of ways, but Rebecca preferred the 'Fairy Hill of the Caledonians'. It was said to be home to the unpleasantly named Blue Hag, who rode the storms and attacked travellers with icy death. On the far slope there was rumoured to be a cave that led directly to the underworld. She and Stephen hadn't hiked up the long trail of its eastern slope, but they hoped to before the week was out.

Thanks to Stephen's reading of the literature Catherine had left in the cottage for guests, they had learned Rannoch was filled with legend. Stephen had been enthralled by the tales of the clans and the caterans, as outlaws were known, and would occasionally drop a story into their conversation as they walked or drove around the loch, pointing out the Gallow Tree, where felons were hanged, and the graveyard with the stone of the heads, where a clan chief had dashed the brains from three children before their mother agreed to leave with him. Most of the tales involved blood, whether it be battles or murder, and Rebecca often had to remind herself that beautiful though her country was, it was steeped in horrors.

She looked directly across from the cottage to a ridge that, if she squinted, took on the appearance of a recumbent head, said to be that of the legendary warrior chief Fingal, sleeping until the return of his master. She smiled. Everywhere she looked in the Highlands there was a memory of the past, whether in fact or legend, and it was something she loved about it.

One part of more recent history she would not be investigating further was the disappearance of Fergus MacGregor. She had reached the decision during the hours of sleeplessness the night before. Frankly, the decision had surprised even her, but Elspeth's admonition about her using work as a means of sabotaging life had resonated. It was true she had let her personal life pass by unnoticed and she was, as Elspeth had also said, too young to allow it to slip away. So, she would let the story go, do her best to get Harry to appear on camera, but the rest of the time she'd enjoy the break and, in particular, her birthday in two days' time.

She had told Stephen of her intention to back off from the story as they sat down to their breakfast. Normally she grabbed a slice or two of toast at most, but as she was on holiday she was treated to scrambled egg and bacon, toast, coffee and fruit juice. It was time for indulgence. Anyway, Stephen had made it, which was just as well, as she could burn cornflakes.

Stephen stirred his coffee. 'You sure about that?'

'Yes,' she said. 'I think it's a non-starter anyway. If Fergus is still around, he obviously doesn't want to be found and it's not my business to rake it all up.'

'And if he's dead? If he met with an accident or was murdered?'

'If he met with an accident, then where's the body? This place isn't that remote that a body could lie undiscovered for years.'

111

'What about that case Harry mentioned? The young lad a few years back?'

Rebecca had checked that out. The young man had been found in a shallow grave by a family picking mushrooms in a Forestry Commission plantation, and a man was subsequently convicted over the death. He had only been missing around a year. Five years had passed since Fergus went missing but there was no real evidence of anything untoward.

'I think to make this work it would take a lot of digging and, frankly, I've got enough paying jobs without something taking up my time that might go nowhere. And we are supposed to be on holiday.'

She didn't know how many times she had to remind herself of that. She didn't know why – had the modern world (*had she?*) become so work-orientated that there was no room for leisure, that the idea of a holiday was little more than an afterthought, even when she was already three days into it?

Stephen buttered a slice of toast, his movements very slow and steady, as if he was considering everything. 'Okay,' he said eventually, but she detected a doubtful note in his voice.

'I mean it, Stephen,' she insisted.

'Sure.' He cut his toast in half. 'I believe you.'

She laughed. 'Your lips say that, but your voice says, "You're full of shit, Becks."'

He bit into his toast. 'I mean it, Becks. If you say you're letting it go, then fine.'

'But you don't believe me.'

This time he looked at her and smiled. 'I believe you believe it. And don't get me wrong – I'm happy that's what you've decided, as long as you're happy.'

She could see that he meant what he said. They stared at each other for a moment and she felt the same wave of affection she had felt before. She reached out and touched his hand, very gently, and smiled. 'You know what, Stephen Jordan?'

He waited for a moment, for her to continue, but she wasn't sure what she had been about to say. Something uncomfortable crept into his eyes and he looked away, covering it with a smile. 'You're going to say I'm wonderful, aren't you?'

'No,' she said, even though she was beginning to think he truly was.

'That I'm the world's best lover?'

She snorted. 'Let's just say you're the second-best lover in this room.'

He gave her a mocking laugh. 'Oh-ho! Kinda full of yourself there, Rebecca Connolly.'

'With good reason, don't you agree?'

He made a show of sitting back and sipping his coffee while he thought about this. 'Well,' he began, then paused. 'Let's just say you're not the worst.'

'Oh, really? And which of the other two women you've shagged was better?'

He had told her that he had only had sex with two other women in his life, which surprised her but really shouldn't have. Apart from Stephen, she only had two notches on her bedpost. There had been Simon, of course, and before him a boy in her year at university who was so nervous he could barely perform, at least the first time. She hadn't been much better, but they each learned to relax into it.

Stephen winced in an exaggerated fashion. 'Really, Ms Connolly, you're so coarse. Shagged, indeed. Your mother would be so proud.'

That warm feeling continued. This was good. This was nice. The anger she had felt yesterday was a memory. The pain and loneliness that had been her constant companions before he came along were so far gone that she wondered now if she really had felt them.

Her phone rang as they sat in silence, each of them with little smiles on their faces.

'Hi, Elspeth, how are you on this beautiful day?'

There was a silence on the line.

'Hello? You there?'

Elspeth finally spoke, her voice overly cautious. 'Becks? That you?'

Rebecca frowned. 'Of course it is, who else would it be?'

'I don't know – the person who answered the phone was bright and cheerful and I thought maybe someone had stolen your phone.'

'Very funny. I'm often bright and cheerful.'

'Yeah, sure,' said Elspeth, 'and I'm going to run a marathon sometime soon.'

Elspeth was not only overweight, she also walked with the aid of two sticks. She should have had her joints looked at years before, but she didn't trust doctors. At least, that's what she claimed. Rebecca had a suspicion that she was afraid of any kind of treatment.

'You sound better today than you did yesterday, got to say.'

'Well, the sun is shining today.'

'Uh-huh,' Elspeth said, scepticism dripping from the two syllables like water. 'I suspect there's more to it. I suspect this is the morning blush after the night before.'

'Is that all you ever think of?'

'No, I also occasionally consider the nature of world events and the damage to our environment, as well as the complete and utter fuckwaddiness of our nation's leaders.' A pause as she sucked on her ever-present cigarette, Julie obviously not being in the vicinity yet again. 'I think I've found your guy.'

Rebecca was momentarily stumped. 'My guy?' Then she remembered – Rory MacGregor. 'Oh, right . . . em . . .'

'He's in Perth, right enough. My pal down in Glasgow checked the cuts and found a court report from two years ago, an assault in a nightclub. He did six months. His address was in the documents. I've emailed it to you. He also checked with a freelance in Perth and it seems your boy's a bit of a player: small-time stuff, a bit of dealing, maybe a bit of receiving, that sort of thing. He may be in with the Glasgow boys.'

'The McClymonts?'

'Maybe, but they're not the only crew in the big city, although they do seem to have their tentacles spread out the length of the country.'

Rebecca had encountered the McClymonts only second hand, more or less by reputation, but she knew them to be particularly tough and ruthless.

'Okay, thanks,' she said, 'but the thing is, I don't think I'll be following this up, Elspeth. Sorry. I only decided in the middle of the night . . .'

'Really?' Elspeth's disbelief was almost tangible.

'Don't you start,' Rebecca said. 'I've just had the same from Stephen.'

'He knows you so well, then. But that's fine, Rebecca. It was only a phone call or two, but I'm glad you're seeing sense. Work is fine, but it's not everything.'

'Yes, I know. I'll finish off the thing for Leo, and then I'm downing tools for the rest of the week.'

'Good,' said Elspeth, and Rebecca could tell she meant it. 'So is the sun really shining down there? It's dull and overcast up here.'

'Yes, it's a beautiful day here in the neighbourhood.'

Elspeth grunted. 'And did you and Mr Wonderful have a good night?'

'I'm hanging up now, Elspeth.'

'Come on, girls tell each other these things – didn't they teach you that at girl classes in school?'

'Bye, Elspeth,' Rebecca said, a laugh tickling her voice.

'You should be drummed out of the Sisterhood.'

'Bye, Elspeth,' Rebecca said again, as she cut the connection and looked back to Stephen. 'That was Elspeth.'

'I gathered,' he replied.

'She found the address of Rory MacGregor.'

'I thought she would.'

'Seems he's a small-time drug dealer in Perth.'

'Harry did say he went off the rails.'

'He was done for an assault a couple of years ago.'

'Goes with the territory.'

'Yeah,' she said.

'Yeah,' he repeated.

They sat in silence for a while as she finished off the rest of her breakfast. He picked up the dirty dishes and stacked them in the dishwasher, then he turned and leaned against the machine, his ankles crossed, his arms folded. 'So,' he said, 'what do you fancy doing today?'

'I don't know,' she said. 'What do you fancy doing?'

He took a deep breath and stared off into the middle distance, as if making a decision. 'I dunno,' he said. 'I thought, maybe – if you were up for it, if you felt like it – that perhaps we'd get in the car and go somewhere.'

She saw something in his face, heard something in his voice, that made her grin. 'Like where?'

'Oh, let me think.' He cupped his chin with one hand and looked to the side. 'What do you say to Perth?'

Elspeth was right. He really did know her so well.

20

Rory MacGregor lived in a block of flats in what would at one time have been a council estate in Perth and was now, Rebecca guessed, a mix of social housing and privately owned homes. She did not know Perth at all, so had no idea if this was a 'good' area in which to live. She knew back in Inverness there were those who sneered at the streets of Inchferry, which she knew very well, and she saw here the same meld of deprivation and what might be called middle-class comfort; some of the small gardens in front of the properties were untidy and had not seen a pair of shears or a mower in some time, while others were neat and trim, or had been paved over and turned into parking spaces. The flats were maisonettes, with a ground-floor flat and an upper floor of two stories, with a corridor-cum-balcony to the front. According to the information produced by Elspeth – or rather by her pal in the Glasgow daily – Rory MacGregor lived on the second floor.

Three young men were strung out across the bottom of the open stairway leading upwards. They all had the same look as the Inchferry youths she had seen many times: dark hoodies draped over lean bodies, complexions pinched and pale, faces bearing a sense of curiosity masked as boredom. There were strangers in their midst and they wondered who they were and why they were here, while also trying not to show it. The one standing in the centre, right in front of the first step, plucked a cigarette from his lips and gave Stephen a quick study, as if weighing him up for future combat, then took Rebecca in from head to foot in a gaze that she had experienced, before, but which didn't stop her skin from crawling slightly. Whether by accident or design, this lingering look at her body, even though she was wrapped in her coat, was both repulsive and threatening, and she felt her shoulders stiffen. She caught sight of Stephen's jaw tensing and willed him not to say anything that might lead to a confrontation.

Nothing was said as Rebecca and Stephen veered away on either side of the trio and began to climb the stairs. She could feel their eyes on her until she vanished round the corner to take the next flight. She glanced at Stephen's immobile face. He would have clients like those young men, would accept at least professionally the way they were, but he was not there professionally. That boy had shown disrespect with his leer and Stephen didn't like that. Thankfully, he had not felt the need to puff himself up in her defence, which was a good thing and it made her proud.

They walked along the corridor, checking the door numbers as they passed, until they reached the right one. Rebecca pressed the doorbell but didn't hear any corresponding sound from within, so she gave the letterbox a solid rattle.

'What do we do if he's not in?' Stephen asked, his voice low.

'I'll stick a note through the door with my card, telling him what it's about and asking him to call.'

'And if he doesn't?'

She took a breath. 'Then we decide if we want to come back and try doorstepping him again, knowing there is every chance he still won't be in or will just ignore us. Or I really do drop this whole thing.'

She heard him give a small chuckle. 'Yeah, that'll be the day.'

There was a flash of movement behind the frosted door panel which loomed into a recognisable male figure. The door swung open to reveal a burly young man with shoulder-length brown hair, wearing a faded T-shirt sporting the logo of an American beer brand. He looked them both over, his eyes clouded with suspicion.

'Aye?'

Rebecca gave him a smile to show they came in peace. 'Rory MacGregor?'

She recognised him from the photograph she had seen online, but she still couched it as a question.

His suspicion deepened. 'Aye. What can I do for you?'

'My name is Rebecca Connolly.' She handed him the card she already had palmed from her pocket. 'I wonder if we could have a wee chat.'

He looked at the card, then back at her, suspicion still pooling in his eyes. 'What about?'

'Your brother.'

He took that in, giving Stephen another glance. 'You a reporter, too?'

'No, I'm a lawyer.'

Amusement ate away at the wariness. 'What? Reporters got to travel with lawyers now, like?'

'Sometimes it feels that way,' said Rebecca. 'Stephen is my' – she hesitated slightly – 'friend.'

'I'm her driver for the day,' Stephen added.

'You her minder, too?'

Rebecca said, 'Do I need one?'

'Sometimes we all need a minder' he glanced at her card, to check her name – '. . . Rebecca. The world can be a dangerous place.'

'Yes, we encountered a little of it at the foot of the stairs.'

Rory frowned and stepped barefoot across the open corridor to lean over the parapet, then smiled. 'They lads are harmless, all looks and posing. You don't need to worry about them.'

He moved back into his doorway. He still hadn't invited them in and Rebecca felt this tandem conversation about lawyers, minders and the threat level posed by the three young men was nothing but a diversion while he processed the reason behind their visit. He leaned against the doorframe, looking at her card again, his smile gradually dropping away. 'So what about my brother? Have they found him?'

'No,' she said, then explained about witnessing the memorial service in the Black Wood.

He tilted his head and squinted, as if considering her words. 'Aye, it would be five years ago yesterday, right enough. Can't believe I forgot about it.'

'Would you have attended the ceremony if you had remembered?'

His laugh was like a short yelp. 'Fuck, no. I'm not exactly welcome in Rannoch. So what's your interest, like?'

'I think it's time the story was told again.'

'Why?'

'In the hope that it might generate some answers.'

'You mean help find him?'

'Hopefully.'

He weighed her sincerity. 'You're really going to do a story on this?'

'If I can, yes.'

'You spoken to Mum?'

'No, not yet. I understand she has never spoken to the press.'

'No, Dad neither.' He laughed. It was a short, bitter laugh. 'Good luck with them.'

'Can we speak to you about it? You were the only one quoted five years ago. Are you willing to go on the record again? Perhaps if we can generate more publicity, some answers might be found.'

He stared at her, obviously debating with himself the wisdom of talking further. Then, finally, he shrugged. 'Fuck it,' he said. 'You'll be lucky to get anything out of Mum or Dad, and if they see me talking it will piss them off right royally.' He stepped back and jerked his head to the side. 'You better come in, but wipe your feet. My girlfriend will string me up if I let someone bring in dirt . . .'

Frances MacGregor hung up the phone and walked from the hallway to the living room, where her husband studied that day's newspaper, again on his tablet. He had been listening to his music earlier, but he had taken the earphones off, she presumed, so he could listen to her side of the phone conversation. 'That was Tom Lester,' she said.

Dan MacGregor looked up from his screen and waited for her to amplify.

'There's a reporter in the village asking questions,' she said. 'About what?'

'Don't be obtuse, Dan, you know about what. It seems she saw me yesterday in the Black Wood.'

He blinked once, swallowed, then turned back to his device. 'I told you that you should have stopped that nonsense.'

'It's not nonsense.'

He ignored her. He often ignored her nowadays.

'She wants to talk to us,' she said.

He feigned interest on the screen, but she knew he was thinking. They had been married for twenty-seven years after all. 'Perhaps we should,' he said at last.

'No.'

He looked back at her. 'You don't think it's worth a try?'

'No,' she said again, even firmer than before.

'It's been five years and no word from him. Don't you want answers?'

'It's family business and of no concern to the world.'

'He's your son.'

She felt her lower lip and chin tremble. She knew he was her son, but she could not bring herself to talk about him to an outsider.

Dan took a breath. 'What does Tom Lester think?'

'He thinks it can't do any harm.'

Dan turned his attention to the tablet once more. 'There you are, then. If you won't listen to me, maybe you'll listen to him.'

'She'll ask about his family life. What do I say then?'

He laid the device down and looked straight at her. 'That's up to you.'

'And if I say nothing and she finds out what happened?'

He thought about that. 'Unless you tell her, that's unlikely, isn't it?' He seemed to be waiting for an answer but she had nothing to say. He returned his attention to the news website. 'Perhaps it's time something was said and the whole sorry mess was out there.'

'No!' She was horrified at him even thinking such a thing. 'Nobody must ever know.'

He didn't look up. 'I wish to God I didn't . . .'

21

Rebecca recognised there was a person with taste and flair behind the decor in the flat and she suspected it was not Rory. The furniture might have been flat-pack and bought from a bargain store, along with the rugs and ornaments peppering shelves and occasional tables, but then so were many of the items in her own flat back in Inverness, which was utilitarian rather than homey. She had nothing of a personal nature on display: no photographs, no items of a sentimental nature. She had pictures on the wall, most of them given to her by her photographer friend Chaz, who believed a bare wall was an affront to decency, but that was it. Chaz's husband Alan had once said that her living room was as welcoming as the waiting room of the Spanish Inquisition. Rebecca knew she needed to warm her home up a bit, buy some knick-knacks, give it more of a lived-in feel, rather than it just being a place she crashed now and then, but she had never quite got around to doing it.

Rory waved them towards a couch shrouded in a variety of thick throws, which was, she surmised, old and threadbare, but when she and Stephen sat on it, it was supremely comfortable. He then asked them if they wanted tea or coffee, his ingrained Highland hospitality still to the fore despite what Rebecca knew of his current occupation. They readily accepted coffee and he stepped into the adjoining kitchen as she removed her notebook, pen and digital recorder from her bag.

She and Stephen sat in silence as they listened to the sounds of beverage-making.

Rory reappeared carrying a tray with three mugs and a packet of digestive biscuits. Rebecca hid a smile, wondering if his girl-friend would reprimand him for not putting the biscuits on a plate. Stephen cleared away some magazines and newspapers from top of the oak veneer coffee table.

'Sorry, no chocolate biscuits.' Rory set the tray down. 'Lily won't allow them in the house. I manage to sneak a wee bag of sugar in when she's not looking, though.'

The sugar was also in a bag, a teaspoon protruding from it like a tongue. Rebecca dug out two heaped spoonfuls, dropped them into her mug, poured in some milk – the carton was also on the tray – and stirred with her habitual extreme prejudice. She had done that since a child, prompting her mother to remark more than once that she would drill through the bottom of the mug if she wasn't careful. Stephen took his coffee black and sugar-free, something that, to her mind, was wrong to the point of being perverse.

She took a mouthful of the coffee. It wasn't bad, but she knew Stephen, who shunned instant, would struggle to keep his face from twisting, though she was confident his inherent cour-tesy would overcome the impulse. 'You have a nice place here,' she said.

Rory looked around, as if valuing it for auction. 'Aye, Lily keeps it nice.'

Rebecca mentally congratulated herself. It's always nice to be right. 'Lily's your wife?'

'Nah, no married. We just shack up. She's been studying up on that feng shui carry-on,' he continued. 'So God knows what she'll do with the place.'

Rebecca thought the trend for the Chinese art of geomancy, of balancing your home to the natural world, was on the wane, though she was impressed that Rory had pronounced it correctly. She still had trouble with croissant. 'Lily's not home, I take it?'

'Nah, she's at work. She works in Matalan down the town.'

He sat down in an armchair which, like the couch, was encased in throws. 'So what do you want to know?'

Rebecca laid her digital recorder on the coffee table beside the tray. 'Do you mind if I record this?'

He regarded the tiny machine as if it were a snake about to strike, then shrugged. 'Sure, why not?'

She clicked record, sat back again and flipped open her reporter's notebook to a blank page.

Rory watched her. 'You take notes and record?'

'Yes. The recording allows me to quote you accurately, if that need arises, but I find taking notes helps lodge things in my memory.' Her mother had performed in amateur drama in her younger days and had once told her that she learned her lines by writing them out over and over again. There was some strange alchemy between the handwritten word and the memory that Rebecca found invaluable. 'So, what can you tell me about your brother?'

Rory sat back and stared at the coffee in his mug for a moment. 'Fergus was . . . Fergus, I suppose. He was my big brother and he looked after me, tried to keep me in line in a lot of ways.'

'Keep you in line how?'

An almost shy smile teased his lips. 'I told you I was the wild one. Well, he tried to keep me on the straight and narrow, if you know what I mean. God knows the number of lectures he gave me about giving myself a shake, stick in at school, make something of myself. I tried to do better, if only for his sake, but . . .' He shrugged again, looked around him. 'Shit happens, know what I mean? Our mum and dad were, well, it's fair to say I was – am – a disappointment to them. Mum's dead religious, not a nut job or anything like that, but she has her beliefs and they're firm.'

'I take it you don't share her beliefs?'

'Nah, used to, like most kids, or at least I thought I did, but I rejected all that from an early age and she couldn't accept it. Neither of them liked some of the stuff I got up to, either, or the company I kept. It was nothing major, me and my pals weren't in a gang or anything, like. You don't get that sort of thing in Rannoch.'

'It's a beautiful place.'

'Aye, but you can't eat scenery. And there's not much to do unless you like walking or shooting guns. Well, not much to do for me anyway. I can't blame the place, or Mum and Dad, for the way I've turned out. It's all me.'

'So what sort of stuff did you do that they didn't like?'

'The usual. Drinking. Girls. Some rowdy behaviour. As I said, nothing major.' He stopped for a mouthful of coffee, then added, 'I got in a few fights.'

'And Fergus tried to set you straight?'

'Aye, he was the sensible brother. Did well at school, went to uni, wanted to be a writer. Never gave them a moment's worry, did Fergus.'

'And was he religious?'

'Fergus?' He smiled. 'No. He wasn't as obvious about it as me – I mean, I would attack it at every turn as soon as I was old enough to think for myself – but he said people should believe what they want to believe, or not believe, if that's what they wanted, and not be questioned about it. He was very even-minded, was Fergus.'

'And your mum accepted the fact that neither of you were believers?'

'She didn't have a choice. She wasn't an ogre, but there was a certain . . . distance, if you know what I mean.'

'With you?'

'Oh, yeah, defo me eventually, but I suppose that was my fault. She never distanced herself from Fergus. Dad was a different story, though.'

126

'He distanced himself from Fergus?'

'Oh aye, it was like a switch was thrown. One minute he was the bee's knees, the next it was like Dad didn't want anything to do with him.'

'Why?'

'We never found out. Things got kinda frosty in the house after that. Even Mum and Dad weren't the same with each other.'

'When was this?'

'Just before Fergus went away.'

'And you have no idea what happened?'

He shook his head. 'Nah. They didn't talk about feelings and shit, Mum and Dad. Certainly not with me.'

Rebecca looked at her notes, as she considered what her next question would be. 'So what do you think happened that day?'

He shifted in his chair a little. 'The day he went away?'

'Yes.'

'I wish I knew.'

'He often visited the Black Wood, right?'

'Oh yeah, he was never out the place. Loved it. Would spout stories about it – about the whole glen – for hours. When I was young I used to love hearing them – it's mostly blood and killing, all that Children of the Mist stuff – but once I was in my teens I got bored with it all and he stopped telling me.' Rory's eyes clouded a little. 'Kinda regret that now. They were good stories.' He seemed lost for a few moments, then found himself again. 'He went there so often he even made friends with the old hermit fella.'

'Cormac?'

He seemed surprised. 'You know about him?'

She gave him a quick bob of the head. 'Yes, he was at the service yesterday morning but kept himself apart from it.'

'Aye, that would be him. Strange guy, so he is. He was the local bogeyman to us kids. Be careful or Cormac will get you, that kinda thing.'

'But he's harmless, right?'

'Oh, aye. Never been any issues as far as I know, but we still wanted to keep away from him.'

'Why?'

He shrugged. 'People don't like anything that's different, do they? And old Cormac, well, he's different. He keeps himself away from everyone as much as he can up there in that cottage of his. Sells his stuff to live, but apparently he had enough cash years ago to buy the place. He wanders the Black Wood and beyond, picking up bits of this and that to turn into art for trendies in the cities. He looks after stray animals, injured birds and the like. Rannoch folk even take animals to him that they've found. Yeah, Cormac's harmless, but he can still be scary to kids, you know?'

'And Fergus befriended him?'

'Aye, if anyone could it was Fergus. He told me they had long chats as they walked the woods together. Even went into his cottage for a cuppa now and then, which is nothing short of amazing cos old Cormac, he doesn't let people over the door usually.'

'Did you go with Fergus to the wood anytime?'

'Aye, as I say, when I was a boy. Not so much later. Fergus would go there, just wander about or sit in that wee clearing, just by himself.'

'Why?'

'He said it helped him think. I said could he no do that on the toilet like decent folk?'

Rebecca smiled. 'So did anything happen just before he vanished? Anything that you think might have prompted him to walk away from it all?'

'Like what?'

Rebecca struggled to come up with any examples. 'I don't know – anything. He didn't drink, do drugs, gamble?'

'Fergus? Fuck no! Sorry for my language. Fergus would have a drink but didn't get pissed. No way was he an alcoholic and no way would he touch drugs. And I never knew him to even back a horse on Derby Day, let alone join Gamblers Anonymous.'

Rebecca knew that many people could hide their demons very successfully. She remembered reading Henry David Thoreau's quote about men living lives of quiet desperation and she believed that to be true. On the outside everything can be normal, but inside they're screaming silently into a void. Was that Fergus? He'd wanted to be a writer – was he disappointed at his lack of success?

'Was there anyone who wished him harm that you know of?'

'Fergus wasn't someone who generated that kind of heat, if you know what I mean. He was a quiet, decent guy who kept out of everyone's way.' He stopped as if something had occurred to him. 'There was all that shit with Shona, right enough.'

'Shona?'

'You don't know about her?'

'Rory, I don't know very much, to be honest. That's why we're talking to you.'

He leaned forward to put his mug back on the tray, his face betraying the feeling that he had said something he shouldn't. He sat very still for a few moments, then said, 'Shona Burnes. Fergus met her at a dance in Kinloch Rannoch. New Year, it was. I was there, too.' He swallowed, his eyes fixed on the table-top as he remembered. 'Christ, I haven't thought about this for ages. He fell for that lassie like a stone, so he did, and I can't say I blame him. She was bloody gorgeous.'

He fell silent again, as if he was lost in the memory.

Rebecca asked, 'And that stirred up trouble, did it?'

As he looked up at her, something in his eye changed. Rebecca couldn't quite understand what.

'Aye, it caused trouble,' he said, his voice no longer as friendly. 'Why?'

He sat back again. 'You really don't know much, do you?'

'Rory, I only learned about your brother's disappearance yesterday. I'm still feeling my way here, to see if there's anything I can do to help.'

'Anything you can do to help? Is that the way you reporters see it? That you help people?'

'I try to help.'

'And it's not about just getting the story? About making money from it?'

Rebecca felt anger flare just a little. She detected a hectoring tone in the man and she wasn't about to be lectured by someone who was involved in the drug trade, even if only allegedly. 'Rory, I won't deny that I do this for a living, and if I can't sell this story on, then there will be no point in me continuing with it. But if I can generate interest, then perhaps that will help in some way.'

'But you can't guarantee it?'

'There are no guarantees, no. We don't know what happened to your brother, but the fact remains that he was never seen again. Your mother arranges this ceremony every year, I understand . . .'

'Yeah, I don't know what she hopes to gain from that.'

'She's grieving, Rory. She lost her son.'

'Yeah.' There was a bitter, sneering tone now. 'She lost both her sons, but she doesn't seem to bother about me, does she?'

His attitude had definitely changed but Rebecca couldn't understand why. She glanced at her notes, saw Shona underlined. That was the point it changed. Who was this Shona and why had Rory's almost accidental mention of her generated this mood swing?

'Why was there trouble over Fergus seeing Shona?'

Rory didn't reply at first, but she gave him time to consider. He looked from her to Stephen, who was sitting silently throughout, then back to her. 'She was a Burnes, if only in name.'

'And?'

130

'And my dad and Alex Burnes, her father, don't get on. The funny thing is my dad, my mum and Alex Burnes used to be pals.'

'When they were children? What happened to change it?'

'They grew up, I suppose. Things are much simpler when you're a kid, right? But then as you get older you find that life isn't that simple, that there's more to being an adult than the kid inside ever realised. Know what I mean? And you do stuff that you would never have thought you would do.'

22

Mist rose like smoke signals from the tree-crusted hills that crowded around them as they turned off the A9, the main route north, towards Dunkeld. They crossed the Thomas Telford-designed bridge over the River Tay into the village, finding a space in a car park that led to the historic cathedral. Stephen had expressed a yearning to visit the place because it was steeped in history and he thought it would make a charming spot for a walk in the soft spring sunshine. First, though, they had a late lunch in a hotel. On the drive from Perth they had discussed what they had learned from Rory MacGregor, but in the dining room Rebecca steered the conversation away from the subject. These matters were not to be aired in such surroundings. They were on holiday and she was determined that her obsession with work did not take up all their time.

They didn't discuss it while they visited the ruined cathedral, either, where Stephen posed for a selfie beside the large stone knight that marked the tomb of Alexander Stewart, the man they called the Wolf of Badenoch because of his allegedly cruel nature. He may not have been as evil as he was painted, Stephen said, for if history is written by the victors, then reputations are made by those still standing. Nor did they discuss it when they visited the grave of William Cleland, who commanded the fledgling Cameronian regiment against Jacobite forces in 1689. They had set their defences in and around the cathedral and eventually put Dunkeld to flame to flush out snipers. Only three houses survived the conflagration and Cleland died in the battle. Rebecca, as usual, touched the stones and caressed the walls, trying to connect with the violence and death from more than three centuries before.

It wasn't until they walked the grassland between the ruins and the dark river, mature pine trees towering above them, that Stephen asked her what she thought about Rory MacGregor and she countered by asking him what he thought, saying that he was better placed to pass any sort of judgement, as he had observed the interview rather than take part to any great degree. Stephen thought about his answer as they walked. He was on holiday, but he was still a lawyer.

'I think he's a troubled young man,' he said. 'There was bitterness in the way he spoke about his parents.'

'Understandably, if what he says is true.'

'Perhaps, but the family dynamic is a tricky thing and what one member perceives as truth is not necessarily the way it truly is.'

'So you think he might have been lying?'

'Not lying, no. I mean, don't misunderstand me here, it may well have been as he said, but I've learned the hard way that often those involved in a situation are the least reliable when it comes to providing impartial testimony.'

Rebecca had learned this, too. A university lecturer had once told her that there are at least three sides to every story: what one person says, what another person says, and somewhere in the middle you might find something a mite closer to the truth if you look for it.

'You said he might be involved in the supply of controlled substances?' Stephen asked, and she nodded. 'Well, I think he may well be sampling the product a little. His mood was change-able, but then perhaps that's the way he is.'

Rebecca thought about his powerful arms. 'I didn't see any track marks.'

133

'Well, you know there are other ways to imbibe. Could be heroin, but maybe something softer. My experience is that the main suppliers tend not to trust any of their sales team, if they are. They'll put up with class C and class B use, most of them are into that stuff too, but class A use is a no-no. It's for selling, not for using. Of course, I'm speaking generally here. I can think of at least two of the big boys who either mainline or powder their nose from the inside regularly. You had experience yourself, with Scott Burke.'

Rebecca really didn't want to think back to the moment when the young gangster, high on his own product, confronted her on a rainswept path beside the Caledonian Canal with murder in mind. Two people died that night, neither of them Scott Burke. He was now in prison. His actions destroyed his family, leaving his mother a grieving shell. The last time Rebecca had seen the woman she was standing over a grave as darkness fell, haunted by the ghosts of her own conscience.

'So you think I should take what Rory said with a pinch of snuff?'

He smiled. 'Well, I can't condone the use of any sort of stimulant, but not necessarily. I don't need to tell you that you're going to have to talk to a lot more people before you can make any kind of judgement here, or even get close to anything like a truth.'

A truth, he had said. There were many different truths and they both knew it. She also noted that he had decided she was going to continue and had known it even before she did. Again, she was amazed at how swiftly this man had come to understand her. She wanted to kiss him but felt that might be frowned upon in a holy place. She wasn't a believer, but she respected other people's beliefs, whatever they may be. Instead, she took his hand.

'So, what's the next step?'

She had to think about his question. She had come upon this story by accident and hadn't really thought it through. Stephen sensed that and said, 'Why not talk over what you know, or think you know, and what you need to know? Sometimes it helps to say it out loud. I do that all the time with Elaine with work.'

Mention of his receptionist-cum-office manager stung at Rebecca – she wasn't sure why. She had no reason to think that there was anything between them – in fact, she was certain there wasn't – but the woman had taken an instant dislike to her the first time they faced one another over the reception desk in Stephen's small office.

'Okay,' she said, her mind flicking through the notes in her head, 'we know Fergus was in the Black Wood when he vanished.'

'No – you know his car was found parked there. There's no evidence to suggest he was in the Black Wood.'

This was good, she thought, it was focusing her mind. 'Fine, so let's assume Fergus was in the Black Wood that day.'

'Okay,' Stephen said, but his tone suggested he was unhappy. 'But as Samuel L. Jackson once said in some film or another, never make assumptions, it just makes an ass out of "u" and "umption". Why would Fergus be in the wood that morning?'

'He often went there,' she said.

'Yes, but he was supposed to be going to Pitlochry, wasn't he? At least that's what he told people. So why go to the Black Wood? His home was on the other side of the loch, so that's a detour.'

'But he wasn't going to Pitlochry. The friend he was supposed to be meeting said they hadn't made any plans.'

'So you think he had always planned to go to the Black Wood?'

'I don't know what he might have planned. But if that plan was to disappear, he could have been going there for one last visit, to say goodbye to somewhere he loved.'

'Evidence?'

'Gut feeling.'

'Hmm,' he said.

She smiled. 'This isn't a court of law, Stephen, we're spitballing here. Gut feelings are admissible. And I've made a career out of them.'

They walked a few paces in silence, as Stephen considered this. 'Maybe, but we still have no firm evidence he was there that morning.'

'His car . . .'

'Someone else could have driven that there.'

'Why?'

'No idea.'

She stopped and faced him. 'You think he's dead, don't you?'

'I think it's a strong possibility. People disappear all the time, certainly, for their own reasons. They can be troubled, they can be escaping something, but so far there's nothing to suggest that Fergus was either troubled or in any difficulty.'

'There was some trouble at home, according to Rory.'

'Enough to make him want to run away? And as you say, according to Rory. I've got to say, I don't think he's the most credible witness.'

They walked ahead as Rebecca turned this over. 'So, did he meet with an accident?'

'He would have been found more or less right away. It's rough country, but it's not desolate and it's not mountainous. The searchers would have found him.'

'So are you saying you think he was murdered?'

'What do you think?'

'I don't know what I think yet.'

'But it has to be considered.'

'We've no evidence of that,' she said, delighted she could fire his own words back at him.

He laughed. 'Touché.'

They turned to walk across the grass back to the cathedral. 'Right,' Rebecca said, 'we've got him maybe visiting the Black Wood, then vanishing, leaving his car at the roadside. Or we've got him going who knows where and someone else leaving his car there. Or we have him being murdered somewhere and the body never surfacing.'

'In other words, we've got a lot of very little.'

'Yeah, that's par for the course, though. But who would want him dead? And it's bloody difficult to completely dispose of a body. So if he is still alive, why did he want to vanish? And why did nobody see him at any point? Sure, this isn't Inverness high street, but there are still people about. Cars, buses, deliveries, walkers. And yet nobody saw him.' She sighed. 'You're right, we've got very little.'

'I think we go back to your original assumption.'

'Oooh,' she said, delighted. 'What happened to umption's ass?'

'All for the sake of argument – and there needs to be some kind of base line here, and until we learn anything else that seems the logical one. He was in the wood that day. We don't know why. We don't know who with. There was some kind of trouble at home, could that be connected to his relationship with that young woman?'

'Shona Burnes,' Rebecca said.

'Yes, Shona Burnes. There was animosity between the families.'

'And yet his mum and dad, and her dad, had been friends once.'

'So what happened there?'

Rebecca looked down at her feet as they walked. 'I'll need to find this Shona and speak to her.'

'There's someone else you may have to speak to as well.'

Her thoughts had been heading that way for a while. 'This guy Cormac,' she said.

'Someone you've been warned against by Catherine and the minister.'

'I was, but if I heeded all the warnings I've had over the years I'd not get much done.'

He walked in silence for a few steps before he said, 'Okay, we'll go see him tomorrow.'

He had said 'we'.

We'll go see him tomorrow.

To hell with hallowed ground, she thought, as she pulled him to a halt, pressed him against the trunk of a nearby tree and kissed him as though they were in a Hollywood movie. When they came up for air, Stephen instinctively looked for anyone watching, but there was nobody around, for which Rebecca was secretly thankful. She kept a challenging smile on her lips, though.

'Where did that come from?' he asked.

'Why? Didn't you enjoy it?'

'Of course I did, but you're not one for open displays of affection.'

'I like to be unpredictable,' she said.

They returned to their rented cottage and finished what they had started against that tree before Rebecca did the honours and made the evening meal. It was nothing terribly complicated because her cooking skills were not about to make Nigella Lawson hang up her skillet – a simple meal of tuna and pasta, fried onions, salad and a dash of tarragon. She still managed to burn the onions, though, and Stephen groaned at the prospect of a stir-in tomato sauce rather than making one from scratch. She pointed out that life was too short for all that malarkey. Food was food to Rebecca. She enjoyed it but didn't spend a great deal of time over it.

After they had eaten, they pulled on warm jackets and sat outside sipping wine as they took in the night sky. It was completely clear, a heavy frost already settling, so the starscape was spectacular. Having grown up in Glasgow and then moved to Inverness, she was well aware that city life was responsible for pollution of all kinds, including the snuffing out of the splendours of the heavens, so she was in awe of the show above her. The black velvet sky was pierced with thousands – millions – of tiny pinpricks of light. They twinkled, they shimmered, and in places coalesced in a milky swathe of frosting mirrored by the glitter on the bare branches of the trees around them and the grass of the small garden. As her eyes had grown accustomed to the darkness, she could make out the dark bulk of Schiehallion reaching up to the stars and the mist floating over the surface of Dunalastair Water.

It was while they were sitting in silence, comfortable in the knowledge that nothing need be said between them, that the peace was shattered by the ringing of her business phone. She felt a pang of remorse at not having switched it off – its artificial, mechanised sound had no place in that moment, in that place – but still fished it from her jacket pocket and checked the screen. Unknown Number, it said. Stephen gave her a glance, but she could not tell from his expression if he was annoyed or curious to know who it was. She considered not answering, but while she did so her thumb slid across the screen. Sometimes her mind had a mind of its own.

'Rebecca Connolly.'

A woman's voice. 'My name is Frances MacGregor.'

Despite her surprise over the woman getting in touch, Rebecca kept her tone businesslike. 'Mrs MacGregor, thank you for calling me.'

Stephen raised his eyebrow when he heard the name.

'I merely called to tell you that I have nothing to say,' said Mrs MacGregor. *No you didn't*, Rebecca thought. *If you had nothing to say you wouldn't have called at all.*

'I understand why you would say that, Mrs MacGregor, but I would appreciate the chance to talk to you.'

'Ms Connolly—'

'Please, Mrs MacGregor, call me Rebecca.' Giving the woman the option to be less formal while continuing to call her Mrs MacGregor might make her feel as if she was in control, which she was, of course. She could hang up, she could refuse to say anything further – she needn't have called in the first place – but she didn't do any of those things. If she accepted the invitation to address her by her first name, then Rebecca was certain she wanted to say more.

Rebecca waited. The line wasn't dead, but Frances MacGregor was silent.

'Mrs MacGregor?'

'I'm here.'

'Is it possible we could meet, perhaps? I find that face-to-face chats are better than phone calls, don't you?'

Another silence, then an exhalation of air. A decision had been reached. 'What would you want to know, Rebecca?'

Rebecca forced the smile from her voice. 'We'll chat is all, Mrs MacGregor. I won't record it, if you're uncomfortable with it. I won't even take notes, if that's what you want.'

'Why are you so interested?'

It was Rebecca's turn to pause. She could spin this, but she knew that in situations like this honesty was always best.

'There is something here that fascinates me, Mrs MacGregor. I know that sounds dreadful, after all you and your family have had to live through, and I am an outsider, an interloper who you will see as sticking their nose in where it doesn't belong, but I really believe that if we can generate some media interest then it might help. You've never talked about it, have you?'

'Not to the press, no.'

'I understand that, I really do. Talking to the media can be daunting and—'

'Can I trust you, Ms Connolly?'

Uh-oh, they were back to being formal. Rebecca let the question lie between them for a beat.

'I could say yes, Mrs MacGregor, but obviously I could be lying. Why don't you meet with me tomorrow, over coffee perhaps, and you can judge for yourself? You can ask me anything you want. You can look me up online and see the work I have done in the past. Then you can decide for yourself if I'm to be trusted.'

In the end, the woman had agreed – 10 a.m. in the lounge of a local hotel. She and Stephen decided that she should attend the meeting alone.

'If she's reluctant at all, I can't go in there mob-handed,' Rebecca said.

'Of course not.' Tilting his head back to gaze skyward again, he said, 'But let's not talk any more about this story, eh? Let's just enjoy this moment for now. Then go inside and I'll open up a whole can of whupass on you at Monopoly.'

'An entire can?'

'Oh, yeah. You'll feel the pinch in your actual bank balance.'

23

Rebecca wondered if Frances MacGregor's features were always as severe, or if it was an expression she had saved just for her. The woman was sizing her up, which was not unusual. People were always trying to make their mind up about her, whether to trust her, or not – whether to tell her everything, or not. It was clear that Fergus's mother had not yet reached a conclusion.

Rebecca had been ten minutes early and spotted Frances already waiting in reception. She had seen Fergus's mother's photograph online, of course, but she had aged badly over the five years. Her hair was grey, her face thinner, the skin sallow and saggy around the jaw, her eyes bagged. Rebecca had introduced herself and told her she had reserved a quiet table in the lounge for them. Frances had nodded and walked immediately to the corner, obviously having been there before.

Now, Frances studied Rebecca across the table, eyes wary and ready to judge. She hadn't touched the coffee she had ordered.

'My husband doesn't know I'm here,' she said.

'Okay,' said Rebecca. Rory had said there was something brittle in the MacGregor household, so she wasn't sure how to respond.

'I don't know why I am here, to be honest.' What might have been a nervous smile tugged at the woman's lips.

'It could be because you feel that something has to be done,' Rebecca suggested.

Frances accepted that with a tilt of the head and stared down at the table, her fingers playing with an unopened sachet of brown sugar. 'There need to be ground rules,' she said.

'Okay,' Rebecca said, her heart sinking. She hated ground rules.

'If I don't want to answer anything, then I won't.'

'Fair enough.'

'I need you to keep me informed regarding whatever you find.'

'I would do that anyway.'

'Good and bad.'

'That's one of my rules too, Mrs MacGregor.'

'I get to read anything you write before it appears anywhere.'

Rebecca knew that one was coming. 'If I write anything – and that's nowhere near certain at this stage – you can read it, but I won't change anything unless you can show me it's factually incorrect.'

The woman looked as if she was about to argue that point, but then she reconsidered. 'What can you hope to achieve here, Rebecca?'

There was nothing fresh she could say other than that which she had told everyone else.

'I don't know and that's the truth. It will bring your son's case back into the public eye, if I can generate media interest – but that's not a guarantee. The media is flighty, Mrs MacGregor . . .'

'Untrustworthy.'

'Yes, I can see why you would think that. It becomes interested in people's lives, then moves on. But sometimes we go back, for whatever reason, and that can help. Time and distance can bring perspective, Mrs MacGregor, and can also help with memory. If I can get some stories placed here and there, then perhaps – just perhaps – it might bring in that one bit of information that was lacking five years ago.'

'And my son would be found?'

'Obviously that would be perfect, but I won't lie to you, it's a long shot. But at this point it's the only shot you have of closure.'

Mrs MacGregor still fingered that sugar sachet.

'It has to be your decision, Mrs MacGregor. If you want to talk to me, then we'll proceed. If not, then we finish our coffee, talk about the weather and go our separate ways.'

She looked up. 'And you won't do a story?'

'I can't promise that.'

'Yes, you can, if you wanted to.'

She had her there. 'Okay, I won't promise that. This is my job, Mrs MacGregor, this is what I do. I believe there is a story here. I also believe there is a strong public interest case to be made.'

'Public interest? What does the rest of the world care about Fergus? Or my family?'

'A young man vanished without trace five years ago, Mrs MacGregor. Your son. Fergus. Why did he do that? What happened? Where did he go?' Rebecca stared at her for a moment. 'And is he still alive?'

A flash then, pain perhaps, in the eyes.

Rebecca kept her voice as gentle as she could. There was nobody else around but she spoke very quietly. 'Don't you think it important that we find out what happened to him?'

'And you think your story can do that?'

'As I said, there are no guarantees, but I also said this was, at this stage, the only chance there is of it happening.'

Frances considered this, then finally took a sip of her coffee, which had to be turning cold by now but she didn't seem to notice. 'Who else have you spoken to about this?'

'Some locals, the police officer who was in charge of the search.' Rebecca waited a minute, debating whether to admit this but deciding honesty was always best. 'I also spoke to your son Rory yesterday.'

Another flash of the eyes, but Rebecca couldn't tell if it was pain or anger. 'You must be careful of whatever he said.'

Rebecca was careful with whatever anybody said. 'Why? Will he lie?'

'No, but' – she searched for the correct way of saying it – 'he has issues. Rory is a troubled boy and he has cut himself off from his family.'

'He seemed fine when I spoke to him.' She didn't mention the suggestion of drug-taking. 'He and his partner have a very nice place.'

Frances's mouth twisted slightly. 'He's still with her, then?'

The coolness in the woman's voice was enough to freeze Rebecca's coffee. There was an ice field between her and her younger son that no amount of global warming would shrink. 'Her name's Lily, if that's the same person you mean.'

Frances MacGregor nodded. It was a curt nod, as if it was cutting off that line of conversation. 'I wouldn't believe what Rory tells you. His memories can be false.'

Rebecca couldn't think of anything he had said that might be false, apart from the frostiness of his home life, but she had seen evidence of that in this conversation. 'He said he could think of no reason why Fergus would want to leave.'

'What makes you think he wanted to leave?'

'He either chose to vanish or something happened. We have to look at both possibilities, Mrs MacGregor.'

After a moment of deliberation, there was another tilt of the head, another acceptance.

'Why don't you tell me about Fergus, Mrs MacGregor?'

'What do you want to know?'

'Anything you like.'

She looked over Rebecca's head, as if looking for her son on the wall behind them. 'He was a good boy. Smart. Funny. Kind. Caring. Handsome, too.'

'And he was a good student?'

'Oh, yes, top of his class in just about everything all his life. It seemed so effortless to him, learning. It was like he was a sponge, simply soaking it all in – facts, dates, names. He could read it once and it was stored away up here.' She tapped her temple with two fingers. 'It was amazing.'

'But he couldn't get work?'

'Not around here. He would have to move to a city and he didn't want to do that. Rannoch was his home and even though both his father and I urged him to broaden his horizons, even though we didn't want him to move to Glasgow or Edinburgh, he had to make his own way, we felt. But he loved this valley and its history, so he took a low-paid job in a hotel in Pitlochry, work well below his capabilities, while he researched and wrote the definitive history of Rannoch. He could have worked with his father on the farm, but he didn't want to do that. Fergus was a sensitive boy and he never could accept that the sheep were assets. Many a time he would be in tears in his room when lambs were sent for slaughter.'

'How had he been in the period running up to the day he vanished?'

When she had been talking about Fergus, Mrs MacGregor had seemed to thaw a little and warmth had crept into her voice, but now the frost settled again in her voice. 'What do you mean?'

'Had he been worried about anything? Had he told you of anything troubling him?'

'No.'

The response was sharp and the woman's eyes darted away, as if looking for an escape route. Rebecca decided to take another direction.

'He had a girlfriend, though, didn't he?'

The eyes came back to her and whatever ease in mood there had been, albeit briefly, was once again gone. 'Where did you hear that?'

Rebecca didn't answer. 'Shona, right? Shona Burnes?'

Frances MacGregor stiffened. 'Yes.'

'Did you approve of this?'

'What do you mean, approve?'

'There's a rift between the two families, right? And yet you and your husband had once been friends with Alexander Burnes.'

The eyes and expression were so frozen that a Norwegian explorer could plant a flag. 'That is none of your concern, Ms Connolly.' They were back to Ms Connolly again. 'It has no bearing on Fergus's disappearance.'

A lie, or at the very least a deflection, Rebecca thought, but she chose to move away from the subject entirely. 'Fergus loved the Black Wood, am I right?'

Frances MacGregor's tone was clipped. 'He was very proud that it was part of our home, yes.'

'He spent a lot of time there.'

'Yes.'

Rebecca could tell she wasn't making any progress at chipping away at this ice face but she kept on trying. 'And he was friendly with the man Cormac who lives near there?'

'Fergus was friendly with a lot of people.'

Including Shona, Rebecca wanted to say, but didn't want to go there again. She had the feeling her knowing about that had damaged whatever trust there had been between her and Frances. 'Have you spoken with Cormac, Mrs MacGregor? I mean, since Fergus vanished. Have you discussed it with him?'

'Cormac is not one for conversation, Ms Connolly.'

'So, you haven't even asked him if he saw Fergus that day?'

'Of course he was asked. I believe the police saw him and my husband spoke to him in the village one day – he doesn't welcome visitors to his cottage.'

'And he hadn't seen him?'

'No.'

'Do you think it was true?'

'We had no reason to doubt it.'

'Did the search party check his cottage out?'

The woman exhaled heavily and her eyes narrowed slightly. 'What are you trying to suggest, Ms Connolly? That Cormac did my son harm in some way?'

'I don't—'

'Because if you are, then put it from your mind. Cormac is a gentle soul and would not harm a fly, quite literally. He cares for God's creatures in a way that I have seen no others do, even vets. He keeps himself to himself and it was a testament to Fergus's loving and caring nature that Cormac felt comfortable enough to allow some kind of friendship. That was Fergus's way, Ms Connolly. He was trustworthy.' She gave Rebecca a pointed look. 'I wish more people were the same.'

Rebecca couldn't tell if she meant her or someone else.

24

It hadn't gone as well as she had hoped with Frances MacGregor. In fact, it hadn't gone well at all. She shouldn't have mentioned Rory. She had misjudged the depth of bitterness between son and parent but wished she knew more about it. She stood in the Square, looking across the bridge to the road leading to the Reverend Lester's church. She considered paying him another visit, but she had the feeling that it would prove equally unfruitful. Her gut feeling was that the secret behind what had happened to Fergus had something to do with the family dynamic. That there was a dysfunction was evident, but the same could be said for many families.

She should get back to Stephen, even though he had told her he would spend part of the morning talking to Elaine back in Inverness and then would go out for a walk. He was happy in his own company, but guilt gnawed at her. She had been ready to walk away from this story, whatever it was. She had made the decision. At least she thought she had been ready and had made the decision – yet here she was, following up on it.

She blamed Stephen. He had encouraged her. Yes, he was a handy scapegoat.

She climbed into the car and backed out, turning the wheel in the direction of the southern road. The Reverend Lester would tell her nothing, of that she was certain, but there was one other person she could talk to who might be more amenable. Or perhaps not. However, she would need a steer in how to find that person.

Frances MacGregor drove home, her mind on the conversation she'd just had with Rebecca Connolly. The reporter would be convinced that she had cut the interview short, but the truth was it had lasted much longer than she had intended. She was certain she had gleaned everything she could of what the girl knew, which was very little. Rory, of course, had been talking, which was to be expected, though still disappointing. He had shown no family loyalty at all, but still he should have known better. They were treading on very thin ice. One wrong step and the crust would break and dirty water would rush through. She couldn't have that. She wouldn't have that. What had happened all those years ago must never come out.

The reporter knew about Shona, and that was a worry. Alex had used every bit of influence to keep her name out of the press and divert any focus from her. There had been a couple of eager hacks who had tracked her down, but like an irritating fly they had been easily batted away. The police had found out, too, and they were not so easily fobbed off, but their inquiries were supposed to be confidential; although Frances suspected someone had told at least one of the reporters about the girl. Frances didn't think this Connolly girl would be so easily dissuaded, but, even so, she would have to do something she hadn't done for many years.

She would have to speak to Alex.

Harry answered the door, his mobile in his hands, looking as if he had been caught with his fingers in the biscuit tin. Rebecca wondered instantly if he had been messaging Ashley. He thrust the phone into his pocket and allowed a smile to cross his lips.

'Ms Connolly,' he said, 'I didn't expect to see you so soon. People will begin to talk.'

She returned his smile. 'Wouldn't be the first time, Harry,' she said. 'And it's Rebecca, remember?'

He stepped back and waved her across the threshold. She walked straight into his tidy living room but didn't sit down.

'It's just a quick visit, Harry,' she said before he could offer her tea.

'I was going to call you this morning anyway,' he said with a nod. 'I've been thinking about this TV programme of yours and I don't want to take part. Sorry.'

Rebecca was not surprised. 'I understand, Harry, but I would ask you to reconsider. I don't think you realise how pernicious these people can be.'

His hand rested on the pocket in which he had thrust his phone, as if he was protecting it from Rebecca's accusation. 'Are you so certain that Ashley is a fake?'

She almost said yes but then thought again. She couldn't say with any certainty that whoever was messaging him was a scammer. He said she hadn't asked for money and any he had given her had been his idea. Of course he might be lying about that, but she had to take it on face value. And without sight of the messages she had no clear idea how she might have manipulated him beforehand.

'No, I can't say that, Harry. But the balance of probabilities is that she is. Or maybe even he. You've never seen her, so you don't know that she really is what she says she is.'

'I've seen photographs on her page and heard her voice.'

'Yes, I've seen them, too, and they could be of anyone. And the person you spoke to could be an accomplice.'

He breathed in deeply through his nose. 'I'm a big boy, Rebecca. I'm old but not senile, despite what my daughter may think.' Rebecca was about to deny that but he raised a hand and waved her silent. 'I know what she thinks, Rebecca. She's made it quite clear that she believes I'm wandered, as she puts it. And yes, I do forget things, but that's natural at my age. I'll bet even you forget things and you're nowhere near my age.'

She couldn't argue with that. His daughter had been unclear about how wandered she thought her father was, and Rebecca had to admit she had seen only a little evidence of it during their conversations.

'I do think you're lonely and I think you're still grieving,' she said truthfully, 'and that combination means you could be an easy target for certain people.'

He glanced away, just briefly, the head movement dodging her words. 'I can make my own mind up about people, you know, and I don't need my daughter – or you, for that matter – to watch over me.'

His tone had become harsh and for a moment she saw the tough man his daughter had told her about edging through the soft exterior. This was the most puzzling thing about this story – he was far from stupid. He had held down a senior position in the civil service for many years. And yet here he was, defending someone he had never met, who was very likely a con artist out to separate him from his cash.

'Of course not, Harry, but Anne really is genuinely concerned for your wellbeing.'

A twinkle returned to his eye. 'Rebecca, you're a nice lass, very polite, but don't kid me. I know what Anne thinks, believe me. She's said it to me often enough. Sometimes I think she's only worried in case I give away her inheritance. And you, charming though you are, just want me on your show.'

She was about to defend herself but then realised it wouldn't get her anywhere. She gave him a little laugh. 'You're right, Harry. And all I can do is respect your decision about the programme. But I must stress that I believe you should appear and tell others about your experience with Ashley.'

'Even though I don't believe she is a – what do you call it? – catfisher?'

'She may well be. Sooner or later you're going to realise that and I just hope not before it's too late. I get it that you're a nice guy, a decent guy . . .'

Something crossed his face just as he averted his gaze once more. 'I'm not that nice,' he said, quietly.

She let that go. 'These people can play a long game, and they eat up nice guys, bad guys and those in between. The TV company has other people like you of all genders and races, from all parts of the country, who have been taken in. Each one of them thought the person they were speaking to was real and that they really cared for them.'

'There's no romance between Ashley and me.'

'I know that. She has appealed to your decency, your caring side. And then she has exploited it. You say she's not asked for any money, that you had to force her to take it. It's all a manoeuvre, and she'll go on doing that until bit by bit she has either bled you dry or you realise what her game is. That's what they do, Harry, believe me, and you need to see that before it's too late.'

He gave her a slight shake of the head that was almost sad. 'You're wrong, Rebecca. Don't ask me how I know, I just do.'

She stared at him for a moment, then decided she couldn't budge him. 'Okay, as I said, it's your decision and I'm not here to force you in any way. But hang onto my card, will you? If you change your mind, give me a call. I'm going to be in Rannoch for the rest of the week. We go back to Inverness on Sunday night. There's still time to include you – they've not started shooting the series yet – and the producers would love to have you on the show. You can help others, Harry, who may fall foul of these people.'

'She's not like that, you have to trust me on this.'

'I hope not, I really do.' She turned to leave the room and he followed. 'There's another thing you can help with, though.'

'What's that?'

She paused at the front door. 'Do you know the Burnes family?'

'Everyone in the valley knows the Burnes family. They own enough of it and a lot more besides.'

'Shona Burnes?'

'I know her to see, certainly. They live in this big old Victorian pile out beyond Bridge of Gaur at the end of the loch. It's on the road that takes you to the moor. Burnes House, it's called, believe it or not. You might not see the house itself from the road, as there are trees all around, but you can't miss the gates. Great big wrought-iron monstrosities. Why?'

'I'm looking into that other thing I told you about – Fergus MacGregor.'

'I see,' he said. 'Well, if you want my advice, I would be careful. Alex Burnes is a very rich man and he won't like the idea of a reporter snooping around his business.'

'It's his daughter I want to speak to, really.'

Harry's smile was thin. 'As far as he's concerned, his family is part of his business.'

After Rebecca left, Harry settled back in his armchair and thumbed open the social media app. He typed that the reporter was gone and waited. He had been chatting with Ashley when she had chapped at his door and had sent a quick message to that effect. Ashley had pleaded with him not to speak to her again, but he felt he had to answer the door. Anyway, he had needed to tell her that he wasn't interested in taking part in the programme. He liked the lass but she was wrong about this.

He didn't wait long. The reply came back almost immediately, as if Ashley had been waiting.

She ask about me?

He smiled. She was worried, but she needn't be.

Of course but I told her I wasn't interested in talking about you any more

He waited for her reply. He had thought it would come quickly but it didn't. Then, finally:

That good dear

Then there was a pause and he was about to respond when he saw the moving dots that told him she was typing something else, so he waited.

We need to chat dear

I thought we were ☺

He hoped the emoji might lighten the mood.

LOL
But we need talk

OK

Not now dear. I need sleep. Early here. I give you chat later. I go to friends house, call from there. It important, dear

OK, I'll be here

Night dear. I sleep now

Night

She had once told him that she didn't like letting friends know about her personal business, as she didn't know who to trust, fearing her cousin used them to spy on her. He stared at the phone for a long time, wondering what was so important that she needed to go to a friend's house.

25

Harry was correct – Rebecca did find the house easily. Or rather, she found the gates, which were tall, iron, black and curlicued, at least she thought that's how the elaborate twists and swirls could be described. They were also closed, and a three-wire fence ran along the roadway on either side, preventing a car from gaining access to the estate beyond. They would do little to deter a determined pedestrian, however, because the fence could be crossed by a simple lift of the leg or, if the person was vertically challenged and didn't wish to risk the top wire becoming entangled in any delicate areas, easily be climbed through without recourse to limbo-dancing. Rebecca considered both options but decided that such trespass was not the sensible choice. She wanted to speak to Shona Burnes and being caught wandering the grounds without an invitation was not the way to gain her trust.

There was an intercom system attached to the gate, so she thumbed the button that said, helpfully, PRESS. While she waited for a response she looked towards the vast Rannoch Moor that stretched brown and desolate all the way to Glencoe. She saw distant mountains, their peaks still covered with snow. There was not a sound, not even a whisper of wind, to disturb the air. She closed her eyes, filled her lungs, enjoyed the silence. The morning sun carried a little heat, but as she let it rest on her face for a moment, a worm of guilt wriggled in her mind. She wasn't sure how Stephen would react to her going off like this. He would have wanted to come with her, but in situations like this she preferred to work alone – even Chaz accompanying her on stories could put her off her stroke, and she knew that sometimes it could be difficult to get people to speak when someone else was present. It occurred to her that his presence hadn't hindered anything with Rory MacGregor . . . Ah well, she was here now.

The voice from the intercom speaker interrupted her thoughts. 'Can I help you, miss?'

It was a man's voice, Scottish but cultured, and she wondered how he knew her gender, then spotted the video camera on top of one of the gateposts. She leaned into the speaker, saw a red light glowing. 'Hi, sorry to trouble you but I wondered if I could speak to Shona Burnes?'

'And you are?'

'My name is Rebecca Connolly.'

'And is Mrs Everton expecting you?'

Mrs Everton. So Shona was married. 'No, she's not, I'm afraid.'

There was silence for a moment. A long moment. So long, Rebecca began to wonder if the guy had lost interest and simply left her standing in front of these big King Kong gates as if she had nowhere else to go. But the red light continued to glow. 'Hello?' she said.

'What is the purpose of your visit?'

Something told her she couldn't tell the truth but neither could she lie. 'It's of a personal nature,' she said, which in a way was true.

Another pause in the conversation, but this time Rebecca was damned if she was going to break it. She wondered what was happening in the house, which she could just make out through some trees. Harry had said it was a Victorian pile and she had expected it to be big and dark. It certainly looked big from here. There may have been turrets, which always suggested big. But it was light in colour, almost white. She had seen Blair Castle from the A9 many times, most recently as they had driven to Rannoch from Inverness, and the colour of Burnes House was similar to that.

The disembodied voice again. 'May I suggest you telephone and make an appointment?'

'Can't I speak to Mrs Everton now?'

Another pause. Was this person in contact with Shona, passing on what Rebecca was saying and taking instructions? 'I'm sorry, but Mrs Everton is busy.'

Rebecca took a gamble. 'Would you tell her it's about Fergus. Fergus MacGregor.'

Silence again and this time Rebecca was certain the man was in touch with Shona at the other end. Or someone, at least.

'Please wait there,' said the voice, and then there was a click and the light died. This time the connection had been cut. Rebecca glanced at the gate, hoping that somehow it would miraculously open, as if someone had said *Open Sesame*. But they remained resolutely locked. She hoped she was not being fobbed off with an upper-class version of being sent for a long stand, but there was nothing to do but wait . . .

However, it wasn't long before she saw a young blonde woman about her age walking down the neat gravel driveway from the house. When she drew closer, Rebecca realised she had to be the most beautiful woman she had ever seen in her life, outside of film, TV or magazines. Tall, slim, dressed elegantly but casually in what Rebecca knew would be designer labels. If this was Shona and not some staff member being sent to fob her off, then she could understand why Fergus had fallen for her. Hell, if she was that way inclined and didn't have Stephen, she might be tempted herself.

'Mrs Everton?' Rebecca asked when the vision came to a halt on the other side of the gate.

'Yes, and you are who again?' Even her voice was beautiful. Low, slightly husky, the Scottish accent like the glow after a sip of fine malt. Rebecca knew she was no bag of spanners herself and her voice was decent enough – there had been a brief dalliance with radio news before she took the job at the *Highland Chronicle* – but she cursed the fact that some people, whether through an accident of genes or the utilisation of wealth, had both the beauty and taste to somehow shine brighter than others.

'Rebecca Connolly,' she said, taking a card from her coat pocket and handing it through the curved bars of the gates. Shona took it, read it. Rebecca saw that the edges were a bit worn and thumbed, and she felt instantly shamed. Way to make a good impression there, Becks, she told herself, handing over a card that looks as if you've used it to pick your teeth.

'You're a journalist?'

'That's right.' She resisted the impulse to say *that's why it says Highland News Agency on the card*. There are times to be smart-arsed, but when you want someone to talk it is never a good idea. She didn't always follow that dictum, though.

'And you want to talk about Fergus?'

'Yes.'

Shona handed the card back through the gate, perhaps not wishing to be tainted by its decrepitude any longer. Rebecca took it back and consigned it to her pocket, crumpling it in her fist as she did so. That one was going in the bin.

'Why?' Shona asked.

'It's five years since he vanished.'

'Yes.'

'I think it's time the case was looked at again.'

'Why?'

Rebecca was beginning to grow a bit annoyed at the resistance she kept meeting over this. Didn't these people want Fergus to be found? She kept her voice steady, however. 'Why not, Mrs

Everton?' Everton, she thought, had she married a football team?

Shona regarded her with cool blue eyes, taking in her walking shoes, her blue jeans, which were designer but not one Rebecca had heard of, and had been picked up at TK Maxx, and her dark blue wool coat from M&S, as though she were taking an account of her worth. 'I'm not sure I can help you, Ms . . .' Her voice trailed away, as if she had forgotten Rebecca's name.

'Connolly, Rebecca Connolly,' she said. 'I just want to know more about him, Mrs Everton. I understand you and he were close.'

Those eyes took on a faraway look, just for a second, then came back to reality. 'Yes, we were. Very close.'

'Then that's how you can help. If I'm to do anything to help, then I need to know more about him.'

'You might try his family.'

'I did.' She left it at that, feeling that Shona would understand, and was rewarded by a very slight nod. 'I think it's important that this be looked at again, Mrs Everton, don't you?'

Shona hesitated and then looked over her shoulder at the house, as if checking if they were being watched. She glanced up at the video camera tilted towards the driveway. Whoever monitored it would see her and her car but not Shona. She looked at the intercom but the red light remained dark. 'We can't be overheard, Mrs Everton.'

'We can't talk here, though.'

'Where, then?'

For a moment, the carefully cultivated cool that had wrapped around Shona Everton like an expensive scent seemed to evaporate, as she struggled to think of somewhere that perhaps they wouldn't be seen.

'How about the Black Wood?' Rebecca suggested.

Frances MacGregor stood in the doorway of the living room. Dan was at the dining table in the alcove, going through some paperwork. He was slightly short-sighted, so his glasses were perched on the end of his nose as he looked at the papers and then peered over them at the laptop lying open at arm's length.

'I met that reporter,' she said.

At first he didn't react. He looked at something on the sheet of paper in his hand, then reached out to tap a series of keys. He laid the paper down, took off his glasses, sat back in the chair and stared at her. 'I thought you would.'

This surprised her. 'How did you know that?'

'Because I know you,' he said. 'You would want to know what she knew. So did you find out?'

She didn't realise she was so transparent to her husband. Once, perhaps, when they were closer, but that had ended when the drifting began.

'She saw your son,' she said.

Dan picked up his glasses again, perched them back on his nose and studied another sheet of paper. 'And how is he?' He had kept his voice distant, as if disinterested in the reply, but she knew he was interested. Rory was his son. Their son. What was part of them was also part of him and no amount of distance would change that. Rory, though, had departed from the values that they had tried so hard to instil in the boys. Everything she held sacred. He had rejected God. He had embraced sin. It was that simple and that complex.

'She said he was doing well. That he lived in a nice flat.'

'With her.'

'Yes, with her.'

'Still unmarried?'

'Yes. As far as I know.'

'Good luck to him then.'

She moved into the living room, dropping her bag on an armchair, but she still hadn't taken off her coat. 'I think this reporter will keep looking into Fergus's disappearance.'

'As I said, it's about time somebody did.'

'She could speak to others.'

'I would imagine she would, but that probably won't get her anywhere. Others have tried and given up when they found nothing new.'

'She's different.'

This made him look up and take off his glasses again. 'In what way different?'

Frances chose her words carefully. 'I don't think she'll give up. She seems determined to me. And I looked her up on the internet. She's no amateur, Dan. She's been involved in some big stories in Inverness. Remember that murder, the one with the man found on Culloden? And then the body in the kirkyard? She wrote about that. She didn't write the book, that was someone else, but she was deeply involved in it. And the young man who was wrongly imprisoned for murdering that lawyer over in Appin. She helped clear his name.'

He took all this in, turned it over in his mind, studied it. She saw all this etched on his face and working in his eyes. She knew he was judging, assessing. He had a way of looking at things in a cold, detached manner that she didn't possess. But that was Dan now. Cold. Detached. He hadn't always been like that. There had been fire once, perhaps too much sometimes, especially when it came to Alex Burnes, and certainly when he was younger. Rory was so much like him, it was true. All that was gone. It had vanished along with Fergus. It died that day, but it had already been mortally wounded.

'So you're saying she may find something?'

'She might,' Frances warned.

He looked back at his paperwork. 'Good.'

She recognised from his tone that the conversation was over. She lifted her bag again and walked into the hallway. She took off her coat and hung it on the rack beside the door, slipped off her shoes and pushed them with her toes underneath, then slid her feet into her slippers. She walked into the kitchen, filled and clicked on the kettle without thinking, took out two mugs – always two, she always made him a cup when she made herself one; old habits die hard even if feelings don't – then leaned on top of the grey work surface, palms flat, and stared at the wall.

She could not understand how he could be so calm. This woman was poking her nose in their family business. Frances was a firm believer that such matters were not for public consumption.

She plucked her phone from her handbag and found a number she had not used in years. It was time.

'It's Frances MacGregor,' she said when the call was picked up. 'We need to talk.'

Shona had hoped to leave the house without being seen, but Alex emerged from his study just as she crossed the wide hallway. He looked at her coat and boots. 'Going out?'

She made a show of looking down at her clothes. 'I can't get one over on you, can I?'

His expression tightened, as it always did when she was a smart-arse with him, but he let her get away with it. He generally did. 'Were you down at the gate just now?'

She regarded him with her usual mixture of stubbornness and disdain. 'Why do you ask, Alex?'

He exhaled loudly. 'Because I want to know.'

She assessed whether he would find out by other means. Of course he would. The staff member who dealt with the security system would tell him. 'Yes, I was.'

'Why?'

She hesitated again, but there was no point in lying. 'There was someone at the gate to see me.'

'Who?'

'Nobody of any importance,' she said airily, as she moved across the hallway to the front door, her car keys already in her hand.

'And now you're going out?'

'Top marks, Alex.'

'Out where?'

'For a drive, if it matters.'

'To where?'

She stared at him, tempted to snap that it was none of his business, but she gave him a smile instead. It might throw him off guard. 'I don't know,' she said. 'Somewhere. Anywhere. It's a lovely day and I need to get the Rannoch sun on my face.'

'Alone?'

'I've been alone in this house for years. At least this way I can pick up some vitamin D.'

He ignored that. 'Why not take Ray with you?'

She opened the front door. 'I don't need a chaperone, Alex. I'm a big grown-up girl.'

His next question startled her. 'Shona, tell me the truth, are you going to speak to a reporter?'

She turned to face him again. 'Yes. How did you know?'

He ignored that. 'And if I forbid it?'

She blinked as a laugh puckered her lips. 'You're welcome to try.'

He stepped nearer. 'You can't trust people like that. She'll tell you she's your friend. She'll tell you that she only wants the truth. She'll be lying. She only wants gossip and scandal.'

Shona's voice was playful, but she knew it concealed her mother's tough edge. 'And we have plenty of that, don't we, Alex?'

He took a deep breath. 'What will you tell her?'

She stepped through the door. 'Anything I want.'

And then she was gone.

26

The silence was deeper here. Richer.

When Rebecca had taken a moment as she stood beside the gate at Burnes House, she had thought the peace was perfect, but now she was back in the Black Wood she realised perfection had degrees, and here it was at its peak. She could understand why Fergus loved the place. Again, she felt that sense of past and present existing in harmony, that this place was a pocket of history that had defied the onslaught of man and climate.

She had picked the location for a reason and not simply because there was nobody to overhear. A tourist or a walker might amble by – the valley was an all-year-round tourist destination – but she was confident they could talk in peace. Rebecca couldn't tell whether Shona was amenable to talking, but it was possible that bringing her to where Fergus may have last been seen might help loosen her tongue.

Rebecca had waited in her car for about half an hour and was beginning to wonder if Shona had simply agreed to get rid of her. Then, in her rear-view she saw a small, red sporty number rounding a bend and she knew immediately it was Shona Everton's car, one that managed to be understated while also screaming, *Look at me.*

The flat shoes Shona had worn earlier had been replaced by a pair of Ugg boots, although the black leggings remained. A thick coat of what Rebecca hoped was fake fur but really couldn't say for certain was draped around her, and her blonde hair was encased in a matching hat. If their walk was going across the steppes of Siberia, then she was all set.

'Thanks for agreeing to meet, Mrs Everton,' Rebecca said.

Shona said nothing, as she lingered at the side of the road, her head turned in the direction she had come. She waited a long time, watching and listening, before she stepped off the verge and they crossed the road to the pathway into the wood.

'Please, call me Shona. I won't be Mrs Everton for much longer, thank God.'

'You and your husband have split up?'

'Oh, yes.'

Rebecca wondered if she should pursue that subject but decided against it. They had other things to talk about.

'Did you choose this place purposely?'

Busted, Rebecca thought. 'Would you believe me if I said no?'

Shona laughed. 'No.' She looked around them as they walked. 'Fergus loved this place, but I suppose you already know that.'

'What can you tell me about him?'

'What do you need to know?'

Rebecca took a few paces before she answered. 'What was he like?'

It was Shona's turn to pause, as she considered how to respond. 'He was . . . funny. He was intelligent. He was loving.'

'I take it his disappearance was out of character.'

A sideways glance from Shona. 'What do you know of that day?'

'Not much. He was supposed to be going to Pitlochry, at least that's what he told his parents, but his car was found back where we parked. He was never seen again.'

'He wasn't going to Pitlochry,' said Shona, looking down at her feet as they stepped on the blanket of pine needles covering the path.

'I didn't think he was. So why was he here, do you know?'

Shona stopped and looked up again, craning her neck to study the tops of the trees, etched against the blue and white sky. 'He used to say these trees were history's witnesses,' Shona said. 'He said that they watched and they listened and they observed, but that they never judged, even when history was cruel to them. These trees have seen a lot, Rebecca.'

'What do you think they saw that day?'

Shona studied Rebecca again. 'I think he was murdered. I think someone came here with intent to do him harm, perhaps not to kill him, but I think that's what happened.'

'Who?'

Shona began walking again. 'I don't know.'

Something in her voice told Rebecca that she had suspicions. She wanted to ask who Shona suspected but took another approach. 'But there is no real evidence of that, right?'

'No, but I still think that's what happened.'

'Why?'

'Because we all act according to our natures and Fergus wouldn't simply vanish like that, no way.'

'How can you be sure?'

'Because I knew him, Rebecca. Because I loved him. And because I know why he was here that morning.'

'Why?'

'He was waiting for me. He was here to meet me. We were leaving this valley, Rebecca. We were going to be together, away from here, away from our families.'

'You were eloping?'

A slight smile, perhaps a trace of embarrassment. 'That's such an old-fashioned word and concept, isn't it? Eloping? It conjures up images of a wild flight in the dead of night pursued by raging parents and ending up over the anvil at Gretna Green. But yeah, I suppose that's what we were doing. We certainly had the raging parents.'

'They didn't approve of you and Fergus?'

'To put it mildly. There's an enmity there that goes back some time, I think.'

'But they haven't spoken for many years, not since she married Daniel MacGregor, am I right?'

'Not a word.'

'And yet they all used to be friends.'

Shona seemed impressed. 'To be honest, I'm not sure Alex and Dan ever really got on. I think there was always rivalry. It began in school, I was told. On the face of it they were friends, but underneath there was something bubbling away. Alex never talks about it, not to me, anyway.'

'So it's fair to say there would be opposition to you and Fergus getting together?'

Shona laughed again, the sound uneasily loud in this cathedral of silence where the trees acted as both spires and chapels. 'That's putting it mildly. But we loved each other. I never believed in love at first sight but that's what happened, for both of us. Can you believe that?'

Rebecca found it hard to accept. She had never experienced anything like it. She'd had boyfriends growing up but nothing serious. She'd been attracted to Simon and had made the first move, but had never loved him. And Stephen? That had crept up on her.

'I'm not sure,' she said, diplomatically. 'So you decided to run off together?'

'Yes. I have some money of my own, left to me by my mother. I'm not Alex Burnes wealthy but it would be enough to keep us. And Fergus had decided he couldn't stay here, as much as he loved the place.'

She looked around her again, as if she might see him one more time moving among the undergrowth, feeling a kinship with the trees that had seen history. Rebecca did the same, but for a different reason. She had felt something prickle at the back

168

of her neck, as if there was something out there, something unseen, seeing them.

'But it didn't happen, did it?' she said, ignoring the sensation and concentrating on the matter at hand. 'Fergus came here, but you didn't. What happened? Did you turn up and he was gone?'

Shona came to a halt and closed her eyes. 'No, I didn't get here at all.'

'Why not?'

Shona's eyes opened again and Rebecca saw fire in the cold blue. 'Alex got wind of it.'

'How?'

'I assume it was Ray who told him.'

'Ray's your brother, right?'

Shona nodded. 'Half-brother. He was there when I met Fergus at a dance in the village. I thought he was going to punch Fergus's lights out – he's more than capable of it.'

'Protective, is he?'

'At that time, to the point of being overbearing. He never let me out of his sight. I had to steal away to meet up with Fergus. Ray's the proverbial apple that didn't fall far from the paternal tree.'

'But did Ray know you were planning to run away?'

Shona shook her head. 'I don't know, I really don't. But Alex found out and stopped me.'

'How?'

They took a few steps before Shona replied. 'He locked me in my room. Can you believe that? He actually locked me in my room to stop me from leaving. By the time I was let out, Fergus was gone.'

'Would Fergus have told anybody of your plans?'

'We both said we would tell nobody, but who can say? Perhaps he told his family, perhaps he felt he had to, but I don't know.'

'Have you spoken to anyone about it? Frances? Her husband?'

'God, no, they won't even look in my direction. I'm a Burnes, remember.'

'What about Rory?'

'Yes, we did speak a few times afterwards. He was the only one who knew about us from the start, apart from Ray.'

'He was at the dance the night you met, wasn't he?'

'Yes, but I don't think he was terribly sure how deep it went, not then. But Fergus and Rory were close, even though they were so different. Have you met Rory?'

'Yes.'

'Then you know what I mean. He's so unlike Fergus it's hard to believe they're brothers.'

'He certainly seems wilder.'

The corners of Shona's mouth turned down a little. 'He was a lovely boy, really. Never as studious as Fergus, certainly, but still lovely. He was Dan's favourite; Fergus was always Frances's boy. He would come with us occasionally, when Fergus and I met – Rory was a sort of beard, I suppose, an excuse to go out to meet me once I'd shaken off Ray.'

'Ray kept tabs on you?'

'Oh yeah, he still watches me a little. I had to drive around to check he wasn't following me today.'

Rebecca recalled Shona taking a long look along the road before they crossed it to walk into the wood. It hadn't been a cautious check for oncoming traffic; it was to ensure she had not been followed. What kind of life had this young woman led in that house?

'Wasn't having a young boy around something of a buzzkill? I mean, you and Fergus would have wanted to be alone.'

A flicker of a smile crossed Shona's face. 'You mean for the kissy stuff?'

Rebecca laughed. 'Yes – and the rest.'

'We managed, is all I need to say. Lust will find a way, Rebecca.'

Oh yeah, Rebecca thought, and again felt that sinking feeling when she remembered Stephen was waiting for her in the cottage, completely unaware that she had gone off on her own. 'So what happened with Rory, then?'

'Well, when I said he was lovely, that was when he was with Fergus and me. He didn't go off the rails big time until after Fergus disappeared. He discovered girls in a serious way, got one pregnant, never married her, got into fights. The police became involved, he was sent to a Young Offender Institution for a time. He tried to contact me, but Ray blocked it and, to be honest, I really wasn't in a place to talk to Rory. He reminded me too much of Fergus, I suppose.'

'They looked alike?'

'No, not at all, but it was just that every time I saw him, I saw the three of us together.'

Rebecca understood completely. Grief was something that remained just under the surface and the slightest thing could stimulate it. In Shona's case it was Rory's face, but it could be a song that meant more than it should, a phrase used by someone but heard in another's voice, a place where memories hung like fine mist. For a long time Rebecca had been reminded of her father in these and other ways. That Shona was here in the Black Wood showed that she had also come to terms with these ghosts of the mind.

Movement beyond where Shona was standing caught Rebecca's attention and she looked into the wood but saw nothing. A bird taking wing, perhaps.

'How is Rory?' Shona asked, not noticing Rebecca's eyes flitting behind her.

'He's in Perth, living with a woman.'

'Is he behaving?'

Rebecca thought about telling her that he was allegedly involved in drugs but decided against it. 'He seems okay. Their flat is nice.'

'Good,' Shona said, and Rebecca could tell she was sincere. 'He deserves to be happy. God knows, he's been through a lot.'

They walked a few paces without speaking, Rebecca casting glances at the trees around them to study the dappled shadows created by the early spring sun on the undergrowth. She recalled the man she had seen the first time she had been in this wood.

'What about Cormac?'

'Cormac the hermit?' Shona smiled. 'What about him?'

'I understand he and Fergus were friends. Did you ever meet him?'

'No, he steered clear of me. I knew he and Fergus had struck up an acquaintance – can't say friendship is what it was. Cormac's a funny old guy and I'm not sure he has any friends. He wanders the woods and the hills alone. In fact, I think I saw him last night, hanging about the garden of the house. Gave me a helluva fright, but once I worked out it was him, it was okay.'

'You weren't sure, as soon as you saw him?'

'No, it's been a couple of years since I've been back here. But he always wears this long coat, you know, like those waterproof bushman's coats? The really good ones? And it has an enormous hood like a cowl, leaves the face in shadow. He was staring in the window and I'm sure he had a scarf wrapped around his neck and jaw – it was bloody cold last night. But I don't know anybody else who dresses like that around here. I didn't tell Ray or Alex about it because God knows what they would do if they thought he was hanging around.'

'What did Fergus tell you about him?'

'Just that he was okay, not the scary bogeyman that we kids were told about. But it was typical of Fergus to get to know him because that's the way he was. Open, friendly . . .'

'So you don't think Cormac would do Fergus any harm?'

Shona frowned. 'I get that you might think that, but really I don't see it. Cormac's creepy, but he's no killer.'

'Do you know his second name?'

'It's Devlin, I think.' Shona gave her a midways look. 'You're not thinking about going to see him, are you? He doesn't welcome visitors.'

'Don't worry. I've been well warned away from him,' Rebeca said, satisfied that she had delivered a negative without actually lying. A non-denial denial, as one of her old lecturers used to say, quoting some old film or other.

Shona accepted it. 'Good, I wouldn't recommend it. He's harmless, but he can be touchy, if you know what I mean. And the poor soul seems to have hurt himself.'

'How do you know?'

'He was dragging his right leg.'

27

Rebecca listened to her phone ringing as she watched Shona turn her sporty little number into the road, perform a perfect – and very swift – three-point turn, then, with a final wave, drive back towards the western end of the loch.

'I really thought I was going to get some peace this week,' said Val Roach, without saying hello.

'And hello to you too,' Rebecca said, brightly.

'Yeah, yeah.' Roach's tone was dismissive. 'What do you need, Becks? I've got bad guys to catch.'

'Paperwork to do, more like.'

Roach tutted. 'Such disrespect shown to the work of Scotland's constabulary. Especially from someone who no doubt wants a favour. Let's have it and let me get back to my paperwork.'

Rebecca smiled. 'Cormac Devlin.'

Roach waited for more, but Rebecca let the name dangle. 'Am I supposed to know who that is?'

'You don't remember? The Fergus MacGregor disappearance. He was the guy, a kind of hermit, lives near the Black Wood. They had become friends.'

'You still following up on that?'

'Yes.'

'On your holiday.'

'Yes.'

'Your birthday break.'

'Yes.'

A sigh. 'Rebecca Connolly, you need to get yourself a life. What does Mr Jordan say about this?'

Roach always called Stephen Mr Jordan. As a solicitor he had often taken police officers to task in court over their evidence and she liked to keep him very much at arm's length. 'He's okay with it,' Rebecca replied.

'Probably glad to get you out of his hair,' Roach said.

'Cormac Devlin,' Rebecca repeated.

'What about him?'

'What do you remember?'

'Solitary soul, lived in a cottage up the hill from the loch?'

'Yes.'

'Nature lover, if memory serves.'

'Did you speak to him?'

'I didn't. I had people for that sort of thing. I also have people here for press enquiries, FYI.'

'I'm still off the books with this. Just feeling my way, so we're off the record.'

'So what are you looking for, Becks? Why the interest in this bloke?'

'I'll bet you were interested in him at the time, too. Strange, creepy guy, lives alone in the wilds, a stone's throw away from where Fergus vanished?'

'My memory is that the cottage was a bit more than a stone's throw from that part of the wood.'

Rebecca heard her phone bleep, alerting her to another call. She flicked the screen and saw that it was Stephen. With no small degree of guilt, she let it go to voicemail.

'We're in the Highlands,' she said, in response to Roach's comment. 'Here there be giants. What can you tell me about him?'

'Becks, what kind of recall do you think I have?'

'Because, Val, I'll bet that after I spoke to you a couple of days ago you dug out whatever notes you've kept on this and read over them.'

'You're certain of that, eh?'

'Oh, hell yeah. You're thorough, Val. You'll have kept your own records because you will always do a good job, even when there may be others around you who don't.'

She heard a small chuckle and knew she had guessed correctly. 'Flattery will get you everywhere,' said Roach. 'Okay, he's from Ireland originally, right?'

'So I understand.'

'Been in Rannoch for a long time.'

'Thirty years or more.'

'Originally County Tyrone, I think.'

'Okay.'

'And that's all I can tell you,' said Roach.

'That's it?'

'Yup.'

'You didn't check his background?'

'I didn't say that. I said that's all I can tell you.'

Rebecca caught something in the timbre of her voice. 'But there's more to tell, right?'

'I didn't say that either.'

Rebecca chewed her bottom lip as she considered. Roach was telling her something without actually telling her something. It was a game they had played before. 'So, if I searched for his name thirty-odd years ago in County Tyrone I might find something?'

'Well, I certainly couldn't stop you from doing that.'

'But I wouldn't be wasting my time, right?'

'Is time ever wasted? Isn't the pursuit of knowledge always a worthwhile endeavour? Isn't there always something we can learn about the present by looking into the past?'

'Jeezo, I wish you would just tell me.'

Roach laughed again. 'Where's the fun in that?'

Stephen was at the kitchen window, wondering where Rebecca was, when a four-wheel drive turned from the hill into the small car park in front of the cottage. He thrust his phone in his pocket and opened the front door to see Alan's face grinning at him from the passenger seat. Chaz was already climbing out the other side.

'How was the drive down?' Stephen asked, as Alan began to alight from the Duster.

'It was jolly,' Alan said with a smile. 'I sang along to the CD – Meatloaf's greatest hits. Chaz loved it.'

Chaz looked round from the back of the car. 'I think that's an overstatement. I ain't never gonna say I loved it.'

'If Meatloaf were alive today, he'd be begging me to duet with him.'

Chaz hauled a large overnight bag from the rear compartment. 'If Meatloaf were alive today, he'd be talking to his lawyer.'

Chaz handed the bag to Alan, then opened the back passenger door and leaned in. He emerged holding a large cardboard box. 'We have the cake,' he said.

'Where is the guest of honour anyway?' Alan asked.

Stephen took the cake from Chaz. 'Thanks for this. Would you believe that Becks is out on a story?'

Alan waved his arms around him. 'What kind of story would she find out here? Is there a psycho deer on the loose?'

Stephen jerked his head at the cottage door. 'Come on inside. I'll make some coffee and tell you all about it.'

Alan turned and looked across the valley to the mountain. 'This is wonderful.'

Stephen followed his gaze. 'Yes, it really is.'

The three of them took in the vista in silence for a few moments before Chaz said, 'And yet Becks is off doing her thing.'

'You know Becks,' said Stephen, something almost sad in his voice.

Chaz and Alan exchanged a glance. 'Yeah, we know Becks.'

Stephen felt the need to defend her. 'She still doesn't know you're coming. If she did, I'm sure she would have been here.'

'Yeah, sure she would.' The humour in Chaz's eyes softened the sarcasm.

They followed Stephen into the cottage. 'So Elspeth still can't make it?'

'We tried,' said Alan, 'but she doesn't do birthdays, she said. I think it reminds her too much of her own mortality.'

Fergus was in his chair again, staring at the dying flames of the fire. Cormac picked up the metal poker and gave them a rake, then placed a few small pieces of kindling on the red ashes to try to resurrect the heat. He watched as the slim wood began to catch flame, then positioned some larger sticks on top. They were bone dry, well-seasoned, and they would catch easily enough. Fergus watched him do this without a word. Cormac tried to keep the annoyance from his face. He did everything else, the wood gathering and chopping, the cooking, the cleaning, the shopping. Fergus could straighten up the place a bit now and then, or at the very least keep the bloody fire going.

'I'll make some soup for lunch,' Cormac said, but received no response from the young man. He merely sat in his chair, wrapped in the blanket, still staring at the fire as the flames began to take hold. Cormac felt his temper begin to slip and he struggled to hold on to it, as he took a can of cream of mushroom from the overhead cupboard and jerked at the ring pull lid to open it. He took two mugs from another cupboard, banging them down on the work surface harder than he intended but still generating no response from Fergus. Not even a flinch. Cormac felt his mouth tighten and his teeth grind as he poured the contents of the can into the mugs, then placed them in the microwave. He should make his own soup, but until he got the time and the ingredients, tinned stuff would have to do. He knew people would be surprised to see his kitchen, for it was clean and modern. Not that anyone other than himself would see it, for he didn't invite people in, and certainly not in the past five years, not with Fergus here. Not even the vet, who came up occasionally to look at the animals, was allowed in the house, for this was his sanctuary.

He watched the mugs turn slowly in the microwave, still feeling resentment towards Fergus for not helping out more. He wasn't completely disabled. He could get around. He could do something for his keep. Cormac knew he should say something, but he didn't like confrontation, feeling it was much better to button up resentment and let it die of old age. That didn't mean he didn't lash out in other ways, though.

'I saw your girlfriend just now,' he said, watching – hoping – for a sign of hurt in Fergus. He wasn't disappointed. The boy looked up and the anguish in his eyes was plain to see, even with the distortion of his features.

'Where?'

'Down in the Black Wood. She was with another young lady. I've seen her before, too, but I don't know who she is.'

'What were they doing?'

'Walking. Talking.'

The microwave dinged and Cormac opened the door to lift the mugs out. He gave the soup a stir with a spoon, then placed them back inside and gave them another minute.

'What were they talking about?'

'I don't know,' Cormac said, watching the slow carousel of soup mugs. 'I wasn't close enough to see.'

Fergus nodded, obviously disappointed, but what did he expect? Cormac certainly couldn't sidle up close to them and eavesdrop on their conversation. Shona had caught sight of Fergus through the window the night before, and given he had been wearing Cormac's coat and scarf she probably thought it was him, so he had made sure he kept out of sight as the women talked. He was used to doing that, keeping out of the way of tourists, for he knew ways through the woods that they wouldn't

179

take. He thought the stranger, the girl with the auburn-hair, had either spotted him or sensed his presence, though, for she kept staring into the trees. She was someone who would bear watching, for he sensed that she was a danger.

28

'I thought you had given up on this?' Elspeth said.

'So did I,' Rebecca said, almost convincing herself.

'Mmm-hmm.' Elspeth was obviously not even halfway convinced. 'I hope you're at least going to take time off tomorrow for your birthday.'

'I thought you didn't believe in birthdays.'

'Only because I've had so many. The march of time becomes little more than a stumble towards incontinence and a desire to wear nylon jackets, so I don't need to be reminded, thank you very much. But you are young and should enjoy the day with your stud muffin.'

'My stud muffin?'

'That's Stephen, in case you didn't realise.'

'Yeah, I cracked that code, thanks. I will enjoy the day, Elspeth, but right now I'm following up on this. My own time, remember?'

'And I take it you need me to do something?'

Rebecca told her of her conversation with Val Roach about Cormac Devlin.

'And you think there's something in this man's background on the Emerald Isle worth finding out about?'

'Worth a shot, don't you think?' Rebecca said. 'I had a look online using my phone, but you know how much I hate that. I couldn't find anything. Thought maybe you could tap one of your mates to check out the cuts.'

Daily newspapers have a vast library of cuttings archived, not only from their titles but others from around the world.

'Again,' said Elspeth.

'Yes, again.'

'You do know he will start charging me for this?'

'I'm sure he does it out of affection for you.'

Elspeth made a noise that suggested she wasn't sure about that. 'Actually, I may need to contact someone down the Smoke for this. She owes me a favour or two.'

That was one of the advantages of working with Elspeth – her career in journalism had touched so many lives, and a number of those in the media owed her a favour or two. Also, her own knowledge was incredible. She had often surprised Rebecca by trotting out some nugget of information that was not only arcane but might be deemed useless by anyone else. Her mind was like an old biscuit tin, she said, with little bits of this and that gathering in corners just waiting for a finger to be dipped into it.

'May take a while,' Elspeth said, 'so in the meantime, you get back to your stud muffin. Remember what I told you, Becks. Don't screw this up. I very seldom say this, but you and Stephen go well together. Don't push him away.'

'I won't, don't worry. Stephen knows what I'm like.'

That noise again. 'That's what I'm afraid of . . .'

'You know what she's like, guys,' said Stephen.

'Bloody Jessica Fletcher,' said Alan, 'that's what. Everywhere she goes, she uncovers murder and mayhem.'

Chaz's face was all innocence when he asked, 'Who's Jessica Fletcher?'

Alan gave him a long-suffering look. '*Murder, She Wrote*,' he explained.

'What's *Murder, She Wrote*?'

'It's a TV . . .' Alan stopped, as he realised he was being wound up. 'Don't start with that malarkey, my lad.'

'What malarkey? Me? I have never malarkeyed in my life,' said Chaz, but the cheeky grin belied his words. 'Is it something you old people do?'

'There we go – even though I didn't bite, you still managed to get the knife in, didn't you? I'm only a few years older than you, remember. I'm far from Methuselah.'

'Who's Methuselah?' Chaz asked. 'Is it someone you met at the senior citizens' club?'

Alan waved him away and faced Stephen. 'I don't know why I put up with him, I really don't. Do you have trouble like this with Becks?'

Stephen laughed. 'No, my troubles with Becks are of a whole different nature, even though the age gap between us is much wider than you two.'

'See?' Alan said to Chaz. 'Just give it a chuck now, okay?'

'Give it a chuck?' Chaz repeated. 'That's something you folks said back in the day, right? Along with fire up the Quattro, what's on the other channel, and gimme that pencil while I tighten this cassette tape?'

'How do you know about that?' Stephen asked. 'That's even before my time.'

'Saw it on Twitty, probably,' Alan said.

'Indeed, I did not,' said Chaz, haughtily. 'I saw it on Facebook.'

Alan sneered. 'Twitty and Fartbook, the twin threats to any kind of meaningful discussion in the modern age.'

'They can be very educational. Very informative. And fun.'

'You don't need their confirmation bias, virtue signalling and general bollocks for that.'

'I know – I have you,' said Chaz, giving him a wide grin.

Alan sighed. 'I don't know why I put up with him, I really don't,' he said to Stephen. 'But anyway – Becks, what are we to do with her? She's supposed to be on holiday.'

That brought the conversation full circle. 'As I said, you know what she's like.'

'And how do you feel about it?'

Stephen took a moment before he answered. He folded his arms and leaned forward to rest his elbows on his knees before he spoke, choosing his words carefully. 'I can't let it bother me because I can be exactly the same. I know she hates the fact that I don't discuss my work, but I think she understands it. And there are times when I'm consumed by preparing for court, or doing something for a client, that I am distracted and, frankly, just not available.'

'Have you brought work here with you?'

'No, but I phone the office regularly.'

'But you're not driving around the countryside conducting interviews, are you?'

'No, but I was glad she went out today because I knew you guys were coming and bringing the cake. I want seeing you to be a surprise, so it works out well, doesn't it?'

Alan sat back on the settee he shared with Chaz and studied Stephen. 'That's not the only reason, is it?'

'What makes you say that?'

'I can sense there's more . . .'

Chaz sighed theatrically and looked to Stephen. 'Alan likes to think he's psychic, but really he's just empathetic. Like Deanna Troi in *Star Trek* . . .'

Alan's head snapped round. 'You know about Deanna Troi but not Jessica Fletcher?'

Chaz shrugged. 'I've seen *Star Trek*, I've never seen *Murder, She Said*.'

'Wrote. *Murder, She Wrote*.'

'Yeah, yeah.' Chaz flashed Stephen a secret smile. 'He can actually size people up very quickly and pick up tiny little tells that others don't see.'

'It's a gift,' Alan said, his modesty not quite surfacing.

'I could do with you when interviewing witnesses,' Stephen said. 'Especially police officers.'

'Don't look now, but your bias is showing. And I'm sure a lot of people tell you lies, not just police officers,' said Alan. 'But setting that aside, why else don't you want Becks's dedication to her job to get to you?'

Stephen remained hunched forward, his gaze seemingly fixed on the low coffee table between them. 'You guys don't know this but I was almost married once. She was a solicitor, too, a good one. But she was like Becks – a workaholic. I can be dedicated, I can work hard, but I do know when to draw a line and say: enough, I want some me time.'

Chaz said, 'Becks doesn't know how to do that, does she? Not really.'

'No, and neither did Kat.'

'Your ex's name was Kat?'

'Short for Katherine. Anyway, she didn't know when to stop, just kept working and working. She'd miss dates, functions, weekends away. We even cancelled a holiday to Tuscany at the last minute because she took on a client with an imminent court date.'

Alan said, 'And this annoyed you, right?'

'Right.'

'And you told her, right?'

'Right again.'

'And the relationship ended?'

'Not right away. She agreed with me at first and promised to cut back, but she never did. We spoke about it again. She promised again. Did the same thing again.'

'So who ended the relationship?'

'I did. I told her I couldn't live like that. You know, work to live, not live to work, all that stuff. She agreed but she said she couldn't see her changing, that she had to work doubly hard because she was a woman, but it wasn't just that. It was simply the way she was. Driven, I suppose. So that was it.'

'You cared for her?'

'Of course I did – we were only two months away from getting married. But I couldn't continue that way. I went through hell for months after that, wondering if I did the right thing, feeling the need to contact her, tell her I'd made a mistake. Because when we were together, when she wasn't working, we were a fit, you know? We really got on together . . .'

'Like you and Becks.'

'Yes, like me and Becks. I don't want to lose her that way, too, so I have to accept that sometimes her work life gets in the way of her private life. Thankfully, she's not as bad as Kat!' He gave them a smile, unfolded his arms and sat back, as if glad he had reached the end of his revelation. 'I think if I'd still been with Kat we'd never have come here this week.'

Chaz and Alan sat silently for a moment before Alan said, 'Well, thank you for sharing, but frankly I was hoping for something a bit more striking. Something with a touch of drama – unrequited love that ends in tragedy, that sort of thing.'

Stephen laughed. 'I'm sorry to have disappointed you.'

'That's okay, I'm used to disappointment.' Alan sent a pointed look towards Chaz.

Stephen began to clear up the coffee cups from the table. 'I suppose we all have broken romances in our past.'

'I don't,' Chaz said, standing up to help Stephen take the dishes to the kitchen.

'Don't worry, darling,' Alan said, 'there's still time . . .'

Rebecca stared through the car window at the loch. The sky was a pale blue with wisps of cloud floating by. The water didn't reflect it back, though. It was a dull grey, and its surface rippled with tiny waves that scraped at the mix of sand and pebbles below the parking lay-by. Through the trees that hung over the edge of the water she could just make out the tower on the island that Harry had spoken about. The Isle of Gulls. Stephen had looked it up later. It was a crannog, an artificial island; the now submerged sandbank that had once been used as a causeway swept towards it from the south bank, even though the island itself was slightly closer to the opposite side. The tower dated back to the nineteenth century, but there had been a structure on it prior to that which had been used as a prison by a local laird. The loch itself was large, but unlike Loch Ness and Loch Morar it didn't boast a monster. Might do wonders for the tourist trade, if one was spotted.

She looked down at the map she had pulled up on her phone, arguing with herself over her next move. She should head back to the cottage, back to Stephen, and wait for Elspeth to dig up what she could on Cormac. She should at least call Stephen back, but then he would ask her where she was and what she was doing now and she couldn't even answer that herself, let alone another person. Especially him.

She studied the map again, working out how long it would take to drive to the destination she had punched in. Not long, she didn't think. A matter of minutes, really, because it was only a mile or two down the road.

She laid the phone on the passenger seat and sat back, one hand on the steering wheel, restless fingers tapping as she studied the road ahead. What are you doing, Becks? You're supposed to be on holiday, not gadding about the countryside on what could be a wild goose chase with no story at the end of it. You've got a guy waiting for you that you're crazy about and . . .

Whoa, she thought, where did that come from? Crazy about him? Really?

But she was, she knew it. She'd known it for some time but had refused to admit it, even to herself. Now she had.

So what was she going to do about it?

It was her birthday the next day and she had promised Elspeth she would take time to celebrate it properly. With Stephen. She wouldn't think about Fergus MacGregor or his family at all for that twenty-four-hour period. She knew he had something planned and guessed he had a gift secreted some-where in the cottage. She hadn't marked her birthdays much in recent years, but she had vowed this one was going to be different. The TV research job was done – Harry had declined and that was that. Which reminded her, she would have to tell Leo.

But that was for tomorrow. For today, she had one more thing to do. She had been warned away, but to hell with it – she had been warned away from people before. And anyway, every-one said he was harmless, if a little strange.

She started the car, pulled into the road and began driving towards Cormac Devlin's cottage.

29

The way from the road to the cottage had begun as little more than a track. Rebecca had debated whether she should try taking the car as far up it as she could, but the rutted path was more suited to a horse and cart than a horseless carriage. Her suspension would never have handled it. So she pulled in a little way along the road, a small inset at the side big enough only for one vehicle, then began to hike up a trail.

It was a fairly steep climb, and she felt the tension growing in her legs and her breath becoming laboured. She was taking steps to do something about her fitness level – having rejected the notion of joining a gym, she had plumped for exercises at home and also very recently taken up swimming, both in a pool and in the wild – but it was hard going. She fully intended taking a dip in the loch, but had not yet got around to it. A challenge for her birthday, perhaps.

The ascent wound through some conifers, not the statuesque Caledonian pine of the Black Wood but the more common Norway spruce, the favourite for Christmas trees. They crowded around her and some towered above her, almost blocking out the light, creating a dense, dark atmosphere as she moved. It was cold, too, the air nipping at her cheeks and nose as if warning her to stay away.

She shouldn't be doing this, she knew that, but sometimes she had to do what she shouldn't. As far as anyone knew, the last place Fergus had been was the Black Wood. Cormac was a regular denizen of the forest and his cottage was just a mile or two away from it. He had also been friendly with the young man. If anyone knew anything, the chances were it would be him.

She felt as if she had been walking for hours by the time she reached an old wooden gate blocking the way ahead, but her watch told her it had only been twenty minutes. A fitter person might have made the climb in half the time. She leaned against the gate to catch her breath, her legs aching now, and looked back down the path as it snaked through the plantation. Stephen would probably have loped up that hill as if it were nothing.

Stephen – she remembered she still hadn't returned his call. He had said he would come with her to see Cormac, but something about this guy told her that two people turning up unannounced at his door would spook him. Even so, guilt, now familiar, crept into her gut as she pulled her mobile from her coat pocket, but there was no signal here. That figured, she thought. She had told him that she would be back by lunchtime, but she had been gone for most of the day. She wondered if he would be worried. Of course he would, she told herself, just as you would be if he had said he would back in a couple of hours and didn't show up.

She sucked in some air and looked up ahead. So far she had not really broken any rules. The path she was on was open to anyone; there were no signs saying it was private property, no warnings that trespassers would be shot, hung or fed to alligators. But the gate blocked the way ahead and a fence stretched off through the trees on either side. The gate was secured by what looked to her to be a new padlock fastened to a chain. Clearly Cormac – if it was Cormac who had fitted it – wished to dissuade casual visitors. If she continued, she would have to climb the fence and at that moment she would technically be trespassing. She recalled a conversation with Stephen months before in which she had stated that there were no laws of trespass in Scotland and he had pointed out that she was wrong.

'Not true,' he said. 'Well, not in the strict sense. Yes, we have what's been termed the Right to Roam under the Land Reform (Scotland) Act of 2003.' Typical lawyer, had to quote the actual legislation. 'But there are restrictions. You can't wander into someone's garden, say, and claim your right to roam. You can't walk where there are crops. You can't go for a stroll through a construction site or onto a military base, among other places. And if you're caught it would be a delict – a civil wrong – and therefore subject to the civil courts. Or, in some cases it might be viewed as a criminal matter, depending, I suppose, on your intention in being there.'

Her intention here was not criminal, although, her being a member of the dreaded mainstream media, many saw her as little more than that. And could the ground beyond this gate be technically called part of the cottage garden? Further up, she saw another much smaller gate set in an old drystone dyke and beyond that she saw the edge of a building. Surely that was where the garden began?

She hesitated. She didn't often hesitate, but she did now. She knew she should not be doing this. She knew she should have at least returned Stephen's call. Who knew what he was thinking at that moment?

But . . .

She had climbed that bloody hill. She was a few paces away from the cottage. Would it hurt to at least reach that garden gate and have a look? Maybe catch sight of Cormac and call out a few questions? It was amazing what people will say when asked. Grieving parents who you would think might not welcome a journalist can invite them in and open up, grateful for the chance to speak to someone about their lost loved ones, to lash out at whatever issue caused their death – drugs, drink, careless driving, or because a young woman cannot walk the streets at night alone.

The flipside was that reporters can also be chased away with a snarl and threats of bodily harm or calling the police. She didn't think Cormac was likely to call the police, but she was here alone and nobody knew it. On the other hand, everyone had told her he was harmless and had lived in the valley for years. If he was dangerous, somebody would have said. Right?

Bugger it, she thought, she had come this far.

She placed one foot on one of the bars of the gate and threw her other leg over. There was a sticky moment at the top when she had to twist herself uncomfortably in order to free her first leg and she was thankful there was nobody present to witness her lack of grace. Once firmly on the other side, she fixed her coat, repositioned the long strap of her bag, which was draped around her neck and across her chest like a bandolier, then trudged onwards.

A quick look, that was all. Over the fence, get the lay of the land, then head back down.

Shona had never seen her father with a book in his hand and yet Burnes House possessed an extensive library. It wasn't the largest room in the building, but it was big enough to house a collection of floor-to-ceiling shelves stacked with a variety of volumes, many of which she swore had never been opened since the day they had been placed there. They were all hardbacks – paperbacks would be a vulgar intrusion – and a number of them were at least a hundred years old. As a child, she had often come here to escape Alex, or to escape Ray, whose attentions were irritating at times. Neither of them came into this room, as a rule. In fact, the only people she had ever seen here – apart from her mother, who had instilled in her the love of reading – were the servants whose job it was twice a year to take down every tome and dust it. It was a long and tedious job, but Shona had helped them a few times, much to Alex's disgust. He was great believer in the order of things, and wiping a chamois across a book, even though it was leather-bound and perhaps worth more than the staff earned in a year, was not something the daughter of a Burnes should be doing. She had never been terribly clear over what the daughter of a Burnes should do, to be honest. She suspected in Alex's mind it was to marry well and have children. She had married, but not well, and there was no prospect of children. She'd never had any intention of procreating with Call Me Rick.

It would have been different with Fergus. She would have had kids with him by now. Two maybe. But Alex would not have welcomed that.

She had come to the library to think after she returned from the Black Wood. Speaking to that reporter had opened up a lot of wounds and she needed time to try to heal them again. What had happened five years before would always be with her, she knew that, but she had learned to live with it and also to use it against Alex, who she blamed for everything. And Ray, of course, but perhaps his guilt was, at the very least, by association with his father. Ray hadn't been the one who had grabbed her as she had made for the front door to leave that morning. He hadn't been the one who had dragged her back up the stairs, wrenching the bag from her hand and throwing it over the bannister. He hadn't been the one who physically threw her into her room, then plucked the key from the lock, slammed the door and locked her in. No, that had all been Alex.

But Ray had been notable by his absence that morning.

She had wept and screamed and cried out as she had been dragged through the house. She had asked Alex why he was doing this, but all he had said was that he could not allow her to associate with Fergus any more. She had told him she loved Fergus. He said he didn't care. And as the key turned in the lock she had banged on the door and told him he couldn't keep her locked up forever. He said he didn't need to. He just needed to keep her home that morning.

In the library she sat with an old copy of *Don Quixote* open before her on a table of highly polished wood. Cleaners did more in this room than a bi-annual book-dusting. She wasn't reading it, although she did love the story, but was gazing absently through the tall window before her over the lawn and then to the moorland. Sunlight streaked through the glass and silence folded itself around her, but she was so lost in her thoughts and memories that she didn't hear the door open and Ray come in. She became aware of his presence when he said, 'I hear you had a visitor today.'

He was standing just inside the room, his hand on the metal door handle, as if he was fearful of stepping inside, afraid he might be infected by knowledge. Ray was not stupid, but he could often be blinkered. Like his father, she had never seen him with a book in his hand. A rifle. A shotgun. An axe. Even a shovel. But never a book.

'Yes,' she said.

'And then you went out.'

'Yes, again.' She twisted round to face him. The memories stirred by talking to Rebecca Connolly were not good ones, and she was in no mood for his passive aggression. 'Was that not allowed? Am I confined to quarters again?'

He flinched. 'No, just wondering who it was.'

He would already know who had been at the gate, although perhaps not why she was there. 'Don't play games, Ray, you know her name. I'm sure both you and Alex had a full report of what she said before I went out to talk to her, and Alex would have told you I was meeting with her.'

He blinked at the vehemence of her tone. 'She wanted to talk to you about Fergus MacGregor.'

'Yes, she did.' She couldn't lie.

'Why was she asking about him?'

'Why do you care?'

His hand fell away from the handle and he looked around, as if afraid the books might ambush him and make him think. 'Because it must be painful for you, and I care about you. Why do you think?'

He had tried to inject some defiance into his voice, but it was a weak attempt. He could never stand up to her; he knew it and she knew it. She had used that against him in the past. She felt some guilt herself now, over speaking to him so harshly. It felt a bit like kicking a puppy. But she kept her own voice sharp. 'You should have thought about that five years ago, Ray, when your father did what he did. You should have come to help me.'

He had no reply to that. He stood in the doorway, not knowing what to do with himself, his head hung a little. What was that about, she wondered – shame? Regret? He opened his mouth to speak but no words came, so he turned and walked back into the hallway, leaving her alone. Not for the first time she asked herself where he had been that morning while she was being dragged through the house. Another reason for that look occurred to her. It may not have been shame or regret.

It may have been guilt.

30

The cottage sat on a slightly elevated position and the upper windows boasted dormers. She had expected it to be, if not derelict, then at least somehow rundown, but it was in top condition, the window frames and door freshly painted, the garden sloping from the front door to the gate neat and tidy. The flower beds were clear and looked recently dug, the rose bushes in a row in front of the house were trimmed and ready for spring and summer. She could see at least one outbuilding clearly: what had once been a garage by the looks of its broad double doors, with a twin track leading from it to another gate and then veering towards her to join the rutted path up which she had climbed. An old Ford flatbed truck sat in front of the garage. Of course, she realised, Cormac would have to have transport, but she didn't envy him the bumps on the way down, although the truck looked as if it could cope with them.

She could not see Cormac. She scanned the cottage windows, hoping he would be looking out at her, but saw nobody. Wood smoke drifted from one of the chimneys, which suggested he was at home.

Okay, Becks, what now? You climbed that bloody mountain without a Sherpa guide. What's the next step?

She knew what the next step was going to be. She had always known it, no matter how she tried to convince herself otherwise. It was as inevitable as the dawn.

She clicked the latch on the gate and stepped onto the narrow gravel path that led to the front door. She waited a moment. No alarms sounded, no pack of ravening dogs attacked her, so she moved onwards and, seeing no bell, rattled the letterbox. She thought she heard movement from inside, as if someone was dragging a bad leg, but nobody answered the door. Shona had said Cormac had a limp when she had seen him the night before. She gave the letterbox another clatter, ears pricked for further sounds, but there was nothing, only the chatter of birds in the trees behind her and, somewhere, the call of a buzzard on the hunt. She looked back the way she had come and saw the edge of the loch and the far bank over the treetops, the water darker now, the shadows on the land deeper as the sun edged lower. She checked her watch. She should be getting back, Stephen would really be worried. She wandered along the row of concrete slabs in front of the house towards the garage and peered around the corner. The gap between the house and the garage was narrow, but she could see the wall and blackened window of a stone outbuilding at the back. A flutter of wings from the garage beside her drew her attention. It was a wooden construct and looked ancient enough to have been built when horsepower was the real thing and not a selling point. She put her eye to a gap between the slats and in the shadows beyond she saw tables with cages, one with something dark and large fluttering inside. He used the garage as his hospital, obviously.

'Mr Devlin?'

She cocked her head to listen, wondering why she did that, because it really didn't help her hearing, but caught no sound of wood being worked on. She called out his name again for luck, but there was still no reply. She darted a quick look back at the front door, still unanswered, before she walked carefully through the gap to the rear of the cottage. It opened up into a small oblong-shaped courtyard created by the building she had already seen joining with another, what looked like an old byre, to form an L-shape. Concrete slabs floored this yard and they were as pristine as when they had been laid. No grass grew in the cracks, no mould clung to the concrete. A couple of large barrels housing flowerbeds sat at either end. Like the front garden, the earth in them looked as if it had been recently replaced. Cormac certainly kept everything tidy, and his love of nature obviously extended to flora as well as fauna. A wooden shelter beside the cottage's back door was stacked high with logs and chopped wood. She had been right about the source of the smoke. Well done, Becks, you're ready for your woodsperson's badge now.

She rapped her knuckles on the rear door and called out, but again there was no reply. She held her ear closer to the door, listening for further movement, but heard nothing. She wandered around the small courtyard, trying the door of the outbuilding but finding it locked. She stood still for a few moments, ears alert for any sound, but all she heard was the birds. Even the buzzard had moved on.

She returned to the front of the house through the narrow passageway, digging in her bag for her notebook. She had spotted a phone line running from somewhere down the hill to a terminal on the upper wall, so she decided she'd leave a note with her card and ask him to call her. She didn't think he would but it was worth a shot. If you don't try, you don't get.

The note scribbled as legibly as she could, the card folded within it, she then dropped it through the letterbox, giving it another rattle as she did so. She waited again, thought she heard the sound of a door closing. Someone was inside, she was certain, but whoever it was obviously had no intention of answering the door. Smoke still floated from the chimney above the room to her right and she eyed the neatly painted window.

She hesitated. She couldn't do what she was thinking of doing. It really was stepping over the line. Nevertheless, she moved closer to the window.

Becks, what the hell are you doing?

A peek, that's all, just a peek. Just a quick look.

She didn't want to stoop and make it obvious. She remained erect, making a show of looking off to the side of the house, as if searching for signs of life. Her glance to the left was casual enough that nobody would think she was snooping, even though she was, in fact, snooping. No wonder reporters get a bad name, she thought to herself.

It seemed to be a kitchen, fairly modern too, from what she saw. The sky was becoming gloomier by the minute and no light had been switched on inside, but logs burned in an open fire, casting a flickering glow onto an armchair beside the hearth in which somebody sat, bundled in a blanket, seemingly staring at the dancing flames. She couldn't see who it was, just the shape of the back of the head and shoulders.

She was about to tap the window when she heard the scrape of a shoe on the path behind her. But before she could turn, something crashed into the back of her head and the colours of the world, the sounds, the smell of the smoke, all melted away, and the notebook she still held in her hand slipped from it as she felt herself pitching forward for what seemed like forever.

Stephen stood by the window, his phone to his ear. The call went straight to Rebecca's voicemail again. He didn't bother leaving a message this time. He had already left two.

'Still no reply?' Alan asked.

'No,' he said.

Chaz asked, 'Okay, am I the only one beginning to grow worried?'

No, you're not, Stephen thought, as he stared through the window where the shadows of the trees were lengthening across the small garden. He reached a decision, one he probably should have made at least an hour before.

'I'm going out to look for her,' he said, stepping into the hall-way to pluck his coat from the row of hooks on the wall. The boys followed him, taking their own coats down.

'No, you guys stay here,' he said.

'We want to help,' Chaz said.

'I know. I need you to stay here in case I miss her on the road and she comes home. Maybe she's lost her phone, maybe it's not working, maybe the battery's flat, I don't know. But if she arrives home and nobody's here, she won't be able to contact me. I need to borrow your car, though, if that's okay.'

Thankfully they didn't even begin to argue, perhaps recognising his reasoning was sound, even though he knew they would see his thoughts regarding her phone as wishful thinking.

'Have you any idea where to start?' Chaz asked.

He had already considered that. 'She was meeting Frances MacGregor.'

'But you don't know where she lives.'

'No, but I know where she was meeting her. And it's a start . . .'

Cormac stood over the unconscious woman, the length of wood he had hit her with still in his hand. There was no blood on its edge, which was a good thing, but he had hit her pretty hard. Hard enough obviously to knock her out, but was it too hard? He knelt beside her, his hand hovering over her back and neck. On the telly they checked the pulse at the side of the neck but that seemed to him to be too much of an invasion of her personal space. He reached out and gripped her wrist gently. Use your fingers, Cormac, he told himself, for your thumb has a pulse. He didn't know where he had learned that – years ago maybe at first-aid classes, when he was a kid. His fingertips found the steady beat of her blood. He hadn't hit her too hard and for that he was glad. He looked up at the front door, where Fergus stood, wrapped in his blanket.

'She was looking at you through the window,' Cormac said. 'Who is she?'

'The lass your Shona was talking to. The one I saw at the memorial the other day.'

Fergus stooped with some difficulty; he seemed to be getting worse instead of better. He picked up a piece of paper from the doormat on the hallway and handed it to Cormac, who unfolded it and looked at the card. 'She's a reporter,' he said, his voice verging on panic. He'd knocked out a reporter. He didn't know why that made things worse, it just did.

'Calm down,' Fergus said.

'But she's a reporter!'

'And that matters why? She was snooping, wasn't she? She could have been a burglar or something, for all you knew.'

Cormac didn't know if that excuse would hold water, but he let it pass.

'Do you think she saw me?' Fergus asked.

'I don't know. Maybe. Probably. In the light from the fire.'

Fergus looked down at her with interest. 'Was she looking for me?'

'Nobody knows you're here. She was probably looking for me. It was my name she called out.'

Fergus nodded, seeing the sense in this. 'You'll have to get rid of her.'

'Get rid of her?' Cormac was horrified. 'What do you mean get rid of her?'

'She saw me, Cormac. I don't want her telling anyone I'm here.'

'I know, but get rid of her? Do you mean you want me to kill her?'

Fergus was shocked. 'No! Nothing like that. You need to hide her away somewhere, prevent her from speaking to anyone, at least for now until we work out what to do.'

'Where?'

'Where you hid me when I asked.'

Cormac nodded, understanding. He had concealed Fergus from the search parties five years before. He had waited until he knew they had searched that place, then in the middle of the night stole the lad across the water and kept him there warm and cosy until the din had died down. Then he fetched him back to the cottage, where he had been ever since. 'For how long?'

Fergus didn't answer. He was looking down the path to the gate. 'She must have a car somewhere. I can't see her walking from the village or wherever to get here. Check her bag for keys.'

Cormac pulled her bag from around her shoulders as gently as he could, laying her head carefully back down. She was breathing steady, he now noted. That was a good sign too. No blood coming from her nose or her ears. He unzipped the bag and looked inside, one hand rummaging around until he found the car keys. 'Got them,' he said, holding them up.

Fergus gave him a satisfied nod. 'Okay, tie her up for now and then get down there and hide her car.'

'Where?'

'You'll think of somewhere. Then we'll have to cart her down the track and get her stashed. Okay?'

Cormac nodded, but he didn't feel okay at all. Fergus sensed this and laid a hand on his arm.

'It'll just be for a wee while, Cormac, don't worry. We'll work this out.'

'I shouldn't have hit her. It'll cause trouble . . .'

'It's done now and we just have to deal with it, right? You did what you thought you had to in order to protect me. It will all be fine, I promise. You've been wanting me to come back to the world and maybe you're right, maybe it's time. I'm feeling so much better now, thanks to you, but I just need a wee while longer, you understand? Just a wee while longer.'

Cormac was relieved to hear that Fergus had decided to reveal that he was still around, but his assertion that he was feeling so much better now troubled him. Because to Cormac the boy didn't look better at all. Not at all.

31

Terri was young, dark-haired, freckled and spoke with a strong
Lancashire accent. She had been on duty in the hotel lounge at
the time Rebecca had met Frances MacGregor. Yes, she recognised Rebecca's description and said she had served her and an
older lady that morning. She wouldn't normally remember, you
understand, because eventually it's just faces, isn't it, coming and
going, ordering and paying, not tipping more often than you
realise, but she remembered them because it hadn't been very
busy, it being midweek and not peak season, and your lady had
left a decent tip. You'd be surprised how many don't. She really
couldn't say for certain how long they were in the lounge, maybe
half an hour. No, they didn't leave together, she was sure of that,
because the older lady – Frances MacGregor, is that the other
lady's name? – well, she left before your friend. No, she didn't
go right away, she ordered another coffee and sat for a few more
minutes. No, she didn't know the MacGregor lady. Well, maybe
by sight, because she'd been in before, coffee and lunches and
such. She seemed nice enough but never left a tip. Sorry, she
didn't have a clue where she lived. Terri wasn't local, you see.
Sorry she couldn't help more.

Stephen thanked her, gave her a tip, then checked if the
receptionist knew Frances MacGregor but again came up blank.
Outside, he checked his phone but there was still nothing from
Rebecca. He tried calling again, but it went straight to voicemail. The sky was growing even darker, what little heat there

had been in the air disappearing fast. *Where the hell are you, Becks? What's happened to you?*

He had tried to control it, but the worry now filled his mind and stiffened every muscle in his neck and shoulders. Becks could be single-minded, sure, impulsive certainly, but not to the extent that she would deliberately stress him out. If she was on a story, on an interview, she would ignore calls, but she always called back as soon as she was clear. Granted, that was more difficult here because her signal was so patchy, so wherever she had gone it may not have been possible to call him.

But something had happened, he knew it.

He had considered calling the police, but Rebecca was an adult, there was no evidence of any accident or foul play, and they wouldn't even begin to take notice until much later.

He could feel the cold air biting at his fingers and he wished he had remembered to pick up his gloves, which had been warming over a radiator in the cottage hallway. He unlocked Chaz's car, climbed in, twisted the ignition and worked out how to turn the heat up on the unfamiliar instrument panel, then considered his next move. As a student he had carried out investigation work for his parents, had been good at it, and although it had been years since he had battered on doors himself to ask questions, being with Becks this week on a couple of her calls had stimulated that part of his brain and now he needed to really tap into that skillset. He needed a timeline, so he sat back and itemised what he already knew.

Becks had left the cottage at around 9.45 that morning to meet Mrs MacGregor. She had made the meeting, confirmed by the waitress, but it lasted around half an hour. Stephen knew not to take this as gospel, though. It could have been shorter or longer. Becks stayed a little longer, though, probably considering what Mrs MacGregor had told her. If anything, because the interview – however long it lasted – might not have been long enough to yield that much information. He would bet that what was said either sparked something in Becks's mind, or she hit on a thought that had sent her off somewhere else. But where?

Frances MacGregor remained his best bet, so he backed out of the parking space and turned towards the bridge, drove past the general store and turned right beyond the fire station to head to the lochside road. He saw the edge of dark waters ahead, the sun already having vanished beyond the moor and the mountains of Glencoe, leaving the sky a mix of red, orange and purple. He stopped at the bottom of the small hill leading to the church Rebecca had visited and, after double-checking the minister's name on the board beside the road, climbed the steps to the doorway. Snowdrops clustered around the small kirkyard like fallen blossoms, while the yellow heads of early daffodils that had thrust their way through the earth around the walls were beginning to droop in the slumping temperature. Behind him, the waters of the loch whispered secrets to the gravel of the shoreline, but if they knew where Rebecca was they were keeping it to themselves.

Lights shone through the high windows on the small white building, which suggested someone was in there, and he hoped it was the minister. He turned the round metal handle on the heavy wooden door and pushed it open. With Becks on his mind, he barely noticed the old, polished dark wood of the pews and the exposed beams criss-crossing the vaulted ceiling, focusing instead on the tall man standing near the pulpit.

'Reverend Lester?' Stephen asked, as he walked up the aisle.

The minister was already coming to meet him. 'Yes, can I help you?'

'The name's Stephen Jordan,' he said, holding out his hand as they neared one another. The minister gripped it firmly. He looked fit, had an ex-military air about him. Stephen had never been in the forces but he had friends who had been and they shared that look of tough determination, of being capable and trustworthy. And sometimes haunted.

'What can I do for you, Mr Jordan?'

'It's about Rebecca Connolly. You met her the other day?'

The minister took a step backward and his tone, which had been open and friendly, became more guarded. Becks had a way of making people do that, Stephen knew. 'Yes?'

'I'm her partner.' No hesitation, straight to the point. He didn't have time for the coy bullshit.

Tom Lester tilted his head. 'Partner, as in business, or partner as in personal, Mr Jordan?'

'Personal.'

'And are you a journalist, too?'

'No. I'm a solicitor.'

Another cautious look. Stephen was used to that. People became more circumspect in what they said in case it ended up being used against them in court.

'Ah. So what can I do for you, Mr Jordan?'

'Have you seen her today, Reverend?'

The minister frowned. 'No, should I have?'

'No, I just wondered if she had come by, maybe this morning?'

'I haven't seen her since we spoke a couple of days ago. Why are you asking?'

'She's disappeared.'

The wary aspect was replaced by one of concern. 'When?'

'I last saw her just before ten this morning.'

'And where was she going?'

'To meet Frances MacGregor.'

The man opened his mouth in a silent *ah*. 'So Frances contacted her?'

'Yes.'

'I wasn't sure if she would.'

'They met, but after that Rebecca seems to have vanished.'

The minister held his hands out in apology. 'I'm sorry, Mr Jordan, but I haven't seen her.'

'Can you tell me where Mrs MacGregor lives?'

'No, I don't think I can do that.'

'I need to find out exactly when she and Becks – Rebecca – parted company. And what was said.'

'I understand, but I cannot in all conscience give you Frances's address.'

'Then can you phone her, ask if she'll speak to me? Can you do that?'

He studied Stephen closely. 'You really are concerned about Ms Connolly, aren't you? Something like this is out of character?'

Stephen hesitated again. Was it really? 'Yes, this is out of character.'

'I see.' He turned on his heel and said over his shoulder, 'Come with me then.'

The minister led him through a door beside the pulpit into a short corridor off which was a small kitchen, a toilet and then a room that might have been called a cupboard in a larger church but was being used as an office. There was space for a small desk, two chairs and a potted plant that had become so large it threatened to engulf them both. Tom Lester caught Stephen's glance and gave him a stiff smile as he dialled the phone. 'I should trim that, I suppose, but I'm afraid I'll kill it if I do. I've no idea about horticulture.'

Stephen knew nothing either so didn't offer any advice.

'Frances?' the minister spoke down the line. 'Tom Lester . . .' He glanced at Stephen as he said, 'Yes, I'm fine, thanks, but did you meet that reporter today? . . . Yes . . . I wonder, can I put someone else on the line? A man called . . .' His eyes searched for Stephen's name. Stephen repeated it. 'Stephen Jordan. He's the young woman's partner and he needs to know where she is . . . Yes, she's not been seen since. He's right here, hang on . . .'

The minister handed the phone to Stephen, who leaned across the desk to take it.

'Mrs MacGregor? Thank you for talking to me.'

The voice was cold and businesslike. 'I'm not sure how I can help you, Mr Jordan.'

'I know, and I won't keep you long. You were only with her for a short time, am I right?'

'Yes.'

'Half an hour?'

'More or less.'

'Did she give you any indication as to where she was going next?'

'No, none at all. We did not part on the best of terms.'

'Why not?'

'I had made a mistake in speaking to her, Mr Jordan, if you must know. I don't want people poking their noses into my family affairs.'

'She's trying to help . . .'

'Yes, that what they all say, all the reporters, but really they just want to pry and turn people's lives into soap opera and I can't have that.'

Stephen didn't want to argue with the woman. He knew Rebecca sincerely wanted to do something that may answer the question of what happened to this woman's son, but he wasn't going to get into the rights and wrongs of her profession now. 'I understand that, but would you mind telling me what you talked about?'

'My son, you must know that.'

'Yes, but what did you tell her?'

'Nothing. As I said, I knew very early in our conversation that I had made a mistake in meeting with her. It was only because the Reverend Lester asked that I did it, but it was an error of judgement on my part.'

'And you told Rebecca that?'

'Yes. And then I left. She was still there.'

'Please, Mrs MacGregor, Becks – Rebecca – hasn't been in touch all day. I'm very worried about her. Was there anything mentioned in your conversation that might have sent her off on another line of enquiry?'

'No.' The woman didn't even think about. 'As I said, we didn't part on the best of terms.'

He knew from experience that sometimes you have to ask the same question again and again. 'I understand, but did either of you say anything that you think might have sparked something in her mind?'

'No. She told me she had met with my son . . .'

'Rory?'

A slight silence after that. 'Yes. He had said enough about our family to make me realise that I didn't want any part in her investigation.'

He heard a man's voice in the background but had the impression Mrs MacGregor was ignoring it. Despite his concern over Rebecca's whereabouts, Stephen's curiosity was aroused by the woman's attitude. 'Don't you want to know what happened to your son, Mrs MacGregor?'

'Whatever happened to Fergus was God's will, Mr Jordan, and I will be none the wiser through the interference of a reporter, no matter what she has done in the past.'

So she had looked into Rebecca's history. That was understandable, he supposed. The man's voice grew louder and then muffled, as if she had placed a hand over the mouthpiece. He could still hear the voices, though, and they seemed to be arguing over possession of the phone.

'Mrs MacGregor?'

The disagreement at the other end continued and he caught Tom Lester's questioning gaze across the desk. Stephen shrugged and gestured with his free hand to the phone to tell him he didn't know what was happening. Finally, the line cleared and the woman's voice was back. 'Leave us alone, Mr Jordan. Leave my family alone. What's done is done. Let it lie.'

'Mrs MacGregor . . .'

'Listen to me – this is our business and nobody else's. Understand? If you continue harassing us, then I will take steps, believe me.'

Stephen felt his own temper rising, but he kept it under control. 'Nobody's harassing you, Mrs MacGregor.'

'This is harassment. Phone calls, meetings, asking people about my family . . . and it will stop, believe me.'

'Is that a threat, Mrs MacGregor?'

There was what might have been an angry growl on the other end before the connection was cut. Stephen stood with the receiver still to his ear but all he heard was dial tone. He handed it back to Tom Lester, who replaced it on the handset.

'That didn't seem to go very well,' he said.

'That's an understatement,' said Stephen, with a small smile. He could feel the adrenaline created by his anger begin to recede and his hand shook slightly as he ran it through his hair. The minister noticed but made no direct comment.

'Frances can be . . . difficult.'

'I think her husband wanted to speak to me, but she wouldn't let him.'

'Dan is perhaps more amenable to certain things. Frances can be intractable. They're very nice, really, but they like to keep their personal business to themselves. I take it you learned nothing that helps you?'

'No, not in finding Becks anyway,' Stephen said, and that was true, but the conversation had told him something. Until now he had been interested in Fergus MacGregor only because Rebecca was. Certainly his curiosity had been piqued – of course it had – but it was in an academic way: he didn't know these people and the disappearance of Fergus MacGregor was simply a puzzle. He hadn't been personally invested. But after that brief but bitter exchange, he made a resolution. Once he found Rebecca he would do whatever he could to get to the bottom of it.

32

Rebecca was floating.

She didn't know where she was – everywhere was darkness, apart from what may have been ethereal fragments of mist snaking through it, but she felt as if she was drifting on warm waters. They were comforting, those waters, like a bath that had been too hot but had cooled to just the right temperature.

She thought she heard voices somewhere, but she paid them little heed. She was far too relaxed to care, to be honest. Let them jibber-jabber away, she wasn't interested. Jibber-jabber. There's a funny expression. Where did that start, she wondered? What's the entomology? No, not entomology – that's insects, stupid. Etymology. What's the etymology of jibber-jabber? When she got back to dry land, she would find out. But that was for later; for now, she was happy just being buoyed up in these dark waters for a while, snug as a bug in a rug. There's another strange expression. Why would anyone want a bug to be snug in their rug? Doesn't make sense. She would have to look into that, too. That was both etymology and entomology, she realised with a smile, and let herself float on into the darkness.

We all float down here.

To hell you with, Stephen King, I'm happy . . .

'She's smiling,' Cormac said, as he dragged Rebecca to the rear of his truck. 'What's she smiling at?'

'She'll be dreaming,' Fergus said, following them. He didn't offer to help, which annoyed Cormac a great deal. He was full of do this, do that, but he didn't do much doing himself. He was glad the boy had reached the decision that it was time to go back to the world. Cormac had been happy to help him when he was sick, but after five years he needed his own space again. This reporter had complicated things, sure, but Fergus said he'd think of something to get him off the hook for that. It might mean she would have to disappear for a while, just like Fergus had, but that was okay.

Even so, he wished Fergus would pull his weight a bit more while he was here. Cormac wasn't young any more, and this lass might look like a wisp of mist but she was a dead weight to drag along the path. The truck's tailgate was already down and he manhandled her into a sitting position, thrust his arms under hers to hoist her upper half onto the flat bed, then hefted her legs. He climbed up and stretched her out on an old duvet, then covered her with a thick blanket because he didn't want her getting cold. An old sack lay beside her and he wondered if he should put it over her head now or later. Later, he decided. Once he got her where she was going.

'You can't take her yet,' Fergus said.

Cormac knew that but he didn't say anything.

'You'll need to wait till after midnight.'

Cormac knew that too, but he still didn't say anything.

'You can't risk being seen.'

Cormac finally gave him a look designed to tell him that he should either shut the hell up or do something to help. Fergus saw the look and nodded.

'Okay, I get it,' he said. 'I'll fetch the bucket and more blankets.'

Finally, Cormac thought.

When the doorbell rang, Harry contemplated not answering. He didn't want to be distracted from his phone, not tonight, for he could easily miss her message and then he'd never know what it was that worried Ashley so, but he hadn't closed the blinds and whoever it was could see his light on. He sighed when the bell rang again, for longer this time, and he pulled himself from his chair.

He could feel himself slowing down lately, and he thought perhaps he should start going for walks again. He had stopped after Mel had died. She had loved to walk the trails around the valley. She loved to pack a picnic and they would drive to Rannoch Station and head along the track to Loch Laidon and up through the woodlands, where they would find somewhere to eat while looking out across the bleak expanse of the moor towards the hills far on the opposite side. He missed Mel and wished he had been a better husband, a better man, a better father. They had never been that close, he and his daughter. His fault, of course. He had wanted to reach out but something within him had always prevented it. Same with Mel. When they were younger he had been full of fire, but as the years wore on it had cooled. Near the end they didn't even touch, not even a kiss goodnight. That pained him now, his distance. It had never been planned; it was something that merely happened.

The doorbell jingled once more as he reached the hallway; through the frosted glass panels he saw a tall figure. When he opened it, the man was familiar, but he couldn't quite place from where. Harry searched his memory for a name, came up with nothing.

'Hello,' he said, the single word both greeting and query.

'Sorry to bother you, Harry,' the man said, 'but I need to know if you've seen Rebecca tonight.'

Rebecca. The reporter lass. He was the fellow who had been with her, her boyfriend, but the name still eluded him.

'Miss Connolly?' Harry tried to remember when he had seen her. He knew it was recently but had it been that evening or earlier? He was tired and sometimes the hours merged together, but he remembered it had still been light outside when she had called. 'No, not tonight, she was here earlier today. I told her that I didn't want to be part of her programme.'

'When was this, can you remember? Was it this morning or this afternoon? Later?'

Harry heard his phone bleep to tell him that he had a message. He needed to send this man away so he could get to Ashley. 'This morning, definitely.' He thought about it. 'Yes, morning, but late, nearly lunchtime.'

'Did she say where she was going?'

Harry struggled to remember. He hadn't paid much attention to what the girl had said, his mind was so full of worry about Ashley. 'I don't know.' He heard the message alert again and began to grow restless. 'She asked some questions.'

'About what? The disappearance of Fergus MacGregor?'

'Yes, but I'd already told her everything I knew.' Remembrance was like a light being switched on. 'She asked about Shona Burnes.'

The man grew very interested. 'Fergus's girlfriend?'

'Yes.' Harry suddenly registered what Stephen had said. 'Really? They were going together? I didn't know that.'

'What did Rebecca want to know, Harry? It's important. I haven't seen her all day, she's not answering her phone and I'm very worried.'

Harry caught the concern in the man's voice, but he needed to get him away now. 'She wanted to know where her family lived. I think she was going to call on her.'

The man nodded and asked for directions to Burnes House, so Harry repeated what he had told the young woman earlier. The man thanked him and then turned away, walking quickly into the darkness beyond the flood of light from the doorway. Harry was relieved to close the door and get back into the living room, where he snatched the phone up and read Ashley's messages.

Hi dear

He hastily thumbed a reply.

Yes I'm here

He sat down as he waited but didn't see the tell-tale dots to show she was typing. Damn, had he missed her? He stared at the screen, willing her to reply. He shouldn't have answered the door, he should have ignored it, to hell with what that reporter's friend would have thought, he should have . . .

The dots appeared. She was replying.

Where were u dear

Sorry, someone was at the door

That okay dear. You here now. That important thing

What did you have to tell me?

There was a pause, then the dots flashed. They flashed for a long time, then vanished, then came back again. Harry knew this meant her reply was either a long one or she was rewording it. That had happened before. He had watched the dots come and go for what seemed like an age before only a single line appeared. This time, though, it was a long message.

Oh baby. I need ur help. U the only one I can turn to for this. I cant trust no one anymore. My cousin. He is making my life hell. I cant tell my aunt – she dont belief me about him. He hide his true self from her. Also things bad for me here now. Too many hate me and I worry for safety

What can I do?

There was another long pause, so long that Harry feared she had lost the connection. That had happened before. He had once asked her about it and she said that although they were in the USA their signal was poor and the router they used was old, so she often dropped out. Had that happened now?

You there, Ashley?
   Yeah baby. I am here. Sorry dear I dont know what say. I dont like asking this
Just tell me what you need, Ashley. I want to help
   Oh baby. You so sweet. I wouldnt ask this if I wasnt desperate. I need to get away from here baby. Only u can help me, I belief. I want to come to u, like I always wanted, so u can care for me. Do you want that, dear? I be good to u, u know that. I make u happy

It was his turn to pause the chat. This was a big step. She was in trouble – this cousin of hers was clearly a piece of work and she needed to get away from him. But to bring her here? Was that a good idea?

   Ur all I got. My cousin scares me so much. He wants me to do things I don't wanna do. He has my passport and he says he will burn it unless I have sex with him. Please baby. Tell me u will help.

He continued to hesitate. She was clearly in real trouble and he believed he really was all she had. Her aunt wouldn't help. She had no friends to speak of. And this cousin, what would he do to her if she didn't do what he wanted?

How will you get your passport from him?
   If u loan me money I can offer him. He will take $s instead of sex. I promise to pay you back dear
How much will you need?
   He take 5 thousnd, I think. Then I get passport and I can come to u, but u need buy me air tkt too.

He sat back. That was a lot of money. He had it, certainly, but it was a lot of cash to send. Before it had been fifty here, twenty there. The most he had sent was a hundred. But five thousand? Plus the cost of an air ticket?

Dear. I know it is a lot to ask and I hate to ask but I wuldnt do it if I didn have to, u know that dear. If u can do this for me, I come to u and we'd be happy, ok? U don need book nothing. I do all that from here. Cheaper that way belief me. OK? U take care of me good. I look after you

He couldn't leave her to face this alone, he knew it. He had to do something. And after all, it was only money.

33

The voice on the intercom at the rather ornate gate seemed bored. 'Do you have an appointment?'

'No,' Stephen said, leaning in. As soon as he saw the gate, he knew getting to Fergus's ex-girlfriend might be a problem, so he had decided to play the only card he had. 'I'm a solicitor and I need to speak to Ms Burnes urgently about a matter of great concern.'

He didn't think he was stepping over any ethical boundaries here. He had not lied once in that statement – he was a solicitor and he did need to speak to Shona Burnes. He hoped that mentioning his profession might prevent any further enquiry on behalf of the remote voice. He was wrong.

'And what is this matter of great concern?'

'I can't discuss it, I'm sure you understand.' There was silence from the speaker for so long he thought the person had cut him off and he was about to ask if he was still there when it crackled again.

'Do you have any kind of identification?'

Stephen reached into his back pocket for his credit card holder and found his Law Society ID card.

'Hold it up to the camera, please,' said the voice.

Stephen looked up to the lens on the pillar beside the intercom and held the card as high as he could. He thought he heard a slight whirring, perhaps a zoom lens focusing on the card.

'Thank you,' said the voice eventually. 'Please return to your car and wait a moment.'

Stephen climbed into the driver's seat, switched on the engine and waited, staring at the gates. They didn't open. He drummed his fingers on the steering wheel. He glanced at the mobile phone sitting on the passenger seat to see if there had been any messages while he was at the intercom. Nothing from Chaz or Alan – more importantly, nothing from Becks. He looked to his right, into the darkness. Where are you, Becks?

He heard a loud click, followed by a grating sound, as the gate swung back over the gravel driveway. He moved the car slowly through some trees towards the lights, which he could see through the bare branches. When he cleared the copse, he saw the Scots baronial-style house, large and ostentatious with turrets at either side of the facade, and a vaulted doorway with a flight of stone steps leading up to it, lit on either side by lamps. He felt the whole place was designed to intimidate anyone who saw it for the first time. He wasn't intimidated. He had faced the ire of police officers and judges. He wasn't about to let a pile of bricks scare him.

He pointed the four-wheel drive into a space beside a Porsche 911 that reflected the lights from the house like twinkling stars. Beyond it was a small sporty number and a red Jeep Cherokee that was slightly more battered and dirty, obviously its off-road capabilities being well used. He climbed from Chaz's slightly lower-end vehicle as two men approached from around the side of the house, one in his early thirties, the other older, but even from this distance he could see they were related. They were both dressed casually, but Stephen could tell at a glance that they didn't buy their gear from Rory MacGregor's girlfriend in the Perth Matalan. They not only looked alike but they carried themselves in the same way. These were men who felt they owned everything they touched, and they very probably did.

221

'What do you want with my daughter . . . Mr Jordan, was it?' It was the older man who spoke, whom he guessed was Alex Burnes. His voice was deep, cultured in a leisurely way, but used to getting answers whenever it posed a question. It was about to be disappointed.

'I can only discuss that with Ms Burnes, I'm afraid.'

'You'll discuss it with us first.' The younger guy was speaking now, more aggression in his voice than his father, and now that he was closer Stephen could see that, although there was a family resemblance, his face had a touch of cruelty about it. Something about the set of the mouth and the way the eyes regarded him almost lazily.

'I don't think I can.' There was no reason why he shouldn't tell them why he was there, but something about them grated.

'Is this about Rick?' The younger Burnes again, but then he shrank back on receiving a glare from his father. Stephen had no idea who Rick was but saw no reason not to use it in a subtle way. He paused for a beat to give the impression that it might just be about Rick.

'I really can't say anything about it, except to Ms Burnes.' He looked directly at her father. 'I'm sure you understand confidentiality, sir.' The use of 'sir' felt bitter, but it was necessary. He had to see Shona and he had to see her away from them.

Alex Burnes studied him, taking in his walking boots, jeans and ancient fleece. 'It's rather an odd time for a solicitor to come calling, isn't it?'

Stephen knew he was on shaky ground here. If this had been a real legal matter, then an appointment would have been made, it would have been during office hours and he would be properly dressed. He tried to think of a reply that would prop up his story, but nothing seemed to work. Shit, he would have to come clean. He was about to admit everything when he heard a woman's voice from the front door.

'I think the gentleman is here to see me, Alex.'

They all turned to face her, as she came down the short flight of stairs, wrapped in a thick fleecy dressing gown.

'We need to know what it is he wants, Shona,' said her brother.

'No, you don't. I understand he said at the gate that it was a confidential matter, so that's all you need to know, I think.'

Someone inside the house must have informed her of his presence then, whoever had been on the other end of the intercom perhaps. Alex Burnes's face took on a weary expression, as he looked from his daughter back to Stephen. 'Mr Jordan, are you in my daughter's employ?'

'No, I'm not,' said Stephen.

'There you are, Alex,' said Shona. 'You're not paying him, someone else is, so you have no rights whatsoever in these proceedings.'

The elder Burnes held her gaze and Stephen sensed this battle of wills had been waging for some time. Finally, the older man shook his head almost sorrowfully, turned on his heel and walked back the way he had come. The younger made no move to go. He stood his ground, studying Stephen as if he was something to be shot at. Stephen would have laid odds that this young man had shot at a lot of things.

'Off you go, Ray,' said Shona, the edge in her voice cutting through the air between them. 'Nothing to see here.'

Ray lingered long enough for his testosterone to be satisfied, before, with a final pointed glare at Stephen for daring to defy not just him but his father, he followed the latter back around the side of the house.

'They're very protective,' Stephen said.

She grimaced, but he had the impression she had enjoyed the exchange. 'That's one way of putting it. So, Mr Solicitor, what do you want?'

She began to walk in the opposite direction from her father and brother, and Stephen kept pace with her. 'I'm here on a personal matter, nothing to do with my job. I didn't say before because I didn't think it would get me through the gate.'

'You're right: it wouldn't. So what do you need?'

'Did you speak to a Rebecca Connolly today?'

'Is she a friend of yours?'

'Yes. We're . . .' His voice hitched, as he again stumbled over how to describe the relationship. 'Involved.'

She nodded in understanding. 'That must be awkward sometimes, a lawyer seeing a reporter. Does it cause conflict?'

She was confident enough to be direct. Being brought up in privilege can make a person that way. 'On occasion, but nothing we can't handle. Did you see her, Ms Burnes?'

'Yes, I did. She arrived at the gate but didn't get through. I spoke to her there for a short time, then we met up and had a longer conversation.'

'Where did you meet?'

'The Black Wood. It was her suggestion.'

Stephen was not surprised. It was perhaps the only place Becks would think of where they could talk without being overheard or seen.

'Why do you ask, Mr Solicitor who is involved with a reporter?'

Stephen wondered if she had forgotten his name, but let it pass. 'Because she hasn't been seen since. She's not answering calls or texts.'

She turned to face him, the levity in her voice replaced by something more sombre. 'Has something happened?'

'That's what I'm trying to find out. I'm putting together a timetable of her movements today. What time did you see her, can you recall?'

Her brown eyes narrowed as she worked it out. 'I got back here about three-ish, I think.'

'And did you see what direction she took when she left you?'

'No, she was still in her car at the side of the road near the Black Wood.'

'Did she give you any idea where she might have been planning to go next?'

'No, she didn't say.'

Stephen was beginning to fear his timeline had wound down. He took a deep breath, trying to come up with another question. 'You spoke of Fergus MacGregor's disappearance, right?'

'Yes.'

'May I ask what you told her?'

'Well, in a nutshell I told her that I was supposed to meet him that day, but I was prevented.'

'By whom?'

She jerked her head back towards the cars. 'I'll give you three guesses.'

Stephen looked at the corner of the house. He wondered why her father and brother had prevented her from meeting Fergus, but that didn't matter now. 'Anything else?'

'Just about Fergus, his family, my family, the events of five years ago.' She laid a hand on his arm. 'You're very worried, aren't you?'

'Yes.'

'She doesn't do this kind of thing regularly, does she? Just drop off the radar?'

'No, she's never done it before.'

Her hand dropped away and she began to walk again. 'Can I ask, was everything okay between you?'

'Why do you ask?'

'Well . . .' She sought the words to explain. 'Look, I've just separated from my husband Rick . . .'

Stephen now understood her brother's earlier question.

'When I was really upset, I would just up and take off, anywhere – a friend's house, a hotel for the night, once I even hopped on a train and ended up at Kyle of Lochalsh. I switched off my phone so he couldn't contact me, or trace me in any way. It was all a means of punishing him, you see. It's spoiled and bratty, I get that, but it was the only way I could get at him, if you understand. So that's why I ask if everything is okay. I mean, did you have a fight or anything?'

Stephen thought about his stupid remark regarding Harry's phone and Rebecca's reaction. He thought about their argument over it. She had been angered by it. And hurt. But they had made up and he was certain that she had put it behind them. 'No, everything was fine. Sure we have our disagreements, doesn't everyone, but everything was fine. Tomorrow's her birthday.' He didn't know why he mentioned that, it merely slipped out. He felt her hand on his arm again.

'I'm sure she'll be alright . . . I'm sorry, I can't remember your name.'

'Stephen.'

'Rebecca strikes me as a very competent person, Stephen. I'm sure wherever she is, she has a very good reason for being there, and she can cope if something has happened. I don't think she's the type of girl to panic.'

Rebecca was panicking.

She had woken up but all was in darkness. This wasn't the comforting, warm darkness of the dream; this was oppressive, cold and damp. There was something tied around her face and something cloth-like in her mouth. Her first impulse was to shout but all that came out was a muffled cry that carried no weight. She tried to move her arms and legs, but they were tied. All she could do was lie there and fight the rising alarm.

Don't, she told herself.

Stop, she told herself.

Focus, she told herself.

She concentrated on her breathing first, until it ceased being dragged into her lungs in jagged shards and became something smoother, more even. She couldn't see anything, could taste nothing but the rag in her mouth, so she focused on her other senses. She shifted slightly, feeling whatever she was lying on move. It was soft but the ground beneath it was cold and solid like stone. She could smell dampness and perhaps rotting vegetation. She could hear the lapping of water but not in her immediate vicinity. The air was chill on her cheeks and there was a draught coming from somewhere.

She was on her back, so she tried to sit up but didn't have the strength. She needed to get rid of whatever was over her head but an attempt to shake it free only made her head buzz, as if there was a horde of angry insects inside her skull. Hurt like buggery, too. She stopped, dizziness spinning her mind as if she had been on a fairground ride and nausea rising in her throat like hot, bitter coffee.

She tried to remember what had happened to bring her here, but her memory was dim and fragmented, images of what she could recall draining away as though they were paintings in oils over which someone had poured turpentine. She forced her mind to sharpen. She saw Cormac's cottage. She had been there, looking through the window. There was an open fire, logs flaming. A red glow. A chair. Someone sitting in it. She couldn't see his face. Then sharp pain, flaring lights giving way to that lovely warm darkness. Someone else had been there, but who? She slowed her thoughts down, tried to replay the events again, but she could feel the world tilting, making her even more nauseous. She concentrated, willing her equilibrium to straighten itself, needing to get back to that cottage. She had been at the door, had called out. Had heard that noise inside, like someone walking, someone with a limp, a step being dragged on the floor. Then she had looked through the window and then something crashed into her and she was falling into darkness.

And now she was here, wherever here was, blindfolded, gagged and bound.

Okay, Rebecca, you've got to face it.

You're in the shit.

Now, how the hell do you get out of it?

All good questions, she thought, but they would have to wait because her mind was seriously off kilter. She felt so very tired, so very tired, so very tired. Blinking was like lifting weights, but she fought the desire to sleep. She shouldn't sleep. She mustn't sleep. But she did sleep and she welcomed the return of the warm blackness.

But this time, she wasn't alone.

34

Rebecca hadn't seen her father or heard his voice for some time but he came to her now. She used to see him regularly. She would awaken, or thought she had awakened, to find him sitting on the edge of her bed. Part of her knew it could not be him because he had been gone for some years. Cancer. A single word for an insidious and hateful disease that is also a sentence. Yet when she saw him in her dreams, in her mind, in her imagination, he was not the man who had faded away before her eyes but as he was when she was a child. Tall, strong, wise. Alive.

Only a year or so before, sight of him was merely a manifestation of her unhappiness, an aspect of the stresses she faced, a means of coping. She had reached this understanding herself, not through any kind of analysis but because, in the final conversation she'd had with him, he had more or less told her. Or she had told herself. Frankly, it was too complex for her to even consider as she lay in the soft shadows of sleep, so she accepted that it was John Connolly, alive and well, back with her.

'Daddy?'

She was always a child with him. Always daddy. Never dad, father or John.

You need to wake up, Rebecca.

His voice simply appeared in her mind without his lips moving.

'I don't want to, Daddy.'

You have to.

She groaned. 'Just five more minutes . . .'

That's what she used to say when he or her mum roused her for school. Just five more minutes.

No more minutes. You have to wake up.

'But why? I'm warm and cosy here.'

No, you're not. You're cold and you're in trouble and you need to wake up and do something about it.

'I don't want to.' Her voice, the one in her head, the one in her dream, was petulant. A stroppy teenager pushing back against authority. God, she had been awkward back then.

Yes, you do. You have to wake up and you have to think and you have to do something.

'I can't do anything. It's too hard.'

You can. You will. You have to do it, Rebecca. You have to do it for Stephen and your friends and yourself. You have to do it for me.

'But I can't!' She didn't like that whiny tone. And neither did her father, because his voice hardened and she knew she had stepped over a line, as she had done many times back then.

Stop that. Stop that now and smarten yourself up. Yes, you're in a tight spot but you're clever and you're strong and you can get out of this.

'But how? I can't even see with this thing over my head . . .'

You need to use your head, Rebecca. Stop whingeing and start thinking.

'I can't!'

Ben. Think of Ben.

Mention of her old dog made her fall silent. Her father waited for her to work out what he meant. He would do that, too. He never gave her an answer to a problem but he steered her in the direction of a solution. He used to say that you only learn by working things out for yourself. So what did

Ben have to do with it? They'd had three dogs while she was growing up and the Lab Retriever had been the smartest of the lot, although sometimes he hid it well. But there was a mind working there; her mum used to say that she could see it ticking behind his eyes, especially when it came to food and the manipulation of his humans in order to obtain what he couldn't obtain for himself. He could work out how to circumvent just about anything in order to get what he wanted. If his bed was placed somewhere he didn't like, it was dragged to where he did. He knew when the post was due to be delivered and watched for it, just so he could bark at the mail as it landed in the basket designed to protect both the letters and the postman's fingers. Not that he ever bit anyone, at least not intentionally. Rebecca had experienced a few nips when she played with him as a pup but that was all. It was his habit of eating everything he found that forced them to get a soft muzzle, to prevent him from picking up something that would one day prove to be bad for him. Her father said there were cruel people out there who would put poisoned treats down just for the hell of it. The muzzle was very pliable and fitted over the edge of Ben's nose with a strap that tucked over and behind his ears. It wasn't too tight, just enough to stop him from picking anything up and chewing.

'He hated that muzzle,' she said.

I know.

Rebecca recalled it didn't take Ben long to work out how to take it off himself. When he was out for his walks he would rub his face along anything he could to try to prise it away. Walls, fences, grass. But soon he realised that he was rubbing the wrong way, scraping the offending muzzle further onto his nose. So he backed up as he rubbed it, pulling it down his black muzzle, and it was an easy thing to hook a claw under and then prise it free.

And at that moment Rebecca knew what her father was trying to tell her. She saw him smile and then begin to shrink. She called out to him, but he kept floating away from her.

You can do this, Rebecca. It's a start.

He vanished and she was awake. She was shivering, but her mind was reasonably alert. Ben used the ground and his surroundings to drag that muzzle off. She could do the same with the hood and at least then she could see where she was before working on freeing her hands and feet. She was on her back, so she twisted her body away from whatever she was lying upon until she was on her side, the side of her head on the hard floor. The hood was loose, she had noticed that when she came to earlier, even though she had been unable to shake it off. She scraped her temple in a downward motion on the rough ground, trying to catch the material and make it ride upwards. She could feel the harshness of the stone and bits of gravel scraping her skin through the cloth but she kept at it, rubbing, rubbing, rubbing against the floor, ignoring the pain that thundered through her skull with every movement, fighting back the need to throw up. She couldn't do that with this rag in her mouth and this thing over her head. Concentrate, Becks, you can do this.

You will do this.

'So, what did that solicitor want?'

Shona found Alex and Ray waiting for her when she returned to the house. She considered refusing to answer but then realised that by actually telling the truth she would be even more defiant. 'He's looking for that reporter I spoke to today.' She saw Alex's eyes narrow. 'The one who wanted to know about Fergus.'

Alex flinched. 'We don't talk about him in this house.'

'I know, and that's perhaps part of the problem. Maybe it's time we did.' She held his eyes. 'It's certainly time I did.'

He tried to stare her out for a moment but saw she was prepared to stand her ground. 'What did you tell this reporter?'

232

'The truth.'

He didn't need to ask what that truth was. He had been part of it, after all.

'I told her she shouldn't have spoken to her,' Ray piped up.

Alex allowed his cold gaze to linger on his son for a moment, as if he had spoken out of turn, then returned it to Shona. 'And will you be quoted in whatever story this journalist writes?'

'I don't know. Probably. I was on the record.'

He nodded, as if he wasn't surprised. 'And why is that solicitor looking for her?'

'He's her partner and she's disappeared. I may have been the last person to see her, it seems, in the Black Wood.'

'The Black Wood,' Alex repeated in a monotone.

'Everything seems to come back to the Black Wood, doesn't it? That's where I was to meet Fergus that day, that's where his car was found, that's where I met the reporter and that's where she was seen last. You wouldn't know anything about what happened to her, would you?'

She couldn't read his expression. Sometimes he was an open book to her, but other times he seemed to retreat into this blank place, a black hole from which no light escaped. His eyes were dead, his voice matched. 'Shona, you seem to think I'm some sort of gangster.'

'I'm not sure even a gangster would do what you did five years ago, Alex. What about you, Ray? Do you know what happened to this woman?'

He gave her a half-hearted, nervous smile. 'Why would I know anything?'

'I don't know, Ray,' she said, truthfully. 'But don't you two think it strange that when a reporter starts to look into what happened to Fergus she suddenly vanishes?'

Ray shifted uncomfortably. Alex was very still. He was always very still. 'Reporters have followed the story before,' he said.

'Yes, when it happened. When the search was on. Appeals, news stories. But there has been nothing much since. The occasional reference, but as far as I'm aware nobody has actually started asking questions here in the glen. And they've certainly not spoken to me. But the minute one does, she disappears, same as Fergus. And from the Black Wood, too.'

'What are you trying to say, Shona?' It was Ray, trying to inject some strength into his voice.

'Nothing. Maybe something. I don't know. I just think it's very strange.'

Ray shrugged. 'Coincidence, that's all. I'm sure she'll turn up.'

'Fergus hasn't.'

'I don't want to talk about this,' Alex said, turning away.

Shona's anger flared. 'Well, I do.'

Alex faced her again. 'Why? What possible good will going over this do now?'

'Because I want to know what happened! I need to know what happened!'

'I have no idea what happened.'

'Why did you hate Fergus so much, Alex?'

'I didn't,' Alex said.

'You still can't bring yourself to say his name.'

He breathed in. Out. Controlling his temper. Controlling himself. She was getting to him and that gave her some satisfaction. 'We're doing this now?'

'Yes, we're doing this now,' she said, anger fracturing the words. 'I've tried before but I was too weak to force you. But not any more. Now, I want to know. Why did you hate him with such passion, Alex? Surely not just because he was Dan MacGregor's son?'

'He wasn't right for you.'

'That wasn't your call to make, was it?'

'Yes, it was. I'm your father.'

'Only through an accident of birth.'

He let that pass. He had heard it before from her. 'It was my duty to prevent you from making a big mistake.'

'You didn't try to stop me from marrying Rick.'

'I strongly advised you against it.'

'You didn't lock me in my room.'

He blinked. 'That was different.'

'In what way?'

'The circumstances were different.'

'In what way?' she repeated with added emphasis.

His jaw tightened and he turned his back on her again. 'I don't intend to go into it.'

'Don't walk away again, Alex,' she called out. 'We have to clear this up.'

He didn't reply. He didn't break his step. He opened his study door, entered and closed it behind him. She turned her attention to Ray, who had watched the exchange like a bystander.

'And what about you, Ray? What have you got to say?'

'About what?'

'Fergus. Me. That day.'

His eyes darted away from her. 'What can I say about it? I didn't lock you in your room.'

'No, you were nowhere to be seen, were you? Where were you, Ray?'

He seemed to grow flustered. 'I can't remember, Shona, it was a long time ago. Probably on the estate somewhere.'

Something told her he knew exactly where he was, but she knew him well enough to know that he wouldn't tell her. But she had another barb to throw at him. 'How did Alex find out about Fergus and me, Ray?'

'I told you, I don't know.'

'But you knew about us, didn't you? You'd seen us together.'

'I saw the two of you at the dance, yes, but I didn't know you were actually seeing him for months after that. You kept that to yourself.' He glanced at the door of Alex's study and shook

235

his head. 'For God's sake, drop this, Shona. No good will ever come of it. You'll just upset Dad.'

'And we wouldn't want that, would we, Ray?'

His temper broke then. 'You know what? You just don't know when to leave things alone, you never bloody did. You pick, pick, pick at things until they bleed. You were a spoiled little brat then and you're a spoiled little brat now. That man in there has only ever had your best interests at heart and all you do is spit in his face. Christ, I wish he cared for me as much as he does for you. Frankly, you don't deserve the love he gives you. Let this go, for God's sake. If you know what's good for you, you'll drop it.'

She hadn't seen him show spine like that in a long time. She knew she had a tendency to be bratty, had admitted as much to Rebecca Connolly, but he had always put up with it. Not tonight, it seems. Tonight she had hit a nerve, but she wasn't about to back off.

'If I know what's good for me, Ray? Is that a threat? What are you going to do? Go get that shotgun of yours?'

He groaned in exasperation. 'Dear God, Shona, you just don't know when to fucking quit, do you? You just don't know that we are actually on your side – then, now, always.' When he shook his head, it was almost sad. 'Or maybe you simply don't want to know.'

It was his turn to walk away. She didn't have any further barbs to throw, so she let him.

35

Rebecca slept again, although without the hood this time. She had no idea how long it had taken to scrape it free – first from her chin, then the rest of her face – before a final shake sent jagged pain slicing through her head. She had managed to take in her surroundings, and even though it was dark – so it was night, which was something at least – she saw bare stone walls and gaping windows. Putting that together with the lapping water, she deduced she was in the tower on the Isle of Gulls. Elementary, my dear Watson. The hood was off, but she still had that damned rag in her mouth and her arms and feet remained bound. She saw nothing that might prove useful to cut the rope, but there were bits of rubble and old stones on the floor. It was too dark to drag herself around to search for something suitable and she was so tired. There was an old duvet half underneath her and a couple of blankets crumpled to the side, as if she had kicked them off while she slept. She could feel exhaustion creep over her again. She tried to fight it, knowing that she should stay awake; but she couldn't keep her eyes open. Just a minute is all she needed. She could rest for just a minute.

That's only half the job.

John Connolly was back again. In her mind he held the discarded hood lightly in both hands, examining it as if for forensic traces.

'I know. I'll get to the rest after I've had a sleep. I'm so tired.'

You shouldn't be sleeping, you know. You might have a concussion.

'I'm okay,' she said, even though she knew he was right. That drew a look that she knew so well from her teenage years. Her father could pack more into a single glance than many could with an entire speech, and this one conveyed both scepticism and rebuke.

'I'm on an island in the centre of the loch,' she told him.

I know. But it's not in the centre of the loch, remember. It's closer to the smooth side than it is to the rough.

'How do you know that?'

He gave her a smile. *I know everything you know.*

She couldn't argue with that kind of logic.

Your first job is to get yourself untied.

'Yes, I know that.'

Then you need to get off this island somehow.

'I know that, too.' She resisted the impulse to remind him that if he knew everything she knew, the reverse was also true – it might provoke a look even more stern than before.

You might need Ben's help again.

She was puzzled as to how her old dog could help her again. Her father smiled and dropped the hood back on the ground.

You'll work it out.

He turned away and began to walk into the darkness.

But you must wake up now.

He was almost gone from her sight.

This darkness is only in your mind. It's daylight.

And then he was gone and she was awake. Grey light slanted in through the open doorway and the uncovered windows, but it was threaded with mist. She shivered and stretched her legs as much as she could to stimulate stiff and frozen muscles, then flexed and extended her knees to get the blood moving. She struggled onto her side to better see through the open doorway.

The waters of the loch kissed the edge of the island, but what ripples there were on the surface vanished into a thick, white mist. A fluttering above her made her crane upwards and she saw some seagulls flapping around the open roof. She hoped it didn't rain. She was cold enough, thank you very much.

Her head still threatened to crack open, but she knew she needed to move. She needed to free her hands and then she could set about getting herself off this island somehow. She couldn't keep dragging herself around the floor, she had to get to her feet somehow. Her feet were numb but she rotated her ankles as much as she could to get some heat back into them. She did the same with her hands, feeling the rope rubbing at the flesh of her wrist. The bonds were tight, but not too tight: she could move under them without risk of burning. That was something at least.

She was still on her side, so she bent her legs a little to gain purchase, then tried to lever her upper body onto her knees, but she was stiff and sore, her head still pounding, and she found it impossible. She wasn't sure she would have managed it, even if she hadn't been stiff and sore. How to manoeuvre yourself while you're bound and gagged was not something you were taught at university. She lay there, her breathing ragged, and looked for something to use to work through the ropes. There was a pile of rubble to her right but she didn't fancy trying to clamber over it in her current restricted state. She studied the corner of the stonework around the doorway. That might work, she thought. It would take a while but she didn't have anything more pressing on her agenda.

Using her knees to push herself along the floor, she began to jockey closer to the opening. Gravel and pebbles pressed through her coat and jeans as she scraped over them, but she ignored them. The material was thick and she had a warm woollen sweater on underneath, so she was confident they wouldn't penetrate to break the skin. The doorway wasn't too far anyway. She had no idea how long it took, but she reached her goal and rested for a moment, her head hanging over the threshold, her breath struggling against the rag in her mouth. She felt sick but reminded herself she couldn't throw up with that thing in her mouth. It would be a shame to go to all this effort only to choke on her own vomit. She took her mind off the queasiness by studying the world beyond the doorway. The mist cloaked everything around, so she could not see either bank. That wasn't helpful, Mother Nature, thanks a bunch. So much for sisterhood.

Taking a deep breath, she used the wall as a brace and struggled to a sitting position, jutting her legs out before her. Okay, she thought, as she positioned her back against the corner, feeling for the correct way to sit before she began to rub the ropes around her wrist against the rough stonework. This may take a while, she realised.

She had no clue how long she had been out of it. She thought maybe one night, but she could be wrong. But if she was right then she was now officially a year older.

Happy birthday, Becks.

Stephen didn't go to bed. Neither did Chaz nor Alan. When he'd returned from driving around the loch in his search for Rebecca, he had told them about his conversation with the MacGregors and his encounter with Alex Burnes and Shona. He had even wandered around the Black Wood, using the torch app on his phone to light the way, in the hope that he would find her there, but all he did was startle a deer, which bounced away into the dark with stunning agility and grace. A mist had begun to seep between the tree boughs and eventually became so thick the beam of his phone simply bounced back. He had to aim it at the ground in order to follow the well-beaten path back to the road. The only sound that broke the overpowering silence was the cry of an owl somewhere in the trees.

The route back became completely alien, thanks to the blanket of white drifting across the headlight beams, so he took the journey slowly. He made it to the cottage without incident, hoping that perhaps Rebecca would be waiting for him.

But she wasn't. And she hadn't called the boys, either.

As he stood in the cottage's hallway, all the strength that had sustained him through the night's travels began to desert him. His muscles, which had been taut for hours, gave way and his mind wilted. His search had been buoyed by hope: that he would meet Rebecca on the road, or that someone would tell him where she had gone or that he had missed her and she was home. That hope was dashed now and his body was ready to collapse. Tears stung behind his eyes and his breath left him in a gush, as if he had been holding it in all afternoon and evening.

It was Alan who spotted the signs and told Chaz to take him to the armchair and settle him in while he bustled into the kitchen. The fire was blazing and the heat began to bring some sensation back to Stephen's skin. He hadn't realised how cold he was, so focused had he been on the task in hand. Chaz poured him a whisky and watched as he sipped it, its peaty warmth firing his blood.

Once he'd finished the dram, drunk the strong, sweet tea and ate the chocolate biscuit that Alan had brought him, he told them what he had learned, which was basically nothing. After Rebecca interviewed Shona in the Black Wood she seemed to have simply vanished.

Eventually they slept, Stephen fitfully in the armchair, the boys wrapped up together on the comfortable settee. Every now and again Stephen woke and threw a couple of logs on the fire to keep the heat in the room. Each time, he checked his phone in case he had missed a message alert while he had dozed. But there was nothing. He even tried calling her a couple of times, but it went straight to voicemail.

He had watched the light beyond the closed curtains merge from black to grey. He stood, stretched his aching muscles and bones, and moved quietly into the kitchen to click on the kettle. He eased the vertical blinds open slightly to gaze out on the wall of grey mist obscuring everything but a patch of wan grass. The fence and trees beyond the small garden were nothing more than hazy silhouettes.

He thought about Rebecca out there on her own. Was she injured? Had she been taken by someone? He couldn't contemplate her lying dead somewhere. He couldn't accept that. She was out there, he knew it. He gave the mist another look. She had been missing overnight and that now merited official cause for concern. He dialled 999.

If she was hurt somewhere and he had missed her, she would have to be found soon before the elements got to her.

Rebecca wasn't sure her exertions were making any difference to the ropes but they were at least warming her up. Her wrists stung where they rubbed against the stone wall. She stopped now and again to tug at the bonds but they didn't seem to be loosening at all. Finally, she decided she wasn't getting anywhere. She took a breather in order to look around for something sharper that might do the trick. The pile of rubble she had noted earlier was her best bet, but the problem was it was against the far wall. She eased herself away from the doorway and began to wiggle backwards, feet flat and pushing her along on her buttocks. She didn't want to lie down again, as she might not be able to struggle upright once more; she had only succeeded the first time with the use of the wall as a brace. She knew this abuse would not do her coat any good, but it couldn't be helped.

A few minutes later she reached the pile of stones and pivoted on her haunches in order to study it. She saw one likely tool, a rock that had once been circular but had split in two, exposing a serrated edge. However, it was sitting near the top of the pile. She wasn't sure if she could haul herself up the unstable heap of rocks, so, she decided, if she couldn't get to the rock, then it would have to come to her. She judged the distance, and believed she could reach it with her feet and pull it down. She leaned back and propped herself up on her extended arms. It was uncomfortable – actually bloody painful – but she ignored it. She then stretched her legs up the fallen stones to catch the edge of the one she wanted with the heel of her walking boot and tried to tip it towards her.

The bastard didn't move.

She swore. She didn't often curse, but she did now and with a fluency that would have made her mother reach for the Palmolive.

Calm down, Becks. Think about Robert the Bruce and the spider. If at first you don't succeed . . . Only, that story was a fake: thank you very much, Alan and your book learning.

She took a breath and straightened her legs again, this time resting both feet on the rock and bending her knees in an attempt to tug it forward. She felt it move, just a little, before her heels slid off again.

She swore once more. This time she would have made a sailor cover his ears.

For God's sake, Becks, put your energy into the task at hand. She sat up to relieve the stress on her arms, her legs resting on the sloping pile. She thought about kicking it with both feet but worried that any mini rock fall she might cause could injure her. She couldn't risk that. She rotated her shoulders as much as her bound hands would allow and discovered that her kinks had kinks of their own. When she got out of here, she would get Stephen to give her one of his massages. She didn't know if he knew what he was doing but it always felt good.

He would be worried sick, she knew that. And he would be looking for her, she knew that too. But he didn't know where she had gone. She should have phoned him, she also knew that. She should have told him that she was going to see Cormac, but she had convinced herself that it was something she had to do alone. Now she knew that she had feared Stephen would have talked her out of it, reminded her that she had been warned away from him. But, she reasoned, as she gathered her strength for another attempt at moving that fucking rock, the warnings had been to protect Cormac from intrusion, not her from harm. Nobody had said he was in any way dangerous. When she got out of here, she'd put that right. She didn't know what he had hit her with but her head still hurt.

Nobody had said that he had someone else living with him in that remote cottage. She didn't know if the person she had seen sitting in front of the fire was Cormac or his guest, but there had definitely been two people. The person she saw and the one who hit her. So who the hell was that?

She had a theory.

But that was something to think about later, because right now she had other things to do. She glared at the jagged hunk of stone as if it was mocking her. Right, you bastard, this is it. This time you're going down.

She edged her butt forward to get more purchase, then leaned back again, aching arms shaking as they supported her, and stretched her legs. With both boots hooked on the rock's edge, she dug them in, feeling the sharp edge against her heel. She bent her knees slowly, moving the rock gingerly. Easy now, Becks, concentrate on it. She pulled at it, some smaller stones dislodging from around its base and tumbling down the surface of the pile. She tugged again and the rock budged even more, two larger pieces on either side stirring with it. She tried to work out their trajectory if they fell but couldn't. If they hit her, they wouldn't cause that much damage, would they? A bruise or two, maybe. She could handle that. She convinced herself that they wouldn't land with enough force to break any bones, and hauled at the rock again. It began to tip out of the space it had held for who knew how long but it still wasn't completely clear. The larger blocks on either side twitched again, but she was ready to try to twist out of the way if they tumbled in her direction. One last go, Becks, what have you got to lose?

She pulled once more and the stone came free, causing further smaller pieces to cascade down the mound of rubble. One of the larger stones slid away too, but nowhere near Rebecca's legs. She pushed herself back and positioned her new tool correctly, then wriggled herself round, looking over her shoulder to see the jagged edge as she twisted her shoulder to place her bound wrists over it.

Here we go, she thought as she rubbed the ropes against this sharper surface.

It was Chaz's phone that rang. Stephen was busy in the kitchen making breakfast; he had to keep himself occupied somehow and making food seemed to be the obvious way to do it. He intended setting out again soon, but he knew he had to eat something, even though his guts were tense and he didn't feel like it at all. He had bacon frying, toast toasting and coffee ready. The ringing continued and he heard movement from the sitting room, then Chaz's voice, slurred with sleep, saying, 'Hello? Elspeth? What time is it?'

Feet padded through the hallway, then Chaz was in the kitchen, the phone to his ear.

'Right,' he said, giving Stephen a nod and glancing at the clock on the wall. 'What? No, we know . . . hang on.'

Chaz laid his phone on the table and hit loudspeaker.

'You're live with Stephen too,' he said.

'Good – Stephen, where the hell is Rebecca?'

'We don't know, Elspeth.'

'What do you mean you don't know?'

Stephen hooked the bacon slices one by one and laid them on a plate. He had to keep busy, had to keep his hands occupied. 'She went out on a story, didn't come back.'

'When?'

He placed the plate under the grill to keep the bacon warm while he cracked open two eggs. 'Yesterday morning.'

'She's been gone overnight?' He had never heard Elspeth worried before.

Another egg. Crack. 'Yes.'

'Have you contacted the police?'

'Yes, but she's an adult and not vulnerable and there's no evidence of any harm having befallen her, but they said they'd send someone out today.'

'When today?'

'They weren't clear.'

He heard an angry sigh. 'I knew something was up. I've been calling Becks since yesterday afternoon and it's not like her not to answer her phone.'

Stephen didn't mention that she had never returned any of his calls either. He poured Chaz a coffee and laid it on the table in front of him. Busy, keep busy. 'Why were you calling her, Elspeth?'

'She asked me to do some digging about this guy down there, Cormac Devlin.'

Stephen felt his fingers tingle. 'Why?'

'She felt he had a history.'

'And does he?'

'Oh yes . . .'

She began to outline what she had learned. It wasn't much, but it was enough, and Stephen's instincts told him where Rebecca had gone.

36

Rebecca felt the fronds of the rope weakening and that gave her the impetus to scrape with renewed vigour, or as much as she could muster given her head still throbbed. She continued to fight the desire to simply lie down and sleep. It took another few minutes before she was able to jerk at the bonds with sufficient force to prise her hands fully free. She flexed her fingers, rubbed the flesh around her wrists and then shook her hands to loosen the numb tendons before she plucked the rag from her mouth, licked her lip and stretched her jaws. The after-taste would linger for a while. Her hands trembled as she unpicked the remainder of the knot on each wrist and let the ropes drop to the ground, then she hitched up her knees and worked at the bonds around her ankles. They were tricky and her fingers were still cold, but she finally managed to ease them apart, allowing her to unwind the rope and kick it free. She pushed herself unsteadily to her feet, rotating her ankles carefully, then gingerly placed her weight on them. They seemed fine, a bit frozen but that would pass. Her progress on stiff and sore joints to the doorway was slow and hesitant, as if she was learning to walk again. She still felt slightly nauseous, but losing the gag had helped with that.

The mist blanketing the water limited visibility to twenty feet or so. The island was not large – little more than a perimeter around the tower – but she walked it stiff-legged, trying not to disturb the gulls sitting on the rocks and grass. She could neither see a bank nor hear anything apart from the occasional squawk of a bird. She tried calling out for help. The first couple of times her voice was weak and hoarse, but practice made perfect and she managed a few shouts at considerably higher decibels. She listened for a reply but the mist dampened all sound. She looked up, hoping to see a blue tinge that suggested it was clearing, but all was a uniform grey.

Okay, Becks, you're on your feet. You're outside the tower. What now?

Frankly, she had no idea.

Val Roach was surprised when she was told Elspeth McTaggart was on the line. She had dealt with her a few times in the past, but since Rebecca had become the mainstay of the agency Elspeth had taken a back seat. Rebecca had her direct number and the fact that she had obviously not passed it along spoke well of her in Roach's mind.

Roach barely got a hello out before Elspeth cut in. 'Have you heard from Rebecca at all?'

There was a worried edge in the woman's voice. Roach knew Elspeth to be hard-headed, even brash: and something must have happened. 'A couple of days ago she . . .'

'She's disappeared and your lot won't do anything about it. Seriously, has she to be found dead before anything is done?'

'Wait,' Roach interjected, used to attacks on Police Scotland and knowing there was little point in retaliating with reason. 'Back up. When was she last seen?'

'Yesterday morning.'

'With Mr Jordan?'

'No, she left him to follow up a story.'

There's a shocker, she thought. 'Fergus MacGregor, right?'

Elspeth's pause conveyed surprise. 'Right.'

Roach knew the woman was wondering how she knew but pressed on. 'And no word from her at all? No phone calls, no messages, nothing?'

'I've been phoning her, so has Stephen. No reply.'

'And he's reported it?'

'Yes, that's what I said. And your lot are doing sweet FA, as usual.'

Roach let that pass again. She knew Elspeth cared for Rebecca and it was emotion talking. 'Leave it with me. I've got friends in Perth.'

Elspeth's thank you was curt and then she was gone. Roach stared at the phone for a few moments. Rebecca was smart and resourceful, but her single-mindedness was apt to get her into trouble, though Roach didn't believe she would be so cruel as to go off the radar for over twenty-four hours. Not willingly anyway. All her instincts told her that this had to relate to Fergus MacGregor.

She'd always known that if anything was to break in this case, Rebecca would be the one to make it happen. She hoped that it hadn't somehow broken her.

Stephen stared at the mist floating across the road, turning over in his mind what Elspeth had told them. Chaz had insisted on accompanying him and was at the wheel, driving as swiftly as he could while remaining cautious. Visibility was down to around twenty feet and the loch to their right vanished in a sea of grey. Alan had remained at the cottage in case the police called in. He had urged Stephen to wait, but he refused. He had convinced himself that Becks had decided to visit this Cormac character. He could kick himself for not thinking of it sooner. Of course she would go and see him, even though she had been warned away from him by locals. It was in her DNA.

He checked the satnav on his phone and said, 'It should just be a mile or so down here. Looks like we have to hike for a while.'

Chaz nodded, his face set in tight lines, either through the driving or what they were about to do, or a mixture of both. 'You sure we're doing the right thing, Stephen?'

'I can't simply sit back there and wait. Becks could be hurt, could be trussed up somewhere.'

'But this guy is supposed to be harmless, right?'

Stephen stared at the phone screen. 'Nobody is completely harmless, Chaz. We're all capable of extreme acts if we feel threatened.'

Chaz's grip tightened on the wheel as he peered ahead. 'You think it's possible he's harmed Becks?'

Stephen didn't reply. He didn't want to think about what might have happened. He just wanted to get to this cottage high on the hill and speak to this man himself. 'Pull in where you can up ahead. There should be some sort of track to the left there.'

Chaz checked his rear mirror and slowed, spotted the opening and steered into it. He studied the rutted track snaking upwards through the woodland. 'I think I could drive us up there.'

Stephen was already opening his door, grateful to be moving and hoping it would ease the tension already stiffening his muscles. 'No, I don't want to warn him I'm coming. And you stay here. I don't know how long it will take me to get up there, but if I'm not back in an hour or so, call the cavalry.'

He saw Chaz was unhappy with this arrangement, but he didn't give him time to argue. He pulled the hood of his thick jacket over his head and began to climb the hill.

Rebecca completed what must have been her sixth circuit of the small island but – surprise! – nothing changed. She felt like a goldfish and the words of Albert Einstein entered her head, that insanity was doing the same thing in the same way over and over again and expecting a different result. The view remained the same, the mist didn't lift, she didn't come upon a boat she had hitherto missed, no rescue vessel emerged from the gloom. She recalled that Harry had told her that the island was once reached by a causeway but Stephen had informed her that rising water levels had encroached on the land so she had no idea if it still existed. She tried calling out again but felt she was doing little more than screaming into a void. And it hurt her head anyway.

Panic began to well up again, but she fought it down. This was no time for that, she told herself; this was a time for thinking. She sat down on a rock, breathed deeply to counter the queasiness in her stomach, and stared into the mist, considering her options. She could sit there and wait for someone to come, perhaps Cormac. He had dumped her with no food or water, surely he didn't mean her to starve? Or perhaps he did . . .

Okay, what were her other options? The mist couldn't hang around all day, could it? Actually, perhaps it could. But if it lifted she could somehow signal to a passing car or someone walking on the bank. The crannog was closer to the north side than it was to the south, but how much closer? She couldn't see either bank at the moment, so tried to gauge the distance from memory, but she had really only viewed the island and its tower while passing in the car.

She was hungry, cold and still woozy from the bump on the head. She hoped she wasn't concussed. She reached up, as she had done a number of times since she had freed herself, to touch the tender spot, feeling a huge lump, but the skin didn't seem broken. Hard-headed woman, that's what her mum and dad called her. As a child she'd had bumps and scrapes, as children do, but her thick skull always protected her from serious injury. It had done it again. Hard-headed woman – wasn't there an old song called that? She wracked her memory for the singer but came up with nothing.

Forget it, Becks, concentrate on the matter at hand, for God's sake. How the hell are you getting off this island?

Stephen made good time climbing the hill track, clambering without hesitation over a wooden gate that appeared out of the mist. It might have been there for a reason, but if it was to keep people out it was severely lacking. A garden wall began to take shape and as he neared it he saw the dark bulk of roofs and walls beyond. He stopped at the gate, squinting through the mist for sight of Cormac himself. He listened for any sound, but it was as if someone had hit a mute button. Not even a bird sang.

He clicked the latch and stepped onto the path. He didn't care if this Cormac character wasn't keen on visitors, he was about to have one. His footsteps on the gravel were unnaturally loud, so any surprise his arrival might have brought was already heralded. He reached the front door and rattled the letterbox.

He waited.

No answer.

He moved to his left, examined the gap between the cottage and the garage and thought about walking along it but then decided against it. He put his face to a space between the wooden slats of the garage and in the dim light beyond saw tables with cages and heard the flutter of a bird. He retraced his steps and tried the door again. Still no answer.

Bugger it, he said to himself. I'm here now, might as well be hung for a sheep as a lamb. He moved back to the narrow passageway and walked to the rear of the cottage, making sure that he made plenty of noise as he did so. He now wanted Cormac to know he was here. The courtyard was deserted apart from a battered old pick-up truck. That didn't mean Cormac was at home, though, because he was known to walk across the moors and through the woods. Stephen tried the back door but it was locked. He wandered to the outbuildings, peeped through windows. One was a workshop, another a storeroom filled with logs waiting to be chopped.

He stood in the centre of the courtyard and wondered what to do next. Smoke drifted from the chimney of the cottage and hung low over the roof, but again that didn't necessarily mean the man was inside. In this weather he would keep the stove burning. But it was worth a look through the windows anyway.

He followed the path back to the front of the house, decided against hitting the letterbox and moved directly to the window at the far end of the cottage. Something in the flowerbed below caught his eyes, a flash of red and white he recognised. He stooped and picked up the mist-dampened notebook. He rippled through the pages, recognising Rebecca's unique mix of shorthand and longhand. There was no way she would throw away her notebook. She had every notebook she had ever used stored in her flat in Inverness, taking up almost an entire bookcase. She'd been here. May still be here.

He stepped closer to the window and cupped his hand against the glass. He saw a kitchen table, some modern cupboards and accessories. The oldest item he could make out was the Rayburn stove that took up the bulk of one wall and had probably been in the cottage when Cormac bought it. Logs burned in the open fireplace, casting a glow around the room, and in it he made out a figure sitting in a chair nearby. He rapped his knuckles against the glass. The bastard must have heard him rattle the letterbox but had ignored it.

'Mr Devlin,' he shouted through the window. 'I need to speak to you.'

The figure seemed to move slightly, but it could have been a trick of the flickering shadow.

'Mr Devlin, it's very important. Can you please come to the door?'

The head didn't lift from the fire. Stephen's anger began to burn. He believed people were entitled to their privacy. He believed they should live the life they want. But Becks had been here, the notebook was proof of that, and something had happened either here or afterwards. He needed to know when she had called, how long she had stayed and if she had told him where she was heading next. If, indeed, she left.

He slammed the heel of his hand angrily against the stone wall and strode to the front door, where he pummelled his fist against the wood. 'I know you're in there, Cormac,' he shouted, 'so open this door. I'm not leaving until I talk to you.' He fell silent, his head cocked for any sound from beyond the door, but there was nothing. His rage finally erupted. 'Damn it, I know Rebecca was here. I've got her notebook. Now open this bloody door or I'll kick the fucking thing in!'

He gave the man the opportunity to reply but nothing came. He stepped back, studying the doorway. It was solid and slightly elevated. His threat to kick it in had been overly ambitious.

'Fine,' he said, settling himself on the step. 'I'll sit here all day if I have to. I'm not going anywhere, Cormac, believe me.'

Rebecca could feel herself slipping a little, her head spinning, her stomach lurching. She was growing anxious and that wasn't a good thing. She needed to do something. She needed to take some kind of action.

What was it her dad had said in her dream? She would need Ben's help again? What did that mean, she wondered? That was the problem with visions in dreams, they assumed you knew what the hell they were talking about. Probably because, on some level, you did. She thought about Ben. Okay, he was smart, he worked out how to remove that muzzle and that had already helped. He was loving, enjoyed a snuggle whenever he could get it, but unless Rebecca could get up close and personal with a seagull there wasn't anything of that nature in her immediate future. He liked food – yeah, he was a Labrador – but as her stomach kept reminding her, Rebecca didn't even have as much as an old dog biscuit on her. Ben barked at the postman but Rebecca felt barking wouldn't help her situation any more than shouting had. So what else did the dog like or do that reflected on this situation?

Her eye fell on the waters of the loch gently brushing at the ground near to her feet. Ben liked to swim. Rebecca recalled a trip to a loch – she couldn't remember which one – where Ben had launched himself into the water from one side of a short spit of land, swum so far out that Rebecca had begun to grow concerned, then came back and climbed back onto dry land on the other side. A quick shake, showering Rebecca with cold water, and then he leaped back in again to repeat the process. Ben loved to swim, in rivers not so much, but in the sea. And in lochs.

She considered it. Could she? Should she? She had been planning on going wild swimming anyway, hadn't she? So what's the difference?

Well, she reminded herself, the difference was that in her case, wild swimming entailed wading into the water and swimming not that far away from the bank, with Stephen keeping an eye out in case she ran into trouble. Here, she had no firm notion of how far she was from dry land other than the island on which she sat. And she would have to do it near naked, because she hadn't had the foresight to wear her wetsuit before she set out yesterday. If indeed it was only yesterday that she had set out – she no longer had any way of telling. She hadn't done her research about the loch. She didn't know what the currents were like, or what lay under the surface. It was winter, so algae shouldn't be a problem. That was something at least.

She stepped closer to the water's edge. It would be bloody cold, but she was already cold. And hungry. And her head hurt. She blinked into the mist, as if visualising the rough side. That would be her best bet, if she was to do this. It was further away, but she remembered Stephen telling her something about there being a sharp dip between the island and the smooth side, and that might mean stronger currents.

Part of her couldn't believe she was even considering this. The loch was maybe a kilometre wide, so that meant she would have at the very least to swim half of that – five hundred metres – before she reached the shore. She had no idea if she had ever swum that distance, but she didn't think so, and not in open water. She picked her way between the rocks to the southern edge of the island and stared into the mist again, wishing she could see a ghost of the bank.

This is a bad idea, Rebecca.

But how long would she have to wait here with no food and limited shelter? She had already screamed for help but she wasn't even sure her voice had reached the bank.

She chewed at the inside of her mouth, a shiver running through her, the pain in her head like a tight band, her guts churning.

Sod it, she thought. I can't sit around here waiting for something to happen. I have to make it happen.

I can do this.

37

A man's voice was complaining loudly about climbing the hill and about the cold and the fact that he was climbing the hill in the cold. The words reached through the mist towards Stephen before he saw the two officers emerge from it and stand at the gate. One was tall and overweight, and probably not as fit as he should have been, and he was the one doing all the moaning. The other was smaller and trimmer, and she looked as if she could have run up the hill and back down again without breaking sweat.

He rose as they came through the gate, the woman in the lead while her partner panted behind.

'Mister Jordan?' she asked.

'Yes,' he said, approaching them and meeting them halfway up the gravel path.

'I'm PC Mann, this is PC Merrick.'

The two men nodded to each other.

'Your friends told us where you were,' Mann said. 'You should have waited for us, you know.'

'I know,' Stephen replied, 'but I've been worried sick.'

'Still no word from Ms . . . Connolly, right?'

'No, nothing, but I think the guy who lives here knows something.'

'What makes you think Mr Devlin knows something, Mr Jordan?'

'I think Rebecca came here yesterday, and if so, this was the last place she was seen.'

'What makes you think that?'

Stephen handed her the reporter's notebook. 'I found this in the flowerbed over there.'

Mann flipped through the pages. 'And this is definitely hers?'

'Yes.'

'She's a reporter, right?'

'Yes.'

'And what was she doing here?'

'Following a story.'

PC Merrick had caught his breath sufficiently to throw in, 'I thought you two were on holiday here. From Inverness, right?'

'We are.'

'And yet your girlfriend was following a story?'

'She's dedicated.'

Merrick's eyebrow flicked, an indication that he either wasn't sure reporters could be dedicated or that perhaps Rebecca wasn't fully committed to the relationship. Or maybe that was just the way Stephen saw it, because it was something he'd been thinking about while waiting on the step, occasionally shouting out to the man inside that he was still there. Once, he had heard some movement, someone with a dragging step, but apart from that there was nothing. No rattle of dishes, no radio playing, no TV. He peered through the window again but the figure hadn't moved from the chair. So, two people in there then.

Mann flicked through the pages of the notebook, trying to read Rebecca's final notes. Good luck with that, Stephen thought. Sometimes Rebecca herself said she needed an Enigma machine to decode her scribbles.

'What story is she following?'

'The disappearance of Fergus MacGregor a few years ago.'

'Aye, I remember that,' said Merrick. 'Yon's a real head scratcher, so it is.' He saw Mann's puzzled expression. She was younger, probably hadn't been in the force at the time. 'Lad went missing around here, never seen again.'

'So what made Ms Connolly think Mr Devlin knows something?'

Stephen looked back at the cottage, thought he saw the flash of a face at the window. 'He's a bit of a recluse . . .'

'Yeah, we know that.'

'He was friendly with the missing man. The last place they know this Fergus MacGregor visited was the Black Wood. Cormac in there' – he jerked his thumb in the direction of the door behind him – 'is always walking round there. I suppose Rebecca just wanted to speak to him, especially because of his background.'

'Aye, we know about that,' said Merrick. 'Your lassie has some connections.'

Stephen didn't understand, but Mann explained. 'It seems there's a DCI up in Inverness who has been in touch with our duty officer, explained all about this guy here and suggested maybe we should follow this up.' She held up the notebook. 'This clinches it, I think.' Despite the fact that she was younger and had been on the job for less time than her neighbour, she was obviously the dominant one of the partnership. 'Okay,' she said, handing the notebook back. 'Let's go see what Mr Devlin has to say then.'

Her pace was brisk as she stepped around Stephen and moved to the door. Stephen was impressed by her decisive action. The older officer hung back, obviously not in wholehearted agreement, or perhaps because he didn't like the fact that Val Roach had interfered with matters outside her own division. Or perhaps he was just lazy.

Mann slapped the door with her open hand. 'Mr Devlin, this is the police. PC Sarah Mann. I'd like you to open the door, please.'

She leaned into the wood as she waited. 'Mr Devlin, please open the door.'

'There's nothing we can do if the guy doesn't want to talk to us,' said Merrick.

Mann held up her hand to silence him, her body tensing as she heard something from inside. 'He's moving,' she said quietly.

Stephen suspected Cormac wasn't about to open the door, but he may have seen the uniforms and that must have spooked him. He drifted to the side to look at the courtyard at the rear. He heard the click of a lock turning.

'He's heading out the back way,' he said and broke into a run along the narrow path. He heard Mann tell Merrick to wait where he was and then her footsteps pounding after him. Stephen reached the corner first and saw a tall man wearing a thick, waterproof bushman's coat, face dark from working outdoors and deeply lined, grey hair springing from his head as if it was electro-charged. But it was what he carried that he focused on.

'That's Rebecca's bag,' he said as Mann surged past to stand between him and Cormac.

'Mr Devlin, I need you to stay where you are,' she said, her voice both firm and somehow reassuring.

'I didn't do anything,' he said.

'Okay, I understand, but you need to let me have that bag and let us talk to you. We can get it all sorted.'

'Where's Rebecca?' Stephen demanded, stepping forward, but Mann raised her arm and blocked him. Cormac took a few faltering paces backwards, putting a large barrel filled with earth between him and them, his face awash with fear and something else. Stephen thought it was guilt.

'Leave this to me, Mr Jordan,' Mann said, without taking her eyes from the man backing away from them. 'Cormac, my name is Sarah Mann, okay? Just take it easy. Relax. We just need to ask a few questions, nothing to worry about, right? Now, can you tell us where you got the bag, Cormac?'

The man's eyes flashed from her to Stephen and back again. He moved away further, clutching the bag to his chest. His head moved frantically, as if looking for a way to escape.

'Please stay where you are, Cormac. We're not going to hurt you, I promise.' Mann's voice was soothing but she didn't try to follow him, Stephen assumed because to do so would appear threatening. 'We just need to know where the young lady is, can you help us?'

Cormac's head tilted slightly to the left, as if he was listening to something. 'I didn't do anything.' His words were stretched thin and reedy through fear.

'We didn't say you did, Cormac. We just need to find her because she may be injured. You understand that, don't you? You wouldn't want someone to be lying hurt somewhere and not have help come, would you?'

His head shook imperceptibly but Stephen couldn't tell if it was in response to Mann's questions or if he was answering someone only he could hear. 'Can't tell you,' he said.

'Where is she?' Stephen asked the question before he knew it, but his patience was non-existent.

Mann shot him a look that told him to leave it to her, then faced Cormac again. 'Tell us, Cormac. We can't help if we don't know what's wrong. Do you know where the young woman is?'

Cormac looked down at the ground. His head bobbed once, twice.

'Okay,' Mann said gently. 'Good. Now, can you tell me, and let me go and fetch her?'

This time he shook his head. 'He won't let me tell you.'

'Who won't let you, Cormac?'

Another head shake, a few more steps away. Then he seemed to crouch and his voice dropped to a whisper. 'Ssh, he can hear us.'

'Who can hear us, Cormac? Is there someone in the house?'

He raised a finger to his lips and looked around him furtively. 'Can't say, mustn't say. He doesn't want me to say. You need to go.'

'I can't go, Cormac, you know that. I need to find the young woman.'

'She left,' he said.

'To go where?'

His head shook again.

Mann's voice was still calm and soothing. She still hadn't taken a step closer to him. 'Where did she go, Cormac?'

'I don't know.'

'Are you sure? Are you sure you don't know?' His nod was strong, but his eyes were not. 'Does the person in the house know?'

His eyes flicked to the open back door just as Merrick emerged from around the corner. 'What's the deal, Sarah? I'm standing down there like a spare . . .'

Cormac was startled by the sudden appearance of the big police officer. He staggered backwards, still clutching the bag tightly to his body with both arms as if it was a trophy he wasn't going to part with. His head swivelled, looking for an escape route, knowing he was hemmed in at the back, before he fixed on a spot beyond Mann. She saw the look and seemed to know what he planned.

'Don't run, Cormac . . .'

No sooner had she uttered the words than he made a break for the space between her and the walls of the outbuildings.

He couldn't move fast, though.

Not dragging his right leg.

Rebecca shivered as she stood near-naked on the edge of the water. Here we go, she thought. She began to wade in, the cold not too bad because her flesh was already frozen. She would try a few strokes, she had told herself, and if she felt she couldn't do it, she would come back. Just a few feet out and then come back if it was too much. She was up to her hips now, the cold biting, but she thought it would improve once she grew used to it and was actually moving. She was a strong swimmer, she was reasonably fit – not tip-top, as her legs had proved when she'd climbed the path to Cormac's house – but she estimated she could do the five hundred metres in less than fifteen minutes. The big threat was hypothermia, but she knew that took twenty to thirty minutes to set in, even in icy water, and the loch wasn't that bad. Even if it did set in, she thought she had a useful time buffer before she would lose consciousness. The problem would be when she reached land: she would have to get dry and find a heat source very quickly, but that was something to be tackled at the other end.

She was up to her chest now, so she pushed her feet against the rocky bottom and began to swim. Nice, easy strokes. Keep going.

You can do this, Becks.

With both Mann and Merrick controlling Cormac, Stephen took the opportunity to slip into the cottage through the back door. He knew he probably shouldn't – he could contaminate any evidence just by being there, and that could be used by a lawyer, like him, to poke holes in any prosecution case – but he wasn't a lawyer today. He was a man who needed to find the woman he loved. He found himself in a small utility room with a door directly ahead opening to a corridor, the boxed-in staircase to the left, a wall to the right, the front door directly ahead. He moved carefully, ears pricked for any sound.

'Becks?' he called out, but there was no answer.

A door to his right led to a nicely furnished sitting room. It was darkened, the curtains drawn, but nobody sat in the comfortable armchairs or couch; the fire was dark and cold, and the entire room felt bleak with lack of use. He turned to the left, past the front door, and headed to the kitchen. Some grey light came through that window from the outside, but not much, although there was still that red glow from the fire. The man he had seen through the window hadn't moved from the chair and didn't look up when he entered. From what Stephen could see, he was bundled up in a number of thick blankets, his face turned away, looking at the fire.

'Hello?' Stephen said.

The man didn't answer, didn't move. Stephen felt something cold creep through his body and slide up his back and neck. As he edged closer he began to see more of the face, and knew that this man hadn't responded before because he couldn't. The shadow of the flames flickered in the hollow eyes, and on the tight discoloured skin stretched back from exposed teeth, and the straggling hair.

A movement behind him made him turn, and Mann said to him, 'What the hell are—' Her gaze landed on the figure in the chair, and her eyes widened a little as she reached the same conclusion as Stephen. 'Jesus!'

'Yeah,' said Stephen, his throat strangely tight. 'I think we've just found Fergus MacGregor.'

38

She had made a serious mistake.

Rebecca didn't get far out before she realised it. Her fingers, which had been numb enough before, became so cold that she no longer felt the water. Her teeth chattered, and shivers – no, convulsions – rippled through her body. She should turn, go back, dry herself as best she could on her shirt and wrap herself in her coat, then wait for someone to save her. The mist couldn't settle forever and she could alert someone, somehow.

She glanced over her shoulder to see how far she had come, but the mist had closed in around her. She couldn't see the island, she couldn't see the tower. She couldn't see a damn thing apart from the mist and the water. If she turned back now, she might miss the island completely – it wasn't that large, after all – and end up in the middle of the loch. Christ, she could even be there already because she wasn't certain she was heading in the right direction.

She had no idea what she had been thinking, but all she could do was keep going. The decision had been made, rightly or wrongly, and she couldn't unmake it. She was like a great white shark: if she stopped swimming, she would die.

She forced herself to keep moving. Concentrated her mind on her strokes – in, out, back, in, out, back. Ignore the cold. Ignore everything but forward motion. In. Out. Back. Legs flexing, extending, kicking. In. Out. Back. Keep going, keep going, eyes fixed ahead for sight of the dark bulk of land forming out of the never-ending grey. In. Out. Back. Flex. Extend.

She was slowing down; she knew she was slowing down. Her arms, her legs, felt so cold, so heavy, so dead.

In.

Out.

Back.

Flex.

Extend.

This was a mistake.

Stop it, stop it. Focus.

In.

Out.

Flex.

Back.

Extend.

Out.

How far had she come? How far did she have to go? Not far enough. Too far. This was a mistake.

Stop it!

In.

Back.

Extend.

Flex.

In.

Out.

Extend.

Was she moving at all now? Was she treading water? She had no way to tell. She had nothing to fix upon. No landmark, no sky, nothing. She could be swimming in circles and, God, she was so cold, so very cold. And tired. Her muscles, those few she could still feel, were like lead weights, dragging her down.

Flex.

Out.

266

Back.

Maybe she could stop, just for a moment, to catch her breath. Just for a moment. Catch her breath.

She stopped, floated for that moment on the still waters, fully intending to strike out again but never doing so. She felt her body go limp and she slipped under the surface. She wasn't that cold now; the truth was, she didn't feel much of anything, not even the water around her, below her, above her. She looked up at the surface and felt suddenly at peace. None of it really mattered: not the cold, not the need to get to safety, not the story, any story. She could lie here all day, just looking up at the surface, at the way it rippled and flowed in tiny patterns. It was soothing, it was . . .

No! She wasn't giving up. She couldn't give up.

She forced her legs to kick back to the surface. It wasn't that far. She broke through, gasped for air, gulped it in, arms splashing. She cried out, she didn't know what, but she did it anyway. It was a watery shout but a shout all the same.

And then she felt her muscles weighing her down again, pulling her back under. She resisted. She kicked and she flailed, but she knew it was useless; she was going under again. Would it really be that bad to just give in to it, Becks? Just let it happen. Slip away, peacefully.

Yes, it bloody well would!

She pushed upwards again, peaty water spouting from her mouth before she could suck in huge lungfuls of air. Coughing. Spitting out more water. Another cry, hoarser, weaker, the movements of her hands and arms and her legs slower, less frenzied.

And then she was under again. It was sudden, it was complete. She was sinking down and down and she didn't have the strength to fight it again, not any more. She had done all she could. She had tried. She had failed. Accept it, Becks, accept the inevitable.

267

She stopped struggling, her arm still outstretched as if trying to reach the surface, which seemed so far above her, so very far, but her limbs were floating free now, her fingers relaxed, her feet still, her muscles atrophying, freezing, dying . . .

But something was moving, something in the water, something black, something familiar. She tried to focus on the shape as it speared towards her. She couldn't make it out at first, but when she did she wasn't sure what she was seeing. It couldn't be . . .

The shape surged around her and she felt something pressing against her back, pushing her upwards, not allowing her to sink, not allowing her to fail, not allowing her to give up. And then the shape darted upwards, grabbing her gently by the wrist, pulling, tugging, guiding her up and away from the depths. She forced her legs to move, thrashing beneath her to help propel her and burst through the surface, the mouthfuls of air grating in her lungs, forcing her to cough up brown water, as hands grasped her to pull her free and something hard and unyielding scraped against her bare flesh. That'll leave a mark, she thought, but it didn't matter, and as she was hauled onto a small boat she looked back to the water and saw the dark shape look back at her, those brown, loving eyes ensuring she was safe, and then it vanished into the grey waters.

'Ben . . .' she heard herself say, and then she slept.

39

'Elspeth tracked down a retired reporter on the *Irish Times* who could tell her about Cormac.' Stephen was perched on the edge of the bed in the cottage, Chaz stood by the door, and Alan sat in an old easy chair – trust him to grab the most comfortable seat in the room, apart from the bed, and there was no way he was going to share that. In fact, Rebecca felt so warm and safe that she never wanted to leave it. The memory of the cold water washed over her and she shivered.

'You okay?' Stephen said, concern obvious in the slight frown and the way he reached out to press the back of his hand against her forehead, her cheeks, his touch warm and comforting.

'I'm fine,' she said, slightly leaning into his hand. 'Just an aftershock.'

'You should have gone to the hospital.' Stephen's fingers continued to brush her skin. It felt good. It felt right.

Rebecca had refused to go to a hospital, although she had agreed to the local GP checking her over. Rebecca didn't do doctors, as she told anyone within earshot time and again, but Stephen was adamant that she be looked at. To be honest, she hadn't had the strength to argue.

'Do you two need some alone time?' Alan asked.

Stephen withdrew his hand and gave him a sheepish glance. Rebecca didn't think it was a bad idea, but she didn't have the strength for that either.

'Sex isn't the answer to everything, Alan,' she said.

'No, sometimes it's the question and it's fun finding out which is which.'

'You're as bad as Elspeth, you know that?' She looked back at Stephen. 'Speaking of Elspeth, what did that reporter tell her?'

He was still worried. 'You sure you're up to hearing all this? Maybe you should get some more sleep.'

She had slept for most of the day, it seemed, because it was dark beyond the bedroom window. 'I've had enough sleep for now. Talk, Jordan – don't make me get out of this warm, cosy bed and slap you about.'

'I'd like to see you try.'

She knew he was right. 'Just tell me, okay?'

He wasn't convinced but he continued. 'Anyway, this reporter had covered Cormac's story thirty years ago. Seems he was a lonely kid. His father was well off, but was much older and pretty stern, his mother a neurotic and they think there might have been some abuse there, but Cormac refused to talk about it.'

'Sexual or physical?'

'Mental, mostly. Parents can do that so easily.'

'Not all parents.'

'No, you're right. Anyway, his home life really wasn't the best, from what I understand. He had no friends – apparently no friends at all – so he created his own.'

Rebecca asked, 'Like a multiple personality thing?'

'Not quite. Apparently, imaginary friends can be a good thing for a kid; it's merely an exercise of imagination and most of them know the friend isn't real, but in Cormac's case it looks as if it was a need to create something, someone, he could confide in, who gave him some comfort in an unpleasant home life. He didn't become them; he came to believe they were real, that they were actually there with him. External manifestations of his psyche. Eventually, though, he was diagnosed with schizophrenia and an antisocial personality disorder. It was all kept under control using antipsychotics.'

'But they didn't think he was dangerous,' Chaz added.

Rebecca could still feel the bump on her head. 'I think I would beg to differ.'

'Ordinarily he wasn't, but he felt threatened by you. And he believed he was protecting someone else. And he was off his meds. Looks like he hadn't been taking them for a while.'

Ignoring her doubts that he meant her no harm, Rebecca prodded Stephen back on track. Val Roach had hinted at something in his past and she wanted to know what it was. 'So what made him leave Ireland and come here?

'A child was killed. Naturally, suspicion fell on Cormac, because anyone who is different must automatically be to blame, right? Also, he had been seen talking to the boy. The child was friendly, apparently, and had managed to penetrate his coyness.'

'Did he kill the boy?'

'No, it was someone else entirely, but a lot of shit was thrown and it stuck. The guy who did it, a church elder apparently, and a thoroughly nasty piece of work by all accounts, was found guilty and sent away, but he claimed he was innocent and there were people who believed it. By the sounds of it, they made Cormac's life a living hell. They smeared dogshit on his front door, all over the handle, too. They made false calls to the fire and ambulance services. He was verbally and physically assaulted on the streets. No smoke without fire, was the way of their thinking, and it didn't matter if someone else was doing time for the murder. Cormac was strange and that was enough for them. It didn't help his mental state any. He was on his own by this time, his father and mother were both dead, he had no siblings, and it was felt that he would be best to move away. With his inheritance and what he made from his work he could afford it, so he moved to Rannoch, where he looked after the animals he loved and kept himself to himself.'

'Apart from befriending Fergus MacGregor.'

'Yes, it would appear Fergus was the only person he spoke to out of choice rather than necessity.'

'So why did he kill him?'

'He says he didn't. He says he found him badly hurt and brought him back to his cottage, tried to mend him the same way as he did with the injured animals.'

'Do you think Fergus was dead all the time?'

'Difficult to say. The post-mortem might show something up, but from the looks of him, Fergus had been dead for some time and Cormac had convinced himself that Fergus was still alive. He became his new imaginary friend. I'm sure psychologists will be able to explain it, but that seems to be the way of it to me. Cormac is just a lonely guy, off his meds, and convinced himself he was protecting a friend.'

'Who just happened to be dead,' said Rebecca, still smarting.

'He didn't know that, though. To him, he was still alive.'

Rebecca suspected she would be more understanding as time went on, but right now she was still bitter. 'You're being very charitable to a man who went all Norman Bates and could have brained me.'

'But he didn't.'

'He could have. I could also have frozen to death on that bloody island. Or drowned in the loch.'

Stephen gave her a long, hard stare. 'Yeah, about that . . .'

Alan suddenly rose and faced Chaz. 'And that, my love, is our cue to go and make some food.'

He ushered Chaz out of the room and closed the door behind him. Stephen was still giving Rebecca a stern look. She had known a lecture was heading her way but had hoped she might avoid it for a bit longer.

'You could have died out there,' he said.

'Yes, thanks to Cormac.'

He had to concede that. 'But in a way it was Cormac who helped save you too. He didn't need to tell us where you were, but as soon as we found Fergus's body he told us what had happened and even where to find the boat Chaz and I took out. And your car, which was tucked away off the road, hidden by trees and bushes.'

'Trying to save his skin, probably.' She was not ready to forgive and forget.

'That'll be for the doctors and the courts to decide.'

'Jesus, can you stop being a lawyer and show me some support here?'

'I will when you stop being a stubborn, pig-headed child.'

'He hit me over the head with something. He dumped me on that bloody island and left me there, trussed like a Christmas turkey. How do you expect me to feel?'

He breathed in deeply and let it out again. 'You're right, I'm sorry. I'll admit, I was angry with him too. I could have cheerfully beaten the living shit out of him, and would have if he'd refused to tell us where you were. Although, there was a female police officer there who I think would have proved quite formidable if I'd tried. But I've had time to reflect on it and Cormac is a troubled soul who really didn't mean to hurt you. I'm convinced of that. He did what he did because he thought – believed – he was protecting his friend.'

Rebecca's lips compressed into a tight line. 'That's all right, then.'

'No, it's not. He's sick, he's confused. Look at it this way, if I was hurt and you had been caring for me for years and someone came who you thought would ultimately cause me harm, or who I said had to be disabled somehow, what would you do?'

'I wouldn't hit them over the head and dump them on an island.'

'Why wouldn't you?'

'Because I'm not . . .' She stopped herself short.

'Because you're not like Cormac. You generally have control of your faculties and your actions. He doesn't.'

Deep down she knew he was talking sense, but she still wasn't ready to accept it. 'Okay.' Then she realised what he had said. 'What do you mean, I generally have control?'

'You didn't have control when you went for that swim. Concussion is a funny thing, it can interfere with the reasoning processes. That's what the doctor said, anyway. I think if you had been firing on all cylinders you would never have attempted that.'

She knew that was the case but she was damned if she was going to give him the satisfaction of agreeing. Maybe somewhere down the line she would admit he was right about Cormac and her own temporary mental condition, but not at that moment. She knew she was being unreasonable, but she felt she had every right to be. She knew Stephen had been worried to distraction because Chaz had told her. She knew he had tried to pick up her trail, had spoken to Mrs MacGregor and Harry and even the Burnes family. She knew all this, so she reached out and clasped his hand. He held her tightly.

After a moment he asked, 'Who's Ben?'

'What do you mean?' she asked, although she knew exactly what he meant.

'You said the name just as we hauled you onto the boat. Ben. Who is it?'

She hesitated, wondering if she should tell him. 'He was my dog, back when I was a kid. Just as I was going down for the last time I thought I saw him in the water with me – he was a powerful swimmer.' She paused, unsure if she should admit the next bit. 'I thought he pushed me to the surface.'

She expected him to laugh, or tell her she was imagining things, to be Scully to her Mulder, but he didn't. He looked thoughtful as he stared down at their intertwined fingers. 'What?' she said.

'It's nothing,' he said.

'It's nothing – but?'

He opened his mouth, took a small breath, closed his mouth, considered, then said, 'We were trying to reach you, in the water. Chaz and I, in the boat. We'd heard you call out, took us a few moments to zero in on you in the mist, and then we tried to get to you but you were already going down, I mean really deep, and I reached in but couldn't get to you. I was going to jump in, dive down to haul you back, but just before I could do it you began to rise towards us.' He paused again. 'As if you were being propelled by something.'

He let that hang between them for a time and she didn't know what to say. Finally, she spoke, but the words came out quietly, because she wasn't sure she believed them herself. 'I probably saw you above me and kicked myself up.'

'Probably,' he said. 'Yeah,' he said. Then, 'But the thing is, you were just hanging there. We could see you, not clearly certainly, but we could see you, just couldn't reach you. And then you started to surge up. And when we pulled you aboard you were pretty much out of it. But you said Ben's name.'

They stared at each other for a long time and her fingers tightened on his. It couldn't have been. It wasn't possible. But she had really thought she saw Ben in those murky waters, had felt his soft mouth on the flesh of her wrist.

Her wrist.

She pulled back the sleeve of the long T-shirt and inspected her skin, saw the very slight indentations. They hadn't been there before, of that she was certain. So what had made them?

Despite the chill on her shoulders and neck, she felt something warm behind her eyes.

40

Rebecca spent a turbulent night, dreams of rushing water, of intense cold and the sense of being unable to breath waking her up with a start. Stephen, beside her, must have been lying only half asleep because each time she woke he sat up immediately and placed his arms around her, soothing her. It felt good. It felt safe. It felt right. She slept again, less troubled but still with visions of water flowing over and around her, the ripples transforming into her father's smiling face, and she heard him say that all was well. And then the black arrow of Ben's body swam from his mouth and circled her.

She didn't feel rested when she awoke but did feel at peace. She could enjoy what was left of her holiday. She had been through hell and she had survived. The mystery of Fergus MacGregor was solved: Cormac had to have murdered him, no matter what he claimed. Chaz and Alan were here, that had been a surprise, and they had celebrated her birthday the night before, eating some of the cake, opening gifts. Stephen had bought her a beautiful 9ct yellow gold Mackintosh-design cross. She wasn't religious, although she knew Stephen did believe in a very basic way, but she loved the necklace. Chaz and Alan gave her a gold Scrivener pen and the new Robbie Williams CD, with the promise that she never play it when they were around. Her fondness for the singer's output puzzled them, not to mention her preference for CDs over digital downloads. She pointed out that it was her birthday and she had been through an ordeal, so they should cut her some slack and let her listen. Her plea fell on fallow ground, so the CD remained in its shrink wrap. She didn't fancy struggling with that damned plastic anyway, which she was sure had been sent by the devil to torment humanity. She'd listen to the CD in the car on the way home, she decided. Stephen wasn't so prejudiced.

The mist burned away through the morning, and, by afternoon, sunlight drenched the valley from an almost unbroken blue. She sat in one of the folding lawn chairs, wrapped in her new fleece dressing gown, a gift from Elspeth and delivered by the boys, enjoying the feel of the sun on her face. It still wasn't strong, but there was heat. Schiehallion looked magnificent, with just a hint of the mist lingering across its face. The warrior opposite still slumbered. Yeah, she thought, where was he when she needed him? Maybe he couldn't swim.

As to her own attempt to swim to shore, she had been wrong and Stephen was right. She hadn't been thinking straight, she knew that now. In fact, looking back, her thought processes had been pretty chaotic throughout, even though she'd had the gumption to get herself free from the gag, the hood and the bonds. She could take comfort in that, but the whole swimming around the loch in her scanties thing was nothing short of madness. Next time she was imprisoned on an artificial island in the middle of a loch she wouldn't try to swim for safety. Lesson learned. Every day is a school day.

The ring of her phone, muffled in the voluminous pocket of the dressing gown, snapped her from her thoughts. She fumbled for it, checked the number.

'Harry?'

'Ms Connolly . . . Rebecca,' he sounded upset. 'I'm sorry to phone you . . .'

'It's okay, Harry, is something wrong?'

She heard a deep breath. 'No. Well . . . can you come and see me?'

Despite her own weakened state, she felt concern rush through her. 'Has something happened?'

He began to speak but the words caught in his throat and he tried to clear them with a soft cough. 'I've been such a fool.'

Ashley. This had to be something to do with that bloody scammer.

'Please,' he said, and she heard his voice was close to breaking. 'Can you come here?'

Rebecca sighed, closed her eyes. She didn't want to do this. She didn't feel able to do it. But she knew she was going to.

Stephen was going to kill her.

In the village shop, Frances MacGregor had heard, or imagined she heard, Fergus's name carried in whispers; and there had been meaningful looks, which darted away as soon as she returned them. Tom Lester had phoned as soon as he heard, of course, and that was acceptable. He was her minister and privy to certain family matters. Not all, though. He must never know them all. She had kept her head high, her back straight. The news that they had found a body in Cormac's cottage had stunned her, had seriously weakened her self-control – she had wept alone in her room for hours through the night, ignoring Dan's attempt at comfort, refusing to let him in – but she refused to let others see her pain.

Before she even came to a halt Dan was in the drive waiting for her. He took the plastic bag of groceries and carried them into the hallway. She steeled herself because she could tell he was building up to saying something. She followed him into the house, into the kitchen, where he placed the bag on the worktop then turned to face her, his face tense.

'I think we should tell the police what happened,' he said.

'They know what happened.'

He cocked his head, frowned at her. 'They don't. We need to tell them the truth.'

'No,' she said and busied herself with emptying the bag.

'We have to, Frannie.'

Frannie. He used to call her that, but he hadn't for a long time. He used to breathe the diminution when they made love, and filled it with a laugh when they were having fun. The gulf that had grown between them, which began to open before Fergus vanished, had meant that there was little in the way of affection. For him to use it now, perhaps as a way of reasoning with her, just made her angry.

She whirled on him. 'No! What happened is family business, you've said so yourself. You will rip this family apart if you tell outsiders.'

'It's already ripped apart, or haven't you noticed?'

Sadness coated his voice in a way she had never heard before, and she felt her own heart begin to crack. 'We can't. You can't.'

'It's the right thing to do. I should have come forward years ago.'

She shook her head, as if the movement would prevent the tears that she could feel stinging at her eyes. 'No . . .'

'He was your son, Frannie. Don't you think he deserves to have the truth out there?'

She looked around her, not sure what she was searching for. Answers, perhaps. Guidance, probably. But she found nothing. 'I can't . . . You can't, Dan. Please.' She felt desperation creep into her voice. 'We're not even sure it's Fergus they found . . .'

He ignored what even she knew was self-delusion. 'I have to, Frannie, don't you see?' His voice was far gentler than she had heard it for a long time. 'I've been thinking about this for hours. Maybe even longer than that, even before they found Fergus.' He reached out to lay a hand on her arm. She hadn't felt his touch in so long and she stared down at it, as if it was something alien. 'We can't live this lie any longer, Frannie,' he said. 'It all has to come out. This has to end.'

She didn't move. She didn't place her own hand on his. She didn't step into him for a hug, even though she wanted to. What he was threatening to do was, to her mind, unthinkable. Yes, the family had been ripped asunder. Yes, Fergus was her son. But to tell the world what had happened was not something she could countenance.

'Please, Dan,' she said, 'let me think about this.'

He removed his hand. 'There's nothing to think about, Frannie.'

'You've sprung this on me. I thought you agreed that what happened was nobody's business but ours.'

'Things have changed. My thinking has changed.'

It was her turn to reach out and grasp his hand. 'I understand, but don't rush into anything.'

'It's been years, Frannie. It's hardly rushing into it. We should have come clean back then.'

'Okay, but please, let me process this. Give me the day. Another day won't hurt, will it?'

He studied their hands clasped between them. 'Fine. I'll not do anything until later,' he said. 'But you need to understand this, Frannie. My mind is made up on this. I'm determined to do it. It's time. We can't let that poor man stand accused of something he didn't do.'

Stephen had tried to talk her out of seeing Harry, but Rebecca argued that this wasn't about a story any more. This was about Harry's welfare. It hit home, but he refused to budge.

'You're not fit to drive,' he said and she saw the sense of that. 'I hoped you would do it.'

His laugh was short and bitter. 'You're kidding, right?'

They were in their bedroom, Chaz and Alan in the living room, so they kept their voices low. Nevertheless, she didn't need raised voices to know this was an argument, and one that perhaps had been brewing for some time.

'No,' she said.

'Jesus, Becks, you really are something. We come here on holiday and you spend most of it gadding about on a story, almost getting yourself killed in the process. And right now you should be resting.'

'You've not left your work behind either.'

'I've made a few phone calls! I didn't swan off on my own for over twenty-four hours!'

'Harry could be in trouble, Stephen. You met him, you saw how he could be.'

'I saw nothing of the sort,' he replied. 'I saw a man who may have been a bit forgetful, but hell, we can all be like that. You forget you're in a relationship often enough.'

That stung. 'That's not true.'

'Isn't it? Did you think to call me before you decided to drop in on Cormac the other day?'

Any answer to that sounded lame, even to her, so she decided her best response was none at all. He took that as an admission.

'That's what I thought,' he said. 'You know something, Becks? You need to have a long, hard look at yourself, at us, because I can't go on like this.'

'Look,' she said, feeling a need to defend herself, even though she knew in her heart that he was right, 'that works both ways. I know you think what I do is unimportant . . .'

'I've never said that.'

'You don't need to, you dismiss everything I do, perhaps not in words but in attitude.'

'You're talking utter pish, Becks. I'm nothing but supportive of your work, even the stuff that really is unimportant.'

'There you go!'

'What? You think telling those first-person misery memoirs for the tabloid magazines is important? And churning out court reports for newspapers?'

'Those misery memoirs, as you call them, help pay my bills. And court reporting is a vital part of local democracy.'

'Yeah, yeah – I've heard all that before. The tabloid articles are voyeurism in the main. And court reports more often than not simply drag the names of people who have very real issues, very real problems, through the press. There's always more to a case than is said in court and these reports of yours don't reflect that.'

'I can only report what's said in court.'

'I know, and that's what makes it all so bloody annoying because these are real people you're writing about, not simply names on a court docket. And they have families and jobs and lives that are severely disrupted by what has happened, and it's made worse by them being turned into fodder for newspapers to fill space between the ads! And you never, ever give a thought to what damage that story may leave behind.'

'That's right – I forgot. Everyone who appears in court is innocent or has made a mistake. None of them are career thieves or thugs or just really bad people who need to be put away. Justice needs to be seen to be done, remember that. Because the minute we stop scrutinising what the police or the courts or governments are doing, then that's the minute we lose a major part of democracy.'

'Christ, we're talking champions of democracy now! You reporters really think you're something, don't you?'

She was already weary, but this argument, even though hushed, was taking more of a toll. The problem was that she knew he was right, not completely, but there was something in what he said. But how they had gone from concern over her wellbeing to the press being the guardians of truth, justice and the British way of life was beyond her. She didn't want to continue with the disagreement any further, but neither did she want to concede anything.

'Look, fine,' she said. 'I know I'm not in any condition to drive, so if you won't take me . . .'

'No, I won't. You should be staying here for now.'

'Okay, I'll ask Chaz.'

'Okay,' he said.

'Okay,' she repeated, and they faced each other across the bed in silence before she gave him a small nod and turned to the door.

'Becks?' His voice was even quieter now and she turned back. 'When you get back, we need to talk, you know that, don't you?'

She blinked at the sudden tears. 'Yeah,' she said. 'I know.'

41

Chaz took the opportunity while they drove to deliver a lecture. At first they had sat in silence, but once they had driven through the village and over the bridge he began, making his points as if he was indicating them on a whiteboard.

She was messing things up.

She needed to realise what really mattered.

Being dedicated to work was all fine, but there was more to life.

She thought the last one was a proxy strike from Elspeth and should have been irritated, but Chaz was merely saying what she had said to herself. He was a few years younger, but beneath all the tomfoolery, when it came to relationships he knew what he was talking about because the bond between him and Alan was strong. They didn't take themselves or each other seriously, but they were very deeply in love.

'You're going to lose him, you know that?' Chaz said.

She did know that.

'He's been good for you. Everyone agrees.'

Everyone. That would mean him, Alan and Elspeth. Mind you, she wouldn't be surprised if Elspeth had phoned her mum in Glasgow and canvassed her vote, too. Normally she would have bristled at the thought of them discussing her personal life but this time she didn't. They *were* her personal life.

'And yet you're pushing him away. I don't get it, Becks. I really don't.'

She sighed. It was deep, it was long, and there was a slight hitch in it halfway through. 'Neither do I, Chaz.'

Dan had to get out of the house to think. He was intent on contacting the police, but Frances had pleaded with him, gripping his arm as if she could hold him back, and would have gone down on her knees if she had thought it would change his mind. His eyes had softened and in that moment his wife had realised that he still loved her, despite all that had happened. Despite all she had done. Finally, he agreed that he wouldn't go to the police, but he still needed time to process everything. She was relieved but remained troubled. There was something in his emphasis that suggested he might go elsewhere.

She stood at the window for a long time after he left. It was another beautiful day, but she barely noticed it. The sun shone and the air was crisp, but darkness had settled around her, as the past again encroached not just on the present but also on the future. She had tried to put what had happened out of her mind, but it was always there, a festering sore that never healed. You can never escape your past. It waits for you, haunts you, mocks you. Mistakes made, decisions taken, words and actions that cannot be withdrawn or changed – they all follow in your shadow.

She looked down at the mobile phone in her hand. Her past was not hers alone; it was shared. Those mistakes, decisions, words and actions had not been made in isolation, and if Dan did follow through with his threat – and she knew him to be a man of conscience who had shouldered the burden of that past for far too long – then it would affect more than just their family. Her husband knew that, of course, and she wondered if he was partly motivated by the need for revenge.

She dismissed the thought almost as soon as it entered her head. No, Dan had never been comfortable with her need to keep what had happened secret. He had wanted to reveal all, but she had prevailed upon him to keep quiet, for the sake of family. And he had agreed, even though he knew it to be wrong. But it had eaten away at him and had affected his personality. First rage, and then guilt, had eroded the man he had been and he took refuge in cold silences. It was never spoken of but the knowledge of it had frosted the air. Only three of them knew what had occurred all those years ago. Only two suspected what it had led to.

She stepped away from the window and for the second time that week dialled a number she had once resolved never to dial again.

Rebecca walked slowly from Chaz's car to Harry's front door. Stephen was right, she shouldn't be doing this. She was washed out, her legs weak, and that buzzing was growing in her head again. She shouldn't have come but she couldn't ignore him. He had sounded beaten somehow, and that was confirmed by his ashen face as he opened the door. He looked past her at Chaz's car, and she could tell he was wondering who the new face behind the wheel was.

'That's my friend, Chaz,' she explained. 'I've had—' She stopped, realising he didn't need to hear about her adventures. 'Don't worry, he'll wait for me in the car.'

He gave her an absent nod and stepped back to let her in. He moved slowly ahead of her into the living room, his shoulders stooped, his legs as sluggish as Rebecca's felt. He eased himself into his armchair and she lowered herself into her now customary place on the settee. She felt like death warmed over, but Harry seemed worse.

'Harry, you're worrying me,' she said. 'Why don't you tell me what's wrong?'

He seemed so small and frail as he hunched into his chair. His eyes were soft, liquid, as if he was on the verge of tears, and they couldn't meet her gaze.

'Talk to me, Harry,' she said gently.

His eyes eased towards her and he said, 'I've been such a fool. A stupid, sad, old fool . . .'

Alex Burnes was obviously anxious. That was new, Shona thought. He was not a man who let his insecurities show; he always held the other person's gaze. In fact, she often wondered if he had any insecurity at all. He had once told her that he had been taught by his father that any display of timidity showed a lack of determination: that was for other people, apparently – weak people, not for men like them. The Burnes men were strong and they took action.

He was also drinking and that was something she had never seen before. Wine at dinner, perhaps a dram now and again, but since she and Ray had arrived in his study he had downed two whiskies. Straight, too. She suspected they weren't the first.

He had summoned them, telling them there was something they needed to hear. Shona guessed it was related to Fergus being found the day before. She had been shocked, but not surprised, because as she had told Rebecca Connolly, she had come to the realisation long ago that Fergus was dead. She wept, of course, when she heard the news. She had wept a lot: for Fergus, for what might have been. She would always miss him, she would always regret the waste of a life, she would always care for him.

And now she watched the man who had forcibly separated her from Fergus edgily pace back and forth behind his big desk. She noted his demeanour in an academic way only and felt no sympathy. Burnes blood would out, she supposed.

Ray sat in a straight-backed wooden chair, staring at his father with concern plain on his face, still flushed and sweat-speckled from the gym. Shona dropped herself into the armchair beside the dead fire and hooked her leg over the arm in what she hoped was a nonchalant manner. She had caught the atmosphere, but no way was she going to let either of them think she cared about Alex's worries.

She raised a quizzical eyebrow. 'Okay, we're here, so what's going on?'

He didn't speak for some time. Perhaps for the first time in his life he didn't know what to say.

DCI Teresa Morgan was very tall, very broad and made a brick outhouse look like a Wendy house. She was the senior investigating officer in the Devlin case, and Val Roach had worked with her when she had been based in Perth. She knew her to be a supremely confident detective.

'You shouldn't be here, Val, you know that,' she said, her Welsh accent still strong despite many years in Scotland.

'I'm not here in any official capacity, Terry,' Roach assured her. 'I do have an interest in this.'

Terry's look grew concerned. 'You've not been obsessing over this, have you?'

Roach had been doing this job for a long time and knew it wasn't a good idea to become obsessed. In fact, she hadn't even thought about Fergus MacGregor until Rebecca had raised the matter again. 'No, but I do have an interest in it.' She leaned forward in her chair. 'Terry, I'm not here to interfere. I just want to look at this guy, Devlin. I need to know if there was anything I might have missed.'

'You didn't.'

'Call it professional curiosity then.' She could see Terry was still doubtful. No SIO wants another officer looking over their shoulder, even if they are work friends. 'Come on, Terry, you know me. I hate a mystery. I hate loose ends. God knows there are enough in this game, but here's one that can be tied off and I'd just like to see it done. All I'm asking is that you let me watch the interview.'

Terry stared at her for a long time and sighed.

*

Harry spoke very quietly, as if he was talking to himself.

'I should have listened to you. You tried to warn me, Anne tried to warn me, but I didn't listen. I knew better, you see, I always knew better. I really believed she was real. I needed her to be real, do you understand? I needed her to be real so that I could help her. So that I could finally do something right for someone.'

He still wasn't looking at her. He was telling himself truths that he had ignored for many years, and such candour, such self-examination, didn't come easily.

'I loved Mel, but perhaps I wasn't loving enough. Over the years we sort of lost touch, her and I, do you know what I mean? We lived in the same house, slept in the same bed, and we laughed and we joked and we shared a life, but we weren't really together, not like we used to be when we were younger. I suppose a lot of marriages go that way.' He paused to consider. 'Maybe not. I don't know. It's not something people would talk about, is it, unless to marriage counsellors? I know I didn't. I suppose I turned cold, in a way. It was the same with Anne. She was, is, my daughter, but I wasn't a great father. My distance extended to her, too. I didn't know how to communicate with her, certainly not as she grew older. When she was a child it was easy, but once she became a person in her own right, not so much. I wasn't cruel to her, not abusive – certainly not, she got everything she ever wanted – but I wasn't . . . loving. But that didn't mean I didn't love her, or Mel. It was just that I was never sure how to show it, always believed that they would know without me having to show it. That's not the way of things, though, is it? We don't show how we really feel to the right person and then they're gone and it's too late. You can't go back, can you? There's no reset button on life. There's just life and love and whether or not you can have one without the other.'

Rebecca felt his words pierce her but she forced herself to focus on him, for this wasn't about her. Her issues could be dealt with later.

'Mel and I were never a demonstrative couple, to be honest – we'd hold hands in public, and when we were younger there was physical contact, but that was youthful hormones in inappropriate places.' He smiled fondly. 'I remember once on a beach over on the east coast, lying in among some dunes and she almost had my trunks off. People were passing by and she was pulling them down my thighs.' The smile faded and died. 'As we grew older we became more circumspect, first in public, then in private. Physical contact was rare. I think, some-where along the lines, something between us had withered. And then she died and I realised that I would never get the chance to say all the things I should have said before. To tell her how much she meant to me. And how much I miss her now . . .'

His voice broke again and Rebecca edged forward in order to reach out and gently lay her hand on his. He looked at it, then at her, and gave her another wan smile, but she could see the tears were threatening to burst. He placed his other hand on top of hers, patted it.

'I suppose I thought Ashley was a way of giving back. I told you Mel was always donating to charities and I continued it, sort of in her memory, you know?' He shot a glance towards the window. 'I always feed the birds, too, because she did.' His eyes crinkled with a memory. 'The result of seeing Mary Poppins when she was a child. "Feed the Birds", you know?' He looked at her and she nodded that she knew.

'Was Ashley also a way of honouring Mel's memory, Harry?'

'Yes. Giving to charities is fine, but you never really know who you're helping, do you? Sure, they send you newsletters about the work they're doing and individual cases, but you're never certain your money is helping an individual, someone you can see. It is – of course, it is – but with Ashley, I thought here was a chance to take direct action, to help someone in need.

Someone who needed my help – a young woman who told me that she loved me. And I believed her.'

A single tear broke free and rolled down his cheek. She squeezed his hand.

'Sad, isn't it? An old man thinking that a beautiful young woman cared for him. Oh, maybe somewhere in the back of my mind I didn't quite believe it, but never underestimate the power of self-delusion. It can overcome many obstacles, like logic, truth. Reason. Even when I transferred all that money the other day, she said to pay off her cousin and to buy her ticket to come over here, there was that little voice in my head telling me I was being foolish, but I ignored it.' He took a breath. 'Here's the thing, Rebecca. It didn't matter to me that she might not be who she said she was. It didn't matter to me if I was being scammed, although I really didn't believe it. What mattered was that I had convinced myself that I was helping someone in need, evening the balance in some small way for the man I had been. I thought that, somewhere, Mel might approve. I didn't have any romantic notions about Ashley, please believe that, although I was flattered and it would have been nice to feel something for someone. I was convinced – I convinced myself – that she was in trouble and that I could help her, that's all. And if she came here I would help her make a new life, not necessarily with me. A life of her own.' He stared at the window again. 'I gave her money to come here and she was to let me know what flight she was catching so I could fetch her.'

Rebecca knew what had happened now. 'You didn't hear anything, did you?'

He swallowed, shook his head. 'And when I checked her social media account, the one we'd been using, it was gone. She was gone. My money was gone. Everything gone.' She felt a tremor course through his body as the tears fell. 'All a lie. Everything. All a lie.'

He bowed his head and sobbed quietly. All she could do was sit by him, hold his hand as she fought back her own tears, and think about the lies people tell to others and those they tell to themselves.

42

Cormac Devlin was lost in a world of his own creation as the two detectives probed into the details of what had happened five years before and since. A duty solicitor sat by his side, occasionally advising him, sometimes urging the detectives to rephrase their questions – not that it mattered, because Cormac did not respond. He was hunched over the table, staring at his hands clasped in front of him. He didn't look up. He didn't nod or shake his head. He didn't move at all.

Roach watched the interview on the monitor, Teresa looming over her like a court appearance.

'He's not said much, and absolutely nothing in the room,' Teresa said. 'He's a poor soul, so he is. He still thinks the guy is talking to him.'

'What's the theory?'

'Well, we're assuming the body is that of Fergus MacGregor for the moment, although we'll need DNA to fully establish it. We're going to get samples from the parents. He'd been sitting in front of that fire for five years so there's not much to go on forensics-wise. The pathologist and assorted boffins will do their best but obviously there's been a lot of post-mortem degeneration. It will be a bugger to work out cause of death unless they find a wound or a skull fracture. The soft tissue has degraded so much that any bruising or bleeding is nigh on impossible to identify.'

'There was no blood found where Fergus MacGregor was last presumed to be. None in his car or in the vicinity.'

Teresa nodded. 'I know, I checked the records. So, unless this fella tells us something, or the pathologists strike it lucky, we might never know what killed that poor guy.'

Roach leaned closer to the monitor to study the man. 'Can I speak to him?'

Teresa gave her a surprised look. 'You know better than that, Val. The boss would have my warrant card on a plate if I let you in there.'

'I'm familiar with the original case.'

Teresa's lower jaw jerked to one side, giving her face a lopsided look as she considered this. Roach had forgotten that she did that when she was thinking. 'Did you speak to this lad back then?'

'No, but I know who he is. I know his background.'

Teresa jerked her head at the screen. 'So do those lads.'

'They're getting nowhere, Terry, you know that. How about it, you and me, just like old times? How many scrotes did we burst together, eh? We were a team. Come on, Terry – if the shit hits the fan I'll get my boss to square it with yours. We're all on the same side.'

'Aye, that'll be the day,' Teresa said, but slowly her jaw righted itself. 'Okay, but I'm running it past my boss first, okay?'

Roach smiled. 'That's the spirit. Thelma and Louise ride again.'

Teresa was already heading to the door. 'They died at the end.'

'Okay, Cagney and Laccy then.'

The door was open and Teresa stepped back to let Roach out of the room first. 'I hated that programme.'

Roach walked by her. 'Jesus, you're hard to please . . .'

The call came in while Rebecca and Chaz were heading back to the cottage. Harry had needed to speak to someone, anyone, to say the things that he had hidden for years, even from himself. Before they left he vowed not to become embroiled with anyone on social media again, even offered to give Rebecca his phone for safekeeping but she declined. She urged him to contact his daughter, to repeat what he had told her.

'Not so easy, you know,' he'd said.

'You said it to me. You can say it to her.'

His eyes were sad. 'Ah, saying it to a stranger is one thing, no offence, but to someone who really matters? That's different.'

Once again that hit home. Stephen was no stranger, but she really needed to say how she felt about him. About them. About their future. It wouldn't come easily, not to her, but it had to be said to try in some way to regain what ground she had lost by being as Harry had been – distant. Disconnected. Unable to see what was good for her, even when it was standing right in front of her.

The sun was vanishing behind the mountains to the west, leaving the water and the land suffused in a pink glow, when her business mobile rang. The caller was unknown and she contemplated ignoring it, but realised it could be work and the agency was really in no position to lose a commission. She ignored Chaz's reproving look as she answered it.

'Ms Connolly, this is Tom Lester, from the Rannoch church.'

'Yes, Reverend, how can I help you?'

'I wonder if you would be able to stop by my home. Would that be possible?'

Shit, she thought. She really wanted to get back to the cottage. To Stephen. But if the minister was calling her it had to be important. She resolved to give him fifteen minutes. Then to get back. A quarter of an hour wouldn't hurt. Would it?

'Believe it or not, I'm literally a few minutes away from the village.'

He thanked her and gave her the address. Then said, 'We'll be waiting.'

'We?'

'I'm with Dan MacGregor.' Rebecca wasn't sure if his pause was for effect or if he was waiting for permission to make his next statement. 'He wants to talk about Fergus.'

43

Tom Lester's cottage was on the outskirts of the village, a short walk from his church. Chaz pulled up outside and dropped Alan a text to let them know they had one more stop to make. Guilt forced its way into Rebecca's conscience. She hadn't let Stephen know they'd been delayed – and frankly didn't have the courage. She wasn't used to reporting to anyone else, but she knew it was something she would have to learn if she wanted their relationship to work. And she did want it to work. They may not see eye-to-eye over some aspects of each other's professions, but what they had was deeper than that. She wanted to take things further with him and that meant she had to be more accessible. Telling him she loved him might be a start.

She didn't feel it fair to have Chaz wait in the car again, so she introduced him to the minister at his door. He didn't seem fazed at all as he led Rebecca and Chaz into a small and cosy living room where Dan MacGregor sat beside a log burner spreading welcome warmth. He was a burly man, his grey hair thin and receding, his face craggy, thanks to years of outdoor work. His eyes were troubled, though.

He accepted Chaz's presence easily as they sat together on a two-seater settee. Tom had settled into what was obviously his regular place in the room's second armchair and they fell into a moment's silence, as if in prayer, but in reality everyone was waiting for someone else to speak. It was the minister who filled the gap.

'Dan has a story to tell.'

Rebecca opened her notebook and was about to dig out her digital recorder when the minister said, 'Before we begin, can I make it clear that at this stage it's off the record. By all means take notes, right, Dan?' After a beat, the man nodded his agreement. 'But please, there can be no story until Dan feels the time is right.'

Rebecca felt disappointment mixed with confusion. 'So if I can't do a story, why are you talking to me?'

Tom looked to Dan, but he seemed unwilling to explain, so Tom continued, 'What you're about to hear is very personal, very troubling. It's background to everything that has happened. If you hadn't begun investigating, then Fergus might never have been found, and Dan is grateful to you for that. He feels he owes you some sort of explanation, especially as you nearly died yourself.'

'If I don't talk about this now, it's possible I never will.' Dan MacGregor seemed to blurt out the words, as if he was breaching some sort of dam.

As Harry had said, you can say things to strangers that you can't say to those close to you.

Rebecca waited as Dan shifted in his chair, as if he were uncomfortable. He seemed to be struggling to say anything further, so she thought she should help him along. She might never be able to tell this story, but she wanted to know what it was.

'Just talk, Mr MacGregor. In your own time. No rush.'

It took him a few moments, during which he turned his attention to the logs burning in the fire. When he finally began to talk, he didn't lift his eyes from those flames. It was as if he was staring through them into the past.

'We were friends for a while, back when we were children,' Dan MacGregor said. 'Frannie, me, Alex. Frannie and Alex were maybe closer, but I had always loved her, even then, even when

I was too young to know what love was, what it meant and how it can twist you until you're in knots. I suppose I was always jealous of Alex. He was a handsome boy, me not so much, and Frannie, well, to me she was the most beautiful creature who had ever breathed air. And she really was, she really was. Time and circumstance haven't been kind to her, and I think I've contributed to that, but she really was gorgeous.'

He stopped as if his memory had drifted ahead of his words.

'Anyway,' he said finally, 'the friendship ended, as they do. You think the friends you have at that age are the ones who will be with you forever, but how often does that happen? Frannie and I went to high school, Alex was sent off to private school, because that's where they make the men who make the country, right?' His laugh was short and bitter. 'I suppose being brought up as a Burnes entails some level of brainwashing. God knows his parents had tried to get him to distance himself from us – we weren't their sort, apparently. They always were a stuck-up pair, and they didn't think it sat well that the scion of the family was running about with the likes of us.' He tried to smile, but it didn't rise to the occasion. 'I hadn't heard that word before Alex used it, scion – had to go look it up – but Alex, the young Alex, had defied them. Spoke well of him, I suppose, but he wasn't the same when he came back for holidays. He thought he was something. He thought he was better than us. I'm not sure if it was the school or his parents who had finally got through to him, but something did.'

Dan took a long breath, let it out as he eased into the memory. 'Anyway, everything changed. That happens, doesn't it? Friendships come and go. And sometimes when you think about some of the people who have been in your life and then faded out of it, you feel as if you have lost something of yourself.'

Rebecca had to agree. There were people from her childhood that she once believed would be her friends forever. Now she barely remembered their names. Life moves on, people move on.

She had new friends, good friends in Chaz, Alan and Elspeth. And Stephen, who she was in danger of losing. And if she did, she would most definitely have lost something of herself.

'The thing was, Frannie was still attracted to him, it was obvious, and he played up to that, even though he treated the rest of us like shit. Sorry, Tom . . .'

'That's okay, Dan,' the minister said, quietly. 'I've heard the word before.'

Another weak smile. 'That hurt, got to say, because I thought we, Frannie and me, I thought we had grown close without him being around. But whenever he came back she was . . . different. I don't think she knew it herself, not at the time, but of course Alex spotted it. Of course he did. He always picked up on these things. He was very empathetic – is that the word?'

Rebecca didn't know if he was asking her, but she replied anyway. 'Yes.'

Dan nodded his gratitude for the confirmation. 'Yes, he was good at picking up on moods and thought processes. I suppose that's helped him in business, too. Some people use that skill to help others, but not Alex. No, not him. He used it to hurt and to further his own ends. And that's what he did.'

Rebecca had guessed what was coming, but she didn't want to interrupt his flow. She sensed that it was important that he get this out.

'I confronted him, told him he was making a fool of her, you know? I told you she was a beautiful girl and all he wanted was to have her on his arm, show her off, to let everyone know that she was his. We argued about this and it developed into more than words. I don't recall who threw the first punch, I think it might have been me. Frannie was there and was screaming at us to stop, but we ignored her. This had been coming for a while, you understand, this fight. It had been building up like pressure in a steam pipe and the fight was the valve that let it free. He'd learned how to box in school, apparently, but I was faster on my feet and I managed to bloody his nose, knock him on his backside, and then I was down there with him, the two of us rolling around on the ground like it was a playground scrap. He threw me off, he was a strong bugger, and he landed one on me. A right hook, it was, and I was pretty much out of it.' He rubbed his jaw as if the memory had brought back the pain. 'I've got to admit that he knew how to hit, but that was pretty much the end of the fight. He might have won on points, I suppose, but he still ran away, crying like a child with his nose streaming. I remember him saying that his dad would have something to say about all this, as if I cared what old Alexander Burnes had to say. Even if he spoke to my parents, which was unlikely, they would send him off with a flea in his ear. They'd give me a talking to for brawling, but I think deep down they'd be happy that it was with a Burnes and that I'd made him bleed.'

Dan's voice had taken on an air of levity as he spoke of how his parents would have reacted, but that vanished with his next words.

'The thing was, Frannie went with him. She asked me what the hell had got into me, blamed me for the fight – and maybe that was true – but she couldn't see that it was for her benefit. She ran after Alex, shouting his name, and left me where I was. That was even more painful than the punch.'

The silence that followed lasted so long that Rebecca felt forced to speak. 'What happened then, Mr MacGregor?'

'That's something I didn't find out for years,' he said. He took another deep breath. 'She . . . he . . . well, she comforted him, do you understand? I don't need to spell it out, do I?'

The minister raised an eyebrow at Rebecca and she nodded her understanding. 'It's fine, Dan, we get the picture.'

Dan blinked a few times, his lips tightening as if he was in pain, which Rebecca supposed he was. 'The inevitable happened, of course. But when she told him she was pregnant, he turned his back on her. Denied the baby was his, even though she hadn't been with anyone else. He would have been terrified his parents found out, but he knew she wouldn't tell anybody.'

Ray stormed from the room after Alex told them that Dan MacGregor had planned to reveal his past indiscretions. Shona had been aware of her sibling's rising rage – not at Alex's failure to support a woman almost thirty years earlier, but by the threat it posed to the family name. It was always all about the family name. Alex called out to stop him, but his voice was weak and had been watered down by the booze.

For her part, Shona sat quietly, struggling to come to terms with the revelation. Fergus was her half-brother. Jesus! For some reason she felt shame, even though her rational mind told her she had nothing to be ashamed of. She stared at Alex as he slumped behind his desk, watching her, waiting for her to react. Perhaps she owed him some credit for finally telling the truth, but she couldn't bring herself to give him any leeway. Confession may be good for the soul, but you have to have one first and she was not sure Alex Burnes did. She had always known him to be a bastard, no matter what her mother thought or said, and in telling her what he had done years ago he had only confirmed that.

In his mind he perhaps thought that by revealing his past sins she might somehow grow closer to him. Certainly he had bared himself to them, more than ever before, which wouldn't be difficult, because he had never revealed anything to his children. She wished he had chosen to reveal something other than what he had – that he had been guilty of insider trading, perhaps, or some other dodgy deal. He had carried guilt around all these years, had never shown any outward signs of it, and was only coming clean now because there was a danger it was all going to come out anyway.

Until this moment, she had felt nothing but contempt towards him, but that had changed. Now she felt hatred.

And she wanted to hurt him.

*

302

Dan finally looked up at Rebecca.

'I know what you're thinking, Miss Connolly. That twenty-odd years ago such things weren't a big deal, but you have to understand the kind of family Frannie came from: very devout, practically Old Testament in their beliefs. Frannie is a believer, me not so much – sorry, Tom.' The minister waved a hand to dismiss Dan's lack of faith. 'And over the years she's become more like her parents, but even then there was no way she would want anyone to know that she'd, you know, been with someone before marriage and, even worse, conceived a child. And she wouldn't, em, consider . . . well, you know . . .'

Being uncomfortable talking about sex was one thing; his inability to say abortion or termination was quite another. He squirmed in his chair, swallowed, blinked furiously. 'Alex even said he'd pay for it to be done privately, despite the fact that he denied he was responsible. But he knew. He knew.'

He fell silent for a moment and Rebecca asked, 'So she turned to you, right?'

His eyes welled with tears. 'Aye. And poor lovestruck sap that I was, I took her back.'

'Did you know she was pregnant?'

A tear dislodged when he shook his head and he wiped it away with the back of his hand. 'No. Well, not consciously. I wonder if it would have made a difference if I had known.'

'The child was Fergus, right?'

He nodded. 'Yes, but I thought he was mine. We were married very quickly, within weeks. I suppose, looking back, it was kind of obvious, but I didn't care. I loved her and she had finally seen Alex Burnes for what he was. She told me she had been a fool, that I had been right all along and I was the one she really wanted and I believed her. To be fair, I think that was true. We . . . well, we went to bed before we were married, which surprised me, given what I knew of her beliefs, but I was full of youthful hormones and love. I didn't question. I didn't examine anything. I had what I wanted and I was happy. And then Fergus came along, prematurely . . . at least that's what I believed. That's what Frances told me anyway, and I loved him.'

A sheen formed over his eyes as he looked away. 'He was a good boy, Fergus. Bright, very bright. Loved his history, loved to learn about the Clan MacGregor. He would talk for what seemed like hours to my mother and me. She was the one who told him a lot of the stories. Rob Roy, the Children of the Mist. We come from the mist and we shall return to it. That's what she used to say. We come from the mist and we shall return to it . . .'

He drifted into silence and Rebecca waited a few moments before she gently asked, 'When did you find out he wasn't yours?'

Dan didn't reply at first. He stared at the flames for a few moments. 'A few months before he disappeared, when we were told he had been seeing the Burnes girl.'

'Who told you about Shona Burnes?'

'Rory. He'd kept it a secret, but he said he thought we should know. It forced Frannie to tell me the truth. I took it badly, I even blamed Fergus, which of course was ridiculous, but for years I had believed that he was my son, can you understand? And then, suddenly I discovered that he was another man's son and that man was Alex bloody Burnes.'

'Why do you think it took her so long to tell you?'

'She had convinced herself that she had been wrong when she thought him to be Alex's and didn't conceive until she was with me.' Dan's head slumped a little. He seemed suddenly tired.

Dan was the second man tonight whom she had watched visibly wilt as they examined their mistakes of the past. In thinking of Harry, she recalled his words – never underestimate the power of self-delusion.

'I wanted to believe it, I wanted to continue the fantasy, but I couldn't. I couldn't handle it, so I withdrew, not just from

Fergus but from Frannie and even Rory. Frannie had deceived me, tricked me, do you understand? On some level I knew I was being unfair, but I turned my rage on myself rather than on them. So what they saw as coldness was really my way of preventing any kind of explosion. Does that make sense?'

The minister inclined his head slightly. 'Does it make sense to you?'

Dan thought about it. 'I don't know. Perhaps I was taking it out on the boys when I shouldn't. But everything I'd told myself was real had suddenly become unreal, do you know what I mean? Frannie and I had been living a lie and it was fine when we lived it, when I believed it, but as soon as she told me the truth that balloon burst. I reacted badly, I see that now, and there hasn't been a day since Fergus disappeared that I haven't punished myself for it.'

Rebecca said, 'And punished your wife.'

Dan's head lowered further. 'Aye, and Frannie. And Rory, who needed my help and I wasn't there for him.'

'Did you know Fergus and Shona planned to run away?'

'Yes.'

'Who told you?'

'Again, it was Rory. He told Frannie, not me, the night before.'

'Why?'

'Because he wanted her to stop them. He didn't want to lose his brother, especially with the way I was by then.'

'Why didn't you tell Fergus the truth?'

'I wanted to, but Frannie wouldn't hear of it. She couldn't bring herself to pull the rug from under him like she had done to me. Think about it: how do you tell your son that the girl he's seeing is actually his half-sister? But we should have. We should have. If we had, perhaps Fergus would be alive today.'

Rebecca thought about Alex Burnes locking Shona in her room to prevent her from leaving the house. 'Would your wife have told Alex Burnes?'

Dan nodded. 'Yes. She spoke to him for the first time, warning him about the relationship, telling him that he had to do something about it, to stop his daughter from meeting Fergus. Frannie thought that if she didn't show up he would come home again. But he didn't.'

'Because of Cormac Devlin.'

His gaze was very level when he turned it on her once more. The tears had dried up and his voice was firm. 'Cormac Devlin didn't kill Fergus.'

This surprised Rebecca. 'Then who did?'

He stared at her, then glanced at Tom Lester, who said, 'You've gone this far, Dan.'

Dan MacGregor breathed deeply as if gathering his thoughts. 'You have to understand, we didn't know he was dead. Nobody did. Not for certain.'

44

Roach had idly wondered if Cormac would respond more positively to being questioned by a woman, but there was no appreciable change in his demeanour as she and DCI Morgan introduced themselves and sat down. The duty solicitor, a grey-faced man with grey hair and a grey suit, nodded to them and widened his eyes as if in sympathy with what lay before them.

'Mr Devlin does not seem to wish to answer questions,' he said. His voice was grey, too, as if he had spent too long poring over documents and dust had lodged in his throat.

'It would be better for him if he did,' Terry said before she addressed Cormac himself, her voice soft and gentle. She had a way with her that often pierced the hardest shell of the hardest scrote. Roach usually preferred doing that with an edged weapon, but that didn't matter, because the deal was that she remain silent during the interview and leave the questioning to Teresa.

'Cormac, love, you need to speak to us. We need to know what happened in the Black Wood.' She waited but still nothing from him, although his eyes did stray towards the paper cup of coffee and the chocolate bar they had placed before him. 'We thought you'd be hungry and need a cuppa,' Terry said. 'Go on, love, wire in.'

Cormac didn't move for a moment, then his hand snaked out to touch the chocolate bar.

'You need to help us understand what happened. We can't help you if you don't speak to us.'

Cormac stroked the packaging with his fingertip. Roach watched him carefully and thought she saw something entering his eyes. A memory perhaps.

Terry's voice was silky soft. 'The Black Wood, love, remember? Five years ago. Fergus MacGregor.'

Cormac blinked and his head tilted to one side. They had seen him do this on the monitors, as if he was listening to something, and Terry told Roach that the uniforms had witnessed him listening to a voice. 'What's Fergus saying, Cormac?' His eyes jerked towards Terry, just for an instant. 'You can hear him, can't you? You can hear Fergus. Only you, right?'

A nod, almost imperceptible, but still a nod.

'He doesn't want you to speak to us, does he?'

He flicked at the chocolate bar's paper with his fingertip, then a tiny shake of the head.

'Why not, love?'

He muttered something while still twitching his finger against the sweet wrapper.

Terry had pushed her chair back from the table because she feared her size would further intimidate him, but she was forced to lean forward a little. 'Sorry, love, you need to speak up a little, we didn't catch that.'

Cormac straightened and raised his voice a little. 'I've to be careful what I say.'

'Say about what?'

He squirmed in his chair. 'You know . . .'

'We don't, love, why don't you tell us?'

The flicking of the paper's edge increased. 'About his accident.'

'In the Black Wood?'

Flick. Flick. A nod and another flick.

'Why have you to be careful, love?'

He still didn't make any eye contact. 'He doesn't want you to know what happened. He doesn't want someone to get into trouble.'

'Who would that be, love?'

Flick. Flick. A whisper. 'Sssh, mustn't say.'

Terry's voice was filled with compassion. Roach had forgotten how good she was at this. 'Were you involved in the accident, love?'

Another head shake.

'But you saw it, didn't you?'

A nod.

'Was Fergus hurt in the accident?'

He didn't respond. His nail continued at the edge of the paper.

'Can you ask Fergus for permission to tell us, Cormac?'

'He can hear you.'

'But does he understand that we only want to help?'

Flick. Flick.

'He says I'll be blamed.'

'Not if you didn't do anything.'

Flick. Flick.

'I always get blamed.'

'We can help, love,' said Terry. 'You need to let us help you. You say you weren't involved, but you won't tell us what happened, and we can't do anything if you don't tell us.'

He looked to the side again. 'I think I should tell them.' His head tilted. 'I know, I know, but they need to know the truth.' He paused. 'I know he didn't mean it, but I'll get the blame if I don't tell them.'

'Who didn't mean it, love?'

He was back at the chocolate bar again. Flick.

'Did someone hurt Fergus, love?'

Flick. Flick.

'In the Black Wood?'

309

Flick. Flick. Flick.

'And you saw it, right?'

The flicking stopped and now he stared at the chocolate as if he wondered what it was. Then he nodded.

'Did someone hit him?'

Another nod.

'And then you took Fergus home to look after him.'

'He was hurt,' said Cormac.

'And you've looked after him all this time. Cared for him. Like the animals you care for.'

He nodded again.

'But he's with us now, love, you know that, don't you? We can care for him now.'

He seemed frozen for a moment, then he began flicking at the paper again.

'But we need to know how he was hurt and who by, can you understand that? I know Fergus doesn't want to get someone else into trouble, but it's important that we get the right person. I don't believe it was you, Cormac, I really don't, but we need to find who it was. You need to tell us. It doesn't matter what Fergus thinks. What do you think?'

Cormac didn't reply for a long time. He didn't tilt his head as if listening to Fergus. He didn't consult his solicitor; it was doubtful he even knew the man was there. Then, finally, he stopped flicking the paper, slowly raised his eyes and gave them a name.

Shona and Alex sat in silence. She deliberately didn't say a word, partly to keep him guessing as to her reaction but also to give her time to control her emotions. She was a Burnes, after all, and they were all about control. She was glad Ray had stormed off in one of his tempers – probably off to further punish his gym equipment. She needed to because she needed to lash out at his father without him being present, because he would always – always – end up backing Alex either in word, attitude or simply his silence.

Alex rested his head on his arms, folded on his desktop, another half-empty glass of whisky beside him. The room was dark apart from the coals in the grate and the slightly orange caste from the desk lamp. When he hadn't moved for some time, she wondered if he had passed out, so she rose from her chair, strode across the room and prodded him with two fingers. He stirred, raised his head and struggled to focus his bleary eyes on her.

'Shona . . .' he said, his gaze sliding beyond her to the clock on the mantelpiece. He squinted to see the face, but it was too dark. 'What time is it?'

'Time you and I had a heart to heart,' she said, her voice harsh.

He grimaced and began to lower his head again. 'I'm too tired for you now, Shona. Leave me alone.'

She rammed her fingers into his shoulder again. 'No, you'll listen to what I have to say.'

He raised himself and slumped backwards in his chair, one hand reaching out to the glass, but she edged it away from him. He sighed. 'Spare me the lecture, I've heard it all before. I'm cold and unfeeling and have made your life a misery. Poor little Shona, so unloved, so abused, so fucking spoiled!'

His voice hardened towards the end and he slammed his open hand on the table to punctuate it. She took a step back, not expecting him to be so assertive.

'Don't try that with me, Alex,' she said, recovering herself. 'I'm not one of your minions who you can bully. But as you've mentioned it, yes – you are cold and unfeeling and you have made my life a misery.'

He laughed – it was a short, humourless sound that was both bitter and sad. 'Misery? Really? The best of everything: education, clothes, whatever you want you get. A husband who grows inconvenient? Toss him aside and Daddy will sort it all out . . .'

'He was a serial philanderer, for God's sake!'

He waved that aside. 'So? You knew what he was like before you married him, but you did it to piss me off. Now you're paying the price.'

'And when will you pay the price for what you have done? To Frances MacGregor. To Fergus.'

He seemed to have a reply, but it deserted him and he fell silent. His body slumped in his chair. 'I did what I thought was right.'

'You did what you thought was right for you. You always do what you think is right for you.'

He laid his head against the back of the chair and closed his eyes. 'Believe what you want, Shona. You always do.'

'Are you saying you rejected that poor woman all those years ago for her own good?'

'She landed on her feet, didn't she? With a man who genuinely cared for her.'

'And your son? Fergus? Did you ever consider him?'

'We don't know he is my son.'

'Then why keep me away from him?'

He didn't have any reply.

'You knew he was yours and you turned your back, as you do with anything that you find inconvenient. A bastard son. A daughter . . .'

'That's not true.'

She ignored him. 'And now you're shit scared that it will all come out because if the police do a DNA check it will show that Fergus is not Dan MacGregor's son. And with Dan MacGregor intent on bringing it all out, it doesn't look good for you and the precious Burnes name, does it? A serious blot on the old escutcheon, I'd say.'

He remained immobile, eyes closed, as if he was asleep. But she saw his jaw tightening when she said, 'I never understood what mother saw in you, why she loved you so much. I tried to find something in you that would explain it, but, frankly, in all these years I've found nothing.'

She waited for him to respond, but he still didn't move. She sighed. 'It's all going to come tumbling down around you. Oh, not the fortune, that's safe, but the Burnes family name will be dragged through the mud because – and believe me on this – if Dan MacGregor doesn't do it, I will.'

She turned to the door but stopped when he said, 'Tell me this. You and that boy . . .'

She whirled. 'Fergus. His name was Fergus, for God's sake. Can you still not say his name?'

His lips thinned. 'Just tell me. Did you and he . . .?' His eyes opened. 'Fergus and you, did you . . .?' He seemed to have trouble finding the words. 'Was there physical . . .' He trailed off.

'Did we fuck, is that what you're asking?'

He closed his eyes as if warding off pain. 'Yes.'

She kept him waiting for her answer, enjoying the feeling of causing him distress. 'No, we didn't.' She saw him relax. 'I wanted to, though, but Fergus was old-fashioned. He had something you'll never have – a sense of decency, a sense of honour.' She sneered. 'He might have had Burnes blood in his veins, but he was certainly no Burnes.'

She saw that hit home and, satisfied, turned back to the door, but she stopped again when a question struck her. 'You tell me something now. That day you imprisoned me in my room, where was Ray?'

Stephen stood outside the cottage, taking in the night air. The mist had risen to hang low over the valley, clinging to the surface of the loch and glowing in the beams of the full moon. He tilted his head back and studied the stars glistening and twinkling above him.

He thought of the night he and Becks had stared in wonderment at the light show above them. It seemed so long ago and yet it was only a few days. The stars, the moon, the mountains all remained the same but the world, his world, had changed.

He didn't think he could do this any more. He thought he could, but it now looked unlikely. He couldn't be the only person invested in a relationship again. He had tried, but it wasn't working. He knew Rebecca was a loving person, though she tried her best to hide it. But she was also committed to her work. She believed that he dismissed that work as inconsequential and, if he was honest, she wasn't all wrong. She had done good things – she had helped clear a young man wrongly convicted for murder, she had helped others when nobody else would, she had exposed suffering and tragedy and held the powerful to account – but there were also the stories that he thought were intrusions, turning real tragedy, real suffering, into little more than soap opera. On the other hand, he recognised bills needed to be paid. The majority of his clients were guilty and he turned a blind eye to that in order to do his job. He had even helped them evade jail. So did that make him any better? Did he have a right to judge her at all?

But . . .

She could have died in that loch. She could have died when she was knocked out. But only a matter of hours later she was off again, chasing another story. At least this time Chaz was with her and he knew where she was. Not that she had contacted him, though, which was typical. Chaz had contacted Alan to say they were making another stop. That's the way it always would be, he feared. Always another story. Always another stop. He had to learn to either live with it or . . .

He heard a footfall in the shadows and saw a figure coming towards him. 'Can I help you?' he said and then saw the shotgun crooked over the man's arm.

*

Alex frowned, but there was something guarded when he said, 'Why do you ask?'

Shona took a few steps back into the room. 'Because I want to know. I was screaming and shouting and crying and he was nowhere to be seen.'

'I don't know,' he replied. 'Out on the estate somewhere, in his gym, why does it matter?'

'It matters . . . because Fergus is dead.'

A beat. 'Cormac Devlin killed him.'

'Cormac Devlin wouldn't hurt a fly and you know it. Whatever happened that day, whatever happened to Fergus, it happened because someone else was there.'

He managed a slight laugh but it was brittle, forced. 'And you think Ray was there? Why would he be?'

'Perhaps you sent him there. While you were preventing me from going, you could have dispatched him to deal with Fergus. Ray would have done it, too.'

'So now I'm party to murder as well? Jesus, you really do have a low opinion of me.'

'You're not wrong, but no, I don't think you would order him dead, but you would send Ray to teach him a lesson, I'm sure of that. And perhaps Ray went a little too far.'

'You think your brother is capable of that?'

'Ray can be a loose cannon, you know that. How many times have you covered for him when he gets out of control? How much cash have you spread to make trouble just go away? He gets himself worked up, call it what you want: gym rage, steroid rage . . .' She saw him flinch. 'Oh, don't pretend you don't know. He pumps his body full of the stuff and who knows what that does to the brain.' She was warming to her theory now. 'Yes, that's it – he goes out to warn Fergus off at your behest and takes it a little too far. Fergus wasn't a fighter, he wouldn't have been able to defend himself against Ray. So, Alex – where was he that morning?'

He took a long time to answer and when he did even she felt his pain. 'I don't know. That's the worry of it. I don't know where he was.'

As he came closer, Stephen recognised Ray Burnes. 'You looking for something?'

The man stopped six feet away, looked around. 'A fox,' he said. 'Catherine's lost some lambs and she asked me to see if I could bag it.'

Stephen had seen people come up with a swift lie often enough in the witness box. The face stiffens, the body tenses, the voice stretches. He saw it all in this man. 'She didn't say anything about that to me.'

'Well . . .' Ray half-smiled. 'You're just a renter, right? I mean, why would she tell you?'

Stephen let that pass. She had mentioned losing lambs, but she was dealing with it herself. She would have warned him if a stranger with a firearm was going to be wandering around her land at night. Ray Burnes craned past him towards the door to the cottage.

'So is she in, that reporter girl?'

'Why do you ask?'

'She's been asking a lot of questions, getting people's backs up.'

Stephen was certain then that he was here to warn Rebecca off. 'That's her job.' Stephen nodded to the shotgun still held easily in the bend of the man's arm. 'You know that should be covered, don't you? Shouldn't it be in a slip?'

Ray looked down at the weapon, as if assessing it. 'If I come across that fox, I won't have time to take it out of the slip, will I? Got to be ready for anything. So, is the reporter girl around?'

'I can take a message for her.'

Ray stopped trying to see round him into the cottage and instead gave Stephen a look to assess his threat level. The humour in his eyes seemed to dismiss him. 'Maybe you should tell her to keep her nose out of other people's affairs.'

'That sounds like a threat to me.'

'Just some advice.'

'When a man holding an uncovered firearm issues advice, it could be seen as a threat.'

'I'm not aiming it at you.'

'You don't need to.'

The man took a few steps to the side, trying once again to see around him. 'So, is she here or not?'

'I don't see that as being any of your business.'

He stooped a little to peer through the window into the living room. 'What if I make it my business?'

'What if I ask you to leave the property?'

He straightened and moved the shotgun from the crook of his elbow to hold it in both hands. 'What if I tell you to go fuck yourself?'

The air between them frosted suddenly and Stephen felt nerves tingle. 'See, now you are threatening me, and I could legitimately report you and see to it that your shotgun licence is revoked. There may also be a substantial fine.'

Ray laughed. 'There's only us here, how will you prove it? I mean, I could do this . . .' He levelled the barrel straight at Stephen. 'And who is here to say that I did it?'

Fear gnawed at Stephen's gut, but he refused to let it show. 'What are you going to do? Shoot me?'

Ray shifted uncertainly and Stephen guessed he hadn't thought any of this through. He had come here with the express purpose of warning Rebecca off, but that was as far as he had planned.

'But since you ask, she's not here, though I'm not alone. I have a friend in the cottage.'

'I don't see him.'

'He's taking a bath.'

A little more confidence returned. 'Then he's not much of a witness, is he?'

'But I am, Ray.'

Light flooded over them and they both turned to the gate leading to the field where Catherine stood, her own shotgun at waist level and a powerful torch held against the barrel. Ray Burnes raised his weapon in her direction. 'Don't be daft, man,' warned Catherine. 'Put that damned thing down.'

Ray became jumpy. If he wasn't dangerous before, he was now. Stephen guessed he had gambled that he could get away with threatening Rebecca in his presence – they were partners, after all, and he could shrug off any allegation as lovers sticking together. But things had changed. Catherine being here was a complication he would not have envisaged. And that made him unpredictable.

'She needs to be told to keep out of matters that are nothing to do with her,' Ray said.

'That's as maybe,' said Catherine, 'but this is not the way to do it.' Stephen was amazed at how calm and in control she sounded, as if she faced down armed men every day. He was on edge, every nerve taut, and he could feel his flesh tremble, but not because of the freshness of the air. Ray had his back to him now, but he occasionally glanced in his direction, and there was a wild flash in his eyes that Stephen recognised from clients who were habitual drug users in need of a fix. They would do anything in that state, some of them, and this guy shared that desperate look. He couldn't tell if it was through drug use or just panic at the situation in which he found himself, but all it would take was one small spark and all hell could break loose.

And that was when Alan came to the front door, a thick dressing gown wrapped around him, his hair still wet from the bath, and shouted, 'What's going on out here then?'

Ray spun, the shotgun rising, Catherine yelled at him to calm down and Stephen called out something, he really didn't know what, and then felt himself moving forward.

Chaz swore long and loud when he saw the driveway blocked by a four-wheel drive. 'I mean, who parks their bloody car like that, blocking the way up?'

They climbed out and looked around for the owner but saw nobody. Rebecca said, 'You'll just need to leave yours here and we'll walk up to the house. It'll be safe enough, it's well off the road.'

He sighed. 'I know, but some people have no consideration. It'll be some rich sod who thinks he owns the world.'

Rebecca smiled as they began to climb the hill. She was tired and her head still throbbed, but only slightly, which was something at least. She thought about the story Dan McTaggart had told them, of families at war, of secrets and lies and how they can twist and destroy. It wasn't over yet, for the name of the person who had killed poor Fergus had to come out, if only to prevent Cormac from being blamed for it. Even though she recognised he was not fully responsible for his actions, she still harboured some resentment for what he had done to her. She didn't want him to be incarcerated for a death he did not cause, though. It occurred to her that Shona would be devastated by the news that she had been dating her own half-brother, if she didn't know already. Poor Fergus. He had been proud of his MacGregor heritage and yet he didn't have their blood in his veins. She hoped they had allowed him to join them in the mist and let him walk his eternity through the Black Wood he had loved so deeply. It was a hell of a story but Rebecca still wasn't sure she would write it at all. Somebody would, though.

They were halfway up the rise when they heard the shout. She thought it was Catherine telling someone to calm down.

After it came another voice – Stephen's, she was certain – crying out the word *No*.

And then the sound of a shotgun blast.

Stephen, she thought. A shotgun, she thought.

No, no, no.

Not again.

She and Chaz broke into a run.

Tears fogged her vision, panic giving her the strength to power her tired leg muscles, the buzzing in her head gone as she had only one thought: reach the top of this hill, get up there, find out what had happened. She left Chaz in her wake as she raced upwards, her mind screaming Stephen's name over and over as if that would erase the fears that had erupted full-grown.

She came to a swift halt as they rounded the drive. Light bled through the mist from the cottage, while a powerful torch bleached it white. A shotgun lay on the pebbled drive, beside it Catherine and Alan knelt next to someone on the ground. Someone who wasn't moving.

She couldn't see who it was.

The image of another night, another figure on the ground, his life soaking away in the rain, flashed like lightning. It couldn't happen again. Not again.

'Stephen!' she cried out. She rushed forward, brushing past Alan as he rose to meet her. She had to see. She had to get a better look at the prone figure.

Alan grabbed her by the shoulders. 'It's all right, Becks, it's not Stephen.'

She looked at the man on the ground, relief flooding her mind, her veins, her entire body when she saw it really wasn't Stephen. And then he came out of the cottage, his phone to his ear, and her legs gave way.

Val Roach stood in the bright sunshine outside the cottage and stared at the view. 'It's quite something, isn't it?'

Rebecca sat in one of the foldaway lawn chairs, Alan in another, while Chaz was stretched out on the wooden bench under the kitchen window, his upturned face catching the rays. She could hear Stephen in the kitchen, bustling about as he made lunch for them all. The drama of the night before seemed so very long ago. She and Stephen had spent the night in each other's arms, promising to do better.

She'd thought she had lost him. When she had raced up that driveway to see the figure on the ground, she'd had no idea what had happened, only that she had heard the shotgun blast and that he was gone. But the man unconscious on the ground was Ray Burnes and the person who had knocked him out was, in fact, Stephen.

'You should have seen him, Becks,' Alan had said, admiringly. 'I've never known anyone move so fast. That bloody shotgun was whirling on me and he didn't hesitate. He launched himself at that idiot and rugby tackled him to the ground. One sock to the jaw and it was goodnight, John Boy.'

Stephen had looked bashful. 'To be honest, I didn't know what I was doing. I just reacted. That guy was so bloody tense that I thought he'd pull the trigger through nerves. As it was, I think it was me tackling him that made his finger twitch and the thing went off anyway, but into the air, so luckily nobody was hurt.'

At that point, Rebecca had stepped in close to him and as he wrapped his arms around her, she made her assurances. She would do better, she promised. She didn't want to lose this man. Ever.

Roach arrived the following morning with news. They had made an arrest regarding Fergus MacGregor's death and she felt that Rebecca would want to know. Off the record, of course. Frankly, Rebecca was having a hard time keeping track of what was on the record in this story. If she ever wrote one, that is, which she still hadn't decided.

When Roach told them who it was, Rebecca was not surprised; Dan had already revealed his other secret the night before.

'Rory MacGregor confessed,' Roach told them. 'I think he was glad to get it all off his chest, to be honest. Cormac had seen him and Fergus arguing in the Black Wood, there was some jostling and the lad threw a wild punch, catching Fergus on the neck. It killed him.'

Rebecca asked, 'Is that likely?'

Roach nodded. 'I've seen something similar, once before. Fight in a pub and the victim was punched on the side of the neck, at the back. It's called a traumatic subarachnoid haemorrhage, apparently. The sudden hypertension of the neck, kind of like whiplash, damages arteries that lead to the skull from the spine and results in bleeding in one of the membranes surrounding the brain. If the boy hit his brother at the front, it could have caused reflex cardiac arrest. It'll never be proved, though. After all this time, there might be no trace on the remains.'

When Rory had returned home, Dan had noted his agitation and asked him what had happened. He told his father that he thought he had killed Fergus. Rory had followed Fergus to the wood, knowing he was planning to leave, and Rory was intent on talking him out of it. Fergus, irritated that Shona was late, had told him to get the hell away and that led to the argument. When he and his father returned to the wood there was no sign of Fergus, and they believed, until that week, that he had merely been knocked out and had left just as he planned. Why his car remained was something they couldn't explain. Or didn't want to think about.

Rebecca told Roach all this and added, 'We know now that Cormac had already taken the body away, convinced that he could help Fergus.'

'And then became convinced he was still alive. He hid him from the search teams, first in his house then on the island for a time. When it all died down, he brought him home again.'

Roach sighed and her compassion surprised even Rebecca. 'He's a poor soul, right enough.'

Rebecca was still not ready to forgive the man for what he had done to her. 'What will happen to him?'

'He'll get treatment. We've urged the PF not to bring any charges, but he'll not be back here, that's for sure. It's sad.'

Stephen shouted to them that lunch was ready and Alan, as usual, was the first out of his chair. Chaz stood, stretched and followed him. Roach took another look towards the mountain.

'I've been here a couple of times, both times job-related, but never really took time to enjoy the view. I once broke my arm over on the other side there.'

'How did that happen?' Rebecca asked.

Roach smiled. 'That's a long story I'll tell you another time. Right now, whatever it is that Mr Jordan is making smells delicious. He must be a handy man with a skillet.'

'It's frozen pizza, so he's a handy man opening a box,' Rebecca said, laughing. 'And he'll probably burn the edges, too.' They began to walk into the cottage. 'Val, are you ever going to call him Stephen?'

Roach's brow furrowed as she considered. 'You know, I don't think I ever will.'

Rebecca stepped over the threshold first. 'Even if him and I get married?'

Roach stopped in her tracks. 'Has he proposed?'

Rebecca turned and beamed. 'What makes you think it will be him who proposes?'

Acknowledgements

Many of the locations mentioned in this story exist in the area around Kinloch Rannoch, which is incredibly beautiful and well worth a visit. Some of the local lore came from material I have gathered during many visits over the years and also from *A History of Rannoch* and *Tales of Rannoch* by A. D. Cunningham. Anyone wishing to know more about the area might seek these out.

Naturally, the events in the book are completely fictitious, and are at odds with the peaceful nature of the location. But that's what crime writers do: bring darkness where it doesn't belong and, generally, chase it away again. The characters and cottages I've described are the work of my imagination, too.

The Black Wood is very real and is one of my favourite places on Earth, while the Isle of Gulls has fascinated me for years.

I am indebted to Professor James Grieve for talking over how Fergus could have died and for suggesting the traumatic subarachnoid haemorrhage, as well as other invaluable tips. If I've got anything wrong, it's all my own doing!

Thanks to Neil Broadfoot, for advice on gym equipment. As a dedicated non-exerciser it's a whole new world to me. Also to the rest of my writing posse: Caro Ramsay, Theresa Talbot, Denzil Meyrick, Michael J. Malone, Gordon Brown. They are always there when I need advice or to run something past them.

I am grateful to the team at Polygon for sticking with Rebecca and to my agent Jo Bell for championing my work. Also to my editor Debs Warner, for keeping me right and spotting my errors.

As usual, thank you to all the booksellers, reviewers, bloggers and – importantly – readers who have supported the series, as well as event and festival organisers who continue to invite me along to talk about my books.